THE OTHER EISENHOWER

Augustine Campana   Marco Di Tillo

WEBSTER
HOUSE
PUBLISHING LLC

Webster House Publishing LLC
Ridgefield, Connecticut

The authors wish to thank everyone who believed in and encouraged the writing of this book, especially the following individuals who gave their astute advice and unflagging support: Jean Campana, Giulia Bondolfi, Dr. Jane Leon, and Fred N. Grayson.

ISBN-13: 978-1-932635-35-5

Printed in the United States of America

10 9 8 7 6 5 4 3 2 1

Dedicated to all who were there, and all who remember.

Table of Contents

Prologue   1

Chapter One—Sunday, 28 May 1944   11

Chapter Two—Monday, 29 May 1944   17

Chapter Three—Tuesday, 30 May 1944   47

Chapter Four—Wednesday, 31 May 1944   83

Chapter Five—Thursday, 1 June 1944   123

Chapter Six—Friday, 2 June 1944   143

Chapter Seven—Saturday, 3 June 1944   177

Chapter Eight—Sunday, 4 June 1944   201

Chapter Nine—Monday, 5 June 1944   233

Chapter Ten—Tuesday, 6 June 1944   255

Epilogue   257

Select Bibliography   263

Authors' Note   265

Prologue

May 1944
London, England

The wallpaper was curling a bit at the seams and water dripped intermittently in the lavatory, but the room at the Villiers Hotel where the seeds of a murder were about to be sown hadn't been chosen for its decor or amenities. It was clean, quiet, and walking distance from Whitehall—perfect for the trysts that had begun three months earlier between Sir Theodore Barnes and Clare Parker, both of whom served at the pleasure of the Right Honorable Oliver Lyttelton, Minister of Production in Churchill's war cabinet. Barnes, a mature Gary Cooper-type, was the primary ministry interface with the military, while Parker, a stunning, thirtyish blonde with curves in all the right places, was his deputy. Unequal in rank and position, they regarded each other with standoffish formality on the job. Away from the office, they were torrid lovers; although on this day, the vagaries of work had managed to interfere.

"What is it, Teddy?" she asked as she pulled the bed sheets up to her neck.

A grunt came from under the covers.

She pushed the linens aside and combed his hair with her fingers. "Come now," she said, her tone masking disappointment. "It isn't like you to come up short this way." The unintended allusion to his inability to perform brought a fleeting smile to her lips.

Barnes looked up at her, his face tinged with guilt. "Clare, we promised never to have work interfere here, but I'm afraid I'm going to let you down. I can't seem to shake the thought of something that happened this morning."

1

Her lips pursed and with raised brows she asked, "And what might that be?"

"I know you've been counting on attending the SHAEF briefing at St. Paul's with me."

"I should say I have."

"Well, Lyttelton advised he can only invite his first-level people, so I'm afraid you're out of it."

Her mouth straight-lined before she replied with a forced smile, "Dear Teddy, it isn't the end of the world. You can fill me in after the fact."

He didn't know it, but what he said next was tantamount to signing his own death warrant. "I'm afraid we're all sworn to remain mum about it. Security is extremely tight and everyone is being cautioned to say nothing. Careless talk costs lives you know."

"A slogan? Is that all you can offer? Do I not need to know what's going on?"

Barnes remained silent as Clare held him to her nakedness, hoping he would relent so she wouldn't have to kill him and put her cover at risk.

"Teddy, certainly you can share it with me."

He pushed himself away from her and leaned back on the headboard, arms folded. "I'm sorry, Clare. There's too much at stake. Please try to understand. It's all military mumbo-jumbo anyway."

Seemingly unfazed, she slipped out from between the rumpled sheets and went for her handbag. "Fancy a fag?" The cigarette case she produced held step one of Teddy's demise. She selected and lit one, careful not to inhale. Teddy went for it like a hungry baby after a pacifier and she lit another and slid in next to him. "At least we can enjoy the afterglow together."

They smoked and cuddled for the several minutes she knew it would take for the drug to work. "Oh, God, I do have to run. I have that report to finish." She patted his cheek. "I promise it will be better next time." She knew damn well there would be no next time.

As he watched her pull on clothes that did very little for her exquisite figure, a bolt of pain shot across his head. "Ow! Bummer!" He rubbed his temples. "I just got a doozy of a headache."

Clare finished tucking her blouse into her skirt and retrieved a tube of white pills from her purse. "Aspirin should do the trick." She dropped two tablets into her palm, handed them to her bedmate, and poured a glass of water from a decanter on the nightstand. "Take them now, and you'll be right as rain before you return."

"I'll be there directly," he assured her.

Before going out the door, Clare watched him swallow the pills and take a second step toward death.

Teddy got out of bed and dressed slowly, allowing for a reasonable gap between his departure and Clare's. By the time he was ready, the headache had gone, and he was feeling quite as well as his lover had predicted. He'd almost reached the halfway point between the hotel and the office when he felt a sudden need to throw up. As he fought off nausea, his left arm began to throb, his jaw stiffened, and an anvil pressed on his chest. Before he could pull out a handkerchief to wipe the sweat from his brow, he collapsed onto the pavement.

Office of the Minister for Production
Whitehall, London

Since returning to her desk, Clare had done little more than shuffle papers, anticipating the news she knew must come. It was almost three in the afternoon when Minister Lyttelton entered her office with a grim look on his otherwise ordinary face.

She stood, "My Lord."

"I say, Miss Parker, I just learned some deeply upsetting news."

She gave a practiced look of concern as he continued, "It seems our Teddy has suffered a heart attack—a myocardial infarction they're calling it—while returning from lunch."

She put her hand to her mouth. "Oh, the poor man. Is he …?"

"He's in hospital, and there is some hope he may get through it. Apparently he collapsed in front of a surgery. A bit of luck there, I suppose."

This time, she didn't have to fake a reaction—her alarm was genuine. He hadn't died!

"My God, what can we do?" she asked, knowing full well what she must do. She had to finish the job.

"For the moment, nothing. We shouldn't want to get in the way."

"Do you mind if I go?"

"That's very kind of you." He smiled a bit too knowingly. "Your presence there may help." Anticipating her next question, he offered, "Miss Calvin has the hospital information." As he left, Lyttelton added, "Clare, I'll be counting on you to fill in for a time. Make certain you have the meeting at Saint Paul's School in your diary. That's Monday the fifteenth."

Her glum nod hid the festival erupting inside her. This was exactly what she wanted to hear.

Saint Thomas Hospital, London

As Clare approached room 309, a nurse came out carrying a tray. "Excuse me, Sister," she said, "but is that Mister Barnes's room?"

The nurse shook her head slowly. "It is, but I'm sorry to say, the poor man passed a while ago."

"Oh, how sad." The stress drained from her as the nurse continued.

"We thought he had a chance when he came around for a time. Even spoke a few words, didn't he."

Clare tensed as a shiver shot up her spine. "Do you know what he said?" she managed nonchalantly.

"I was right there when it happened. Incoherent he was. Something about being poisoned. 'Clear, or queer,' he kept saying. I'm not certain."

The hairs on the nape of Clare's neck stiffened.

"Like I said, incoherent he was," the nurse went on. "Doctor was obliged to phone it in, just the same. A constable is in there now. Was he a relative?"

"Oh, no. Only an associate at the ministry."

What *had* he been to her? An intelligence source? A sex toy? A victim? Like a pinball spinning into a jackpot hole, her mind settled on what he had really been—the enemy, the goddamned enemy!

"Then you was work mates," the nurse was saying, adding as she started down the hall, "Just the same, I'm sorry for your loss."

Clare went quickly in the opposite direction telling herself no one could ever really understand how great a loss she and her beloved Führer had just suffered. There would be no returning to work for her, and no chance to attend the meeting and learn the details of the Allied invasion. None of that was possible anymore. Her true identity would certainly be discovered and she'd be lucky to escape with her own life.

Headquarters, Sicherheitsdienst Security Service (SD) Berlin, Germany

Obersturmbannführer Willy Henkel, a product of the early Hitler youth camps, ran his fingers through his mop of light brown hair as he plowed through the decrypted message traffic on his desk—suspected troop movements, security slips, the activities of the British Home Guard. Among the usual scraps of information that would become part of the intelligence mosaic about Allied operations, one paper grabbed his interest. It concerned Clare Parker, code-named, "Magdalena," an operative in London who had spent four years infiltrating and rising in rank within the British wartime hierarchy. The report said her cover had been compromised and the opportunity to learn the plans for the invasion lost. She wanted a new placement.

Henkel grabbed his phone handset. *"Connect me to Standartenführer von Kroit's office. I must speak with him immediately!"*

Headquarters of General Bernard Law Montgomery
St. Paul's School, London

Montgomery peered out from behind an auditorium curtain at the balcony filling up with high-ranking military personnel and civilian dignitaries, including Minister Lyttleton, "My God, Ramsay," he muttered to the uniformed man standing beside him. "are we mad exposing Overlord to all these people?"

"It *is* a bit sticky," Admiral Bertram Ramsay agreed as he surveyed the crowd, "but we do need to keep the Crown and our COs informed," adding in a lower voice, "although, as Eisenhower makes perfectly clear, it is the PM we are here to win over."

"Right. He is ever the conciliator." Montgomery scanned the room again. "So long as they don't muck up the place with their smoking. I reminded everyone of it, including our fearless leader."

"I should think smoke is the least of it, Monty," the admiral observed. "The entire effort could be defeated with a single well-placed bomb here."

"By God, you're right!" The general squinted as he surveyed the scene. "There are more brass here than I've seen in one place before." A glint of light off a polished helmet caught his eye and, when he spotted the accompanying ivory handled revolvers, he added, "I see the decoy commander has deigned to grace us with his presence."

Montgomery was referring to Lieutenant General George Patton who had entered and taken a seat on one of the tiered benches. He sat rigidly erect, his demeanor offering little hint that, after two slapping incidents involving battle-fatigued soldiers, he had been relieved of command. As public furor over the episodes had faded, he'd been named Commander of the First U.S. Army Group (FUSAG), located near Dover. Few Allied personnel and virtually no Germans knew FUSAG was an absolute sham. The so-called "ghost army" was comprised of cardboard and inflatable vehicles and weapons, empty tents and huts, and enough personnel to appear convincing. Its only mission, supported by a bogus battle plan, tactical intelligence leaks, and scripted messages the Germans were allowed to intercept, was to deceive the enemy as to where the invasion of France would occur. Nazi reconnaissance planes were permitted aerial photos of the area, while British and American air forces fiercely defended against surveillance of the actual build-up farther south. Patton turned and offered a nod and a cool smile to the other guests, clearly aware this was not his day.

As Montgomery and Ramsay continued to watch the guests take their seats, from behind them, a familiar voice with an easy Kansas inflection prompted, "All right, gentlemen, let's do this."

The civilians present rose politely and the military came to attention as the staff of Supreme Headquarters Allied Expeditionary Force (SHAEF) strode onto the stage and stood behind their chairs. The last person to appear was General Dwight David Eisenhower.

Moments later, Prime Minister Winston Churchill entered the balcony accompanied by his long-time friend, Field Marshall Jan C. Smuts, Prime Minister of South Africa. Churchill's bulldog-like countenance morphed into the face of one of Raphael's cherubs as he raised his arm to the crowd, an unlit cigar in his fist.

Finally, and without pomp, His Royal Majesty George VI appeared and was greeted warmly. Looking fit and military in his dark blue naval uniform, the monarch joined Churchill at the front center of the balcony. He shook hands with the PM, nodded to the others present, and took a seat. The group settled onto their benches and Eisenhower, known since childhood as "Ike," strode confidently to a lectern. As he did so, the curtain opened on a huge plaster relief map of northwest France from Le Havre to Cherbourg. The display depicted the coastline, geographical features, and the names of key towns and villages. It also showed the planned areas of assault and incursion of the Allied forces at the beaches and farther inland.

Union Jacks identified beaches code-named Sword and Gold, while the Canadian Red Ensign sat on a section of the shore called Juno. The Stars and Stripes adorned the two landing zones of Omaha and Utah, as well as Point du Hoc, where it was reported that six 155-millimeter cannons sat atop a high cliff. Arrows traced the paths of the invasion forces onto the mainland, and models identified air routes and parachute and glider landing zones, along with the flotilla of ships in the channel. Known German emplacements and unit locations were also represented.

Ike looked up to the crowded balcony, flashed a confident grin, and began. "Your Majesty, Prime Minister Churchill, honored guests, for those of you whom I have not met, my name is Dwight Eisenhower, and I have been given the role of Supreme Commander, Allied Expeditionary Forces in the European Theater of Operations. As allies, we here have been assigned the mission of invading the European continent, defeating the forces of the Third *Reich*, and restoring liberty to the oppressed lands and people. By doing so, we will also diminish the threat to our respective countries. The plan for achieving this goal is code named Operation Overlord, and the men who developed and are charged with its implementation will now describe the various segments of the invasion. Let me introduce the SHAEF officers sharing the stage with me and give each the opportunity to present the operational portion of Overlord for which he is responsible."

Lieutenant General Carl Spaatz, Commander of Strategic Air Forces in Europe, gave an awkward reading of the transportation plan, describing the pre-invasion bombing of railroad lines and transit facilities.

Air Chief Marshal, Arthur Harris, Commander of the British Bomber Command, rose and spoke solemnly of the threat posed by the German V-1 rocket sites and how they were being systematically targeted. He ended with the inflammatory comment, "One must point out here that the efforts of Operation Overlord will of necessity impede the effective accomplishment of these raids on the enemy's missile emplacements." A hum rose from the audience and the usually affable Ike glared at Harris as he returned to his seat.

Next, Air Chief Marshal Trafford Leigh-Mallory, Commander of the Allied Expeditionary Air Force (AEAF), described the air program designed to provide cover for the landings on Normandy. He went on to outline the integrated air operations that would bring paratroopers and gliders filled with troops and equipment into the battle zone behind enemy lines.

Admiral Ramsay, Commander of the Allied Naval Forces, followed with an overview of Operation Neptune, the naval portion of Overlord. His comprehensive description of the coordinated movements of thousands of ships, including support and landing craft required for a successful crossing of the channel, was possibly the most complicated segment of the entire review. Since the landing areas had no natural ports, man-made harbors, code-named "Mulberry," would be towed in once the beachheads were secured. By the time the admiral had finished, the guests understood the challenge of moving the equivalent of a medium-sized city as much as 100 miles in a matter of hours while providing firepower cover for the landings.

It then came time to discuss involvement of the Army and the troops who would be slogging it out on the shores of France, fighting to take back that country and gain access to the rest of Europe. Lieutenant General Omar Bradley, Commander of the U.S. First Army, part of Montgomery's 21st Army Group, explained the tactics for landing at the two American beaches, Omaha and Utah, and the ranger assault on Point du Hoc. When he spoke of the German defenses known as the Atlantic Wall, he described the build-up of Rommel's bunkers, mines, and beach obstacles and explained how they would likely produce high numbers of casualties. The mood in the room darkened with the realization of what the future might hold.

Montgomery followed with yet another sober commentary on the overall army plan of attack, incursion, and build-up, starting with the tactics for taking the beaches of Juno, Sword, and Gold. The memory of the terrible British losses at Dunkirk four years earlier tempered his talk, and he chose his words deliberately, not wanting to foster any expectations that such a tragedy might be repeated. In the process, he stepped onto the map like some military Gulliver and explained how and where he believed the Germans would respond, concluding with the assurance that, "We have prepared and trained well and our soldiers are motivated. They have faith in the plan and in God that this is the right thing to do." Aware that Ike had already chosen early June when the tides and moonlight were right for the invasion, he added, "We should not delay, for the chance of success diminishes with each day."

As Montgomery returned to his seat, Churchill stood, and fully aware of the host general's well-known aversion to tobacco, lit his cigar and took a great puff, relishing the smoke. Montgomery's ruddy complexion took on a tinge of vermilion as he fought to hold his temper in check.

"Gentlemen, you say this can work," the PM's face was granite as he addressed Ike and the other presenters. "I say it must work! You know by now of my grave reservations for the enterprise and my enduring fear that the channel will run red with the blood of our brave men." He puffed again and continued, "I am hardening toward it," then he slowly looked around the room before pointing to the map with his cigar. "I repeat, I am now hardening toward it."

Ike and the others chose to believe the PM's ambiguous phrase meant he was finally "hardened" in favor of the operation. Their conclusion was confirmed when Churchill went on to make a rousing appeal for rallying behind the effort and trusting in the might of the Allied war machine, the countless hours of planning and preparation, and the dedication of those who would accomplish the mission. When he finished, the PM again scanned the audience, as if daring anyone to challenge him.

Then, underscoring the force of his determination, he held up his hand in a victory symbol and applause overtook the room.

As Churchill sat, the gathering once again fell quiet. George VI stood and paused for a long moment. When he finally spoke, his words were slow and measured, as he worked to defeat his stutter. In his brief remarks, the man who had never expected to be king, much less a wartime monarch, recognized the enormity of the undertaking and asked the Lord's blessing upon the plan and all who would carry it out. He ended with, "May God save us all."

The King then descended the balcony steps, followed by Churchill and Smuts, and before departing, shook hands with each presenter and took the time to comment on their respective responsibilities. When the royal came to Eisenhower, the supreme commander assured him, "Your Majesty, with thousands of planes overhead and backed by the greatest armada in history, Overlord will succeed."

After King George departed, Ike ended the proceeding with a strong caution for maintaining absolute secrecy. "If the enemy were to discover our plan now, our chances of winning the war may well be lost."

On D-Day, the day the offensive was to be launched, the operation would involve over 150,000 troops, 11,000 aircraft, almost 7,000 sea-going vessels, including some 4,000 landing craft and 1,200 combat ships, and many thousands of combat and support vehicles. It was to be the greatest invasion force the world had ever seen and the success of the mission rested on the shoulders of one individual—a general named Dwight Eisenhower. Operation Overlord, for which he was responsible, was vital to the future of Europe and possibly the freedom of much of the world.

At the time, the Supreme Commander was unaware that another Eisenhower, a simple London postman named Paul, might cause the entire endeavor to fail.

Chapter One

Sunday, 28 May 1944

Cock and Rose Pub
Camden Town, London

"Blast!" groused the graying, middle-aged man when his dart struck the board well outside the bull's eye. Stroking his moustache, Paul Eisenhower took aim again and sent a second missile into the dead center of the target, winning the right to throw first.

"There it be, Jeremiah," he told the ashen, lanky man draped over a nearby chair. "Still fancy sixpence a round? We don't need to wager, you know."

"Naw, sixpence is what we always bet, and today will be no different. Give 'em a go, mate."

Paul's first attempt scored a treble twenty and his second hit the yellow nineteen wedge. Pausing a moment to smooth the flights of his third dart, he let it fly and hit the narrow outer ring of the nineteen, doubling up and closing out the wedge.

"The luck of some blokes," the tall man muttered as he stepped to the line. Despite the fact that he had only won a few dozen matches in the five years they'd played together, Jeremiah Jamison stubbornly refused to give in. The more he lost, the more he longed for victory. His hopes and dreams had by now far surpassed his abilities and he would have been satisfied with a single win, but it was not about to happen this evening as, once again, he came up short and went down to Paul in all three matches.

"I suppose I'm a fair source of income for a postie the likes of yourself," said Jeremiah as he slapped two coins down on a wooden tabletop. "I'll get you next time, Paulie." He took a hat from the rack and turned to leave.

Paul caught him by the sleeve. "Oy, can you still look in on me pets? Five days, is all."

"I said I will, and I will," Jeremiah assured him. "Don't give it another thought. I'm on late, but I can get over there after work. Enjoy your holiday, mate."

As the pub door closed, Paul carried his half-full pint to the bar where John Mackenzie, the burly, auburn-haired publican, observed as he polished a glass. "Bested him again, eh Paulie?" He leaned over the bar. "Couldn't you give the bloke a pass now and then?"

"Me dad taught us better," Paul replied. "'Always fight at your best,' he would say. 'That way if the bloke happens to win, he can be proud of going up against an able player.'"

"Sounds like a smart fellow, your dad," observed the barman.

"Good, sensible stock from the Saar."

"Then your family came here to get away from the Hun."

"Oh, no. Me ancestors first sailed to America in the 1700s."

John's heavy eyebrows shot up. "When they were our colonies?"

"Yeah, back then, the name was 'Eisenhauer,' spelled with an a-u-e-r on the end."

"So you're a Yank, of sorts."

"Hold on. Born here I was, and me family are in England for a good long time. Me great-great gran came from Pennsylvania and settled up north in the last century."

"And are you at all related to the good general?"

"I may be, who knows? Not that it'd be worth a farthing."

Suddenly, the pub door burst open and a patrol of the local Home Guard entered; Paul instinctively cringed at the sight of their weapons.

"Johnny, me and the lads are sorely thirsting. Pints all 'round, if you please," called their leader, Thomas Doyle, a sandy-haired, fit man with three sergeant's stripes on his sleeve. He was clearly older than the others in the group, three of whom appeared to still be in their teens.

"Right-o, Tommy," the barman replied. "You all look like you've earned it."

"We were on patrol for the better of twelve hours," Tommy said as the youngsters retreated to two tables by the dartboard. "The bloody handbook says not more than eight per watch, but our relief never showed until a bit ago. Some sort of breakdown or Lord knows what."

Paul gazed up at the rafters and recited, "Page twenty-seven of the Home Guard Pocket Book also says 'no man should be on duty more than one night in five.'" He eyed Tommy. "You blokes are always at it."

"Aye, we do what we must," the sergeant replied. "And you needn't throw your bleedin' memory in my face, to boot."

Paul put his hand on Tommy's shoulder. "Sorry mate, I wasn't thinking. I know, to a man, you all do what needs doing. Anything going on?"

"Naah! Bloody quiet out there. A few warning sirens, but that was it. No bombs or gunfire, just a lot of gadding about and observing." He patted Paul's back, "Everything was Bob. No guns, no danger. Your sort of mission."

The rest of Tommy's group overheard the comment and sniggered. "Eh, go easy Sarge, you're talkin' to an Eisenhower," said one.

"Yeah," another added, "some 'Ike' old Paul would make." And a third chimed in with, "Aye, too gun-shy for the guard, so they put him out to pasture."

"Here!" warned Tommy, "You lads show respect for a veteran of the Big War. This gent saw action over there."

The group hushed and Paul said modestly, "I was an ambulance driver in France, was all."

"They also serve who only stand and wait," observed John. "So said the poet."

A corporal looked up from his beer. "Amen, mate. Yeah, amen to that."

Tommy nudged Paul, "You didn't just stand and wait, did you, mate." It wasn't a question but a statement.

Paul's face flushed a bit. "Truth be told, I had to lie about me age to serve. I hate war, but I love England more."

"Sorry about the remarks, mate. We're getting some boys too young for the regulars, and they're in need of a bit of bloody hell raising."

"It's okay. I'm used to it by now." Paul thought a moment and added, "It isn't at all like I'm some fanatic, now am I. It's how I was raised. Me family were pacifists. No war, that sort of thing. I'm no regular churchgoer, but it be in me blood."

John jumped in with, "Still, you did your part."

"Listen, Paulie," Tommy said. "I know you don't care for weapons, but we all do appreciate your helping us out the way you do with the bell tower and all."

"Oh say, that reminds me!" Paul exclaimed, his expression brightening. "I have a bit of leave from the post and I aim to take a holiday up to Blackpool. Here's the key for the tower. You might be needin' that."

"You know travel is a problem anywhere along the coast, do you?" Tommy said, pocketing it.

"So I've heard, but I need to get away, don't I."

The sergeant shook his head. "Going off just when I was about to ask a good turn of you."

"Good turn? What might that be?"

"I wanted to ask you to collect some documents from the War Office."

"What sort of documents?"

Tommy shot the barman a furtive wink. "Oh, just the top-secret plans on how we're gonna blow the Jerries to kingdom come."

The beer in Paul's glass sloshed as he took a nervous sip.

"I'm joking," Tommy told him, grinning. "They've given me quartermaster duties and I need some forms and manuals. I'd be asking nothing more than your regular mail duties. A postman's holiday of sorts."

"Not the holiday I had in mind," Paul took out his pipe and pouch, and tamped a wad of tobacco into the bowl.

Tommy added, "It'll be a lark. Just collect the documents and deliver them to … hey Johnny, is it all right if he drops them here?"

John shot him a thumbs up and Tommy explained to Paul, "We need them for training and incident and strength reporting and the like."

"Well, I guess …" Paul shrugged.

The sergeant pressed his case. "Look, we've been at it for a long day and I need to get some rest. Besides, we're off to training in the morning. Now, they want us to learn anti-aircraft, don't they. He reached into his pocket. "Here's the order form. I'll write the name of the office and explain how you're representing me.

Paul read over the note signed by his persuasive friend and he smiled. "I'll go down first thing. I shouldn't think it will matter delayin' me holiday a half day. Do anything one can for the war effort, I say." Glancing at the rifles the troopers had lined up against the wall, he added, "Well, almost anything."

"We have a deal then." Tommy said, shaking his hand. "Let's have another pint for Paulie, John."

"Hold on." The postman held up his hand. "No more for me. I'll finish this and be off." He glanced at the wall clock. "Oy, look at the time! By now Old Frank is frantic and Odette no doubt has her knickers in a twist wondering where I got off to."

"Better mind your pipe once it gets dark," Tommy cautioned as he pointed to the ceiling. "The glow you know."

"Ain't nearly dark yet, but I will and all," Paul assured him.

Regent's Park Road, London

Paul's flat was a bit more than a mile away, located just opposite the park at the foot of Primrose Hill. It was a typical two story, red brick terrace house with a letterbox at the door. On the ground floor, there was a parlor and a large kitchen where the aroma of onions and fried fat lingered. In its midst sat a wide wooden table where Paul took most of his meals—alone, save for his two pets, a parrot and a basset hound, whose scents also contributed to the flat's ambience.

A door led out of the kitchen into a small courtyard where he grew what herbs and seasonal vegetables he could, despite the unpredictable English weather. The garden also held small quince and pear trees which yielded flavorful, if somewhat undersized, fruit. Upstairs, a carved headboard looked out of place in the plain bedroom. It had been made by his father when the senior Eisenhower sought to supplement his income as a carpenter, and Paul could not part with it. There was also a bathroom and a space with a small desk and wardrobe. Next to it, a basket served as a doggy bed.

Paul opened the front door and called out, "Hello."

"Allo, Allo," screeched Old Frank as Paul came in past a foyer rack holding a postal satchel, hat, and jacket. From his perch, the bird repeated the greeting, his head bobbing up and down. Meanwhile, coming down the steps on her stubby legs, the hound emitted a soft "woof!" as she reached the bottom, and proceeded to nuzzle his leg and whimper.

"Oy, Odette," Paul said, opening the door to the courtyard. "All right, all right. I know what you want. You see to your needs there, and I'll see to them here." The dog obediently waddled out and made for her favorite relief area.

"Eat!" Old Frank demanded as he climbed around his wooden perch. "Eat!"

"Here you be, mate." Paul filled the container on the parrot's stand with sunflower seeds and held out a cracker, which Frank snatched with a gnarled claw and crunched with his beak. Paul rinsed and refilled the dog's water dish and scoured the food bowl labeled "Oscar," after Odette's late father. He retrieved a few leftover scraps from the refrigerator, added some kibbles, and dropped the concoction into the bowl just as Odette returned to attack the mixture noisily.

"Now, me friends," Paul announced. "I'm off to freshen up. I have a full day tomorrow." He raised a finger. "And don't forget, I'll be away for a bit. I have a mate seeing to you, and I expect you both to be on best behavior."

As he approached the stairs, Paul glanced out a window to the flat across the way and glimpsed a flash of red hair through the sheer curtains. The sight brought to mind the lovely face, full figure, and captivating smile that went with the fiery tresses. They belonged to his neighbor, Miss Emily Crowley, a piano teacher he guessed to be in her mid-thirties, who had moved in several months earlier. The strains of a classical piano piece that began wafting from her open window completed the fantasy. During the week, the serenades had become ritual after her day working with young students. This being Sunday, Paul knew her music would be lighter and more joyful than usual. As was often the case, the melody buoyed his spirits and brought with it a warmth much like the personality of its player. Sitting down on the steps to listen, Paul found himself wondering what it would be like to share life with such a fine woman, only to conclude when the music ended, "Not for a bloke like me, I'm afraid."

Chapter Two
Monday, 29 May 1944

Hitler's Berghof
Obersalzberg, Germany

Adolf Hitler, bent and haggard for his 55 years, stood at the stone wall of his mountain retreat's terrace, gazing at the misty evergreen forests that ascended from the Bavarian village of Berchtesgaden. Next to him, his German shepherd had her front paws up on the wall, also watching. She was the one being he trusted most in the whole world.

The *Führer,* wearing a simple brown military tunic over a white shirt, black tie, and dark trousers, bent down and whispered in one of her soft ears, *"You see, Blondi, all this before us and well beyond, practically an entire continent, is part of the Third Reich.* He stood erect and hammered the top of the wall with his fist. *"There are those who would wrest it from us and destroy all I have accomplished. And I shall not permit it! The Reich shall endure for a thousand years!"*

Suddenly, something caught his eye in the woods, and his voice mellowed. *"Blondi, look, our mighty stag,"* he said as a large buck with great antlers and a distinctive mottled coat emerged from the morning mist.

Fascinated by the magnificent deer, Hitler paid little attention to the driveway below where a black Mercedes-Benz pulled up and stopped at the base of the long, stone staircase that led to the *Berghof* entrance.

Walter Schellenberg emerged from the vehicle immaculately dressed in the gray uniform of a *Waffen SS* officer and carrying a leather briefcase. The insignia he wore was that of an *SS-Oberführer,* roughly equivalent to a brigadier general, but he appeared far too young to hold such an exalted rank. In fact, he was only slightly older than the strapping major who welcomed him. The two military officers exchanged salutes.

"*Good morning, Herr Oberführer,*" the major said, indicating the stairway. "*This way please,*" adding as he started up the steps, "*It is good to see you again.*"

At the top of the staircase, the pair walked under the arches on the right, through the main door, and into the great room, with its magnificent art, comfortable chairs, and imposing chandeliers. Opposite the door, a huge picture window offered a majestic panorama of white-draped mountains catching the morning sunlight. Schellenberg paused and took in the view before following his guide left through a living room and into a solarium.

"*If you will kindly wait here, I shall inform the Führer.*"

The visitor nodded and watched the aide disappear out a glass-paned door to the terrace. A minute later, the major held the door open. "*If you please, sir.*"

Schellenberg strode out onto the terrace, passing a grouping of cushioned white deck chairs and a table holding a silver tea service. The view again seduced him, and he nearly bumped the table with his briefcase. As he nimbly sidestepped to avoid it, he saw Hitler and the dog looking over the wall to the forest below. The young general walked to within a few paces of his *Führer*, and receiving no acknowledgement, came to attention with a click of his heels.

Hitler's gaze did not shift as he said, "*You know Schellenberg, stags are such wonderful animals. They are lithe and beautiful, but have magnificent, deadly antlers for conflict. Wouldn't you agree?*" He regarded his visitor and added. "*I see you have brought the documents.*"

"*Yes, sir. There are maps, photos, detailed reports by the Luftwaffe, and of course, the latest from your intelligence operation. Based on what we have seen, all the generals agree that the invasion will come at the Pas de Calais.*"

"*Ah, so I understand. You know, it is so difficult these days to have all the generals agree on anything.*"

"*Yes, my Führer. They do have their differences. It is one of the reasons they are asking that you make clear the roles of von Rundstedt and Rommel. There promises to be a clash of command.*"

Hitler glowered at the young officer's brashness and again looked to the forest. Seeing that the stag had disappeared, he turned back.

"*Rommel is creative,*" he said crisply. "*What he has done to strengthen the defenses at the Atlantic Wall is most gratifying to me. He is a man of ideas and so he will command much of the mechanized force with Army Group B.*"

However, Gerd is OB West commander and so he will remain." His probing eyes burned into the general's soul.

Schellenberg looked away and began to open his case but froze when the dog growled and showed her teeth.

"*It is okay, my Blondi,*" the Fuhrer said, stroking her. "*He is not here to harm us.*"

"*Excellency, these clearly show a major Allied build-up at Dover, less than forty kilometers from the French coast,*" Schellenberg said, pulling out a stack of reconnaissance photos. "*Radio traffic and other intelligence support what we are seeing. Thus, the common belief regarding the Pas de Calais. In which case, having von Salmuth and Dollman join the forces of the seventh and the fifteenth armies there will pay off.*"

"*Most convincing, Herr Oberführer,*" Hitler said, studying the pictures as Schellenberg laid them out along the crown of the wall. "*Most convincing, indeed.*" He frowned. "*Maybe too convincing.*" He picked up and squinted at aerial photos showing hundreds of tanks and armored vehicles in a field, then another of lines of heavy artillery, and demanded, "*Who is in command there?*"

"*The word we have is—Patton.*"

"*Patton! A thorn in the side of the great Eisenhower?*"

"*Yes, my Führer, there were some incidents; however, they will be forgiven. Patton is their most effective field commander and Eisenhower knows it.*"

"*Rommel knows so as well. But I doubt that mad dog Churchill will allow the Americans to run the whole show.*"

Schellenberg shrugged. "*Probably not, sir.*"

Hitler scowled. "*Probably? Of course not! Which can only mean there is something else afoot. Some detail we are missing. Some information we lack.*" He waved the photos in Schellenberg's face. "*The English are sly foxes and the Americans are smart dogs. They are masters of deception and I don't trust the lot of them. Nor should my generals—especially you.*"

"*Yes, my Führer.*"

"*I rely on you, Schellenberg. Your most important mission is to discover for certain where and when the invasion will come. It is your highest priority and I want you to keep me personally informed of your progress.*"

"*Of course, my Führer.*"

The German despot slapped the photos into his palm before handing them back to Schellenberg. "*How and where I deploy the panzers and infantry will depend greatly on the reliable information you provide, and never on the guesses of my warrior generals. I know you will not disappoint me. Now, let us discuss this further over tea.*"

Supreme Headquarters Allied Expeditionary Force (SHAEF)

SHAEF was located at Camp Griffiss, a sixty-acre plot behind the walls of Bushy Park, some fourteen miles southwest of central London. Commonly referred to by its code name, "Widewing," this former headquarters of the American 8th Air Force took up most of four sets of long, camouflaged buildings. There were also a number of smaller service buildings and Nissen huts, many of which had been erected along Chestnut Avenue, named for the stately trees that lined it as it made its way through the park to a large fountain that was also under camouflage. The command center, the place where the Overlord plans were amalgamated and their progress tracked, was a beehive of activity. The air hummed with conversations and the sounds of ringing phones arising from manned stations along the sides of the spacious room. Strategic and tactical maps of England, France, and Western Europe lined the walls. One that detailed the northwest coast of France hung near a large conference table, which was actually several smaller tables butted together. Around it sat Montgomery, Ramsay, and Leigh-Mallory from the 15 May briefing. They were joined by Air Chief Marshal Arthur Tedder, Ike's deputy.

"Well chaps, before you is the latest Overlord release," Tedder said, looking down at the folder in front of him. "All the codes and go signals, including those for Neptune."

Montgomery picked up a copy and riffled through it. "Must it give away the entire endeavor? One should think the codes alone would suffice."

"It also defines the signal cue for the French resistance, does it not?" Leigh-Mallory asked.

"Quite so," answered Tedder. "They will receive word in two parts. The first warns them the invasion is coming, and the second will be broadcast hours before it actually begins. Those chaps certainly need to know the big picture of what's what so they can focus their efforts in the proper areas."

"Or, stay the hell out of the way, I suppose," Montgomery added.

Ramsay spoke up, "My ship captains will need notification immediately, as they are due to leave port early on."

"Exactly, sir," Tedder answered, deferring to Ramsay's length of service, "this is being forwarded by courier or, when needed, transmitted in encrypted message. Our intelligence sections are handling it." Tedder checked his watch. "We have some time before we meet with Ike. Are there any topics of an unusually pressing nature?"

"Yes!" Leigh-Mallory raised his voice uncharacteristically. "The fifth of June! I have a problem with it!"

"Easy, old boy." Ramsay made a lowering motion with his hand. "What's wrong with the fifth? The moon will be right and the tides with us. Low, you know, so the landing craft can spot and avoid Rommel's beach obstacles."

"It gives us more ground to cover," Montgomery piped up, "but at least the men won't be landing into the teeth of Jerry's defenses. Quite the opposite of what the crafty Desert Fox might have thought."

Leigh-Mallory's face was stern as he regarded his comrades. "Well, the tides might be in our favor, but the skies are another matter. The forecasts show high winds, cloud cover, and generally poor visibility through the seventh of June. Doubtful we'll see the moon at all." He leaned forward with his hands palms-down on the tabletop. "Straight away, I need to launch over nine thousand aircraft and complete more than twice that number of sorties."

"Look, old boy, it isn't going to be a stroll in the park for any of us," Ramsay said quietly. "What's really troubling you?"

The Air Chief Marshal bristled. "How in God's name have we come to be commanded by a Yank? Worse yet, one with a German surname? Generations of British Kings must be tossing in their graves at this very moment! Moreover, may I remind you all that the general has seen not a moment of real military action."

"Would you rather his name were Windsor?" asked Montgomery, reminding him that the current royals, of the German house of Saxe-Coburg and Gotha, had changed their family name a few decades earlier. He suspected that Leigh-Mallory's grousing about Eisenhower was likely rooted in the fact that he had expressed the strong desire to have SHAEF headquarters close to his own. However, after some assurances from Ike's chief of staff, Lieutenant General Walter Bedell Smith, a failure of communication had led to the selection of Bushy Park, which was almost twenty miles away from Leigh-Mallory's AEAF digs at Stanmore.

Montgomery continued his defense of Eisenhower. "Look, old man, Ike may come up short on combat experience, but he's no fool. Jerry surname or no, he demonstrated considerable military skill in the African and Italian campaigns." He regarded his compatriots for a reaction. "I say our American cousins have proved themselves again and again. Still, I don't in any way discount the superiority of our own military strategists. Don't you agree, Tedder?"

"Monty, you were a master at demonstrating that very thing a fortnight ago," the deputy commander cajoled. "The timing and content of your briefing to the PM and King left the distinct impression that you were the prime mover behind Overlord."

"Quite so," Montgomery replied, breaking into what for him sufficed as a smile. "Quite so."

"However, my friend," Ramsay said, adding a footnote, "it was clear to everyone in the room, including His Majesty and Winnie, that Ike was in charge."

Montgomery frowned. "Right. He certainly knows the politics of it all. Then, there's that blasted boyish grin."

Whitehall, London

It was not yet ten in the morning, but Paul was already warm and a bit sweaty as he pedaled down Whitehall, the reading glasses he usually used to make out addresses swinging back and forth from a chain around his neck. He was thankful he wasn't wearing his Royal Mail uniform, yet grateful to have the use of his postal satchel and bicycle. Turning onto Horse Guards Avenue, he headed to the main entrance of the War Office.

Once he leaned the bike against the massive baroque building, Paul retrieved his satchel from the rack at the front of the handlebars and made his way around the huge pile of sandbags to the entrance where an armed guard regarded him with a suspicious frown.

"Where might you be going?" asked the soldier.

"I'm here on official Home Guard business," Paul told him, pulling out the papers Tommy had given him. "I have to visit the quartermaster is all."

Still frowning, the sentry read the note and said, "Quartermaster is in the basement, down the stairs and to your left."

Paul started for the door and again the guard stopped him. "Hold on, then. Not here, is it. You need to use the Whitehall entrance around the corner.

The Royal Corps of Signals, located on the second floor of the War Office overlooking Whitehall, occupied a long, wide room stretching half the length of that side of the building. Desks lined the wall under the row of windows and a reception desk sat at the front. As were most military offices, it was stark but busy with telephones ringing, clerks at file cabinets, idle chatter, and hushed conversation.

American Army major, Ed Bradford, well over six feet tall, dark-haired, and confidently military, entered carrying a brown dispatch case and approached the desk of the civilian secretary seated by a pair of tall oak doors. "Excuse me," he said. "I'm here to see Colonel Hocking. I believe he's expecting me."

Before the prim young woman could hit the intercom button, a door opened and British Army Colonel Ralph Hocking, a ringer for actor Ronald Coleman, greeted the major.

"Ah, Bradford old man," he said, extending his hand. "Your office rang and said you were on your way. I understand you have documents that might be of some, shall we say, passing interest to us, what?" He chortled at how he'd played down the importance of the Overlord papers Bradford was delivering. "Care for a tea or coffee?"

The major shook the colonel's hand. "Coffee sounds great."

Hocking looked to his secretary. "Miss Dickman, if you please." She nodded and the colonel ushered the visitor into his office. Once the door was closed, Bradford reached into his bag and pulled out a folder containing copies of highly classified Overlord plans, codes, and signals.

Putting on his reading spectacles, the colonel ignored the cover sheet warnings and paged through the top copy. He looked up with a stern expression. "Inform SHAEF we will get this out immediately, and assure them I shall give it to my most trusted men to handle."

"Absolutely, Colonel."

Hocking pulled out a handkerchief and wiped his brow. "Blasted hot today. They say it may approach a record you know."

"I didn't know. It's still a lot cooler than my home state of South Carolina," answered Bradford.

"Right," said Hocking, reminded that he was speaking with a Yank. He went to a window, set the folder on a wide marble sill, and pushed up the sash. Standing there for a moment, the colonel enjoyed the cool air coming from the outside, then turned and hit an intercom key on his desk. "Carling. Please come and bring Bowles, Ashford, and Newton."

The speaker crackled, "Yes, sir."

Hocking leaned on the edge of his desk and picked up a handy folder to fan himself. "So, I'd say things must be hopping at HQ."

"Yes, sir. We have been very busy. But it's starting to get really ..."

Suddenly, when Miss Dickman entered carrying a tray with cups and serving pieces, the open door and window created a stiff cross breeze. The resulting torrent of air lifted Miss Dickman's skirt well above an acceptable level of modesty and moved papers, folders, and pencils off the colonel's desk.

"Blast!" Hocking slapped his hands onto the contents of his in- and out-baskets as the persistent gust blew open the folder on the sill. The major leapt over a chair and went for it, but before he could reach it, all twelve copies of the Overlord codes sailed out the window, beyond the balustrade, and fluttered to the street some thirty feet below.

Bradford quickly closed the window as Hocking's face went as white as a tablecloth at Claridge's. The distraught colonel slumped into his chair.

Red faced, Miss Dickman managed to set the tray on the desk, pull down her skirt, and tend to the office door. She went to close it just as a lieutenant colonel and three majors arrived. They all snickered when they saw the flummoxed state of the colonel, a man known for his decorum.

"Good God, men! Are you all balmy?" Hocking shrieked and pointed to the window. "Classified documents of the highest nature have escaped out onto Whitehall. Now, get to it and rescue them at once! And don't return until you have!"

The threesome snapped to and raced out, heading for the steps.

"There are twelve copies," Bradford called after them. Then to Hocking, who was holding his head as if it was about to topple from his neck, he said. "I should go help them."

Contemplating the end of what up until that time had been a stellar military career, the colonel murmured, "Don't bother."

Emerging from the War Office building, Paul Eisenhower went around the corner to retrieve his bicycle and never saw the staff officers on the Whitehall side frantically dodging passersby and gathering up papers from the sidewalk and street. He set his bulging mail pouch on the rack and decided not to strap it down as it was surely heavy enough with books and papers to stay in place. As he pedaled off, merging with the traffic on Horse Guards Avenue, a cat ran into the path of an oncoming Morris. Swerving to avoid hitting the animal, the driver brought the car to a panic halt, but not before striking the mailman's bicycle and upsetting its rider.

As Paul went down and hit the ground with a thump, his flailing arms broke the chain around his neck and sent his spectacles skittering across the pavement. The postal satchel flew off the bike rack and dumped most of its contents.

"Shite!" Paul shouted. It was his first accident in nearly twenty-five years with the post office.

"Are you hurt?" asked the driver who appeared to be no more than twenty and wearing a Royal Army uniform with the insignia of a second lieutenant. He bent over Paul. "It's all that bloody cat's fault. You saw it, didn't you? It sprang out and I swerved so as not to run it over. What could I do?"

"You might have hit the bloody cat is what," Paul said indignantly.

The lieutenant helped him up. "Hold on now. Move gingerly until we're certain you're all right. Here, sit in my car and I'll see to your things." He looked around and spotted the eyeglasses, which he rescued and returned to Paul.

The postman accepted the spectacles with a grunt. "What about me Home Guard supplies you mucked up?"

The soldier grabbed the satchel and set about gathering up the errant books and papers that lay scattered on the street and sidewalk.

Meanwhile, the postman grumbled as he tried to repair his spectacle chain and finally gave up and put the glasses in his pocket.

"There you are, sir." The lieutenant held out the packed postal satchel. "I believe I got them all."

"Oy, so it's all okay now, is it?" Paul demanded. "You've damaged me bike—Royal Mail property—and me guv will be bloody fuming. You should have to pay for repairs."

"Of course," the soldier said, pulling a paper and pencil from his pocket. "I'm Second Lieutenant Philip W. Davis, nine Sydenham Avenue, just off Crystal Palace Park Road."

"Not on me route, but I know it," Paul replied as he pictured a map of the area in his head.

"You can write there," the young lieutenant assured him. "My father will pay everything. I'm only here for the day. Must get back to my unit, you know."

"Oh, right, the invasion and all. There was some talk at the post office."

Phil looked around. "Mind you, one shouldn't mention it."

The postman persisted, "I'm against war but someone has to deal with those bloody Jerries once and for all!"

"Sorry, no comment. I've got to go. Goodbye, Mister ...?"

"Eisenhower."

"Are you joking?" asked the bewildered soldier.

"Actually, no. It's the family name," Paul said matter-of-factly as he picked up the bike. He and the lieutenant set about restoring it as best they could.

With the handlebars realigned and the rear wheel reasonably straight and no longer scraping the crumpled fender, the young officer bid him a good day and returned to his car.

"Good luck, Lieutenant Davis," Paul said sincerely, before adding a dash of sarcasm. "And thank you on behalf of that bloody cat!"

As the Morris continued down the street, Paul strapped the mail satchel onto the rack and walked his bicycle across Horse Guards Avenue, heading for a shady respite from the heat.

Colonel Hocking had his elbows on the desk and his head cradled in his hands, while Major Bradford slouched forward in a chair, arms dangling between his legs. The door handle rattled and the staff officers sent to retrieve the errant documents entered bringing an air of jubilation with them.

With a big smile, Lieutenant Colonel Will Carling waved the copies. "We have them, sir."

Hocking's skin flushed with new life. "Good show! Damned good show! Did anyone gain access to any of it?"

Bowles reported, "We very much doubt it, sir. The sidewalks were busy, but no one paid much attention.

Carling added, "They'd hardly just landed, sir, when we arrived." The others nodded agreement.

"So you got them all. Show me."

Carling counted as he laid each set of pages on the desk. "One, two, three, four, five, six, seven, eight, nine, ten, eleven ..."

Hocking paled again. "Is that it? Eleven?"

Sheepishly, Carling replied, "It appears so, sir."

"There were twelve!" the colonel exclaimed his face turning ashen. "Gadzooks! Did you not see the control number on the cover?" He picked up one of the documents. "This is copy five of twelve." He did a quick check and came up with, "Number seven is missing."

"We'll go back," said Carling.

"Then, get cracking, by George!"

Once again, the four men raced out of the office and down the stairs.

This time Bradford didn't bother to ask. He trotted after them.

Paul's bicycle moaned and squealed as he arrived at a grassy, treed area behind the Banqueting House. Despite the sparse shade, he decided it was good enough. Tired and getting sorer by the minute, he retrieved the mail pouch and set it at the base of a scrawny oak, using it as a headrest as he reclined in the grass.

His forty-four year old body, while in good enough shape, needed a rejuvenating break; but, something kept bothering him. Here he had made this special trip for the Home Guard forms. Could he have lost some of them as a result of his run-in with the lieutenant's car?

Opening the satchel, he took out Tommy's order form and began taking inventory. Ten training manuals, 300 strength report forms, 200 incident report forms. He hefted the stacks and estimated that they were intact. Then, he saw it. The cover page was unlike anything he had collected earlier.

Supreme Headquarters Allied Expeditionary Force (SHAEF)

It was stamped "U.S. SECRET, British MOST SECRET" followed by the word "BIGOT" all in large red letters. A red-bordered box contained the following warning:

"THIS PUBLICATION AND THE INFORMATION
CONTAINED HEREIN MUST NOT FALL INTO THE HANDS
OF THE ENEMY."

In the upper left corner it was typed, "Copy no:" followed by the handwritten numerals, "7 of 12."

"Oy, what's this?" he asked himself. "Tommy said no classified." The security warnings had piqued his curiosity and, unable to resist temptation, he pulled out his glasses and opened the document. The title page told him he was looking at:

OPERATION OVERLORD
PLANS, CODES, and SIGNALS

Invasion of Northern France
May 1944

Ignoring the "Eyes Only" and other security warnings on each page, he read on. It was all there—the Normandy landings, the code names for the beaches, the airborne drop zones and glider areas, the signals that would launch the attacks, and the two part radio message to be broadcast to the French resistance:

Les sanglots longs des violons de l'automne (The violins of autumn).

Blessent mon coeur d'une langueur monotone (Wound my heart with monotonous languor).

The lines were from a popular song based on a poem, *"Chanson d'automne"* by Verlaine. The first line was to be sent immediately to get the attention of the underground and initiate certain acts of sabotage. The second was to be broadcast as a signal that the invasion was to come within forty-eight hours. The range of dates for D-Day was 5–7 June 1944.

Paul finished reading and, despite the heat, shivered a bit, and a lump grew in the pit of his stomach as he realized that this could not possibly be part of the package Tommy had sent him to pick up. What in God's name was he to do with classified material? And where had it come from? The lieutenant who had caused him to fall off his bike? Yes, of course! That was the only possible explanation. But what would a young fellow like that be doing with top secret documents? He decided he would turn it in to someone he was certain would handle it responsibly. But who? And how?" He was certain of only one thing, he shouldn't keep the document.

Paul Eisenhower had just become privy to many of the same Overlord details that were revealed to the Crown, the PM, and the top brass on 15 May. Few lower echelon commanders and virtually none of the troops involved had this level of knowledge of the momentous military event that would soon take place. It was a heavy burden, and he wanted to be rid of it as quickly as possible, but he had to protect himself in the process. He certainly didn't want anyone to think he had somehow stolen the papers. "Buggers! They well might lock up a bloke in such possession. Ike or no Ike, with a Jerry name like mine, they'll bloody well lose the key."

Then, he spotted it. Just across the street stood a guard post at the entrance to the Horse Guards Parade. There it was—a way out. Paul, with his thick reading glasses still perched on the end of his nose, braved the Whitehall traffic and approached an armed sentry.

"Excuse me, mate," he said, "I need your help. You see, I have this document …"

With that, Paul told of his encounter with Lieutenant Davis's car, explaining how the papers in his satchel had gone flying and how Davis had gathered them up for him and left an address in case he needed to be contacted.

The sentry showed little interest in his dreary tale of woe, but the well-meaning postman pressed on, relating how he had discovered the document in his satchel and his belief that it belonged to the lieutenant. He pulled out Phil Davis's information. "Here you are. This is him."

The sentry took the paper. "Right, an army officer is he? I'll just enter this in my log." He got a book from his guard shack and, as he wrote, he asked, "Now what about this bleedin' top secret document?"

Paul opened the flap of his satchel. The underside showed where he had inked his name in bold letters, EISENHOWER.

When the sentry saw the red warnings on the papers, he exclaimed, "Blimey! What in hell do you expect me to do with that?"

"Maybe the War Office can trace the bloke down," Paul suggested.

"I'll get it over to them right away. Just wait here while I notify someone!" He got on the phone in his shack. "Hanes, post three here. I need a security courier right now. Right! I have a classified paper ... No, I'm not ... I don't know what's in it, and no I shouldn't want to find out. Just get on over here!" He hung up the phone and called out, "You wait here, mate. They'll want to hear your stor ..." Paul was gone.

The postman had ridden off into blissful anonymity. He would deliver the Home Guard documents to the pub, do some quick packing, and catch a train to Blackpool. Then it struck him that he needed to report the accident. Sighing, he peddled the bike faster, determined not to let this mess spoil his holiday.

Headquarters, Security Service (SD), Berlin

The severe statues and paintings in *Oberführer* Walter Schellenberg's office gave it the look of a gothic movie set, an apt setting for the general's ominous "fortress" desk equipped with two automatic machine guns that could be activated by a single button. Schellenberg leaned forward, elbows on the desktop, and looked intently at the man sitting before him in an unyielding wooden chair. He was Colonel Deider von Kroit, the very antithesis of an Aryan. Short and stocky, with cropped black hair, and a single bushy eyebrow that went across his forehead, he had the default expression of a man about to burp. Certainly not the type to ever be chosen by Schellenberg, he was acquired during the dismantling of the *Abwehr*, the foreign intelligence service of the *Oberkommando der Wehrmacht* (OKW). A few months earlier, it had been absorbed by Schellenberg when its powerful director, Admiral Canaris, was disgraced and put under house arrest because of several ineffective and questionable intelligence reports to Hitler.

The general clasped his hands together before him. *"So, Herr Standartenführer, I cannot overemphasize the great importance of this undertaking. You must, by whatever means possible, discover the Allied plans for an invasion of Europe."*

"Yes, Herr Oberführer, your words have been very clear. I will employ a multi-faceted approach to ensure we learn precisely when and where the attack will come."

"Stengel and Kimmel before you failed miserably in this endeavor," the general reminded him. *"For this, they now serve at the front lines in the east. I'm sure you do not want to experience their fate."*

As he spoke, the general stared directly at von Kroit just as the *Führer* himself had done to him.

The colonel, clearly uncomfortable, looked away and redirected the conversation. *"It is most regrettable we have lost so many agents in England,"* he said. *"The British have clamped down most effectively there."*

"However, the ones who remain are well-experienced and under deep cover." Schellenberg tapped a pencil impatiently. *"The time grows short. I must know by the end of the week and inform the Führer immediately thereafter."*

Von Kroit regarded the two ports in the desk from which black gun muzzles peered and he blurted, *"Sooner, if at all possible, Herr Oberführer!"*

The general gave a patronizing grin. *"Good, Kroit. Very good. I believe you will work out well here. I shall see to it that the Führer himself learns of your success."*

The colonel managed a stiff smile, but his eyes never left the gun muzzles. In his mind, he heard the general's unspoken, *"or failure."*

Post Office
King's Cross, London

The clerk at the equipment section desk wrote slowly and meticulously, pausing now and then to carefully check the formation of the letters, the punctuation, and the spacing between the words. Paul Eisenhower had already endured twenty minutes of the painful process of making his incident report. Now, with his patience worn thin, through clenched teeth, he attempted to speed things up. "Pardon me," he said, "but do you have any sort of estimate as to how much longer this might take?"

The man went on writing without raising his head. Then, as if he had suddenly been struck by an idea, he dropped the pen on the desk, twisted his handkerchief into his ear, and began an awkward operation of personal hygiene. Upon finishing, he asked, "What did you say?"

"I was wondering how long this will take. You see, I'm on holiday."

"Well, then what were you doing using your post bicycle?"

"We already covered that; it was official business for the Home Guard," Paul said impatiently. "Can't you go any faster? I have a train to catch."

The clerk licked the pencil tip and continued engraving Paul's information on the form.

"You see, once I've finished writing," he explained, "I have to proofread it to make sure there are no mistakes and then send it to my supervisor for his signature. He'll want to read the report thoroughly before he signs it, and he doesn't like to be hurried. For my part, I shouldn't be much longer."

"Very well. I'll wait." Paul settled onto a wooden bench and pulled out his pipe. He filled it but couldn't locate a book of matches anywhere on his person. "I don't suppose you have a light."

"I am sorry. I gave up smoking last month. My wife gave me an ultimatum. She forced me to choose between herself and cigarettes, and I must admit that I half thought of choosing cigarettes. But it would be too quiet without her. I love the clank of the pots when she cooks, and the dishes being washed as I read the Times. Or, just watching her tidy up or knit by the fireplace, listening to the wireless while I sip my tea. I miss my cigarettes, but I couldn't live without my Beryl."

"I understand," Paul nodded and almost bit through the pipe stem, reminding himself not to ask any more questions.

"Are you married, Mister Eisenhower?"

"No," Paul grunted.

"Then you don't really understand, do you? A married man's life can be extremely routine sometimes, and we find joy where we can."

"Married men ain't the only ones who live dull lives," mumbled Paul.

The War Office
Whitehall, London

Colonel Hocking's face was buried in his arms crossed atop the rescued sets of Overlord plans. He had scarcely moved since the five officers left in search of the missing twelfth copy.

There was a tap at the door and Hocking looked up, his eyes red and skin dented with the wrinkles from his sleeves. "Yes, come in."

Miss Dickman entered. "Sir, a courier from the Horse Guards is here with a delivery."

"Horse Guards?" Hocking groaned, looking up at her. "What on earth?"

She shrugged. "A package of some sort."

He smoothed his hair, stroked his mustache, and fixed his shirt and tie. "Please show the fellow in."

A sergeant with a holstered pistol at his waist entered carrying a dispatch case. "Sir, I have a classified document that I believe belongs at this office," he announced, "possibly to one of your officers, a Lieutenant Philip Davis."

"No, no one by that name here."

"Excuse me, Colonel, but I made several inquiries and apparently this is in your bailiwick. Royal Signals, isn't it, sir?"

Pulling a file from his case, he handed it to Hocking who leapt to his feet and just barely suppressed the urge to hug the sergeant.

"By George, seven of twelve!" he exclaimed, cradling the packet in his arms. "I say, smashing! You've made my day, Sergeant. Where in God's name did you find this?"

"Oh, it wasn't me, sir. It was turned into one of our sentries who passed it on to the secure courier service."

"Great Scott! Turned in? By whom?"

"The sentry wasn't sure. Some middle-aged bloke with glasses. It's here in his report, original and three copies."

The colonel found the report form with carbon copies attached and scanned it rapidly. "So, what does this Lieutenant Davis have to do with it?"

"The sentry wasn't sure how the lieutenant was involved at all. He got his name from the bloke what brought it to him. Said he looked like he was a postman—riding a bike and carrying a mail satchel, but no uniform. The report also mentions the name Eisenhower."

"Eisenhower?" Hocking's brows shot up. "My God, is Ike in on this?"

"No, we think that might be the postman's name. It was on his satchel."

"Do we know if he read the document?" asked Hocking.

"I questioned the guard about it and he said he didn't think so. The bloke could hardly see with the thick glasses he was wearing. Said he just found the papers and turned them in. Then he disappeared."

"Marvelous! You've done a bang up job, what? I am most grateful. You may pass that on to the sentry."

"Sir, if you'll sign at the bottom and give me the top copy, I need to show that you received it."

"Of course." The colonel scrawled his name, tore off the copy, and handed it to the sergeant."

"Thank you, sir. If I can be of further assistance, please contact me at the Horse Guards security section. Benny Jobson's the name."

Turning crisply on his heel, the courier departed, leaving Hocking to call off the search and bask in the fact that the nightmare was over.

Post Office, King's Cross

Another twenty minutes had passed and the clerk was still laboring over the accident report. "Let's see, Philip W. Davis, number nine Sydenham Avenue. What does this W stand for? William, was it?"

"I've no idea. He wrote a W is all I know. It shouldn't really matter now, should it?"

"My supervisor is very fussy about this sort of thing."

"We've got his name and address. Surely that narrows it down a bit."

"Would you care to explain that to the supervisor? How long have you been working for the Royal Mail, Mister Eisenhower?"

"It will be twenty five years in a few months. Why?"

"Supervisor Bowers has been in service here forty years. He has been in charge of this section more than twenty of them and I have never met a more precise and careful man. Do you know that I have never seen him come in late, not even a second? At eight sharp he comes in through that door and at five p.m. he leaves. Order is all he cares about. That's why our reports have to be so well-written. The word 'mistake' is like the word 'devil' to him. Do I make myself clear?"

"As a bloody bell, thank you."

"No need to be sarcastic," the clerk cautioned as he handed Paul a copy of the report. "But I will say this. You were right to have informed us. I'll contact you about the repairs once Mister Bowers approves."

"Thank you." Paul took the paper and paused. "Say, you wouldn't know if there are forms for authorizing travel to restricted zones—say to the seashore?"

"Not this department. You might try 3-D down the hall. It'll be for official purposes only, of course."

When he got to room 3-D, Paul found it deserted. Scanning the sample authorizations on the wall, he located the one for official travel and committed it to memory. Then, he searched the rack behind the desk for the proper blank form, pulled two copies, and hurried out the door.

The Normandy Coast of France

From a massive blockhouse overlooking the shore at *La Madeleine*, Field Marshal Erwin Rommel observed through his binoculars as teams of men and machinery made their way down the beach. Four groups were toppling sharp, metal objects dubbed "Czech Hedgehogs" onto the sand. Meant to interfere with enemy landings, they resembled giant pieces from a kid's game of jacks. "Volunteers" who had been pressed into service from the nearby town helped the soldiers bury mines and, from small boats, set the explosive devices on poles just below the water line.

Rommel lowered the glasses and turned to his aide, Captain Hellmuth Lang. "*Well, Lang I wish I had millions more of each. Although, if I did, we likely would not have the time to deploy them.*"

"*Yes, Herr Generalfeldmarschall.*"

"*They may never come into play here because I believe the invasion will come at Calais. But then, I consider them insurance that will deter the enemy and send him north to the heart of our defenses.*"

"*Will it be soon, sir?*"

"*Any time now. I would say in no more than two weeks, and when it does come it will be fierce—a true test. As I have said before, it will be the longest day.*"

Cock and Rose Pub, Camden Town

"My word, don't you ever look like you need a pint," John said from behind the bar as Paul, stooping under the weight of his mail satchel and his recent ordeal, appeared in the pub door. "I thought Tommy said that errand he sent you on would be a lark."

"Oh, that part was nothing," Paul told him setting down his pouch. "No problem getting the quartermaster papers. It was what followed that did me in. First off, me bike and I got run into by a car. Then, there was this mess with some papers and a bloke at the Horse Guards. The worst of it was when I had to report the accident to the post equipment section. There it is. The day is about gone and ..." He broke off as Tommy came through the door. His military utility garb was wrinkled and dusty from a day of training and so was he.

"Paulie!" he exclaimed. "What the hell are you still about for? I thought you'd be off to Blackpool by now."

"Tommy, I've got to talk to you about something. It happened in Whitehall and I don't know which way to turn." Seeing that John had instantly become interested in what he was about to say, Paul led the sergeant to a table in the far corner of the pub and related the tale of his discovery of the classified Overlord papers.

"My God, sounds serious! Do you know what's in them?" Tommy asked.

Paul fidgeted in his seat and his eyes shifted from the table, to the pictures on the wall, and back to Tommy. "I don't know a thing. I—I turned it in to a sentry and never read it." It was the first of many lies he would have to tell in order to avoid being labeled a traitor.

SHAEF Headquarters

Major General Bill Terry, a native of San Antonio, and a graduate of Texas A&M, had recently been promoted into the job of Chief, Operational Intelligence. He was just returning to his office from the break area where he had helped himself to his eighth cup of black coffee when he found Major Bradford waiting by his office door. "Ed-boy, I'm glad you finally made it back. What's this dang delay you couldn't tell me about? Where the hell have you been?"

"Two questions, one answer, sir."

Bradford proceeded to explain everything that had happened at the War Office: the twelve copies that had blown out the window; the race to recover them from the sidewalk below; the return of eleven; and the unexpected delivery of the twelfth from the Horse Guards.

"No shit!" Terry exclaimed. "A copy of the whole crappin' Overlord plan missing for how long? So who knows what the hell happened? What if it was compromised?" He eyed the major. "And you're one-hundred-percent certain you weren't involved?"

"I give you my word, General. Only in the recovery. I had nothing to do with the window incident. That was all Hocking."

"Heads will roll over this. Worse yet, the Krauts may get on to us. How do we know they didn't see it?"

"Sir, we don't. All we know is the document was turned in to the sentry in what we think was a half an hour or so after the window incident."

"Okay, then maybe there's some Limey out there with it all in his head. What if he's a spy? Who is this guy, anyways?"

"It's all here, General," Bradford said, pulling a copy of the sentry's report from his inside breast pocket and handing it to Terry.

The general scanned it and looked up. "What's the involvement of this Philip W. Davis?"

"We're not sure, sir. Apparently he ran into this guy on a bike. A sack of documents went flying and the lieutenant picked up this guy's papers for him. Apparently the Overlord plan somehow got into the sack."

"Or, maybe he found the plan earlier, read it, and decided this was a convenient way to pass it off onto the bike rider. What if this Davis is a spy?"

"Sir, he could just be a bad driver who ran into this other guy on a bike."

"Look, we can't take any chances. All we need is for the damned Nazis to be ready to pounce on the troops when they make the beach. We gotta track this lieutenant down."

He looked back at the report. "Now, what about this other fella—the bike rider. He possibly works at the post office? And what's this about the name Eisenhower?"

Bradford shrugged. "It's what the guard reported, sir."

Terry handed the report back. "Get on it now! Check with the Brits about this Lieutenant Davis, see if he's on the BIGOT list, and get some G2 on the postman, if that's what he really is."

The BIGOT acronym was code for the ultra-high clearance required to know the Overlord plans.

Terry took another swig of coffee. "And for God's sake, keep this under wraps for now. Maybe it's all just an innocent screw up. If not, we're gonna have to report it up the chain. You know Ike doesn't like it when we kick problems upstairs if they can be fixed right here. I'm not looking to lose a star over some Brit's negligence. *Comprende?*"

"Yes, sir!" Bradford said smartly. In fact, he *comprended* all too well.

Camden High Street
Camden Town, London

Home Guard Sergeant Thomas Doyle opened the door to his flat located among a row of unremarkable houses on the nondescript street. He turned the lock behind him deliberately and set the pile of papers and manuals Paul had fetched for him on the kitchen table. Taking off his uniform shirt and hanging it over a chair, he unlocked a cabinet and reached behind some bottles. "Ah, so," he said softly as he pulled out a green glass container with a stag on the label below the word, "*Jägermeister*." It was less than half-empty, having been used sparingly over the years for special occasions. He regarded the bottle and smiled before pouring himself half a shot glass of the herbal liquid. A sip brought a rush of memories of the days in the training camp outside

Munich. The site was a faithful reproduction of an English village where young men dedicated to Hitler were immersed in every aspect of British life while also being indoctrinated in the methods of Nazi espionage. Of course, a give-away like *Jägermeister* was forbidden during his eighteen months there, but he and his fellow future agents found ways to skirt rules they considered pointless. Rupert Zimmerman had even managed to bring this very bottle with him when he arrived in England as Thomas Doyle some ten years ago.

One more taste was all he allowed himself before going into his bedroom where he opened a wall closet, reached in, and removed a panel situated between two shelves. Behind it sat a radio set and telegraph key next to a wooden box containing an odd-looking typewriter with a row of rotors across the top and a plug board with several wires in front. The device, known as Enigma, was a German invention used for message encryption and decryption.

Placing the machine on the lower shelf, Tommy consulted an instruction booklet of dates and settings before raising the inner cover and configuring the rotors to the positions prescribed for the first message of *29 Mai 1944*. After resetting the counter and changing the placement of the wire patch cords, he picked up a pencil and pad and was ready to begin encoding his message.

Regent's Park Road, London

Happy to be back home in his flat, Paul soaked for a time in a hot bath while he sipped a bit of brandy. When he was quite relaxed, he dried off, pulled on his favorite dressing gown, and went out into the garden to pick some fresh herbs and lettuce for his evening meal.

"Good evening, Mister Eisenhower," a melodic voice drifted over the stakes that divided the garden. Paul's attractive neighbor was waving a small spade and smiling at him with a set of perfect white teeth framed by seductive lips. She was wearing a white cotton dress that, even under a work smock, revealed enough to tweak Paul's imagination.

"Oh, I'm sorry, Miss Crowley. I didn't see you," Paul said, pulling his robe closer about him. "I hope I haven't embarrassed you."

"Oh, never mind about your dressing gown, Mister Eisenhower. You look quite refreshed. Besides, it's a time for happiness. Have you heard the war will soon be over?"

"That would be most welcome news, wouldn't it. And where might you have come upon it?"

"Oh, along the way and in the shops. It's all anyone talks about these days. We're about to give Hitler the what-for very soon, we and the Americans. We'll invade France in a few days and the war will be over. That's what they're saying. A Yank General was at a pub bragging about how we'll all be drinking French wine soon. What's the matter, Mr. Eisenhower? You don't look pleased."

"Of course I am," Paul said, forcing a smile but determined to end the conversation for fear that he might inadvertently mention the secrets that had bubbled to the very top of his consciousness. At the same time, he was finding it difficult to go inside.

Miss Crowley eyed the parsley and basil in Paul's hand. "Oh, how lovely. You know, I just never get mine to grow as well."

As she bent over to pick some of her own herbs, the neckline of her dress fell open to reveal more of her creamy skin.

Paul tried to look away, but couldn't. She was a magnet and his eyes were two steel balls.

"Look," she said, holding up a sprig of parsley, "it's small and just not as firm as yours."

Thoughts of Overlord were displaced by a tingle in Paul's groin.

"Maybe you can tell me your secret sometime. Fresh herbs are quite wonderful, don't you agree?"

"Right-oh." He swallowed hard.

"Are you cooking up something interesting, Mister Eisenhower?"

"A bit of fish chowder is all." Then, taken by her charm and beauty, he blurted out, "Say, would you fancy some? I'd enjoy the company."

She frowned. "Oh, but I don't eat fish. An allergy, you know."

"Maybe another time, perhaps?" came Paul's pre-programmed response from years of being turned down by women.

"I'd like that," she said, smiling.

He started away when it occurred to him that he must be daft to pass on a chance to have dinner with a smashing bird like this. "On second thought, I could make something that suits you," he said, turning back. "A steak, perhaps?"

Her face glowed. "Oh, would you? I haven't had beef in ages. I'd be delighted, Mister Eisenhower."

"Please call me Paul."

"Then you must call me Emily."

"It would be a pleasure. Say in an hour or so."

"Lovely! I'll fetch some wine," she said with a look that was at least as intoxicating to him as the contents of any bottle she might bring. "I've a student coming in a bit, but I'm free after."

Once inside, Paul asked himself what he thought he was doing. For years he had had the uncomplicated affection of Odette and Old Frank. Wasn't that enough?

"No," he exclaimed aloud. "No, it's not."

Only when he heard himself say the words, did he realize the truth of it all.

Emily Crowley's flat was modest but the epitome of tidiness, consisting, as it did of an appealing bedroom, a practical kitchen, and a sitting room with two comfortable chairs and a console radio. Off to one side sat her most important possession, an upright studio piano that was the source of both her enjoyment and her livelihood.

She'd hung up her smock and had just finished washing the garden dirt from her hands when the doorbell rang. She dried off and opened the door to find a freckle-faced boy looking up at her. His red hair matched the color of her own and some might mistake them for mother and son, but it was not so. He was Jimmy Johns, the one student she had agreed to see after her normal teaching hours as his mother insisted that he finish his schoolwork before taking any music lessons.

The weekly prospect of expressing himself on the piano was a great motivator for the young lad, to say nothing of the chance to be with the wonderful Miss Crowley. To him, she was so comfortable and unthreatening, not because of her beauty, which he was too young to fully appreciate, but because of some other quality which he found difficult to express. Maybe it was the trace of lavender that he smelled whenever she came within a few feet. Maybe it was her soft voice. Certainly, he could never picture Miss Crowley shouting and nagging him the way his mum did. Whatever the source of his fascination, he always looked forward to spending time at her flat, even though the next day, he would receive the usual ration of teasing from his mates. They chided him about playing piano and even got after him for taking lessons with a teacher who looked like the American actress, Rita Hayworth, a reference with which Jimmy disagreed. Miss Crowley was much more interesting than any movie glamour girl could ever be.

"Did you practice the lesson?" she asked, as they settled themselves at the piano.

"... ehm ... a bit ... well not much," Jimmy told her, not meeting her eyes.

"I see," she said softly. "Is it your father again?" She sat next to him on the piano bench. "Would it help to talk about it? Should we skip the lesson?"

"Oh, no, I'm fine. Really. But I think about him all the time. He has to ... he should ..."

"There," she said smoothing his hair. "Take your time."

"You see, it's just that my dad is off in Portsmouth, and everyone is saying they'll soon go to France to fight Germans." There were tears in his eyes as he looked up at her. "What if he never comes back?"

"I know, Jimmy, I know how difficult this is. We're all so helpless to do anything about it. But we just have to hope and be brave, don't we? In the meantime, why don't we save Chopin's etudes for next week?"

The boy frowned. "But if I miss this lesson, Mum may not allow me to come again. She has me play what I learned, and if I can't ..."

Miss Crowley turned toward him and held him by his shoulders. "It shouldn't be a problem, I'll see to it. But you have to promise to practice every day and be that much better prepared next time. Can you do that? Promise?"

He smiled and nodded. She held him close to her for a moment and his world brimmed over with strange and confusing emotions—heaven with a lavender scent.

"Fancy a treat?" she asked him leading the way to the kitchen where she proceeded to cut a thick slice of bread from a crusty loaf and removed a round piece from the soft center.

"My gram used to make this for us," she told him, melting lard in a skillet and adding an egg, some sugar, and a dash of cinnamon to a bowl. "She called it 'egg in the basket.'"

Emily came from a farm in Devonshire where, for decades, her family raised animals and cultivated the good earth. She and her folks had the relative luxury of living off the land, but even with that, life was never easy. It was, however, always full of joy. The talent and love of music she inherited from her parents made her dream of someday playing with the London Symphony. But of course, the war had changed all that.

"Care to help?" Emily asked, handing him the bowl and a fork. "Beat that around until it's all bubbly." Setting the bread in the pan to fry, she asked, "Would you like to tell me about your dad?"

The invitation opened the lad up and he recalled for her how his father would tell him bedtime stories—ones he had made up himself. His favorite was about Bobby Bunny, a strange rabbit who loved a squirrel named Daisy. He taught her to eat carrots and she taught him to eat acorns and climb trees. Daisy wasn't sure she could get used to the chewy sweetness of the carrots, and Bobby was not overly fond of nuts. To make matters worse, he often fell trying to duplicate her moves up and across limbs and branches. But they loved each other and eventually had three little ones—two boys and a girl, all with furry tails, droopy ears, and a love for nuts and garden vegetables. "And they were great acrobats," Jimmy added.

"My, my. What an interesting story," she told him, turning the bread over in the pan.

Jimmy continued, finding it impossible to stop.

"Dad takes me to the Arsenal's football matches at Highbury Park, too," he told her. "He says that, when I was a baby, they won the championship over the Wolverhampton Wanderers by a single point. We have great fun together."

As tears filled the boy's eyes once again, Miss Crowley put her hand on his. "There now, I think that's mixed well enough."

He handed her the bowl and she poured the mixture into the hole in the sizzling bread, and it smelled wonderful. As Jimmy sniffled, wiped his tears, and smiled, she found herself wishing that all of life's problems could be so easily solved.

In the flat across the courtyard, Paul stood at his stove wearing a large apron to protect his best suit. As he coated the boiled potatoes with butter and added a dash of salt and dill weed, he kept expecting to hear the discordant sounds of piano practice echoing in the courtyard, but there was nothing. About to put two steaks into a pan, he hesitated, wondering whether he'd only imagined the chance meeting in the garden and his neighbor accepting an invitation for a meal.

To his delight, Emily arrived right on time with a bottle of claret, and the two of them began an evening of good food and casual conversation. She was very easy to be with and he found himself looking beyond her dazzling charms to her kind manner and gentleness.

"I must ask," she said as Paul served, "how did you come by such fine meat—and real butter? Have you a connection at the post?"

Paul felt a small twinge of guilt as he explained about his mate Freddy Martins, the butcher. "He's on me postal route and he gave me the steaks out of gratitude after I delivered a letter saying that his son James broke his arm in France and was coming home."

"France? So, we do have our boys over there."

Paul tiptoed around the invasion. "It was a special mission with the underground. That's all he knew, or at least all he would say."

Not wanting to go down that path any farther, he took a scrap from his plate and fed it to Odette who was waiting expectantly at his feet. Old Frank, taking his cue from Odette, flew to Paul's shoulder, screeching, "Bikits! Bikits!" in his ear.

"Oh, how simply adorable," Emily observed as she took a sip of her wine. "What other things does he say?"

"You shouldn't want to hear most of them," Paul told her, scratching Frank's head. "He's rather rude."

"He does so well for a parrot."

"Shh." Paul held his finger to his mouth and whispered, "He don't know he is one now, does he."

Emily leaned forward, her breasts touching the edge of her plate, and asked in a soft voice, "Does he eat steak?"

"Oh no, only Odette," Paul said, averting his eyes with difficulty. "No, and he's already had his fill of seeds and biscuits."

After dinner, Paul and Emily adjourned to his cozy parlor, where sitting side by side on the settee, they finished their wine and talked about all sorts of things, including food, music, work, and the weather. Everything except the war. Each time that subject came up, Paul carefully avoided any mention of the Allied invasion that it seemed all of England knew was in the offing.

Headquarters, Security Service (SD), Berlin

General Schellenberg was stretched out on his black leather sofa, boots off, and balancing a glass of mineral water on his chest. There was a knock on the office door.

"*Come,*" he called out as he held the tumbler to keep it from tipping.

Colonel von Kroit entered excitedly. "*Herr Oberführer, I have important news. It's about the invasion!*"

"*So, Herr Standartenführer, do you have the information I asked for?*" the general said, sitting up and setting his glass on the floor.

"*Not exactly, but we are very close.*"

"What does that mean, Kroit?" his superior said, pulling on his boots. "You felt the need to disturb me with 'very close?'"

"We received a transmission from our man in London, Thor. He has learned that the invasion plans have been compromised. A postman somehow obtained a copy of the document that outlines the entire operation."

"Did Thor acquire this copy?" Schellenberg moved to the chair behind his desk.

"No sir, the postman turned it in, but Thor suspects he read it and knows its contents. So ..."

"So, we find this postman."

"Sir, Thor knows him. He sees him nearly every day."

"Then why didn't he simply interrogate him?"

"For two reasons, if I may. First, Thor has been under deep cover more than ten years as a bank employee, currently serving as a home guardsman. He could not be fully certain that this postman had actually read the document and didn't think it wise to reveal himself on a guess."

"Ah, yes, I do recall him. We used him on Bacchus I believe. I must say that with so few agents left, we would be foolish to lose him. Go on."

"Second, the postman has gone on holiday to Blackpool and Thor will likely not see him again for days."

"What's his name?"

The colonel hesitated, "Er, Eisenhower, sir."

"Eisenhower!" Schellenberg squinted. "Are you certain?"

"Yes sir, I thought it odd and had him retransmit. It caused a delay, but I wanted to be sure we had it right."

"I see. In that case, have one of our itinerant agents handle this. Make that happen at once."

"Yes, Herr Oberführer."

Schellenberg regarded the report while the colonel stood there in silence. After a few awkward moments, he looked up and asked, "Is there something else, Kroit?"

"Yes, as you will see, there is the name of a Philip Davis, a British lieutenant, who may also have come into possession of the document."

"What!? Two unlikely Englanders with such knowledge. I smell a very large rat. Or, maybe we are the rats and they are the cheese."

"Yes, sir. Can we take that chance?"

"Find both these men and test their stories. You understand what I mean by 'test' don't you?"

"Absolutely, Herr Oberführer."

"Use our best assets to track them down. Quickly Kroit! Do it quickly. We cannot afford to lose a minute more."

"Yes, sir." Von Kroit raised his arm, proclaimed, *"Heil Hitler,"* and left.

Regent's Park Road, London

Night had descended and blackout curtains covered all the windows, adding to the flat's coziness and the budding closeness of the two neighbors. When the evening ended at about ten-fifteen, Paul turned off any lights that might escape to the outside and saw Emily to the door.

He offered her his hand, but instead of reaching for it, she leaned in and gave him a moist kiss on the cheek. "We must do this again. Soon, I hope."

He smiled quite dreamily for a bloke his age and was about to close the door when a thought struck. "Say, might I impose on you?"

"Oh, that depends," she teased. "Nothing naughty, is it?"

"N-no, not, not at all," he told her, so disconcerted that he had to pause to re-board his train of thought. "You see, I'm going on holiday to Blackpool and I, well, I wondered if you would look in on Odette and Frank for me— you know feed and maybe talk to them. Odette just needs to be let out, usually twice a day, but she's gotten by on once. She does her business and comes right back." He smiled and added, "I should return Saturday. I had asked one of me mates at the pub, but he would be coming around late, and seeing as you're right here, and you've met them …"

"But Paul, there are travel restrictions. It's been in the press. The invasion, you know. The shore is closed unless you live or have business there."

"I have that covered, don't I. Nicked me a Royal Mail travel authorization. I'll fill it out all proper and it should clear the way—no problem."

"I see," she said with a disappointed frown.

"Here. Please, Emily, understand I'm not that kind of bloke, but I really must get away. Been two years since me last one, and I'm just up to there with work. It does no one a bit of harm, does it?"

"Well, I suppose …"

"Then you'll do it? Watch me pets?"

"I'd be delighted." She flashed a glowing smile that might warrant a warning from the Air Raid Patrol.

"Good, I'll ring me mate and let him know." He beamed. "Oh, this is so good of you. The key will be under the mat at the back door."

"Going alone are you?"

Paul wished he could say, "Why don't you come with me? We could start out in Blackpool and end up wherever we fancy—together for the rest of

Augustine Campana & Marco Di Tillo

our lives," but common sense prevailed. "Quite alone," he told her. "I'll take the train up in the morning."

"Well then, I shall look forward to seeing you when you get back. Not to worry. I'll tend to everything here. Your garden, as well."

"Help yourself to anything, and thank you."

"My pleasure, Mister Eisenhower."

Playfully flipping his shirt collar, she turned and headed to her door, a vision in white, waving over her shoulder before dissolving into the shadows. Paul closed his door and again had to recover from Emily's presence before he turned on the light. It would take some doing, as he discovered when he went to pick up the wine glasses and found her fragrance lingering in the living room. Happily lightheaded from the wine and the scent of a beautiful woman, he cleared the table and washed the dishes. Then, with plates and glasses drying in the rack and Old Frank safe in a covered cage, he got his mail satchel from the rack and man and dog went upstairs—one to sleep in her basket and the other to get down to serious business.

At the desk, Paul took the travel authorization form and, with a fountain pen, carefully duplicated the information he had seen on the sample. He wasn't sure what to put in the destination box. What if Blackpool was closed to all civilians? Taking a chance, he wrote, "All restricted areas of England." He practiced the signature he remembered from the sample and then wrote it perfectly on the form.

With that chore done, he made a note to phone Jeremiah in the morning, then completed his usual nighttime ablutions and slumped into bed. He was lying there happily reviewing the events of the evening when less pleasant memories intruded: the accident with the bike, the discovery of the document, and the sentry at Horse Guards. He'd hoped he'd gotten rid of all that worry, but there it was, haunting him.

Maybe he should never have turned it in. Maybe he should have tried to locate that Davis fellow and given it back to him. Because that was where it had had to come from, wasn't it? That young lieutenant must have dropped it in his bag. But why would he have passed a secret document onto a man he'd just knocked off his bike? Whether Davis had properly possessed the plan or had stolen it from one of the offices in Whitehall, Paul decided he must forget Blackpool for a time, find him, and get to the truth of it.

Chapter Three
Tuesday, 30 May 1944

SHAEF Headquarters
Office of the Chief, Operational Intelligence

General Terry was swigging his first morning coffee when Major Bradford entered looking disheveled and drained.

"Ed-boy, you look dang awful."

Bradford straightened his tie. "Sorry, sir. Long night."

Terry pointed to his coffee carafe. "Grab a cup and have a seat."

The major poured himself some of the dark brew, added milk and sugar, and took a taste.

"Now, whatcha got for me?" asked the general.

"Well, sir, I have a lead on this Eisenhower guy. He does work for the post office. I verified it in their official records, and I know he delivers mail."

"Postmen usually do. Is there some sort of link between that and the reason why he had the document?"

"Not really, sir. Not so far as I can tell."

"Okay, what do you know?"

"After gathering more G2 on the postal system, I went to the main post office in London. They're open around the clock, but it took some doing to get access to the records section. They had me cooling my heels for over an hour before I could even talk to anybody. Finally, in the quote, 'spirit of cooperation with you Yanks,' they let me search their files."

Bradford took another drink and continued. "Let me tell you, that was a real mess. The filing system is unlike anything I've ever seen—probably dates back to Henry the Eighth or something. But I did wade my way through it and the good news is, he's the only Eisenhower they have.

He lives near Regent's Park and works out of the King's Cross office. They had a picture of him they couldn't let me have. We tried to Photostat it, but it didn't turn out. It was old and probably wouldn't have helped much anyway. Since he's the only one by that name, I figured he'd be pretty easy to find. But when I went there, they said he was on vacation—you know, holiday—for a week."

"So, you went to his place."

"Yes, sir. But he wasn't there, either. I checked with a neighbor." He pulled out a notepad and read from it. "A Miss Crowley, and she said he was taking the train to Blackpool."

"Blackpool?"

"Yeah, it's a resort area on the northwest coast up well past ..."

"Dammit!" Terry stopped him. "I know where it is. The place is swarming with troops. So, why aren't you up there instead of here telling me about this?"

"Sir, because of the travel restrictions, it isn't likely he went there."

"You sure of that?"

"I checked at the train station nearest to his apartment." He again consulted his pad. "The one at Euston. They said it would take a special authorization for a civilian and they had no record of an Eisenhower going anywhere. They even contacted other railroad stations and verified it with them. No deal. By that time, it was curfew, so I spent the night on a bench in the waiting area."

"Shit! The trail has gone cold," Terry summarized, "and it's looking more and more like this guy is a spy. He might be flying out on some Kraut plane back to Berlin right now. What the hell am I gonna tell the brass?"

Bradford returned the notepad to his jacket pocket. "We aren't sure of anything yet, sir. I think you're safe to hold off. I doubt the Brits are inclined to announce it anytime soon. Colonel Hocking seemed content that all the copies had been recovered."

"Just the same, I'll have to say something. I doubt our friends at Whitehall are downplaying it. God forbid Ike gets it from them first."

Bradford nodded. "Amen to that, General."

"Now," Terry said, leaning forward, "what about this other hombre, the lieutenant?"

"Davis. That's where I'm heading next, sir. Back over to Whitehall to find out where he got orders for."

"Make sure you get a picture. You need to know who you're lookin' for."

"Will do."

"What about BIGOT? Is he cleared?"

"No, sir, not according to our records or the list at the War Office."

Terry stood, prompting the major to do the same, and came around his desk. He put his hand on the major's shoulder.

"Ed-boy, dig up whatever you can on this Davis," he said, "and let me know if you need some added horsepower to get the Brits to open up." He backed away. "And grab a shower before you go, but don't waste a dang minute."

"Yes, sir." Bradford saluted and left.

Terry returned to his desk, slurped some coffee, and grumbled, "Crap! Am I ever screwed."

Crystal Palace Park, London

Toting a worn but sturdy piece of leather luggage, Paul Eisenhower got off the number three bus at the corner of Sydenham Avenue and Crystal Palace Park Road. As he walked down Sydenham, he saw he wouldn't have to go far to get to number nine, the home of Lieutenant Phil Davis. It was another warm morning, and he had already hiked from his flat to the bus stop in Camden Town. Needing a rest, he spotted a shaded wooden bench just off the sidewalk near a rose bush full of pink and red blooms. A perfect spot he thought, to pause and rehearse his reason for calling on the Davises. Looking beyond the flowers, he saw a half-dozen or so people working in a garden: weeding, planting, and building plots.

A white-haired curmudgeon in a plaster foot cast was directing the effort. "Come on," Paul heard him shout. "Hurry up! Move those stones over there!"

A woman, a near bookend of the man, came Paul's way puffing and sweating, and joined him on the bench.

"Lord, ever since Colonel Hamilton dashed his foot to pieces, he's off work and has taken to using the garden to brush up on his bloody leadership skills." She smirked. "Needs a whole lot of brushin' if you ask me."

Paul inquired, "How'd it happen? The foot, I mean."

"He hacked into it with a garden hoe on Saturday, in the early afternoon. He'd only just arrived. They had to take him to hospital immediately. Lucky he didn't lose a toe."

She looked down at his luggage. "Of course, you couldn't know a bit of this, could ya. Not from around here, eh?"

"I'm afraid not. I am after someone in the neighborhood about a postal matter."

"A postman are ya?"

"Aye, about to go on holiday, but I must see to this first."

"Maybe I can help. I'm Maggie Tracy. Our family has lived in Crystal Palace for near a hundred years. I don't want to boast, but I do know every soul here."

"What can you tell me about a young officer by the name of Philip W. Davis?"

"Philly Davis? Yes, of course!" She wiped her hands on her garden smock. "That would be Farley's son. I saw the lad just yesterday—so handsome in his uniform. His folks live just up there on the left. The big house with the fence, it is."

Colonel Hamilton shouted from a distance, "Mrs. Tracy, quit your prattling and get to it!"

"The old warhorse seems to have found more work for me," she said wearily. "I'd best go before he cultivates more problems than potatoes. Good-bye and give my regards to Farley and his wife Janet!"

"I will," said Paul as the old woman returned to her gardening. He walked to the Davis house ready to dig further for the truth, even if it meant lying in the process.

Farley Davis, a big, balding man with muscular arms and a barrel chest, was sitting in an overstuffed chair, intently working on the crossword puzzle in the *Daily Telegraph* as he puffed on a carved meerschaum pipe. Blue-gray smoke encircled his head and filled the room with a bittersweet perfume of tobacco and citrus.

"Hmm. Bush at the center of nursery revolutions," he mumbled. "Hah! Of course, mulberry!" He jotted in the answer and sang, "Here we go round the mulberry bush."

His wife Janet, crocheting in a wing chair, smiled at his childlike enthusiasm for his puzzles. She was a slim, gray-streaked brunette wearing a neatly sewn dress she had made herself—the sort of woman who did things properly and always had tea ready at four o'clock. Besides being an able seamstress, she taught sewing classes, and every Thursday night ran a meeting to organize aid and assistance for wounded soldiers and families whose sons had been lost.

The serenity of a spring morning at the Davis home was shattered when the front door knocker clanked twice. As usual, Farley didn't budge, so

Janet set down her work and went to answer it. There stood a middle-aged man with luggage in hand and a smile on his face.

"Hello," he said. "Me name is Paul, and I'm here about a matter concerning a Philip Davis."

Janet eyed him up and down. "One of Philip's mates, are you?"

"No, I'm a mere postman."

"A postman? Where's your uniform?"

"I'm about to go on holiday," he explained, "but I needed to stop by here first."

Janet caught her breath, and told him to come through. If he had come about Phil, something must be wrong. Were they now sending postmen to carry devastating news about a son or husband serving in the military?

"I'm Philip's mother, Janet," she said as she ushered him into the parlor, "and this is my husband. Farley, this has to do with Philip."

"Philip? What about Philip?"

"The gentleman says he has news, isn't that so, Mister …?"

"Eisenhower, me name's Paul Eisenhower."

Farley set his paper and pencil aside, "Eisenhower? Is this some sort of prank?"

"No, it be me family name," Paul shrugged. "No relation to the good general that I know of. Now, I don't want to worry you. It's just that yesterday, your son and I had a bit of an accident."

Janet's eyes grew wide and her hand went to her mouth as she sank onto a chair.

Farley set aside the paper. "An accident? Good Lord! Is Philip injured? Damn, I told the boy to be careful. Sit down, Eisenhower and explain what this is all about."

"Believe me, it ain't nothing serious at all," Paul assured them. "His car contacted me post office bike in Whitehall. There was a bit of damage to the mudguard and the rear wheel."

"I do recall the boy mentioning something before he left last evening," said Davis, drawing on his pipe.

"So, he's gone, has he?" Paul asked.

"Back to his post."

"Blast!" The blurted word startled Janet. "I'm sorry, Mrs. Davis. But you see, our equipment department at the post office is strict about such things. They want him to sign a report. If you give me his address, I'll pass it to the person in charge of this matter and he can write to him there."

"I can pay for the damages," Mr. Davis offered, taking several pound notes out of his pocket and tossing them on the table between his and

Paul's chair. "That should take care of it. Enough there for a whole new bi-cycle, I'd say."

"I'm afraid he needs to sign the form," Paul persisted. "If I might have his address, I'll not bother you with it any longer."

Farley stiffened. "Just leave it and we'll send it on."

"It has to go directly to him to be official," Paul said, thinking fast.

"Oh, Farley," said Janet, "Let's just give him the boy's address and be done with it. After all, it *is* official business."

Knocking out his pipe, her husband scowled at Paul. "We don't know that, do we? Don't know this fellow either. Do you have Royal Mail papers?"

"I do," Paul responded as he reached in his pocket, took out a wallet, and unfolded his identification.

Davis looked at it and nodded to his wife. "Give him the address."

"It's in the Bible." She disappeared leaving the two men alone for a few long, silent minutes. When Janet returned, she copied their son's address onto a pad and tore the sheet off.

"There you are," she said, handing it to Paul. "I hope you can read my handwriting."

"D company, 2nd Battalion, Ox and Bucks Regiment, Tarrant Rushton, Dorset," Paul read aloud. "Thanks, Mrs. Davis. I've deciphered a lot worse in me time."

"He has a military post office address," she explained, "but he claims his mail arrives faster this way."

"I'm not surprised." Paul stood up, still looking at the address. "What's this Ox and Bucks?"

Janet said proudly, "His regiment is the Oxfordshire and Buckinghamshire."

Farley glared at his wife. "Now I think we've told you enough. Maybe more than we should."

Paul grabbed the handle of his luggage. "Thank you very much. You've been most kind. And now I have to be on my way. I was aiming to get away on holiday yet this morning. Oh, and a Mrs. Tracy sends her regards."

Mr. Davis's face brightened, "So you know Maggie?"

"I only just met her on the way here, didn't I. A kindly sort."

"Humph." Farley's face went dark, and although he shook Paul's hand, it was clear that he was still appraising him.

Sensing the man's distrust, it occurred to Paul that perhaps Davis's father knew more about the invasion plan than he was letting on. Out on the sidewalk, he recalled a newspaper article warning the people to pay attention to anyone acting suspiciously. There were German spies in

England and every citizen was duty-bound to report any strange occurrence or person, no matter how seemingly insignificant. He thought about the young soldier. Had he put the papers in the mail satchel by mistake? If so, when Davis discovers his error, what then? Would he come after Paul and attempt to retrieve the plans? Would he believe he had turned them in at Whitehall? If the lieutenant was a German agent, would he try to harm Paul or possibly even kill him? The postman shuddered. He could go to the authorities, but with what? He had no proof of anything, and all that would accomplish would be to arouse speculation. Without Davis to back him up, he might find himself in a real fix. No, this was something he had to resolve on his own. It was his first chance to do something meaningful for his country since the big war.

When Paul walked past the garden, he found the old woman sitting on the bench. The colonel had apparently given up for the morning and she was enjoying a respite.

"Well, did you find them to home?" she asked.

"I did. Ta," Paul answered as he set down his suitcase and sat next to her. "Maybe I can ask your help again."

"Be happy to, so long as the colonel is away."

"Alls I need to know is whether a bus goes to Waterloo Station from here?"

"Well, the three is the only one that comes by, ya see. To go to Waterloo, you'll need to get back on it and change. It will get you to Camden Town, but you'll be asking the conductor what one to take next."

Paul knew how to get there from his home area, but let it pass. "I'll do that." He stood. "Thank you, and enjoy your gardening."

"I will, won't I, so long as that old man stays out of it."

"We all have our crosses, then, don't we," Paul said as he headed back to Crystal Palace Park Road.

SHAEF Headquarters
Office of the Supreme Commander

General Eisenhower sat behind a dark, wooden desk in his large, modestly appointed office. Behind him, the flags of the United States and Great Britain were joined by the red standard of an army general officer, with its four white stars. His neatly organized desktop included two phones—one a secure hotline to President Roosevelt and the other a scrambler—along with in- and out-baskets, family photos, a coffee mug, and an ashtray.

Ike pulled off his reading glasses and set down a report on the results of the previous day's air attack on aircraft factories at Wiener Neustadt, Austria, pleased that the bomb groups had achieved a high level of success while suffering few losses. The continued softening of Germany's capacity to wage war was heartening to him—so much so that it raised his hopes for the invasion that was only days away.

There was a light tap at the office door followed by the appearance of Lieutenant Commander Harry Butcher, Ike's naval aide and frequent confidant.

"Come in, Butch," the general said. "What's up?"

"You've heard from Leigh-Mallory, sir," the commander said holding up a manila envelope. Butcher was referring to a letter that Eisenhower had asked the air chief marshal to write after he had expressed serious apprehensions about the airborne operation on D-Day. He believed the mission could fail, resulting in the needless slaughter of two divisions of men. In response, the supreme commander employed the military dictum, "PTSIW"—which in polite circles translates as, "put the stuff in writing"— by requesting a letter expressing his concerns.

Ike stood and Butcher handed him the envelope without further comment. The general took the letter out of the manila envelope and scanned its contents.

"Well, he's true to his word," Ike concluded. "He's included every point he made earlier, and then some. According to him, losses could go as high as seventy percent for the gliders."

"Yes, sir. That'd be awful and a damn show stopper."

"It well could be," Eisenhower agreed. "I assured him he had every reason to bring this to my attention. It was his duty, and I'm glad he did it. It doesn't make things any easier, but it is something I needed to know about."

The commander nodded, "Yes, sir."

"Please, ask General Smith to step in."

When Butcher left the office, Ike read Leigh-Mallory's letter in greater detail. His brow furrowed and he reached for a pack of cigarettes, captured one with his lips, and lit it, never taking his eyes off the document.

The door opened and General Smith entered.

"You wanted to see me, Ike?"

"Beetle, Leigh-Mallory has put his concerns about the airborne mission in writing. A sure sign he feels very strongly."

"We knew he did, but this does take it to another level."

"Yes, and there's really not much else to do in terms of planning. There's no need for more advice or consultation. It's too late for that. The operation will either fail or succeed, and we've done everything to assure the latter, but he does make some valid points. I'd like to know if you've sniffed out any other reservations among the chiefs. Are we kidding ourselves here?"

"Ike, I can tell you there have been some differences, but I believe Tedder and Ramsay are on board. Monty has become a cheerleader for Overlord, and the others—Harris, Spaatz, Bradley—are all ready to go. Now, you know it isn't all sweetness and light among any of them, but they see that it can work and are ready to give it hell."

"I wish I could be confident of it," Eisenhower said, "but that will likely never happen, will it? At least not in the next several days. Anything else I need to know about?"

"One thing, but we don't have all the facts yet."

"Please, I don't need any more speculation."

"Ike, you have to hear this. It has to do with security."

"By God, not another loose-lipped general, is it? I hated doing what I had to there," he said, referring to recently busting and sending home a major general for bragging that we would soon be in France enjoying the local wines.

Beetle shook his head, "Not at all. We just got it and have verified the major events with the War Office. I was on my way here with it when Butch ran into me."

"Okay, let's hear it."

"It seems that yesterday, a stack of the Overlord signal documents blew out a War Office window and onto Whitehall."

"Christ!" Ike ground out his cigarette. Those goddamn documents outlined the entire plan, including landing sites, didn't they?"

"Yes, sir. There were twelve of them, and all but one was recovered almost immediately."

The supreme commander simmered. "Damn! What the hell happened, Beetle?"

"This is where it gets foggy. The missing copy showed up at signals more than an hour later, but no one is certain it wasn't compromised."

"Then, we have to assume it was."

"Right, and the Brits are taking action to find and isolate anyone not BIGOT-cleared who might have come in contact with the document. Our man Terry, in G2 ops, is also bird-dogging it with his people."

Ike lit another cigarette. "Where does it stand?"

"As far as anyone can tell, there are two names that popped up of people that had unauthorized access— the guy who turned in the missing copy and a Brit lieutenant whose name he reported to the guard as possibly having lost the plan. The first fellow claimed this lieutenant ran into his bike, sent him ass-over-elbows and the papers he was carrying all over the place. The lieutenant picked them up, but when the bike rider checks his bag later, he finds the classified document."

Ike nodded. "Then he returns it and disappears before he can be debriefed."

"Exactly. The sentry and courier who handled the plan after it was turned in have been cleared."

"So, the other two are still out there." He took a long, reflective drag.

"The kicker is that the guy that turned in the copy is named Eisenhower."

Ike almost gagged. "What? A potential spy using my name?"

"We don't know that. Nothing suspicious came up on any of the rosters. The Brits think it's legit. Apparently, he's just a postman."

"So, this postman named Eisenhower may be walking around with the invasion plans in his head. And the lieutenant?"

"Davis. He's stationed at Tarrant Rushton airfield in Dorset. He's due to go on Operation Tonga."

"The bridge capture. Poor son-of-a-gun. That could be a rough one."

"Right. The Brits plan to put MI6 on him covertly. They're concerned about morale among the troops if the lieutenant is openly identified as a spy."

Ike glared. "Morale would be a helluva lot worse if German guns are awaiting their arrival." He paused and looked down, letting the steam subside. "Of course, they're right. We don't want one of their officers being hauled off so close to H-hour. What about the postman?"

"He's nowhere to be found. Word was he had planned to go to Blackpool on vacation, but that never happened."

"And no one has seen him since? Good God! It sounds like he's the person we should be going after. Dollars to doughnuts, if he's not a spy, he's likely to be a prime target for German agents."

"We haven't been able to confirm anything yet."

"Beetle, let's be sure to ride herd on this. I mean tight control."

"Absolutely. It's top priority."

For the first time in the conversation, Ike appeared to relax. "Oh, and when you have a spare moment, see if you can find out if this postman is any relation."

Headquarters, Security Service (SD), Berlin

Oberführer Schellenberg was at a multicolored wall map of the entire Third *Reich* with highlighted areas indicating where intelligence assets were located. It also showed troop and mechanized deployments, along with places that had been fortified and hardened for expected battles. He ran his hand over the coastline of northwestern France and said to an otherwise empty room, *"I must know. For the Führer! For the Fatherland! And by God, I shall know!"* And then, diving into a deep abyss of thought. *"It will happen. They must invade or concede. With the cock-sure Americans in it, there is no chance of the latter. No, they will come. But where? When?"*

A knock at his door brought him back into the moment.

"Come!" he called.

Colonel von Kroit entered, saluted sharply, and stood at attention.

"You have news I take it."

"Yes, Herr Oberführer. We have engaged an agent in the London area. A woman named Magdalena."

"Ah, yes. I did not know she was available after that unfortunate incident at the war ministry." A smile crossed his lips and his eyes dimmed as he repeated her name, *"Mag-da-le-na."* Von Kroit cleared his throat and the general resumed a stern demeanor. *"And what did you tell her?"*

"I gave her both names—Eisenhower and Davis—and filled her in on their backgrounds, as much as we know. I told her about the lost document and the fact that either or both of them may have had access to the invasion plans. She said she would attend to them immediately."

"Immediately? Kroit, we have already lost more than a day. Do you not understand the need for haste here?"

"Yes, sir. The radio traffic is difficult right now. There is a lot of jamming. Besides, she needed to get to her Enigma device."

"Yes, yes. It is always something. What does she propose to do? How can she possibly attend to both at one time? Has she somehow learned to divide herself?"

"She has chosen to track down this Lieutenant Davis first because she believes he is more likely to have knowledge of the plan and ..."

"Davis! He's in the army. He'll be hell to contact and isolate for interrogation. Why doesn't she go after the postman?"

"Her reply, which came about an hour later, said she had attempted to trace him, but apparently he has dropped out of sight, sir."

"Wonderful—that's simply wonderful! Time is the enemy. Had we moved sooner ..."

Von Kroit headed off the hypothetical. *"She said one of them is all we need. We lost contact before I could ask anything further. She is out of touch now and in pursuit of Davis."*

"Hah! Like some sort of cowboy bounty hunter in one of those foolish Western novels Eisenhower—the real Eisenhower—is said to love so much."

Unsure where to go with that, von Kroit managed, *"Yes, Herr Oberführer."*

The general picked up the swagger stick from his desk. *"We cannot allow either of them to escape our interrogation. Understand?"*

"Yes, sir."

Schellenberg beat the desktop with the stick. *"Do—you—understand?"*

The colonel came to attention, clicked his heels, and cried out, *"Yes, of course, my Führer!"*

The general smirked at von Kroit's slip. *"Good."* He sat and took a more conciliatory tone. *"So, we must do something and we must do it now. Don't you agree?"*

"Yes, sir!"

"We all make sacrifices for the Fatherland, yes?"

"Indeed we do, sir!"

"You may be at ease, Kroit. Take a seat and I will tell you my plan. I propose that you ... you who know this entire story ... you who brought it to me and gave me so much hope ... you go to England and find this postman. You will find him and learn what we need to know to save the Reich! Yes?"

"I—I will go gladly for the Reich and the Führer, sir," von Kroit replied. *"But my English is barely passable, certainly never as good as yours."*

"I have prepared for this very eventuality," the general assured him, opening a folder and pulling out a passport and several other official looking papers. *"You will go as a Dutch expatriate, a language professor who is being employed by the military to teach American and British soldiers Deutsch. Your accent will actually add to your cover."*

Given the *oberführer's* overwhelming determination, there was, of course, no protest. But it did not escape the general's notice that, as he left the room, von Kroit looked as though he was about to face a firing squad.

Telegraph Cottage, Kingston

The gabled cottage, located about three miles from Widewing, was off the beaten path, relatively small, and a perfect retreat for the supreme commander. In the tidy kitchen, Sergeant John Moaney, Ike's valet since 1942, was putting the finishing touches on several sandwiches, while an attractive, leggy brunette in a military uniform poured two cups of coffee from a percolator and put them on a tray. She was Lieutenant Kay Summersby, possibly the most fascinating chauffer of the entire war, having earned this distinction not only because she was Ike's military driver, but also due to the persistent rumors linking her romantically with the general.

Born in County Cork, Ireland, the daughter of retired Lieutenant Colonel Andrew MacCarthy-Morrogh, of the Royal Munster Fusiliers, she had worked, before the war, as a film studio extra, dabbled in photography, and eventually became a fashion model. Married and now divorced, she had retained the name of her ex-husband, and when Britain entered the war in 1939, joined the Mechanised Transport Corps. Throughout the blitz, she had driven an ambulance. After the United States entered the war in December 1941, she became one of many drivers of high-ranking American military officers. Ultimately, she was assigned to Major General Dwight Eisenhower when he arrived in London in May 1942.

"There you are, Lieutenant," The sergeant said, adding the plate of sandwiches to the tray.

"Thanks for your help, Moaney. I'm sure General Ike will enjoy them."

"Well, with Sergeant Hunt off getting supplies, it was my pleasure. I just hope the general is even considering food. He's been doing a lot of smoking and thinking about something since he got here. Not usual for him to bring the office home with him."

"I know, and it concerns me," she admitted as she picked up the tray and headed into a bright living room that looked out on a lovely lawn and garden. There, Ike, tie loose and tunic off, was sitting in an easy chair, hunched over a coffee table.

"You've been beavering away for quite a while, sir," she said, setting the tray down in front of him. "How about taking a break? Could it be that you've been violating your own rule about bringing the war into your sanctuary?"

"You caught me, Kay," he admitted with a weary grin. "I needed to get away and think, but I promise I'm done with it. I've made up my mind and that's final."

"It's always good to come to a conclusion," she said as she sat in a chair opposite his.

"Actually, I came to it earlier when I weighed all sides. Leigh-Mallory had concerns about the airborne mission, but after all the planning and training, and the fact that we've addressed every possible threat, I can't change it. I phoned and told him we go as planned."

"So, now you have second thoughts."

"I did, but I'm over it." Ike lifted the top piece of bread on one of the sandwiches and offered her a mock frown. "Chicken again? Not that I'm complaining. I'm happy just to come here and get away from it all for a while. I have to tell you Kay, this place has meant the world to me, and you and the boys have made it particularly pleasant. Where is everyone, anyway? I'm in the mood for a few hands of bridge."

"T.J. is around somewhere," she said, referring to T.J. Davis, Ike's adjutant. "And I saw Mickey out dog walking."

The Scotty dog had been presented to the general on his birthday in October 1942. He had named the pup Telek after Telegraph Cottage and Kay, two bright spots in his life.

"Oh, and I believe Butch is back at Widewing, sorting out some things with General Beetle," she added.

Ike looked out at the garden full of bright, multicolored rhododendrons, roses, and poppies. "In that case, join me in a bite. Then how would you ..." he made a point of using the British vernacular, "... fancy a stroll?"

She smiled. "That would be lovely. After which I need to collect the mail for T.J."

The general frowned, "That reminds me. There's something else I need to be concerned about—a postman who could well be a fly in the ointment."

Kay suppressed a sigh, knowing as she did, that no matter what he was referring to, the man she had come to love would not rest until he had found a solution.

Waterloo Station, London

The postman showed the document stating that he, Paul Eisenhower, was an official courier. Once the name was compared with his Royal Mail identification, he was allowed to purchase a ticket for the trip into the restricted area of southwest England.

The train to Salisbury arrived thirty-five minutes late, which, for the times, was punctual. It rolled to a stop and Paul looked in the windows and spotted a vacant compartment in the middle coach. As he boarded, two Yank soldiers followed him in—a corporal who looked to be about twenty years old, and a private not out of his teens. They greeted him, put their duffels in the overhead, and sat across from one another by the windows. As the last call whistle sounded, a priest opened the door, excused himself, and stowed his bag. A few years older than Paul, he wore wire-rimmed glasses and was dressed entirely in black except for his Roman collar and the straw boater on his head.

"Hey, Father, you from the states?" the private asked.

"No, just outside of London, actually," the priest told him, smiling. "The name is Dawes, Father John Dawes, S.J."

"Oh, so you're a Jesuit," the private replied. "Well, you look like you're from back home. I'm from Boston. We got lots of priests back there."

The corporal slapped the private's leg. "Hey Tony, you dope, priests look the same all over, ain't that right, Father?"

"So I would guess," answered the clergyman as he took out a small black book from inside his coat and held it up. "If you don't mind."

"Yeah, come on, Tony," the corporal said, pulling out a deck of cards. "My deal."

"Hey, it's always your deal."

The twosome settled into a version of rummy, and the priest commenced reading.

The journey was just less than 100 miles, but at the rate the train was moving, it was sure to take at least three hours. Paul wondered how he could occupy himself. He'd forgotten to pack a book, and his mind's eye saw his copy of *War and Peace* sitting on the nightstand beside his bed. He sighed and closed his eyes, picturing in his head the epic's pages he had already read. He eventually did doze off for what seemed like a few minutes before being awakened by the private, who had just lost another hand.

"Jesus Christ, Ray, don't you ever lose?"

"Please! Leave Our Lord out of it," the priest cautioned. "Remember, my son, we must all have patience and persevere, especially in these troubling times."

Paul knew it was a lesson for him, as well.

SHAEF Headquarters

General Bill Terry was on the phone. "Yeah, I'm tellin' you, my ass was grass and General Smith was a big ol' lawnmower. He was all over me for holding onto this thing for as long as I did."

The voice on the other end of the line was Major Bradford's. "What can I do to turn it around, sir?"

"Beetle said Ike was leanin' toward the postman being the possible culprit. The Brit lieutenant is an operational type. We doubt he's involved. The postman—this Eisenhower guy—is the only one we know for sure had access to the plans. He might have given Davis's name to the guard to throw everyone off his own scent."

"Yes, sir."

"So, what you can do is find this goddamn postman and grill him. Go back to his apartment and trace his steps. Go by the post office where he works and see if any of them have seen him. Contact the train stations again. Maybe they have an update on his whereabouts."

"I'm right on it."

"And for God's sake, keep it low key. We don't need any more bad press about Yanks harassing Brits. When you pick up this guy's trail, go right after him. Take the staff car or whatever you need to get to him. Ed-boy, you're my eyes and ears on this one. If you need authority to do anything, use my name. If that doesn't do it, have them call me pronto. I'll use Ike's name."

After hanging up the phone, Terry put his hand to his forehead and took inventory of the situation. Bradford was a good man and one good man ought to be enough for the job. If he loaded up on operatives, he might lose control and risk the chance of a further breach of security. "Nah, Ed-boy can do it on his own," he assured himself. "Shit, he'd better!"

The Train to Salisbury

When the train squealed to a stop as it pulled into Basingstoke station, Paul awoke in time to see an attractive brunette in uniform at the corridor side door window. Her eyes traveled over him and the card players, who, sensing her gaze, were momentarily distracted. When the priest looked up, her face froze with fear and she quickly disappeared.

"What's her problem?" asked the corporal.

"Hey, you looking for some action, Ray? A little old, ain't she?"

This time his smart mouth earned Tony a jab to the belly.

"Magdalena," the priest muttered almost inaudibly, rising and grabbing his black bag. "I believe I know exactly what her problem is." He quickly exited into the corridor.

"Crap! Did you catch that?" Tony asked. "What in hell are we missing?" He looked at Paul. "You taking off, too?"

Paul shook his head, "I believe I'll stay put."

Tony observed, "Something fishy's going on. Ain't that right, Ray?"

"Can it, Tony."

"So," Paul looked at one then the other, "Ray and Tony."

Both men nodded.

"Coming back from leave are we?"

"We can't say," answered Ray.

"Yeah," Tony added, and putting on a British accent, "It's all rather hush-hush, you know."

Ray eyed Paul. "What about you? What's your story?"

"I'm looking for someone," Paul told him. "Official Royal Mail business. Can't say a word about that either. But perhaps you blokes can help me. I'm on me way to the Tarrant Rushton base in Dorset. Do you know it?"

"Nah," said Ray, "We're lucky we know where our own camp is."

"Yeah, the place is crawling with GIs," said Tony. "Kilroy's all over England. Some of us Yanks are even billeted in the towns."

Ray banged Tony's knee with his own. "Ouch!"

"Hey, you dope, we ain't supposed to say any of that. What if this guy here is some kinda spy? Keep your big trap shut!"

"What?" countered Tony, "I'm not saying nothin' more than name, rank, and serial number."

"Yeah, what about being billeted in the towns."

"Now, who's blabbin'! You shut your trap. How's that!"

"Hey, hey. Respect the stripes." Ray turned his arm and flaunted his two corporal's chevrons.

"Yeah, okay, okay. Sorry. Do I need to call you sir?"

Ray waved a clenched fist at Tony, "Go ahead. Just try."

Paul intervened. "Here, I'm no spy. But right you are. Mustn't go running off at the mouth."

Tony took off his military cap revealing a crop of curly, black hair. "Not that they tell us much. We know something is coming, but we don't know what."

Ray pulled rank. "One more word and I'm turning you in."

"Okay, okay. Let's play."

They went back to rummy and the compartment turned silent while the train sat in the station. When it finally lumbered on and gained speed, the door opened and the priest returned to his seat.

"Welcome back, Padre," said Tony. "Hey, did you hurt yourself?"

Father Dawes took out a handkerchief and blotted the small wound on his forehead. "Silly me," he said. "I walked into the door jamb on the way to the W.C. It's nothing."

Tony asked, "Did you catch up with that lady?"

The priest shook his head. "I thought I knew her, but I was mistaken."

He opened his prayer book, but the young private persisted. "Maybe put some holy water on that cut," he said. "That should be good for it."

Dawes forced a smile. "I have some in my bag. I'll try it later." His eyes dropped to his book, but Tony failed to take the hint.

"So, where you heading, Father?" he said, shuffling the cards.

The priest looked up, exasperated. "I have souls to tend to at various installations. I'm afraid that's all I can say."

Glancing surreptitiously at what was clearly, to his mind, a knife wound on the priest's forehead, Paul concluded that whatever had happened to him, it had nothing to do with the church.

Templehof Air Field, Berlin

A twin-tailed cargo airplane, an *Arado* Ar 232B, one of the aircraft used by the *Reich* Air Ministry for special missions, sat on the apron, the pilot running up each of its four powerful Bramo 323 Fafnir engines in turn. The plane rested on its tricycle landing gear, used for normal operations. However, under the fuselage, it also had eleven sets of small auxiliary wheels, for which it was dubbed *"Tausendfüßler,"* or "Millipede." Its versatile gear and high-mounted engines made it well-suited for use on unimproved landing strips.

In the cockpit, the navigator, a brawny, fair-haired *oberfeldwebel*, or master sergeant, who was also responsible for manning the MG 131 machine gun in the plane's nose, sat reviewing his charts. Next to him, the pilot, a *Luftwaffe* captain, was setting switches and checking dials while behind them, the radio operator, a *funkmeister* who also ran the power-operated dorsal turret and its MG 151 machine gun, was at his console. Aft in the bay, a tall, Aryan sergeant, whose other function was that of the plane's loadmaster, climbed into the rear turret with its MG 131 machine gun. The sole passenger, riding in one of the comfortable seats that had been added to the cargo bay, was Colonel von Kroit. He wore the garb of a Dutch country gentleman, and was talking on a radiotelephone.

"*Yes, Herr Oberführer,*" he said, "*I am ready to go. We are cleared to depart within minutes and the pilot informs me that the flight will be approximately seven hours, with a stop near Calais for fuel.*"

Von Kroit pressed the black headset to his ear, laboring to hear Schellenberg's voice over the engine noise and tolerating the pause due to the scrambler delay.

"*Kroit, the aircraft must be back in Berlin by ten tomorrow morning. The Reichsführer has need of it. If you cannot return, it must.*" And then, without waiting for the colonel's expected concurrence, the *oberführer* asked "*Have you contacted Magdalena yet?*"

"*Yes, sir, I have. She has located Davis's unit at a camp in Dorset, England. Tarrant Rushton.*" He looked at his wristwatch, "*She is on a train to Salisbury now. Over.*"

"Good. The idea is to divide and conquer. She'll pursue Davis and you go after this Eisenhower. With both, we can make doubly sure we have valid information for the Führer. I'm counting on you, Kroit."

Railway Station
Salisbury, England

As the train slowed for its arrival, the railway guard came by and announced that there would be a delay for anyone exiting at this station. When they came to a stop, Paul watched out the window as a squad of local police boarded and cordoned off the very coach he and the others were in. No one was allowed to detrain while two constables carried off a sheet-wrapped bundle. They laid it on a bench where a bearded gentleman carrying a leather case was standing.

"Looks like a doctor," said Paul as he observed the man open his bag, take out a stethoscope, and pull back the sheet. Instantly, Paul recognized the face of the woman he had seen in the window earlier. The red blotch on the front of her uniform jacket startled him. "Blimey!"

The doctor opened her jacket and shirt and examined a bloody wound just below her sternum. He listened to her chest and neck with his instrument, then re-covered the body. He called over a nattily dressed, gray-haired man, spoke with him briefly, and left.

Detective Inspector Miles of the Salisbury police summoned another plainclothesman, a detective sergeant. "Canniff, check with the guards for that carriage and the ones on either side of it. Account for any traffic through it since Basingstoke. Apparently, that was the last time she was seen alive."

"Already asked the guard, Guv. No one went through at all."

"Good, we can release the others and concentrate on the coach where it happened. It shouldn't have been long, the body's still warm, for God's sake."

Paul watched as one of the men standing by the body passed the word to the officers guarding his carriage. Shortly thereafter, passengers detrained from the other railcars and were allowed to leave the station. At the same time, the riders in Paul's car were taken off and brought to a dreary waiting room guarded by four constables.

Paul looked around and realized that nearly every traveler in the room was military—mostly Yanks and a few Brits. There were also two women wearing the same type of uniform the dead woman had worn. Paul could now see that they were members of the Mechanised Transport Corps, probably on their way to chauffer VIPs or drive ambulances and support vehicles. Then there was the priest, wearing his own kind of uniform, leaving Paul as the only one of the group in civilian clothes. Wishing he had taken his Royal Mail jacket, he mingled with the others and did his best to blend in.

After about ten minutes, the two men who had been by the body entered. The man who was clearly in charge of the operation announced, "I am Detective Inspector Miles. As you may have guessed, it appears a crime has been committed in the coach in which you all were traveling, and we need to sort it out. We have established that the victim's assailant did not leave your carriage after the time the crime could have taken place. We must then assume that person is still here, in this room. We will begin your interviews shortly. In the meantime, please give your papers to Detective Sergeant Canniff."

"I say," the priest spoke up, "Here are mine." He handed Canniff a packet. "However, do you have authority to check the identification of these military chaps? Most of them are our allies. I'm just a priest, but it seems to me proper to bring in the military police to conduct this."

"The father got a point, Guv," Canniff, a grim faced fellow with a gravelly voice agreed.

"Right," the detective inspector waved it off. "We'll skip that for now."

Carrying the priest's papers, Canniff nodded to his boss, and left.

The inspector continued. "We want to get this cleared up right away and have some standard questions. Quite routine under these circumstances, as I'm sure you understand."

The irrepressible Tony spoke up. "Excuse me. We all have places we gotta be. Look none of us left our seats. Can't you dismiss us first?"

"Good idea. However, that will take some time to ascertain. Please bear with us. I beg your patience." Inspector Miles began his interview with the two women, asking them basic questions. "Where did you board? Were you on the train in Basingstoke? Did you move from your seat at any time? Did you know the dead woman?" Surprisingly, both MTC drivers answered in the negative to the last question. Although she wore the same uniform, they had never seen her before.

Just as the interrogation moved to an American private, Canniff returned and whispered something in the inspector's ear.

Miles calmly walked over to the priest. "Father, would you please come with me?"

The man of God calmly complied and the two men left the room.

This got a rise out of Tony, who jabbed Ray. "See that?" he demanded. "What in hell ...?"

Paul ignored him, absorbed for the moment in the memory of the wound on the priest's forehead when he had returned to the compartment. Being more tired than curious, he sighed, leaned his head back, and closed his eyes, letting his mind wander; however, the bladder he had not emptied since that morning began to nag him. He got up and went to one of the constables.

"Sorry, mate, but I'm in need of the facilities."

The young policeman gave a curt nod and followed Paul out. "You can't go into the main terminal. You'll have to use the one down there." He pointed to a narrow basement access. "Down those stairs, right, then left, then first right." He posted himself at the top of the steps. "There's no way out, so you'll need to come back this way."

Paul descended the stone stairway into the musty basement of the station. Once down, it became clear the young policeman's directions were wrong, and he began searching with increasing desperation for the toilet. The ceiling was low, and cobwebs clung to mildewed beams above his head. The dank place seemed to consist entirely of narrow corridors and locked doors. The only illumination was the occasional naked light bulb hanging from an electric cord. Finally, Paul came to a door set slightly ajar on which someone had crudely painted W.C. Once he had relieved himself, as he buttoned up, Paul was aware of voices coming from a metal grate on the wall high above the commode. It was an air duct, and he was about to disregard it until, recognizing the clipped intonations of the priest from the train, he stood on the commode and strained to listen.

"You can well imagine, Canniff here was quite surprised to find this note among the papers of a priest." Paul recognized the voice to be that of Inspector Miles.

"The collar is merely a ruse, inspector," Father Dawes replied. "A passport you might say, to gain entry into places I might otherwise have difficulty going."

"Here we were considering having you perform the last rites over her," Paul heard Canniff say.

"I will have the remains seen to," Dawes assured them. "For now, treat this as a suicide and leave the rest to me. Give it some time to look convincing, you know, then let the others in the waiting room go on. Now, I'll need to ring my office. In private, if I may."

The sound of a door opening and closing was followed by the staccato clicking of a phone dial and the priest's voice saying, "Yes, Kane here," and something about level five clearance and no encryption. And then, after a pause, "The deed is done. Not the way we should have liked, but she is no longer an issue. I followed her onto the train at Waterloo. At Basingstoke, she recognized me and bolted. She knew it was over, and I thought she'd do the right thing and bite the capsule. Instead, she came after me with a blade, leaving me little choice. The police are cooperating."

Faint phone sounds drifted from the vent.

"I have no idea what she was after. She wore an MTC uniform, if that's any clue. It'll all come out sooner or later, I suppose. I'll be returning to London forthwith."

More muffled noises.

"You do? Who?"

Paul pressed his head against the duct grill.

"Lieutenant Philip Davis? What's he have to do with anything?"

The postman shivered.

"Whitehall did what? By Jove, that's quite incredible. What! Someone named Eisenhower?"

The jolt provided by hearing his name nearly knocked Paul off his perch.

"I see. Not that Eisenhower. The Yanks are involved? Yes, I had better, then. Have someone collect the body and I'll tend to things here."

The shaken postman held on to a water pipe desperately trying to keep both his balance and composure.

"To Tarrant, immediately. Ox and Bucks. Of course. Niles. Saint Mary's. Yes, that should work well considering my present masquerade. Cheerio."

The phone clicked and so did Paul's mind. What had he just heard? The priest was not a priest at all, but some sort of agent. But what kind of agent, and working for whom? The Jerries? If so, would he be after Paul for what he knows? Or, if the priest was with British intelligence, might he be coming after him as a spy? Something had gone terribly wrong.

Paul rushed back through the dank halls, propelled by a fear that was quickly spinning out of control. It must have helped him navigate the confusing labyrinth because in less than a minute he was standing, pallid and panting, in the waiting room.

Inspector Miles was announcing that the woman's death had been judged a suicide and foul play was no longer suspected. He told the group they were free to leave, but Paul just stood there, even more frightened and bewildered than before. He needed time to put the pieces of this puzzle together, but he knew when he did, he might not like what he saw.

Arado Ar 232
Somewhere over Northeastern France

"She was what? Over." Von Kroit was again on the radiophone, shouting over the noise of engines. It and the scrambler-descrambler delay were maddening.

Schellenberg repeated, *"She has been neutralized. Done for. Do you understand?*

"Yes, sir. I understand. Kaput! Over."

"Correct, and we have no time to waste. It is bad news, but we must carry on. I have no other assets readily available, so I want you to divert to this Tarrant Rushton airfield. You must take Magdalena's place. Find Lieutenant Philip Davis."

"But sir, what about the postman? Over."

"Kroit. Stop with the 'over.' I know when you are finished. Now, Magdalena went after Davis for a reason. We don't know what that was, but I must conclude she had evidence that he was the more likely target—the one who could divulge the plans to us. At any rate, we must work with what we have. Tell the pilot that there is a remote landing area just west of the town at fifty degrees fifty-one north by two degrees zero five west. I will make arrangements to support you there."

Von Kroit repeated the landing coordinates to himself, committing them to memory.

Schellenberg continued, *"Someone will come to meet you. If not, it is only a short walk to the White Horse public house. It is on the main access road to the base. Helga, cover name Ruth, is your primary contact."*

There was just time for Von Kroit to say, *"Heil Hitler,"* before the phone went silent.

Railway Station, Salisbury

Paul hustled along the station platform following a sign for autobuses and, wishing to avoid the man he knew to be a killer, picked up his pace when he spotted two olive-drab military buses waiting at the curb. When he boarded the one for Tarrant Rushton – Blandford, the corporal behind the wheel held up his hand like a traffic cop. "Sorry, mate, no civilians. Bases are closed to outsiders. Maneuvers, you know."

"I'm on official business," Paul countered, pulling the Royal Mail document from his pocket. "There's me authority."

The driver glanced at it. "You can come on, but I got me orders too, don't I. You might try in the morning. Do you want Tarrant or Blandford?"

"Tarrant," Paul replied.

"I can drop you in town. There's a pub. That'll have to do you."

Paul was about to take the first available seat right behind the driver when he heard, "Hey, mister, there's room back here."

He lugged his bag down the aisle avoiding the rucksacks and duffels of the soldiers who were already seated. Most gazed emptily out the windows or attempted napping in the uncomfortable seats.

In the back of the bus, he spotted two faces he had not expected to see again. "Hi, mister," said Tony.

"How's it goin'?" asked Ray.

"Looks like we are all goin' to the same place," he observed, taking a seat across the aisle from them.

Tony responded. "We couldn't say. Right, Ray?"

"Look mister," said the Yank corporal, "like I said on the train, we can't say a thing. Let's keep it that way."

"I understand I won't be able to get onto the Tarrant Rushton base tonight," Paul observed. "The driver said there is a pub in town. Do you know it?"

Ray's nod to Tony was apparently permission for him to speak.

"Yeah, there's a few, but we go right past one," he said. "Nice place, if you like warm beer."

Ray smirked, "You're pretty okay with the warm girls, though."

"Now who's giving away secrets? If my Anna ever finds out …"

Paul headed off further comment, "The pub?"

"Yeah, they have rooms there. You should be okay. Hey, what's your name anyway? We been spendin' all this time together and we don't even know what to call you."

"Frank, Frank Jason." The lies were becoming easier for Paul and he was feeling good about how it all was going until he spotted Father Dawes at the bus door. The bogus priest exchanged a few words with the driver and was allowed to board. Clearly, he had been correct about the collar gaining him access to just about anywhere. Sliding down behind the man in front of him, Paul was relieved to see Dawes take the seat behind the driver. He prayed Tony and Ray didn't call the Jesuit back, but he needn't have worried. They showed little interest in receiving another dose of his moral guidance as they gladly returned to their hands of rummy.

The White Horse Pub
Tarrant Rushton, Dorset, England

The pub was located along a main street of the tiny hamlet and Helga Reichenhoff, a long-time Abwehr operative now part of Schellenberg's domain, was its owner. Its location close to two military bases made it ideal for gleaning information let slip over pints of beer. She was a blue-eyed blonde who was as hefty as a Munich barmaid, which is exactly what she had been earlier in her career.

In 1929, she was still a teenager when Adolf Hitler spoke before members of his National Socialist German Workers Party at her beer hall. Helga had become instantly transfixed by the emotion, ideals, and extreme nationalism of the charismatic man. Soon afterward, she joined the movement, and because she had been a World War I refugee, raised in Bexley, England until she was twelve, she was eventually chosen and trained for covert operations in the U.K.

Using the cover name, Ruth Rice, she had worked first in Devon, then London, until three years ago, when it became clear that the English would not be easily defeated. She took ownership of the White Horse, after the then owner, Tom Smyth, was found dead of an apparent suicide. Ruth arrived from out of nowhere to mourn him and, as the papers she brought with her proved her to be his closest living relative, claim ownership of the pub. It hadn't taken long for the plain living folks of the area to accept her as one of their own.

Now, she was standing out front of the pub as a truck, the contents of its stake bed covered with a tarpaulin, drove up and stopped.

The driver, a pot-bellied, dark-haired man wearing a leather apron and a stained shirt, climbed down from the cab and greeted her. "How be things today, Ruthy?" he asked pulling the tarp aside to reveal an array of wooden beer kegs.

"Not at all busy," she replied. "None of the usual blokes from the bases, was there."

"Right. Been quiet all over for almost a week."

She indicated the barrels. "Just one will do, and there's an empty in the storage."

As he hoisted the beer onto his back, the publican asked, "I suppose your trade on base has picked up."

"That it has." He eased the keg to the ground and rolled it to the door.

She followed him into the pub. "Any word of what's happening? Don't seem to be the usual practice drills, does it?"

"Nay, not likely. Great deal of activity. But who knows? I don't condone a bit of it. We'd be better off accepting the Jerries just like the Frenchies did. They seem to be getting on all right. We've suffered long enough, I say."

"I have to agree with you," she said, eyeing him speculatively. "You know, Malcolm, we've always seen eye-to-eye on it. I believe the takeover is going to happen no matter what, and we have to be ready for it."

"I suppose you're right, Ruthy," he said as he hoisted the keg and set it on end, unaware of the smile spreading across her broad face."

London

After getting all the information he could on Lieutenant Davis, Ed Bradford spent the afternoon tracking down the postman named Eisenhower. He'd returned to Paul's flat and checked again there. Miss Crowley was gone, but a nosy neighbor in a faded blue housedress was happy to share whatever information she could, including the very recent gossip about Paul and the attractive music teacher, even though Ed took pains to assure her that he was only interested in locating Eisenhower.

Making a pointless attempt to smooth down her scraggly gray hair, she offered, "You might drop into the Cock and Rose. He spends quite a bit of time there, doesn't he."

Armed with directions to the pub, Bradford went on what he figured was likely another wild goose chase. When he arrived at the Cock and Rose, he asked the barman if he knew Paul Eisenhower.

"Who wants to know?" Johnny responded.

Ed introduced himself and explained that Paul had been involved in an accident with a military man, and he was just following up.

"Yeah, I heard him mention that, but wasn't the bloke British?"

Ed scrambled for a second. "We're allies, all working together. So, you do know him?"

"Know him? Of course I do. Spends a lot of time here. Poor devil. Seems like he has no place else to go. He's usually in every evening, after his duties for the post. The bloke delivers letters all day and seems to remember every bloody address. We have him read articles in the daily and challenge him. He'll quote them back word for word. Won a few bob and pints at it up till we all got wise and quit wagering. He's right good at darts, as well."

Ed made a mental note of the memory claim. "Well, would you know where he might be now?"

All the major was able to get out of the man was confirmation that the postman said he was going to Blackpool on holiday. On the chance that Eisenhower and the lieutenant were in cahoots, Bradford drove to the Davis home in the Crystal Palace Park area. There, Farley and Janet told him Paul had been there earlier, but they had no idea where he might have gone.

"He said he was going away once he contacted our Philip," the lieutenant's mom added.

"Did he say what he wanted from your son?"

Farley spoke up, "Only that he needed his address to send him an accident report to sign."

"So, you gave him the address at Tarrant Rushton?"

The pair traded surprised looks and Farley asked, "Here, how did you know that?"

Offering no explanation, Ed thanked them, excused himself, and hurried to the door.

As he drove back down Sydenham Avenue, he saw the victory garden crew leaning on their rakes and spades. On a whim, he stopped and sought information about his elusive quarry. The ever-accommodating Maggie Tracy gave the major one of the biggest leads of the day when she told him that, after Paul had visited the Davis house, he'd asked about the bus route to Waterloo station.

From his earlier experience tracking the postman's movements, Ed knew trains did not go to Blackpool from Waterloo. Driving as fast as traffic would allow, he got to the station in minutes and was dealt yet another stroke of luck. The ticket master remembered Paul because of the special travel authorization he had presented, and confirmed that, hours earlier, the postman had indeed purchased a fare to Salisbury.

"Oh, and by the way," the agent added, "he inquired about a connection to Tarrant Rushton. There is a rail, but it's no longer in regular service."

As far as Ed was concerned, that cinched it. Paul was definitely planning to link up with Lieutenant Phil Davis. Could this really be a spy ring? Ed ran out of the station and hopped in his jeep, determined to find out.

The Bus to Tarrant Rushton

The ride to the town was slightly over twenty miles, but because it was by way of narrow country roads, the cautious bus driver stretched it to almost an hour. Paul watched out the window as they traveled by rolling farmland and through nameless hamlets identified only by signs with military insignia revealing some kind of armed forces installation nearby. Tony was right; there were camps all over the countryside.

As the bus was about to enter yet another village, it stopped at a crossroads. When the driver turned back to speak to the priest, Paul could just make out what he was saying. "Father, this be as close as I can take you. St. Mary's is just up that street. Not Roman though, is it. It's Church of England."

"That's perfectly fine, Sergeant," Father Dawes replied, and picking up his black bag, he stepped to the open door. "We work closely with vicars all the time, especially for the war effort. You have been most helpful."

Paul breathed a sigh of relief as the vehicle rolled on and turned left. If what he had overheard back at the railway station meant what he thought it did, the more distance between himself and Father Dawes, the better. About a half mile farther down the road, the driver slowed and stopped again. He called out. "Oy, mate. If you're interested, the pub is just there."

"Indeed I am." Paul picked up his luggage.

Tony waved. "Hey Frank, take it easy."

Ray added, "Maybe we'll see you again. Who knows?"

"Aye, who knows?" Paul replied as he headed down the aisle, unable to dismiss the thought that, with what they would be facing, even their loved ones might never see the Yank soldiers again.

St. Mary's Church, Tarrant Rushton

St. Mary's was a beautiful little fourteenth century church of flint and stone, built in the form of a cross, with sections that dated back to the Normans. Its gothic windows were boarded up to protect the stained glass from war damage.

Inside, Father John Dawes stood in the south transept shedding his priestly garb. Out of his jacket and undoing his collar, he heard the main door creak open and close with a thud. He glanced into the nave and saw a slight, balding man toting a leather suitcase coming quickly down the center aisle.

"Ah, Niles, good to see you," he said, extending his hand. "On the spot as always, what?"

"Yes, sir. At your service, as ever."

Dawes was, in reality, Sir Harold Kane, code-named, "Jackdaw," one of MI6's most capable and decorated agents, and one with a license to kill.

"The vicar here was kind enough to allow us this—you know, being ecumenical, et cetera—so let's make the most of it, shall we?" Sir Harold declared. "He has no clue who I am, and I'd prefer keeping it that way."

And with that, he went on to explain that his goal was to abduct Lieutenant Philip Davis and keep him out of circulation until after the invasion, when any classified information he might have would become irrelevant. Should the opportunity present itself, he was to do the same with the postman.

Niles Peters, a mouse of a man, but a most resourceful agent, had been called upon many times to aid Sir Harold and had never once come up short. He produced a Royal Air Force uniform jacket with four stripes on each blue-gray cuff, and held it up for inspection.

"Group Captain?" Sir Harold observed. "I say, that's a bit of a demotion."

"Yes, sir. Can't be a general every time. It was all I could manage on short notice. We didn't anticipate your going back out so soon."

"Nor did I. A quiet evening with friends awaited me, but duty called."

Niles sat in an old deacon's chair and watched Jackdaw transform himself into a military officer.

Once Sir Harold put on the tunic, he checked its inside breast pocket and examined the papers he found there. Satisfied with his new identity, he pulled on a pair of well-polished boots and was about to top off the costume with a service cap, when Niles reminded him they were in a church and handed him a pistol.

"That may come in handy, and there are the usual aids in the uniform," the slight man offered as he gathered up the cast off clothes and put them into the luggage. Finally, he produced a dossier with a picture of Lieutenant Philip Davis and handed it to Sir Harold, who examined it with "Hmmm" and a "Right-o."

"Will there be any further need for my services, sir?"

"A ride someplace where I can spend the night," the man who gone from priest to group captain replied. "I shouldn't want to attempt getting on the base until morning, even in this getup. They say it's sealed tight."

"Yes, sir. I do know of a local pub with some rooms that might do."

"Good show. We can go over my cover story in the car."

Cock and Rose Pub, Camden Town

Home Guard Sergeant Tommy Doyle bellied up to the bar, once again looking worn out from his tour of duty, and ordered his usual.

"A pint it is," the publican replied cheerfully, pumping a full glass of brew and setting it on the bar.

Doyle took a long drink. "Lord, that's what I needed? Another slow day, was it?"

"It's been that way of late, I'm afraid," John told him. "What with so many blokes off to war and money being what it is. Besides, word is, they have the military confined to their camps. All London is quiet. Well, save for the racket overhead. But I did have one interesting visitor earlier. A Yank, and you know we don't get many of their kind. He was this major asking after Paul."

"Did you get his name?" Tommy asked nonchalantly.

"Ah, let's see, Bradley. No, Brad something. He said it but I can't … hold on … Bradford! That was it, Major Bradford. Like the name of the town up by Leeds where the wife has family."

"I don't suppose you could tell him much."

"Only that Paulie was off to Blackpool."

"And did that do it? Was it all he wanted?" Tommy asked.

Receiving a nod back from the barman, the sergeant drained his glass and set a coin on the bar. "I've had it for today, Johnny. Need to go home and have a good soak and some rest." He walked almost too casually to the door, "Till tomorrow, mate."

Headquarters, Security Service (SD), Berlin

Schellenberg was gazing out his office window at gathering storm clouds when there was a knock on his door. *"Come,"* he called as he turned and walked back to his desk.

An aide, *SS Sturmbannführer* Klaus Earhardt, entered carrying a folder. *"Herr Oberführer, this report just arrived from Thor."* He opened the folder and handed over a yellow paper.

"Ah, Thor. Maybe good news, yes?"

Earhardt shrugged. *"Possibly, sir."*

"Thank you, you may go."

As the aide left, Schellenberg leaned on the desk and read the report. *"Hmmm. A Major Bradford. He may have been sent to control the situation. But why an American?"*

The White Horse Pub, Tarrant Rushton

The glass of beer Paul was sipping had done little to satisfy his hunger, and his stomach grumbled as he waited patiently for his order of shepherd's pie. Finally the kitchen door swung open and Ruth approached with a tray. "There you be, love," she said, setting the plate in front of him. "Is there anything else I can get for you? Another pint, perhaps?"

"Oh, no. This'll do. Then I'll be off to bed."

"The room is to your liking, is it?"

"It's fine. I even dozed off for a bit, but my stomach held forth and here I am." Paul dug into his meal of potato and carrots, mingled sparsely with lamb. The dish was more peppery than he would have liked, but his hunger and the luxury of having meat two days in a row swelled his enjoyment.

He was about to finish it off when he saw a familiar face in a not-so-familiar outfit enter the pub. The man in the RAF officer's uniform was carrying a black bag that Paul also recognized. The priest who was no longer a priest was coming straight for him. Diverting his eyes to his plate, Paul worked at keeping everything he had just deposited in his stomach from making an encore appearance.

The officer passed without a hint of recognition and asked the publican if there were rooms available. She said there were several and commented that it was unusual for an officer to be staying there. He explained that the base was under quarantine for maneuvers and he needed a place for the night.

"Please sign the book" Ruth said, "and that'll be one crown, sir." He scribbled a name in the register and handed her a coin, receiving a key in return.

"It's first floor up the stairs to the right. Number's on the key."

As the officer walked back past him, Paul recalled that upsetting phone conversation and concluded that the ex-priest had assumed a new disguise and was going after Lieutenant Davis. For the moment, he felt safe in his anonymity.

★ ★ ★ ★

Outside, Ed Bradford's jeep arrived from the direction of the base and the major hopped out and strode quickly to the pub door. He entered and assessed the place—the sot standing at the end of the oak bar, the few patrons at the tables, and the woman wiping and stacking glasses. There was nothing remarkable about any of it, but his three years in intelligence had taught him to observe every one and every event closely.

Paul watched as the new arrival requested a room for the night. The palaver was similar to the previous one, except this time his stomach was calm.

"There you be, Major ..." Ruth squinted at the signature on the register, "... Bradford is it?"

He nodded. "Right, Bradford."

She handed the new guest a key. "Welcome." Then adding as she eyed his uniform, "So, a Yank, are ya?"

"Yes, ma'am. I tried to get on base, but they turned me away."

She lowered her voice. "Something big happening, is it?"

Ed dodged the question. "No, just training exercises. Anyhow, I was happy to find your pub."

"Oy," she waved him off. "It's our pleasure."

Bradford grinned and went back outside to the jeep.

According to a wall clock, it was after nine. As the pub owner pulled blackout drapes over the windows, Paul headed for the stairs, unaware that the man who was doggedly pursuing him was only a few steps behind.

Tarrant Rushton Air Base

The runways and taxiways of the RAF installation were clear, but the parking apron was lined with rows of Horsa and Hamilcar gliders, and larger Halifax bombers that had been modified for use as tugs. Several twin-engine fighter-bombers were parked by large hangars where the gliders were assembled and the powered aircraft maintained. The rest of the installation consisted of a control tower, support buildings, tents, and temporary barracks rimming the airfield. The latter housed the enlisted men and officers who were about to risk their lives to liberate Europe.

Inside one such structure, designated officer quarters for the Second Battalion, Oxfordshire and Buckinghamshire Light Infantry, Lieutenant Phil Davis sat on the edge of his cot and watched daylight slowly fading outside.

Lieutenant Trevor Lunt, his cubicle mate, stood by the window smoking. He took a final drag and tossed his cigarette into the red tin he was holding. "I say it's time to go," he said, setting the tin on the floor with a deliberate clank.

"I don't know, Trev," Phil replied. "It's a colossal risk."

"Say mate, where's your pluck? What in hell can they do to us? Exclude us from the mission? I'd call that an act of kindness, wouldn't you?"

"No, they'd likely consider it an act of treason and shoot us for deserting," Phil said, rising reluctantly. "Besides, I really want to go to France. You'd risk anything to get into a bird's knickers, wouldn't you? To me, it isn't worth it after all the bloody anticipation. I'd as soon be done with it and on the way over."

"What's the chance of anything happening in the next few hours?" Trevor said impatiently. "Come on Phil, the girls are waiting."

"And you're certain your scheme will work?"

"I've been tracking it for days," Trevor said, checking his watch. "Look, the beer lorry shows up at the same time every night. In a few minutes it'll be parked behind the club."

"Right. Provided …"

"It will be, trust me. Then, after his delivery, the driver heads back to the village. Just like clockwork."

"So, all we have to do is what?"

"Secret ourselves among the kegs until we get away from the base and we're home free."

"And how do we plan to return?"

"No need to till dawn. We show up and tell the gate guards we're joining our unit. Mind your papers."

Taking his tunic off a coat rack, Phil checked for documents in the inside pocket. "Oh, God," he said wearily. "Why do I listen to you?"

"Look, there it is." Trevor watched as the beer truck rolled past. "As expected, he's headed for the club. Come on."

Outside, the two officers approached the parked truck. "Slowly," Trevor cautioned. "Don't want to attract attention, do we."

They waited for the beer man to finish hauling kegs to and from the delivery dock before making a move to the back of the vehicle.

"Here!" Trevor whispered, jumping up onto the truck's bed. "Under the tarp."

It was stifling beneath the canvas and that, together with the smell of rancid beer, made Phil gag by the time the driver returned. They could hear the beer man humming as he got in, cranked the engine, and turned the truck back down the main road toward the gatehouse.

"What will the girls say when they smell us?" Phil insisted.

Trevor slapped his hand over Phil's mouth. The vehicle paused for a minute and they could make out an exchange with the guard before the driver was allowed to proceed. They had made it.

The White Horse Pub, Tarrant Rushton

The burden of the Overlord information, mixed with the over-spiced shepherd's pie, kept Paul tossing and turning; even his reminiscence of the wonderful evening with Emily failed to relax him. Finally, he figured a drink might be in order, and since it was only quarter past ten, he decided to go down to the pub. As he descended the staircase, he found the place wreathed in quiet except for the radio speaker carrying the sound of Vera Lynn singing about meeting again some sunny day. By the time he reached the bottom step, the song filled him with nostalgia and longing for the days when it was peaceful and secure in this country he so loved.

From behind the bar, Ruth called, "Ah, Mister Jason, what can I get for you?"

"A good glass of claret, if you would," Paul said, going on to explain that he was having trouble sleeping. He took his glass to a table in the corner where he could listen to Vera Lynn sing about bluebirds and the white cliffs of Dover in peace, only to find, to his dismay, that the RAF officer he had first met as a priest on the train was heading right for him carrying a drink. Paul shrunk down into his seat, but it did no good. The man pulled up a chair and sat across from him. "Oh, God," he thought, "what do I do now? The bloke is a killer and he's right here in front of me."

"Hello again," the officer said, extending his hand, "I'm sorry to disturb you. We never were properly introduced. I'm, ... oh, names matter so little these days ... John Dawes will suffice. You do remember me, of course. I suppose I owe you an explanation."

Paul shook his hand and nodded almost too vigorously. "I'd welcome that. I really would."

"Right, and so you shall have it. As you might suppose, I'm working undercover—neither, actually, a priest nor an RAF officer. My job is security and secrecy." He looked deep into Paul's eyes. "This is where you come in."

"How's that?" Paul's mouth was so dry that he could scarcely utter the words.

"I am in pursuit of a possible security breach of the gravest nature," the RAF man explained in a low voice.

Paul figured he had surely been found out, and the agent was toying with him. "How long," he wondered, "before I, an innocent postie doing a mate a favor, turn up dead?"

His frightened expression spoke for him and Dawes asked, "Is there something wrong? I don't mean to alarm you, but I do need your cooperation. You've seen me as two different people, and I need to ensure that you never reveal what you know. You are aware of the official secrets act, what?"

Since all postmen had been briefed on the act and how it applied to them, the only question Paul needed to ask was, "What must I do?"

The officer regarded him genially. "Simply forget you ever saw me as the priest."

Emboldened by the possibility that he was not going to be killed after all, Paul voiced his own doubts. "I have to know who in bloody hell you work for," he said. "You might be a spy. A bloke like me wouldn't know about such things, now would he."

"I assure you, I'm on your side. I am an agent working for the Crown. That's all I can say, and I can't show you identification because I don't carry any other than for the role I am playing at the time. You simply have to trust me as I must trust you." He regarded Paul for a moment. "What is it you do and why are you here?"

Paul was spared having to devise an answer by the arrival of two army officers each with an arm around an attractive damsel. As they went for a table, Paul recognized one of them. So did Sir Harold. It was the person responsible for setting them both on this little adventure. Paul took the occasion to make his escape, if only temporarily. Whatever was going on in the spy world, he needed to make contact with Lieutenant Davis.

When Paul approached the group, Phil not only recognized him but remembered his name. "Eisenhower the postie. What are you doing here?"

"We need to talk ..." Paul barely got out the words when the two lieutenants shot to attention, respecting the four stripes on Sir Harold's sleeve.

"I say, should you chaps be out and about at this hour?" asked the senior officer as he joined them.

Phil was the first to speak up, albeit irrationally. "You see, sir, we have, er, we, I ..."

"No excuse, sir," blurted Trevor.

"Your name?"

"Lieutenant Trevor Lunt, sir. Second Ox and Bucks."

The group captain turned to the other man. "And you?"

"Lieutenant Philip Davis, Second Ox and Bucks as well, sir."

Sir Harold was delighted to learn that the object of his mission had landed right in his lap, but he took pains not to show it. "Yes, well, I recommend you return to your post. Lieutenant Lunt, if you will, first see the ladies home."

"Yes, sir!" Trevor gathered up the two confused women, saluted smartly, and left.

Phil was still at attention when Sir Harold took pity. "Rest easy, Lieutenant. You may sit." As the young officer did so, the group captain regarded Paul and asked, "Now, my good man, who are you really?"

"Me? I'm no more than a simple postman. I really don't know how I got caught up in all this, but it all began with this bloke here."

"And, your name is Eisenhower, eh?" Sir Harold asked, and when Paul nodded timidly, he exclaimed, "Good-oh! I say, we *are* making progress. It seems I have you both together in one place."

"And I have all of *you,*" Ruth said as she pointed a deadly MP 40 machine pistol directly at them.

Chapter Four
Wednesday, 31 May 1944

Arado Ar 232
Over Dorset, England

Colonel von Kroit gazed out the round window by his seat at the farmland and forests barely discernible in the misty moonlight. As the aircraft banked and turned to the right, the pilot feathered the engines and glided almost silently over the village, then headed back toward a field located at the coordinates provided by *Oberführer* Schellenberg. As the Ar 232 rumbled across the bumpy furrows of fallow farmland, its rigid wings and fuselage shuddered noisily until it came to rest. Von Kroit checked his watch and noted that they had landed in Tarrant Rushton at eight minutes after one in the morning, local time. Looking out, he saw the outline of a truck waiting at the edge of the field.

As soon as the aircraft's engines had spun down, the Nazi colonel walked forward to the cockpit and demanded, *"Captain, you are to await my return for as long as possible."*

"Yes, Herr Standartenführer. So long as we are in Berlin before ten in the morning for the Reichsführer."

"I understand this and remind you, local time is one hour ahead of Berlin. If I do not return in time, you are free to go, in which case, you are to inform Oberführer Schellenberg's office."

"Yes, sir. Good luck."

"Thank you. Expect me well before dawn."

The navigator opened a side door behind the cockpit. Setting out a small ladder, he helped von Kroit to the ground while the loadmaster handed the colonel the leather case he had packed specifically for this mission. The ersatz Dutchman waved and walked quickly to the truck, where Malcolm the beer man waited.

The White Horse Pub, Tarrant Rushton

In the pub's storage room behind the bar, Paul, Phil, and Sir Harold sat lashed to wooden chairs with their hands bound behind them while Ruth stood across from them, holding her MP 40 and eyeing the captives like a cat watching a captured mouse. When Sir Harold yawned and closed his eyes, the postman and the lieutenant feigned boredom, as well.

"It will be exciting enough soon," the pub owner told them. "I expect our guest at any moment."

Paul looked at Phil, who responded with a raised brow and a shrug.

On the radio, the deep, mellow voice of Vaughn Monroe crooned that the lights would someday be going on again all over the world.

"Bloody wireless!" Ruth stomped out into the main room and the music went silent. In her absence, Harold carefully eased a small blade out of the cuff of his tunic and began rubbing it against the ropes binding his hands.

"Our world! It will be our world!" Ruth raved as she returned and eyed the prisoners, stopping when she got to Sir Harold. "You! I know of these two, but why you? Who are you?"

"I, Madam, am merely an instrument of war dedicated to wiping out the blight of Nazism and the likes of your kind," Sir Harold told her, ignoring the fact that she was now pushing the muzzle of her weapon directly against his forehead.

"You are nothing," she said with a sneer. "The others are important, but there's no reason to keep you then, is there."

She cocked the gun in the same moment that a voice called from the outer room. "Ruthy, it's Malcolm. I have done as you asked. We're here." The lorry driver appeared, followed by a dark man in tweeds, carrying a case.

The publican turned to greet her guest. *"Ach, Herr Standartenführer, wilkommen."*

"Helga, it has been many years." As they shook hands, von Kroit eyed the trio of captives. *"What have we here?"*

"The very ones you seek. May I introduce Lieutenant Philip Davis and the postman Eisenhower."

Von Kroit broke into a toothy smile which faded as soon as he saw Sir Harold. *"I know this one,"* he snarled. *"He is a British agent known as the* Jackdaw." The Nazi visitor took a step closer. "But you be really Sir Harold Kane, *ja?"*

Augustine Campana & Marco Di Tillo

Harold's head dropped to his chest in apparent submission.

"Fine," said von Kroit as he went for his case and opened it, revealing four glass vials and an equal number of hypodermic needles. He eyed Phil and Paul. "I deal with you two here." Turning to Sir Harold, he added, "But you, Jackdaw, come to Berlin with me. I present you to *Oberführer* Schellenberg."

The lorry driver, apparently hearing more than he wanted to, said something about having to be on his way and turned to leave. He took a single step toward the door before Ruth pointed the machine pistol at him.

"Stop there!" she shouted, adding when Malcolm stopped and faced her, "My friend, you have seen too much, I'm afraid."

"I won't tell a soul. I only want to ..." It was as far as he got before bullets tore into his chest and splattered blood out his back. He fell against the wall and slid to the floor, painting a smear of red as he went.

When she turned back to the trio of captives and eyed them with contempt, they surmised that, when they were no longer of any value, they would be disposed of in the same way.

The noise woke Ed Bradford, the only pub lodger who was not up and about. As the cloud in his mind cleared, he leapt to the window. Outside, a somber blue-gray sky was busy with Allied bombers droning and backfiring. He scratched his head, yawned, and concluding they were probably returning from a mission, went back to bed.

Von Kroit broke the glass cap off a vial of amobarbital, long used by the Germans as a truth serum. Picking up a hypodermic needle, he sucked the clear liquid into its reservoir and looked over at Phil. "*Ach*, you first because you are reason for *mein* mission. *Ja?*"

As the Nazi colonel moved closer to the lieutenant, Harold intercepted him. With the chair still tied to him but both arms free, he grabbed von Kroit and used him as a shield against Ruth's weapon.

"*Helga, nicht schießen!* Not shoot!" von Kroit screamed.

Harold slapped the syringe from the Nazi's hand and crushed it with his boot. As Ruth tried for a clear shot, the MI6 man kept von Kroit in the line of fire as he worked his way to the man's case. Pieces of the wooden chair fell away, freeing him even further as he reached his objective and dumped the case's contents onto the floor. Sir Harold stomped them, breaking all the vials.

Ruth aimed the MP 40 at Paul. "If this one ain't part of your mission, maybe he's disposable now. Well, are you?"

Paul closed his eyes and his face blanched.

"Wait," Sir Harold cried. "Don't do it!"

"Release him," she demanded.

The MI6 man complied and Ruth backed him up against the wall, jamming the gun muzzle under his chin. She sneered. "A catch dead or alive, are you?"

Von Kroit looked down at the scattered broken glass and spilled serum that was oozing into the wooden floor. "*Scheiße!*" he exclaimed. "*What must I do now?*"

"*Take the lot of them back,*" Ruth suggested.

"*Of course. Having them is as good as having the plan. Then, we can do what we want with them in Berlin.*"

Von Kroit took the pistol from Ruth and controlled the others as she retied Sir Harold's hands. Making sure their hands were tightly bound, she freed Phil and Paul from their chairs and the captives were ushered into the pub's main room and out the front door to Malcolm's truck. Seeing there was no chance they would all fit into the vehicle's cab, he handed Ruth the weapon and told her to keep watch.

With surprising agility, the stocky colonel climbed onto the vehicle's bed and began rolling the kegs off onto the ground. Thump, thump, thump. The last one landed on two others and broke apart with a resounding crack.

The noise wasn't quite loud enough to wake the dead, but it did rouse one Ed Bradford sleeping just above. As he got to the window, he saw two of His Majesty's officers and a civilian being driven off at gunpoint. He quickly donned his uniform and raced out to the jeep where he retrieved the pistol he had stowed under the seat and drove off in pursuit.

The truck was well ahead of him, its blackened taillight barely visible in the night mist. Eventually he lost sight of it completely so he slowed to a crawl and tried to pick up the trail. Then he smelled it. The stench of rancid beer signaled its course. He grinned when he imagined General Terry saying, "As sure as shootin', they went that-away."

Sniffing the air as he drove, Ed followed the smell to the right, and farther down a narrow lane, veered left into a thick stand of trees at the edge of a field. Pulling the jeep onto a side path, he killed the engine and lights, and watched as an unfamiliar aircraft taxied to one end of the field, and with a low scream of its engines, took off. By the faint moonlight, Ed could make out the German *Luftwaffe* markings on the side and a swastika on a stabilizer. Impulsively, he grabbed his .45, aimed it, then decided it would be a waste of ammunition. Besides, if he did get lucky and hit a vital fuel or oil line, he could be killing three British patriots. Holstering the gun, he threaded the case onto his belt. A check of his watch told him it was 2:33 a.m.

Ed waited no more than a minute longer before the beer truck passed by on its return trip. He followed it to the White Horse, and watched from a distance as Ruth got down from the cab and rushed inside, apparently failing to notice the missing jeep out front.

The Yank major stole into the pub and crept toward the only room with a light on in back of the bar. From behind a keg, he observed Ruth wrap what appeared to be a body in a blanket and secure it with rope before proceeding to drag it out in his direction.

"Hold it right there!" Ed cried, gun in hand, as she came abreast of him.

"Ah, Major Bradford, isn't it?" she said with remarkable composure. "I'm afraid we had a terrible accident tonight. The lorry driver who brings my beer was playing with an old gun and it went off. Poor man. I could use your help with him, if you would."

In the instant it took Ed to consider her outlandish story, he dropped his guard and she reached into her apron pocket. Pulling out the pistol she had taken from Sir Harold earlier, she let go two rounds, but the major's reflexes were better than her aim and the slugs went harmlessly into the wall. His return shots, however, put splashes of red next to the third button of her blouse, and she dropped to the floor.

"You're too late," she gasped as he bent over her. "We have them. Heil Hit …"

Ed watched as she expelled her final breath. He had never killed anyone at close range before and it shocked him deeply. He dropped his gun and held his hand to his mouth as vomit oozed through his fingers. After retching over the bar sink, he wiped his face with a towel. With steeled determination, the major picked up his gun and sprinted for the door.

Telegraph Cottage, Kingston

General Dwight Eisenhower was at the kitchen stove, an apron protecting his uniform shirt and trousers, making pancakes and sausages, while a pot of coffee was rhythmically percolating on the back burner. Cooking was one of Ike's many hobbies, and like the others—golf, oil painting, and fishing—he had become quite adept at it. Given the chance, he enjoyed preparing meals for groups of ten or twelve, but today, it was breakfast for one, or so he thought until Lieutenant Commander Butcher suddenly appeared.

"You're up and at 'em early, Butch," Ike greeted him. "How about some breakfast?"

"Good Morning, sir. I thought you'd like some company. I'll just take some Joe if that's okay."

"Big day today. You'll need more than that," Ike said as he grabbed a plate from the shelf and plopped the two pancakes and a couple of sausages on it. "Here, eat up."

"Thank you, it smells great but we don't have anything unusually special today, just a weather briefing and a luncheon."

"Butch, from here on out, every day is a big day." The general poured the batter for two more pancakes. "How about the weather? Has Stagg come up with anything decent?" He was referring to Group Captain James Martin Stagg, the RAF meteorologist who was the chairman of the committee charged with providing reliable weather predictions for the invasion.

"Well, sir, as of late last night, it looks like it will hold for D-Day. That's what the last agreed-to report said."

Ike frowned as he flipped the pancakes. "I wish I could count on it. We can't afford to wait!"

"Well, so far so good. Stagg and his experts are the best we have," the commander replied, slathering on butter and adding some maple syrup.

Ike switched subjects. "Are we all set at Portsmouth?"

"Yes, sir, SHAEF Advance will be fully operational on time. Tents and trailers are all in place, and they've finished putting in electric and comm."

"Good," the general said as he retrieved two sausages for himself, flipped the pancakes one more time, and deposited them on his plate. "I hate giving up this place, but when the balloon goes up, I want to be as close to the action as makes sense."

"Absolutely, General. I think you'll like your trailer. All the comforts of home." He looked around the room. "Well, almost."

Arado Ar 232
Over the English Channel

Forward in the plane's cargo bay, von Kroit was sprawled across two seats, dozing. He had decided to wait until they stopped in Calais for fuel to grill Phil and Paul about the invasion and break radio silence to report to General Schellenberg. He ached to find out what he needed to know quickly and proclaim his mission a success.

Farther back along the port side, the Englishmen were lashed to cargo straps, their hands bound behind them. Lined up right to left were Phil, Paul, and Sir Harold all swaying side to side each time the plane bounced. The turbulence ranged from mild to quite violent, and after almost an hour of it, they were all a bit queasy. The headaches from banging the overhead each time the *Arado* hit a particularly nasty air pocket didn't help.

The situation was made even worse for Paul as he was forced to explain himself to the man swinging next to him. "That's what happened, Sir Harold. I swear it."

Before the MI6 agent could react, Phil demanded, "Why in bloody hell did you give them my name?"

"I bloody well found the papers after you ran into me, didn't I?" Paul replied defensively. "I thought they were yours."

"I never had any papers. I only picked up those I found and put them in your sack."

"Gentlemen, please," Sir Harold interceded, "let's say you were both victims of circumstance and be done with it. Now, we must work together to free ourselves. Davis, when we first came aboard, I noticed a leather utility case hanging just forward. I believe it's a few feet to your left, shoulder height. The metal handle tells me it may be some sort of cutter."

Paul asked, "No more blades up your sleeve, Guv?"

"All out, I'm afraid." Sir Harold replied dryly.

"I see the case, but it's out of my reach," Davis reported. "Wait, there's a strap. It's almost … arrgh! Bloody hell, I can't quite grab it!"

The rear gun turret clanked and Phil quickly straightened up and faced the same direction as his mates. Removing his headset, the tail gunner climbed down and walked stiffly to the snoozing von Kroit.

Like a sleeping dog, aware of activity near him, the colonel's eyes opened slowly and he growled, *"Yes, what is it?"*

"Excuse me, Herr Standartenführer. The pilot says we will be landing at Calais in twenty minutes."

"Ach, yes," he said, closing his eyes again. *"I have a special package awaiting me there. Wake me when we land."*

As the turret hatch banged closed behind the sergeant, Sir Harold rolled into Paul. Having caught the words *"Zwanzig minuten"* and " *Calais,"* he whispered, "Tell Davis we'll be landing soon. He can give it a go then without all this bumping. With any luck, we can beat this thing before that bastard manages to kill us."

Tarrant Rushton Airfield

Ed Bradford paced back and forth across the floor of the gatehouse shack sucking on a half-smoked cigarette and flicking the ashes into a red can on the floor while, at a desk, Sergeant Nathaniel Newkirk listened to the phone receiver pressed to his ear.

"Yes, sir, I understand, but we are sealed up here," he was saying, and then in response to a muffled grumble which erupted on the other end of the line. "General Eisenhower? No, sir, I'm only the NCO of the watch, there's no need to get him involved." The remark elicited more muffled grousing.

"Yes, General, I will arrange it immediately," he replied and handed the phone to Bradford. "The general would like to speak to you, sir."

"Ed-boy!" Terry sounded awake and fully engaged. "Since we talked, MI6, the Brit cloak and dagger boys, passed on that one of their agents posing as an RAF officer may be on that plane. He stayed at the same pub as you and was after Lieutenant Davis."

"I think the lieutenant was with him." Ed slapped his forehead. "Damn! So close. But I saw three of them."

"Who knows, maybe it's the postman. Listen, I don't give a real hoot-in-holler who the third man is, but, for God sake, don't even think about shootin' the plane down unless you absolutely have to. We sure as hell don't want to go killin' an MI6 type. Got it?"

"Wilco that, sir."

"Oh, and Ed, you were right about that plane. It's an *Arado* Ar 232. Very few of them built and they're easy to spot. Hitler's staff has been known to use them, so a Berlin destination is a good bet."

"Yes, sir. I hope to catch up with it and track it in flight."

"Good luck, Ed-boy. This one could make you a hero."

"Yeah," Bradford mumbled as the line clicked, "It could make me a dead one." A fleeting negative fantasy of his wife and kids standing by a flag-draped coffin went through his head.

Newkirk came out from behind his desk, sounding a lot more conciliatory than when Bradford had first demanded access to the base. "Major," he said, "I'll personally see to it that you have what you need."

"General Terry will appreciate that, I'm sure." The major's face turned deadpan. "Look, Sergeant, I haven't got a minute to spare. I need a fast plane out of here. The people the Krauts kidnapped may have top-secret information. Their plane took off well over half an hour ago and is probably heading back to Germany. I can't let that happen."

"Understood, sir." He picked up the phone and dialed the three-digit number for operations. "Yeah, Kelly, this is Newk. Right, I got the duty tonight. Look, no time to chat. I have a top-level SHAEF request for a pursuit aircraft immediately." He waited for and weathered the expected response from a bloke who wasn't happy about a change in mission plans. "I know, but it's an emergency, isn't it, and I need one now. I'll have this Yank general clear it with Wing Commander Pope in the morning, unless you want to rouse the old man now. Right, then. Let's go with that. Be there in a mo. Thanks, mate."

The sergeant held the door for Bradford, and together they skirted the sandbags piled at the entrance as Newkirk informed the guard on duty that he was leaving on a most urgent matter.

It took slightly more than four minutes to arrive at the airstrip, clearing a fight line security checkpoint as they went. Expecting to make the trip in one of the tug aircraft, Ed was surprised to see a de Havilland DH 98 Mosquito on the apron outside a large hangar with three members of the ground crew readying it for flight. Awaiting them was a lieutenant wearing coveralls, leather jacket and boots, life vest, and harness for his parachute and dinghy pack. Next to him, an NCO cradled a pile of similar gear in his arms. Saluting, they introduced themselves as Flight Lieutenant Charles Mason and Sergeant Jake Kingsley, flight engineer. The pilot explained that they were about to launch a reconnaissance flight when word of the major's mission reached them.

"Here you are, sir," Kingsley said, offering the flight gear. "You'll be taking my seat."

"Look, fellas," Bradford said, stepping into the coveralls, "I know I might have fouled up your mission, but it's very important that we catch up with this plane."

"Yes, so I've learned, sir. No worries," Mason assured him. "The Mossie is one of the fastest in the inventory. They routinely go off an hour or more later than the bombers and catch up before they make their IP."

"We're chasing an *Arado* 232," Ed advised as Kingsley helped him into the parachute harness.

"Yes, sir. I just learned that. Your General Terry thought it appropriate to ring our wing commander and fill him in."

"That doesn't surprise me," Bradford told him. He shook his head at the sergeant's offer of the flight boots, preferring to hold on to the GI footwear he had so carefully broken in.

"At any rate," Mason went on, "I've been against one of them before. They're armed, but one might say, they're sitting ducks. We're a lot faster and have a range over twice as far."

"Can we make Berlin if we have to?"

"And return, with petrol to spare, sir."

Bradford finished dressing for the flight, adding a helmet with goggles, earphones, and oxygen mask, while Sergeant Kingsley picked up the unused boots, wished the two officers good luck and headed back to the hanger.

"Well, sir, it's time to meet the lady," Mason said as, with the help of the ground crew, the pair headed for a narrow metal ladder which led up into a hatch in the aircraft's belly. The lieutenant went first, climbing into the left seat, while Bradford took Kingsley's right-hand seat next to and a few inches back from that of the pilot. The ladder was stowed, and they strapped in as the ground crew chief wished them, "Godspeed" and closed the hatch.

Mason quickly ran through his final preflight procedures and checked to see that the propellers were clear before he pressed the black buttons to start the plane's twin Rolls-Royce Merlin engines.

Bradford reached into his flight coveralls and touched the .45 case. Then he felt his army jacket for his extra clips of ammo. As he pulled the oxygen mask close around his face, he gagged from claustrophobia, but the pilot advised, "No need for that now, Major. We're pressurized. Save it for an emergency."

Mason pointed to the two small screens on the console in front of Bradford. "That's our radar. The left is height, the right is bearing. It should come in handy later on as we close in." He said no more as he busied himself with the flight controls, obtained clearance from the tower, and taxied the Mossie out to the end of the main runway. Suddenly, with a roar that rumbled inside Ed's chest, they were airborne. The chase had begun.

Marck Airfield
Calais, France

It was 0327 hours, German Central Time, and the airfield lighting painted a yellow glow on the Ar 232 being serviced by a tanker truck and refuel crew. Inside the cargo bay, the light filtered through the windows onto three figures hanging like mummies on the wall.

Earlier, immediately after the plane had landed, Colonel von Kroit instructed the rear gunner to watch over the prisoners. He left and was followed by the pilot, navigator, and radio operator, all in search of a toilet. There was one on the aircraft, but it was small and smelly. Everyone except the rear gunner and the captives used the opportunity to relieve themselves in comparative comfort and stretch their legs. Not to be left out, the gunner emerged from the shadows of the aft bay and walked to a phone booth-size compartment behind the cockpit bulkhead marked, *"Toilette."*

"How close are you to that strap?" Sir Harold asked Davis.

"It settled back when we landed, and it sits just outside my reach."

An idea struck Paul with crystal clarity. "Oy, why not work out of your boot enough to give you those few inches?"

"There's a thought," the MI6 agent encouraged as Phil began pressing the toe of his right boot against the heel of his left and slowly wriggled his foot free. Keeping his toes clenched, he held as firm as he could against the inside of the upper part of the boot. Slowly, the lieutenant maneuvered his toe in between the strap's loop, raised his foot behind his back close to his hands, did a reverse kick, and grabbed. "Damn it all," he grumbled, as he missed it and the strap dropped to the floor. With an eye on the toilet door, he worked fully out of his boot and managed to wrap the leather thong around his sock. Awkwardly, he again raised his foot behind him and was able to stretch enough for his left hand to reach the strap.

"He's got it!" Paul exclaimed as Phil jerked to his left and yanked the implement out of its case. As Sir Harold had surmised, the handle held a sharp blade. There was just time for him to hide the prize behind him and force his foot back into its boot before the German emerged, grumbled to himself about the smell, and scarcely glancing at them, went aft to his station.

As the gunner reached for his gun turret hatch, there was a loud, metallic rapping on the rear cargo bay doors. He quickly went to a handle located just below a sign that read, *"Warning! Do not open during flight,"* pulled down on it, and servo motors whirred as they opened the plane's clamshell doors.

As the gunner busied himself deploying a ramp from the bay deck to the ground, Phil whispered, "Eisenhower, turn your back to me and don't move about. The blade is quite sharp." Paul obeyed, and the lieutenant set about removing the bindings from the postman's hands. The last of the ropes were cut and the knife was passed to Paul just as a team of workers pushed a dolly holding a large wooden box up the ramp and into the cargo bay.

Phil nudged Paul. "When you can, free me and then see to the group captain."

"I will mate, but what about them?" Paul nodded at machine gun toting guards climbing the ramp. "You're making me out a bloody hero and I ain't one."

The soldiers were followed by the pilot and rest of the flight crew, and finally, Colonel von Kroit. He had changed from his civilian attire into the sharp uniform of an SS officer complete with highly polished boots and swagger stick. Despite his compact stature, the outfit made him appear menacing. *"Be careful,"* he warned the workmen as they removed the box from the dolly. *"The contents are fragile."*

Once the workers and guards left, the rear gunner retracted the cargo ramp, and pushed the door lever up, causing the hydraulic motors to return the clamshell to a closed position. As it shut, von Kroit went forward and ordered the radioman to contact General Schellenberg, but the annoying cacophony of grating static and high-pitched whines that followed were more than the Nazi colonel could take. He told the operator to try again later, when they were away from the Allied jamming, and he returned to the bay, where he stood before the captives. "So, now we see I have little surprise for you." All three of them instinctively looked over at the box. "Yes, correct. In the box it is." He smiled wickedly, and batted the swagger stick into his gloved palm. "But too long have we stayed here. We must continue on." He pointed the stick directly at Paul's nose. "Later will come your treat." The postman felt sick to his stomach, but this time it wasn't due to the turbulence.

Schellenberg Apartment, Berlin

General Schellenberg heard the clock in the hall chime four and he knew there was little time before he had to rise. Normally, waking up at five in the morning was no problem, for he rarely got more than four or five hours of sleep; however, he had scarcely slept a wink all night. He grunted, rolled over, fluffed his down pillow, and tried to salvage some rest, but the fate of Colonel von Kroit's mission preyed on his mind. He beat his pillow one more time and rolled over again, this time managing to disturb his wife, Irene.

"Walter, dearest," she said groggily, *"if you must stir, can you do so with less vigor?"*

"Sorry, my love, I may as well get up and face the day." He threw off the bed linens and swung his feet over the side and into a pair of well-worn mules.

His wife picked her head up. *"Is it something so terrible?"*

He threw on his dressing gown. *"A stupid mistake on my part. I sent a buffoon on a vital mission when I should have gone myself."*

"So, he has failed?"

He cinched the robe's belt around his waist. *"Not yet, but I suspect he will bungle it in the end, and if he does ..."*

He was interrupted by the sound of a telephone ringing, and hurried out into the hall to take the call, fully expecting to hear the voice of von Kroit at the other end. Instead, it was a senior agent with urgent news.

"Herr Oberführer, this is Henkel. We have just discovered the signal that will announce the invasion to the resistance. Under interrogation, an operative of the French Maquis told of a poem by their poet Verlaine called 'Chanson d'automne.' The first stanza will be sent to alert the French partisans and the second will confirm to them an invasion is imminent."

"So, we will now have notice of the attack, but do we know where."

"Herr Oberführer, all indicators continue to point to the Pas de Calais."

"Yes, that is precisely what concerns me. Keep me informed of your progress, Henkel."

Schellenberg hung up the phone. *"Maybe, I should have sent him."* He continued down the hall to the bathroom.

Arado Ar 232
Somewhere over France

When the aircraft reached its cruising altitude and had leveled off, von Kroit left his seat and made for the captives, only to become the victim of the worst sustained turbulence of the trip which left him struggling to remain upright. As for the three Britons, they were forced to hold on desperately to the canvas cargo lining, fighting to keep from being tossed free, thus revealing that they were no longer bound in place.

"Keep hanging fast, boys," Sir Harold encouraged. "I believe we can flush out and best that old fox."

Regardless what course or altitude the pilot chose, the plane continued to be jostled for another forty minutes. When von Kroit was convinced the ride had settled down sufficiently, he again approached the hostages. Standing before them akimbo, his right hand gripped the swagger stick. "So, you think I not hear you whisper to one another when I am sitting. I have most fine ears." He stepped close to Phil and whacked the stick on the canvas next to the lieutenant's head. "I am happy that you are wanting to talk. The more you talk, the more happy I am. You see, I bring here something to help you say what I want to hear."

Phil had had enough and was about to pounce when Harold's frown and slight sideways motion of his head told him he had better wait. Von Kroit walked aft and banged his stick on the gun turret. *"Feldwebel, help me at once."*

The hatch opened and the gunner descended to the deck. *"Yes, sir, what is it you need of me?"*

"Come, I shall instruct you in a moment. Stand by that crate."

Von Kroit returned to the captives. "And now, my three English friends, I have the upsetting news. You see, unable I was to—*bekommen*, er—obtain—the chemicals the Jackdaw destroyed earlier. I believe you say 'truth serum,' *ja?*"

Paul nodded and von Kroit zeroed in on him like a teacher coaching his brightest student. "You see, this chemical is most difficult to replace. None in all of Calais." He moved to Phil. "However, is good news! I have way to make you talk most effective." He looked the lieutenant directly in the face, "You do want talk ..." Then abruptly turning to Paul, he asked, "... do you not?"

When there was no reply, the colonel clasped his hands around the swagger stick behind his back and walked slowly from man to man. "Come, come! We know how it works. I ask question, you say answer. So, tell me of invasion and we all enjoy rest of our voyage."

The hollow silence was broken only by the drone of the aircraft's engines. Von Kroit sneered. "I see. Perhaps to begin, an easy one." He gazed up at the overhead of the bay. "Capital for Nepal, is what?"

"Kathmandu!" Paul blurted out with a grin on his face. "The capital of Nepal is Kathmandu."

His pride was short-lived. The stern look Sir Harold shot at him made the postman want to crawl into a hole and hide.

"Very good," The German touched his stick to Paul's shoulder. "You are up warmed. So, next, tell me of invasion. Where and when it comes?"

He waited. When all he received was another loud silence, the Nazi inquisitor sighed. "Gentlemen, I have not time for this." He looked to the sergeant standing by the box. *"Feldwebel, remove the lid from the crate."*

Undoing four hasps, the gunner pried off the top and shouted, *"Ratten!"*

"Oh, shit," Sir Harold grumbled, "Rats."

"Yes, Jackdaw," von Kroit replied. "This time you win prize. Rats! Many, many rats. *Feldwebel, take the civilian and drop him into the crate."*

As the soldier came his way, Paul realized what was about to happen. He felt a warm, wet trickle run down his trouser leg. "Buggers!" he cried, "I don't know a thing."

A burst of adrenalin gave the postman the presence of mind to wrap the rope that had been binding him around his hands and quickly fashion what might, in the dull light, pass for a knot. Even though it was holding nothing, the gunner was fooled. He hoisted Paul onto his shoulder like a sack of coal.

"Please, no. Not rats!" the postman screamed as he flung himself about wildly.

The sergeant held him tighter and, in the process loosened his grip on his weapon. "Now!" Harold shouted as he leapt on von Kroit.

At the same time, Phil grabbed the cutter and went to help Paul, who was crazily shifting his weight back and forth in an effort to avoid being dropped into the crate. The postman's movements were enough to give Phil the chance to attack with the cutter. The big German swung Paul around trying to knock him into the lieutenant, who dodged him just as the plane was once again buffeted by heavy turbulence. As a result, they all wound up sprawled on the deck.

Phil held the blade to the sergeant's throat and relieved him of his weapon as Paul scampered to where Harold had pinned the struggling von Kroit. The lieutenant pointed the gun right between the German's light blue eyes as he tossed the cutter to Paul, who surprised himself when he actually caught it.

"Give it here," Sir Harold said, and taking the blade, held it against von Kroit's chest with one hand while he grabbed his neck with the other. "Now, old man," he snarled, "the shoe is on the other foot."

The colonel gasped. "Why speak of shoes and old men? Never I will …" Von Kroit went out like a dead light bulb thanks to Sir Harold pressing the carotid artery on the side of his neck and stopping the flow of blood to his brain.

The agent regarded his handiwork. "That should hold him for a time."

Before Sir Harold could get to his feet, the gunner pushed Phil away, ducked behind the wooden box and began to rock it back and forth until, on the third try, it overturned. Scores of rats scurried all over the deck, giving the German time to disappear through the forward hatch and slam it behind him.

"Step lively!" shouted Sir Harold as he made his way to the rear of the bay, kicking off squealing rodents as he went. "Now's our chance to get the hell out of here!"

"Wait! What do I do?" cried Paul as he tried to knock off two large rats.

Phil aimed the gun at Paul throwing the postman into such a spasm that the vermin were thrown to the deck and scampered away.

Square packs hanging from straps below a sign that said *"Fallschirm"* were neatly arranged next to the ramp door. "Parachutes," said Harold as he pulled one down, stepped into the harness, and yanked on the shoulder straps. "Hurry gents! Follow my lead, now!"

Paul and Phil each copied Harold's actions. As they finished getting into the harnesses, the forward hatch opened and two large figures with guns were silhouetted by the light of the morning sun streaming through the cockpit.

Sir Harold quickly pulled on the cargo door lever and the clamshell motors responded. As the hatch opened, the change in pressure caused the aircraft to dip and a small tornado-like torrent spun into the bay. The MI6 agent shouted over the roar of the engines and the scream of swirling wind, "Look here." He showed Paul and Phil a metal handle on the chute harness. "Once you clear the aircraft, pull this firmly. Understand?"

Gunfire reverberated off the tin can-like bay as the German soldiers waded through the eddies of rats, firing their weapons as they came. Shots struck all around the Britons, but the conditions—the wild air currents, the rats, and the instability of a plane flying with its cargo hatch open—kept the enemy bullets well off the mark. The Englishmen held on to the side webbing at the ramp as the western sky was revealed.

When the cargo hatch had opened sufficiently, Harold cried, "Now!" and dropped to the deck. He let himself slide down the ramp, and disappeared over the edge.

Phil had experience with parachute training and copied Harold's exit; however, this was all completely foreign to Paul. He closed his eyes and let himself be thrown to the deck, and, as the vacuum of the plane's wake grabbed him, flew off the ramp and into the morning air, spinning like a pinwheel. When he opened his eyes and reached for the chute's ripcord handle, pulling it as hard as he could, nothing happened. He could see the open canopies of Harold and Phil growing larger and the ground rushing toward him. He yanked again. Still nothing. Paul fought off his mounting panic and checked his parachute to discovered he had been pulling on a harness buckle. This time, he grabbed the correct handle. The strap broke free and the chute opened gloriously above him while below rose the fields of a farm near the German town of Leuth.

Meanwhile, the pair who had been pursuing them watched from the cargo plane's ramp as the three chutes drifted to earth.

The Cockpit of the DH 98 Mosquito

Flight Lieutenant Mason had taken the aircraft well near its operating ceiling of 37,000 feet, with an airspeed that hovered near 400 miles per hour early in the flight. After passing over the English Channel and the French coastline, he pushed forward on the dual throttle controls, causing the whine of the twin engines to assume a lower pitch and the plane to slow noticeably. "I reckon we have been high and fast long enough to make up the lost time, sir," he told Bradford. "We shouldn't want to overrun them. They likely had to stop for petrol.

"Good thinking, Lieutenant. It's like looking for a needle in a haystack as it is."

"They should help," Mason said, indicating the radar screens. "The Ar 232 has an operating ceiling well below ours. We'll enter that regime for a solid go at it." He brought the aircraft down some 20,000 feet and leveled off. "Our pace will seem a bit of a drag, but we do need to match the *Arado*'s air speed."

"Roger that," Bradford replied, feeling optimistic as he alternately watched the radar screens, then scanned the horizon, fighting the morning sun for a clear view.

Mason reached into a rucksack next to him and pulled out a pair of binoculars. "Here, these should help, Major. Mind the sun."

Bradford took the glasses, scanned the horizon and, on the chance they were still higher than the *Arado*, checked as much of the airspace below them as he could. Another half hour passed before he saw blips pop up on the radar screens. When they disappeared almost as quickly, the major guessed the Mossie had overrun the bogey. He quickly searched to his right and down and caught a flash of reflected sunlight from a gun turret canopy. Through the field glasses, he could discern the outline of a plane which was definitely not a fighter, but more like the one he had glimpsed near Tarrant Rushton. "I think we have them," he declared. "Four o'clock low."

"Two tails with a box, high wings, and four airscrews?" Mason asked.

Bradford observed through the binoculars. "I think it's the one I saw earlier, but I can't be sure."

Mason guided the Mosquito into a bank turn to starboard and executed a 360-degree spiral that put his plane 2,000 feet above and as far to the rear of the *Arado* where, by throttling back, he allowed his objective to open up the distance between them. When the gap had widened sufficiently, he boosted power enough to match the cargo plane's airspeed. "Let's just see what they're about."

Another few minutes passed before both Mason and Bradford saw the *Arado's* cargo doors begin to split open and the rear of the plane dip slightly. Bradford glued his eyes to the glasses once again. "Holy crap!" he exclaimed. "Do you see what I see?"

"Indeed I do, Major," Mason replied as he proceeded to close in on his quarry.

The binoculars gave Bradford a clear view of a figure sliding down and off the rear cargo ramp. As a chute opened, another jumper repeated the action of the first. While two parachutes drifted to earth, a third jumper twisted and spun off the ramp and dropped like a twirling rock toward the field some 14,000 feet down.

"The last guy is in trouble." Bradford watched until finally the third chute opened.

"Are they the ones you're after, sir?" asked Mason.

"Yeah, I think so, Lieutenant. At least, I have to assume it's an escape. No one just jumps out of a plane that way without a good reason, do they?"

"Not that I've ever known." Mason made another banked turn back to the west. "I'll come in low and slow so you can egress."

"I've only done this once before. Any way we can land?"

"I'm afraid not, sir. There's a huge airfield at Venlo, held by Jerry, and the Mossie doesn't do well in potato fields."

As the Mosquito continued to fly in the opposite direction of the Ar 232, Bradford became more and more determined not to blow this chance to complete his mission.

The Cargo Bay of the Arado Ar 232

Colonel von Kroit slouched over in his seat and held his head with both hands.

"Sir, is there something I can get you?" the gunner asked.

"You fools, you let them escape. You can get them back for me, that is what you can do!"

"But sir, we must fly on to Berlin."

"Tell the captain I want to return and land immediately. We cannot allow the three Englanders to get away."

Von Kroit tried to stand, but unable to manage it, cursed the man he referred to as, *"that bastard Jackdaw."* He was still grumbling to himself when the gunner returned with the navigator who explained that the pilot could not land due to the unknown nature of the terrain.

"*Sir, we believe it is quite rocky as there are gravel pits in the area. However, the airfield at Venlo is close to the drop zone and Düsseldorf is less than 50 kilometers away.*"

"*We must not lose sight of them!*" von Kroit shouted. "*I order him to land in the same field where they escaped!*"

"*Sir, he doesn't want to risk disabling the aircraft. Reichsführer Himmler is expecting to have it available in a few hours. We can deliver you, after which we must continue on to Berlin.*"

"*So, Venlo will have to do,*" von Kroit sneered. "*But see that I have swift transportation awaiting my arrival.*"

"*Yes, sir. We will turn back immediately.*" The navigator returned to the cockpit.

Von Kroit stood and kicked away a rat that was nibbling at his boot. "*Feldwebel!*" he barked at the gunner. "*Get rid of these infernal vermin. I hate the little bastards!*"

A Field in Leuth, Germany

Due to his period of rapid descent, Paul landed at about the same time as Sir Harold, and Phil arrived just after him. The lieutenant was the only one who tried to stay on his feet, running with the pull of the chute, only to fall forward, twist onto his back, and be dragged along on his empty chute pack. Sir Harold did a classic landing fall, tumbling from feet, to side, to buttocks, in a v-shaped roll, while Paul simply hit the ground and executed a series of awkward somersaults. It wasn't a graceful landing, but the soft earth was quite forgiving and they all came through it with no more than minor bruises.

Farmer Jan Dekker, who had seen their parachutes descending while he was raking hay, arrived panting, as they were each pulling in the shrouds of the chutes and removing their harnesses. "*Guten Morgen!*" he called. But as he got closer and saw the two uniforms that were unlike those of his homeland, he was taken aback. "*Mein Gott. Sie sind Ausländer!*"

The agent masquerading as a group captain answered, "*Wir sind Engländer.*"

"Ah, English," he smiled. "Come the invasion, yes?"

Paul and Phil did double takes as Sir Harold, sensing he was in friendly territory, traded introductions with the man and explained, "We are on a special mission and are in need of help. Can you tell us where we are?"

"Near here is the village of Leuth, by the Nette," Dekker told him.

"We are in *Deutschland*, then, not Holland?" asked Sir Harold.

"Very close. *Niederlande* is just there," the farmer replied, pointing to the northwest.

The escapees finished stowing their chutes as best they could, and the farmer regarded them for a moment and asked, "This help. What is it you need?"

Paul answered first, "To get back to England." He looked at the others, "Well, that's it, isn't it?"

Phil chimed in, "Back home would certainly do."

Sir Harold harrumphed and said, "Short of that miracle, our immediate need is for shelter. A temporary refuge. You see, old boy, the Nazis are after us."

"Ah, yes," the farmer frowned. "Nazis. Then you must come with me. Quick, quick!"

As they hurried after him to the farmhouse, Phil spotted a familiar fighter-bomber flying over and wondered why a Mosquito was in the area. He dared to hope it was a good sign.

Lieutenant Mason turned the wheel on the control yoke and pointed his Mossie back toward the field where they had seen the parachutes. Surveying the area, Bradford spotted the three jumpers following a fourth person to a farmhouse. Through his binoculars, they appeared to be going of their own accord as the leader waved them on and showed them to the door.

"Hah!" he exclaimed. "That guy looks like he's welcoming them. Maybe he's on our side."

The major had barely gotten the words out of his mouth when bursts of gunfire came at them from their five o'clock high position. Mason immediately dove the Mossie and turned out of the line of fire, but not before four scorched holes appeared in the Madapolam fabric of the right wing.

"Crap!" Bradford shouted. "We're hit!"

"We'll be fine. I need to …" grunted the lieutenant as he worked the flight controls, "… get her steady and away from those buggers."

As the other airplane passed above them, they saw it was the Ar 232.

"Blast!" cried Mason. "Didn't expect that. I reckoned them long gone." Taking his plane over the treetops, he went into a curling climb that had Ed holding onto his stomach and yelling obscenities.

"Shit, Lieutenant, next time warn me."

"Get a good hold, Major. We're about to go inverted."

And with that, the skilled pilot executed a perfect Immelmann maneuver, climbing into a half loop and putting the ground directly above them as they momentarily hung upside-down from their harnesses. A half roll returned the Mosquito to level flight and put it well above and flying in the same direction as the enemy. With the *Arado* at twelve o'clock low, the lieutenant declared, "Now, for a bit of turnabout."

As they dove, Mason aimed the DH 98's nose directly at his target and fired the cannons so that tracers showed a direct line of ripping splashes along the plane's spine, from the cargo bay to the cockpit. The forward turret and part of the canopy shattered and the aircraft banked sharply to port as Mason followed up by strafing the rear turret. In seconds, the *Arado* was struggling to maintain controlled flight until its pilot managed to put it into a slow climb before leveling off again.

When Mason turned his aircraft back in the direction of the Ar 232, he and Bradford saw a side hatch open and three jumpers exit the crippled plane. As their parachutes deployed, the *Arado* again lost control and nose-dived into a stand of pines a farm away. The orange flash and billowing black smoke that followed told the rest of the story as the chutes floated over a field just north of where the earlier trio had come down.

"I shouldn't think you'd want to drop near here now," Mason said as they flew over the landing spot."

Bradford wagged his head. "No, I sure as hell don't want to run into any Krauts, and the place will be crawling with them. I'm only interested in the first guys that jumped. They're on our side. At least I hope they are."

"I say," offered the lieutenant, "maybe we can locate a decent carriageway to set her down. I believe I spotted one not far back across the border." He headed the plane to the west and the relative security of the Dutch countryside. "You may have to tramp it a bit, but you'll be a damn sight safer."

"I'm for that," Ed told him, grabbing the harness of his parachute. "I don't really trust these things." He looked down at the scenery slipping by. "Slow down so I can get my bearings." He gazed through the field glasses. "There's the river, and that road leads right where I want to go."

Mason pressed a button on his yoke and reconnaissance cameras recorded the topography below them on film. "This will give HQ some idea where you are," he explained. "We'll try to land a mile or two from here. I don't need much of an airstrip, provided there are no trees."

Leuth, Germany

None of the German jumpers had had an easy time of it. The navigator, his body limp and bloody, was dragged some twenty meters before coming to rest. The wounded loadmaster attempted a fall and roll, but once down, he lay there motionless. Von Kroit came in awkwardly, with both legs stiffly extended and heels angled to take the brunt of the shock, but instead he went down hard on his buttocks and pelvis before being dragged by the chute. The worst of it happened when, struggling for control, he reached down with his right hand only to have it snap back, causing him to flip end over end and crack his head on a two-meter high monolith in the center of the field.

Responding to an earlier call that three parachutes had been spotted, a *Gestapo* staff car accompanied by a truck carrying six soldiers arrived minutes later. Inspector Georg Weber, wearing a dark suit and hat, got out and surveyed the smoke rising from the more distant crash site and the parachutes in the field billowing slightly, each anchored by a motionless body.

"Feldwebel," he called. *"Half of you check the wounded here and send the rest to see about the aircraft."*

In response, the sergeant jumped from the truck, directed a corporal and private to do the same, and ordered the vehicle and remaining soldiers to the crash site of the downed aircraft.

"Is he dead?" asked Weber, as the sergeant bent over a contorted von Kroit.

The soldier pressed his ear to the colonel's chest and listened. *"No. He is breathing and his chest has heart sounds. But he has serious injuries, sir."*

"I see." Weber looked around. *"Check on the others."*

"Ferdi," the sergeant called, *"how is he?"*

The corporal standing over the rear gunner answered, *"Not so good, but alive."*

"This man is dead," reported the private as he pointed to the navigator.

Weber hustled back to his car and directed his driver to call for an ambulance at once. While they waited, the soldiers who had been sent by truck to the crash site, returned to report that there were no survivors. In fact, the wreck was so complete, they hadn't found any bodies.

Moments earlier, Paul, Phil, and Sir Harold had been salivating from the aroma of a breakfast of sausages and eggs being prepared by Frau Inge Dekker when a loud explosion shook the house. Jan rushed to an upstairs window and the Britons followed. From there, they watched as black smoke curled into the sky from amid outlying pine trees, while closer in, three parachutes landed at an adjacent farm.

"Oy!" Paul exclaimed, "They're coming after us."

The farmer squinted at the scene and concluded, "The three who come from the sky are not so fortunate like you. They do not move."

"Look," said Phil, "vehicles are on the way."

Sir Harold eyed the arriving car and truck. "*Gestapo*, I'd say. Rather a quick response."

"Maybe they came for us. Three and three, isn't it," offered Paul.

Sir Harold shrugged and they all watched in silence as the activities in the field unfolded.

When the ambulance departed, followed by the other vehicles, the farmer concluded, "I think, you be okay now."

"Right-o," said Sir Harold, "we may be in the clear. I wonder if that might have been the Jerry colonel's plane that went down."

"I don't think it was that Mossie. There were too many chutes," commented Phil.

"Whatever it was, I'm happy it ain't us," said Paul.

When they returned to the kitchen, breakfast awaited them, complete with fresh milk and warm bread. Jan bowed his head and the others did the same as the farmer gave thanks for the meal. As they ate, Sir Harold asked the farmer about getting in touch with the local underground.

"Of course, the L.O. in Venlo, but we will wait," their host told them. "We must cross the border and that is better later, after the guards are full and lazy."

"What is this L.O. in Venlo?" asked Phil.

"Part of the Dutch resistance called the *Landelijke Organisatie*," Sir Harold explained. "They help those poor souls who are hiding from Jerry."

"It is true," said Jan, "Maybe they help you poor souls as well."

Inge turned away from the sink and dried her hands on her apron. "Perhaps you need the rest as well as food, yes? We have beds for you. The boys they leave to the fight, and you can use."

Phil's eyebrows went up. "Fight?"

Jan raised his hand. "Oh, not what you think. They escape to England, like the *Niederlande* queen, to serve there. Much of us here think ourselves more Dutch than German."

Paul cleaned his plate, stretched and yawned. "I don't need to be invited twice, do I. Where did you say the beds were, Frau Dekker?"

"Come, come." Inge led the way.

As he and the others followed her, Paul wondered what was waiting for them in Holland and whether he would ever make it back to his flat and Emily.

Near Venlo, the Netherlands

The Mosquito sat on a remote roadway west of Venlo with its engines idling, while in the cockpit, Ed Bradford prepared to deplane and continue his mission.

"How will you get away with that big airbase so close by?" he asked Lieutenant Mason. "If they spot you, your goose is cooked."

"Not to worry, Major. First of all, they have to see me, and this old Mossie is a problem for their radar. Mostly wood, you know."

"Right. I've read that," responded Bradford, as he rapped on the panel next to him. "I'll be darned."

"Even if they do pick me up," continued Mason, "she'll outrun the lot of them. That's what she was built for, to outdo the *Luftwaffe*." He patted the machine gun button on his control yoke, "I can do the rest, should the need arise."

"Well, good luck." The major worked himself out of his harness and pulled off his leather helmet. "Oh, one thing. I'd like to report back to my general. Is that possible?"

"Yes, sir. We use Morse. My sergeant usually handles it, but I have a decent touch."

"It's okay. I can manage," Ed told him, switching the radio on. "Do you have a frequency … ah never mind. I see the book."

Turning the pages of the small manual to 31 May 1944, he adjusted the dial to the prescribed frequency, and using a key, sent a series of dits and dahs over the airwaves. Long moments passed before he heard similar sounds in his headset. Taking a pad and pencil from a compartment, he proceeded to decipher what he was hearing until, after several minutes, he said, "I think I have a line to General Terry. Now, to tell him where we are, what happened, and how I'm going after the three suspects."

The pilot scanned the roadway before and behind them as Ed listened for a reply. When the response came back, the major's face grew grim as he continued to scribble away.

"'Final authorization," he read aloud when the exchange was completed. "Kill Eisenhower and Davis if necessary. Spare MI6 agent if possible." The major shook his head. "Shit! There has to be another way. That's nothing I ever wanted to do."

"Sir, I expect it's a matter of two lives versus hundreds saved." Mason looked down at the radio. "Do you need to respond?"

"Yeah," Ed sent code for "understood" and turned off the set.

"War is hell, as they say," was all the lieutenant could offer.

Bradford leaned forward and twisted the handle on the hatch down by his feet. As he did so, he noticed the red warning, "Beware of Airscrews."

Simultaneously, the pilot cautioned. "Crawl back along the fuselage. I'll see you clear before I go. And take this escape and evasion kit. It contains maps, a compass, money, some dried food, and medical supplies. That sort of thing."

After checking his gun and ammo supply, Bradford stuck his weapon back into the holster under his flight coveralls, grabbed the E and E kit, and signaled a thumbs-up. "Thanks, Mason," he said just before he disappeared through the escape hatch. "It's been one hell of a ride!"

SHAEF Headquarters
Office of the Chief, Operational Intelligence

"Crap, Beetle," Bill Terry told General Smith who was sitting across the desk from him, smoking a cigarette. "I damn well hated doing it, but if the Krauts find out the locations now, they have enough time to shift their defenses and we'll lose thousands."

"That's exactly right, Billy," Ike's chief of staff replied. "But I don't see any way around it. We have one, maybe two men out there who could doom the whole shooting match. I hope they're able to avoid capture until the balloon goes up, but if not, they need to be silenced."

"What about this Eisenhower angle?" Terry asked, sipping from the ever-present mug. "Do we know if this postman is related?"

"We're still checking. It's very remote. Ike's family settled in Pennsylvania in the eighteenth century."

Terry shrugged. "What would it matter anyway? I don't believe he's working for the bad guys, but if he is, it may already be too late. If not, he has no espionage skills and he'll crack the minute they grill him."

"What about Lieutenant Davis?"

"Whitehall gave us the go-ahead on taking him out. They see it the way we do. His name was linked to the BIGOT documents and he's considered as big a risk as the postman. Besides, it was a Brit screw up in the first place. Can you believe it, letting classified papers fly out of a goddamn window like that?"

"Earlier, Bradford reported that, according to the owner of the pub he goes to, this Eisenhower has some kind of photographic memory," Terry said, his face grim. "If he did read the papers …"

Both of them knew what had to happen. Guilty or innocent, Eisenhower was too great a threat to be allowed to stay alive.

Headquarters Security Service (SD), Berlin

The *Oberführer* was at his desk, lost in paperwork, when the door crept open and there stood a stern Heinrich Himmler, his dour countenance made even more menacing by the black suit he wore.

"Ah, Herr Reichsführer, to what do I owe …?" The Wagnerian villain's expression on his visitor's face stopped him.

"Herr Oberführer, this is not a social call," Himmler said, quietly closing the door behind him. *"Quite the contrary. I have received word that the Arado aircraft I had reserved for this morning has crashed. I believe you may know something about this."*

Himmler made a point of moving a chair to one side, out of the line of fire of the fortress desk's machine guns, before sitting.

The general dropped into his seat and once he gathered his thoughts, responded, *"Yes Excellency, I sent the plane on a special mission to England, but the last I was aware, it was on its way back safely to German soil."*

"And that is where it lies, in the soil of the Fatherland, never to fly again. Apparently, most of the crew was lost along with your precious cargo."

Himmler's words stung Schellenberg. *"Herr Reichsführer, this is terrible news!"* he exclaimed. *"And it is my fault. I sent an Abwehr dolt to do the job of an experienced SD agent. Amazingly, he had succeeded, or that is what I thought. He had captured two Englanders with apparent knowledge of the invasion plan, and a top MI6 agent to boot."*

Himmler remained cold. *"There were two survivors. One is possibly your dolt, a standartenführer. The other, a feldwebel of the crew. No sign of the Englanders. The wreckage was quite destroyed by fire."*

"Yes, the standartenführer would be my man, von Kroit. What did he have to say?"

"As of a few minutes ago, nothing. He is seriously injured, as is the other man. They are both comatose."

"Kroit may have interrogated the captives before they all died. He must be awakened. I believe the attack will come from England at any time now. We will discover where. The Führer must know!"

"Exactly, Schellenberg," Himmler glared. "This is why I want you there to ensure the information reaches me without delay. I shall inform the Führer. Are we clear?" Himmler stood and Schellenberg did the same. "The crash site and hospital are close to Fliegerhorst Venlo. Of course, you know the area well. I need not remind you of the Café Bacchus affair." The *Reichsführer* was referring to the 1939 sting operation in which then Major Schellenberg, using the name Schämmel, helped abduct two British agents from Venlo.

As soon as his visitor was gone, Schellenberg beat the top of his desk with his hand. "That bastard Kroit! Why did I ever test him this way? Now, he tests me."

Going to a cabinet in the corner, he pulled out a piece of pre-packed luggage.

"I thought I was over all this." He looked at the portrait of Hitler on the wall and said, quite simply, "I do this for you, my Führer."

Near Venlo, the Netherlands

The four-kilometer trek that Bradford's survival map had led him on, added to the fact that he had not slept well for two days, finally took its toll. Before reaching the border, he found a spot among rows of bushes and crawled in for a short nap, using the E and E kit Mason had given him as a pillow. The Yank major slipped into the arms of Morpheus for a much-needed rest only to awaken in a panic when he saw that six hours had passed. Taking deep breaths to calm himself, he prepared to take on the challenge of crossing over into Germany. Of course, he would avoid the roads where there were sure to be guards, but the map showed many farm areas where border coverage would be spotty—or at least that was what he hoped. As it had proved over and over since he joined the army, in times of war, destiny was a major player.

Leuth, Germany

It was mid-afternoon before Jan's house guests awakened. Paul was the first to get up and head for the facility down the hall. When he went to put on his trousers and carry the rest of his clothes with him, he discovered they were neatly folded and his shirt smelled like it had been laundered, all courtesy of Frau Dekker. As he passed the room next to his, he could hear Sir Harold snoring away without an apparent care or concern. Creaking sounds of pacing coming from behind the next door told him Phil was awake, probably worrying about his predicament, and whether he would get back to England and his unit in time.

Paul completed his wash-up in quick order and when he opened the bathroom door, there stood Phil waiting his turn. His arms held clothes fit for a farmer.

"Well, Lieutenant, did you ever expect Germans to be so very kind to us?" Paul wondered. "Here, I was thinking they all favored the *Führer*. Gives me hope for humanity and makes me believe we've a chance in this bloody war."

"Call us lucky, I'd say," Phil responded as Paul descended the steps to the kitchen where Frau Dekker was busy preparing a meal.

"Ah, Mister Paul, you sleep well?" she asked.

"Very well, indeed, Frau Dekker."

"Please, Inge."

"Inge. Of course. I'm afraid we lolled longer than what we had planned. Your husband wished to leave a bit after noon." He checked his watch. "It's nigh unto three."

She looked at the wooden wall clock. "Only near two it is."

"Oy, I forgot the time difference. We're an hour ahead. Double summer time, you know." He adjusted his watch.

Phil arrived moments later and joined Paul at the table. Once again, the meal consisted of sausages, this time with sliced potatoes, boiled red cabbage, and beer instead of milk. Just as they began enjoying the hearty fare, Sir Harold showed up, looking very much the farm hand. He gave a cheery greeting, as he might at some English inn, and expressed the group's appreciation to Inge in her native tongue. His charming delivery made the sweet-faced, buxom woman blush.

Jan arrived moments later and took a seat at the head of the table where Inge set a full plate before him. Her kiss on his cheek and her tender term, "Schatzi," made Paul long for such a bond. His thoughts went back to Emily and the blossoming relationship he hoped for with her. He was determined not to let it be his impossible dream. The very thought of it inspired him.

As they prepared to leave, Frau Dekker handed Paul a package. "Here, Mister Paul, you men need this for trip, yes?"

He looked inside the used flour sack and found a loaf of bread, a half dozen hard-boiled eggs, and three dried sausages. He kissed her cheek and she blushed again.

As the farmer and the fugitives walked across the barnyard, Jan explained. "Safer if we go on foot. Not a kilometer to the border. Five or six more to the L.O."

"Is the border well-guarded?" Paul asked.

"That we shall see," Jan replied as he led them across the same field where they had arrived that morning. "The roads they are patrolled, and the rest is sometimes and sometimes not. Often not in afternoon." He pointed to a line of trees in the near distance. "*Niederlande* is there."

Holland was, Paul realized just across the water from England, but with what might lie ahead, he wondered if he would ever get there.

Venlo Hospital, the Netherlands

General Schellenberg paced back and forth as Doctor Adriaan Kuyper, a rangy man sporting a strawberry blonde goatee and wearing a white medical coat, leaned over the still, ashen body of Colonel von Kroit. The patient's head and arm were enclosed in plaster casts, and his chest was wound with heavy gauze. Kuyper placed his stethoscope under the edge of the bandage and listened.

"*Well, Kuyper. Is he still alive?*" the general demanded.

"*Most certainly, Herr Oberführer. However, he remains in a coma.*"

"*And when might his condition improve? I have been here for almost two hours and I see no signs it ever will.*"

The doctor shrugged. "*It is not easy to determine.*"

"*What of the feldwebel?*"

"*Herr Oberführer, he is worse off than this man. He has bullet wounds in his chest and neck.*"

"*Bullet wounds?*" Schellenberg erupted. "*Then the crash was not an accident. Why wasn't I informed of this earlier?*"

"*I am only a doctor, but it is my opinion the crash was the result of an attack.*"

The door opened and a nurse went to the doctor and whispered something in his ear. He nodded and she left.

"*What is it?*" asked Schellenberg.

The doctor shook his head. "*The other man just died.*"

"*So, this poor bastard is my only hope!*" He glared at the doctor. "*You must do something.*"

"*Sir, we have done what we could. Now, we will let nature take its course.*"

Schellenberg stomped his foot on the oak floor. "*I have no time to await nature. Do something. Now!*"

The doctor stroked his chin. "*We can try a stimulant. Adrenaline, possibly cocaine, but it will tax his heart and he may die in the process.*"

The general walked up to Kuyper and grabbed him by the lapels. *"Herr Doktor, I don't care what <u>might</u> happen. Unless you can wake him, I know what <u>will</u> happen. The Reich will suffer. Do I make myself clear?"*

Kuyper nodded nervously, and releasing him, the *oberführer* allowed the doctor to hurry out of the room. Going to the bed, Schellenberg looked down at the mangled mess that was once von Kroit. *"So, you are not as big a blockhead as I thought. I don't wish to lose you Kroit, but I must attempt this for the greater good."*

The doctor reentered accompanied by the nurse carrying a tray holding two hypodermic needles and a vial of clear, greenish liquid.

"Please prepare it," instructed the medic.

The nurse sucked the cocaine into one of the syringes and handed it to Kuyper.

The doctor explained to the general, *"We will attempt a partial dose at first."*

Pointing the needle to the ceiling, he squeezed out a spurt of liquid before locating a vein on von Kroit's good arm and sending about half of the syringe's contents into his bloodstream.

Von Kroit's eyelashes fluttered for a second and he emitted a low moan.

"Hah! Progress! Good!" observed the general. *"Can you give him more?"*

"We risk killing him, Herr Oberführer. Then you would learn nothing. Please give it time to work."

The colonel moaned again, and the general took over the bedside. *"Kroit,"* he said. *"it is Schellenberg. You had an accident. I must know what happened."*

"Enemy attack from above," von Kroit whispered. *"Crew wounded. Three of us jumped on chutes."*

"The Englishmen! What of them?"

"They escaped before the attack. They jumped also."

"Bradford! Do you know the name? An American major? Was he with them?"

"No Bradford. No Bradf ..." Von Kroit's eyes closed and again he lost consciousness.

"More, use more!" the general demanded.

"Please, I have an oath," the doctor pleaded, *"I must not do harm."*

"You have sworn a greater oath to the Fatherland!" Schellenberg reminded him as he grabbed the syringe and pumped the rest of the solution into von Kroit.

This time, the colonel responded almost immediately. His eyes opened and he held his chest with his good hand. *"Oh, God,"* he gasped. *"Help me."*

"Kroit! Kroit, listen. Did you get the information?"

"Information? Information?" His face went blank and his eyes took on the dead stare of a shark as he lapsed into silence, never to speak another word.

The doctor pushed the general aside and checked von Kroit with his instrument. *"He is gone. Murderer!"*

Stern-faced, Schellenberg picked up his hat and case and calmly left.

Leuth, Germany

Major Bradford met no obstacles, either human or mechanical, as he made his way across the border. When he discovered the smoldering wreckage of the Ar 232, it told him for certain he was in Germany and close to the field where he last saw the trio from the air. Burned into his memory was the fact that it was a mile or less southeast of the crash site. After checking his compass and map, he pivoted in the correct direction, and ever wary of being spotted, once again used the hedges bordering the fields for cover as he went.

The first farmhouse the major came across was too close to the crash site to be the right one, so he kept going, arriving at what seemed a more likely location minutes later. When he got there, he weighed his options. The farmer appeared to be friendly to the three jumpers, but Bradford wasn't even sure the men were the ones he was after. They might have been Germans being welcomed by a Nazi sympathizer. But this was war and it was time for a bold move.

The knocking startled Inge as she was pulling loaves of bread from the oven. Wiping her hands on her apron, she went to the door, worried that the *Gestapo* had returned. Instead, she opened it on yet another stranger who, to her amazement, announced that he was an American.

"Amerikaner? "she exclaimed. "With the others, are you? The Englanders?"

Ed breathed a sigh of relief at her words. "No, but I need to find them."

"Come, come in. No one should see you. "

He followed her into the kitchen where the aroma of baking captured him for a moment.

"They go with mine husband to Venlo. Help is there." Inge motioned him to a chair just as the sound of vehicles arose outside. She went to the window and paled at what she saw. *"Mein Gott! Gestapo.* Please, you come."

The farmer's wife led Bradford to a hallway where she moved a rug, revealing a trap door which she pulled open.

"In here," she told him. As he looked down at an earthen vault about a meter deep and the width of two coffins, with its sides shored by wooden slats, she explained, "We use when the bombs come. Hurry! You must!"

Fighting off claustrophobia, the major crammed the E and E kit into his tunic, dropped into the damp crypt, and lay down as Inge replaced the panel.

Bradford could hear a banging at the door, then the sound of heavy footsteps and what seemed stern threats coming from above. Boots stomped directly over him and went in all directions, followed by shouts that he assumed meant they were finding nothing. As the harsh dialogue continued, he remained as still and quiet as a corpse. From the direction of the kitchen, he heard a slap and a woman's scream. There were scuffling noises amid her protestations, as the sounds traveled to the yard outside. More shrieks were followed by what seemed to him a confession punctuated by sobs, and then, at last, he heard the vehicles drive off. As he wondered if it was safe to show himself, the eerie silence left behind by the *Gestapo* was slowly being overtaken by a low rumble and a distinctive crackling and popping. Then he felt it—heat creeping into his refuge. His oxygen was disappearing, making it more and more difficult to breathe. Desperate for any kind of relief, Ed pulled down the support slats and used two of them to dig out the walls of his tomb. His lungs felt like they were going to burst as he gasped for air, but he kept digging with every ounce of energy left in him.

The Monastery at Venlo

After an uneventful hour and twenty minutes of avoiding guards and miscellaneous other military, Jan and the three fugitives reached a small stone chapel in Venlo. The picturesque village, once a fortress of the Hanseatic League, had suffered collateral damage from the bombing attempts to neutralize the German airbase; however, many of the quaint buildings and infrastructure were relatively unscathed.

Jan led them to a basement door located beneath the chapel that was part of a large monastery complex built in the late fifteenth century following the *Kulturkampf* the Germans waged against the Catholic Church. Rapping on the door first three times, then two and then one, he waited until he heard the sound of footsteps. "*Hans, It's me, Jan,*" he called in a raspy whisper.

Slowly the portal opened and they were hustled inside by Hans Rijkers, a big, handsome Dutchman wearing traditional work clothes. The cellar smelled of the grapes and wines that had been processed and stored there over hundreds of years. It was musty and dark, and slowly their eyes adjusted so they could make out their surroundings—a man at a radio set, a couple writing at a table next to a hand-operated printing press, and a dark, gray-bearded elder fussing over an array of weapons ranging from handguns to rifles and machine guns.

"*These are Englanders,*" Jan explained. "*They escaped from the Nazi plane.*"

"*Ah, the one that crashed in Leuth,*" Hans said, eyeing the fugitives closely before speaking to them in English. "You are most fortunate to survive."

"We got out before the accident," Sir Harold clarified. "Came down on chutes, don't you see."

"Yes," Jan added, "right into my field."

"So," the Dutchman walked around to the back of a desk. "Now, you want that we hide you."

"Oh, no," Phil corrected. "We're on the move. I need to get back to my unit. As of now, they believe I am a deserter."

"And I must return for other security reasons," Sir Harold added. "I don't believe I have any knowledge they'd be interested in, but I would be a prize, a bargaining chip as it were, if I should fall into Nazi hands."

"I see." Hans looked at Paul. "And you?"

"All I want is to return to me life as a postman," Paul told him. As he said it, a vision of Emily came to him.

"So, you think because the others return, you ride along with them?"

Paul fidgeted from one foot to the other. "Since you'd be protecting the lieutenant here and Sir Harold ..."

"Wait!" Hans interrupted, "I want no names. The little I know, little I can say."

Paul scrunched up his face. "Sorry, mate."

"My friend here is being modest," Sir Harold explained. "It's vital he get back to England, out of reach of the enemy."

"We are fleeing the *Gestapo,*" added Phil.

Hans looked them up and down for a second time. "Why should the *Gestapo* want you?"

Phil nudged Paul. "Tell the man."

Avoiding the classified aspects, Paul related the story with his fellow Britons filling in, as appropriate. He wrapped it up with, "If the Jerries found out what I know, it could cock up the whole invasion. This bloody war could go on years longer."

"*So, you help them?*" Jan pressed Hans who nodded. "*And so,*" he added, clearly relieved, "*I go back to my wife and farm.*"

There were expressions of thanks as the farmer departed, leaving the Englishmen he had done so much for in the hands of the partisans.

"You see, we have extensive operation here." Hans said with a hint of pride. "We must not have it interrupted. I will not introduce you to anyone. I am your only contact and I will see that you are transported and, what is it you say? Ah, 'handed off.'"

Harold leaned forward. "Handed off to whom? Where?"

"That depends on what you want to do. You have options. Directly to the coast, as to south of *Den Haag*, then a boat from there to your homeland. Maybe Antwerp, for access to the sea. Or by land to Brussels, then south to Paris. The resistance can help along the way."

"Oy," Paul concluded, "so it's up to us blokes to decide, is it?"

"Let the chap finish, old man," Phil cautioned.

"It's okay," Hans assured. "You see, it will depend on the level of exposure and threat at the time. As of today, the route along the seashore in my country is the most dangerous because the enemy prepares for an invasion."

"It must be the same all along the coast," Sir Harold said. "Is such not the case?"

"Oddly, France is the more open because the Nazis have concentrated their power in the big port cities such as Le Havre, Calais, Cherbourg. Although it is fortified and heavily mined, we are told the Germans do not expect the invasion to come at Normandy."

an's last word caused Paul to catch his breath before he quickly offered, "Well then, I vote for Normandy."

Harold shrugged. "It all sounds like a gamble and I'd rather like to know we have the best odds, what?"

"When do we leave?" Phil asked.

"There is much to prepare first," Hans told them. "You need papers and suitable clothing. Does anyone speak German?"

"I do," said Sir Harold. "Fluent enough, I would say."

"And I speak French," Phil added. "Studied architecture there for a year before Jerry arrived."

Everyone looked to Paul who explained, with a grin, that he was still working on his English, but was sure he could learn enough of another language to get by.

Thus began preparations for the trip back to England, and hopefully, to safety.

Leuth, Germany

A few hundred meters after Jan Dekker crossed the border he saw a sight that sent an icy chill up his spine. His farmhouse sat smoldering in the distance. The smoke curling into the late afternoon sky numbed his brain. Squatting, he tried to catch his breath, but there was no relief. Clearly, disaster awaited him, and he could not bring himself to approach it. The next few minutes dragged by as the farmer dug deep to find the resolve to go on. He had to discover what happened, but in the back of his mind, he already knew.

When Jan got there, he found a few walls of the smoldering house still standing, but the barn was a pile of charred rubble. Animals were scattered dead and dying everywhere, and among them, he glimpsed the multihued dress Inge had on that morning. Looking closer, Jan discovered his dear wife on the ground, her crimson blood adding to the print of the fabric. *"Oh, my Inge,"* he wailed, cradling her limp body in his arms. *"What did they do to you?"*

"They forced me to tell," she gasped, in a voice so weak he could scarcely make out the words. *"They made me do it, Jan."*

"Don't speak, my love," he wept, holding her close to him. *"I am here now and I promise to make this better."* Lifting her in his arms, he began the trek back to the border.

Gestapo Field Office
Venlo, the Netherlands

"Weber, as of this moment, you are relieved." General Schellenberg snapped his fingers. *"Just like that, you are gone. You allowed my captives to escape and all you have to show for it thus far is a ravaged farm and a tortured woman. I do not consider these worthy results."*

He looked around the office of six desks and agents who appeared to be busy with work.

The general demanded, *"Who is second in command here?"*

No one responded and the *oberführer* scowled.

"Ullrich, sir," Weber said finally. *"He is not here."*

"Get him here immediately. He will run the operations against the L.O. Understand? Now, what do we know about the Dutch resistance?"

"They are clever and efficient ..." Weber swallowed hard, *"... and, extremely adept at covert activity, sir."*

"Covert? Does this mean you don't know where they are?"

"I'm afraid it does, Herr Oberführer. They regularly move from place to place."

"When Ullrich gets here," Schellenberg told him, placing emphasis on each word, *"we shall plot their annihilation."*

Rommel's Headquarters
Château de La Roche-Guyon, France

Field Marshall Rommel rarely sat behind his ornate desk situated in a ground-floor chamber of the twelfth century castle he had converted for military use, as he preferred standing over it to do his work. The office around him, while beautifully appointed, lacked any indication of his personal tastes or who he was. For him, it was simply another place where he could gather his thoughts and scheme his plans. Now, as he reviewed weather information, there was a tap on the door and in strode his aide.

"You sent for me, Herr Generalfeldmarschall?"

"Lang, please assure me this is the latest on the weather. I feel in my bones that the attack is imminent. The only obstacle for the Allies is a storm I am told is developing in the North Sea."

"Yes, sir, I have checked, and this is the latest data from the weather staff."

"I see. As you know Lang, I would like to return to Germany for my wife's birthday. If the weather materializes, as they predict, I may be able to do that. So, be prepared and make certain I take those new shoes I had made for her." He tossed a weather map aside. *"Remind von Tempelhof I would like him to accompany us, if I, in fact, am able to go."*

The Convent at Venlo

Jan Dekker carefully set his wounded wife down on the grass and rapped frantically on the chapel basement door. *"Hans! Let us in."* Getting no response, he rapped again and cried out, *"Hans! Please!"*

From behind him came a soft voice. *"The ones you are looking for are no longer here."*

He turned and saw an Augustinian nun.

As she approached him, she looked down and saw Inge. *"Oh, dear Lord, we must help you."*

The nun and the farmer carried Frau Dekker to the nearby convent where, with the help of two other sisters, they opened an unused room and brought medical supplies to treat the woman's wounds.

When she was satisfied the patient was out of immediate danger, the nun, who Jan had learned was called Sister Maria, did her best to comfort the farmer who was sitting in a corner crying like a baby. *"There are serious injuries, but they appear treatable,"* she told him, placing her hand on his shoulder. *"She can survive, if she has the will."*

Inge groaned and raised her hand to her forehead. *"The pilot. What happened to him?"*

"Inge, my darling. Don't you remember, I led them all away. They are safe with the L.O."

"Jan, I mean the American," she said, startling her husband. *"He came in search of the others. When the Gestapo arrived, I put him in the safe cellar. I never spoke of him to them."*

"The cellar!" Jan exclaimed. *"My God, he must be dead."*

"Please," she pleaded weakly, *"he may have escaped. If he has, you must find him. Unless you do, I will always think he died because—because of me."* And with that, she closed her eyes and lapsed into unconsciousness again.

Leuth, Germany

It was twilight when Jan Dekker re-crossed the border and approached what once was his farm. A fine rain was falling and his first reaction was, *"Ah, good for the crops,"* before he realized there would be no more crops. Not here, not for him.

The embers from the blaze had been doused by the rain and he found his way through the demolished kitchen to the trap door and the safe cellar. Opening it, he discovered the encrusted body of Ed Bradford. Jan reached down and pulled the major up by his flight coveralls. *"You poor man, you are cooked like a lamb."* As he did so, he realized the crust was a layer of dirt. Somehow, the major had managed to bring soil down on himself and insulate his body from the heat.

Once he was sure the American was still alive, Jan made him as comfortable as possible on the floor. He found an unbroken half-liter of *Jenever*, a Dutch gin, in the cabinet and force-fed him a healthy swallow.

Bradford coughed himself into consciousness. "Holy shit, what is that? And who are you?"

"The husband of Inge, my wife you see earlier."

"Oh, God, that's right. Is she okay?"

"They destroy my farm, but not my Inge." Jan held up the bottle. "Here, you have more. And then we go."

Once Bradford had recovered reasonably well, Jan led him on the same course he had taken the three Britons earlier. When they got to the border, Jan went first and Ed hid in the brush. The farmer was about to signal the major when he saw a figure coming toward him. By the fading light, he could make out the silhouette of a German army helmet.

"Halt!" cried the guard. *"Identify yourself."*

"I am a local farmer searching for my lost cow," Jan told him. *"I did not realize it might have crossed the border."*

The guard pointed a rifle with one hand and shined a flashlight on him with the other. *"Papers!"*

As Dekker reached in his pockets, Bradford came from behind, grabbed the guard's head and twisted it violently to the right. There was a crack before the major allowed the soldier's limp body to fall to the ground.

"Mein Gott!" exclaimed Jan. "What do you do?"

Ed looked at him quizzically, "Eliminated a threat. Here, help me with his clothes."

Together they stripped the body and Bradford swapped uniforms, trading his army dog tags for the German's, and putting both sets of identification papers—his and the guard's—in the E and E kit. The switch was complete except for footwear. The soldier's boots looked two sizes too small and he didn't intend to have aching feet for the rest of his mission. After equipping himself with the German helmet and rifle, Ed and the farmer continued their trek, leaving behind what appeared to be the corpse of a downed American.

They met no further interference as they entered Venlo, although it was slow going. Once, for a brief time, they played the roles of a German soldier escorting his captive as they cautiously passed a *Wehrmacht* half-track parked in a small square. It turned out the charade was unnecessary as the machine was empty.

It was almost midnight by the time they reached the convent, and when they arrived, Ed stayed in the shadows while Jan rapped on the door. One of the nuns let the farmer in and escorted him down the hall until he assured her he knew the way. Once she disappeared into her cell, Jan returned to the door and waved Bradford inside. They found Inge asleep and Sister Maria sitting by the bedside reading.

Jan entered first and the nun looked up and put her finger to her lips. *"Shhh, she is resting well. Oh Lord!"* Her face blanched when Ed stepped into the doorway.

"Don't worry. He is our American."

Hearing the word *"Amerikaner,"* Ed nodded and the nun cautiously smiled back.

She went on to explain that Hans, the resistance leader, had come by earlier and she'd told him Jan and Inge's story.

As the conversation progressed, Jan translated for him. "Sister Maria says the L.O. must meet you to see you are not enemy agent."

"What's this L.O.?"

"The resistance, loyal to the Dutch crown."

"Is it where the Englishmen are, with them?"

Jan shrugged and turned to the sister. *"Maria, have you more appropriate clothes for this man?"*

"Only the robes of a monk, I'm afraid. Will that do?"

"It will have to," Hans said as he slipped into the room and addressed the farmer. *"Jan, I am afraid that, for safety, we must move both you and your wife now, before the first light."*

Sister Maria returned with the robes, and when Bradford began changing, Hans asked for the German uniform.

"Later, in return," said the L.O. leader, "maybe we provide you more suitable clothes and papers."

"What about money?" Ed felt for the kit in his tunic. "I have some gold coins, a few British pounds, and Army scrip. Any of it will raise a red flag."

"We will arrange for *reichsmarks*." He looked the American up and down. "That is, if you are permitted to go anywhere."

Chapter Five

Thursday, 1 June 1944

A Road from Venlo, the Netherlands

Early morning found the three Englishmen being driven to Brussels. The 1938 Citroen was noisy and uncomfortable, but the passengers were most grateful to have wheels under them—wheels that would take them closer to home and away from the nightmare of recent days.

Hans was driving, Phil was riding up front, and Sir Harold was giving Paul German lessons in the back seat. He would hold up a common phrase page of a *Deutschland* tourist guide, and amazingly, Paul would look away and recite it back with great precision. Harold's tutoring was suspended when the car approached the checkpoint outside of Venlo. Fortunately, the guards there did not converse with the travelers. They simply took their papers and returned them routinely before waving them through. Hans knew it would be much more difficult at the Dutch-Belgian border.

As the lessons in the back seat resumed, Hans turned to Phil. "So, I have something I must know," he said. "Do you know a Major Bradford of the United States Army?"

Phil shrugged. "Anyone back there know a Yank major by the name of Bradford?"

"Here, isn't he the bloke I saw sign in at the White Horse," Paul replied. "That was his name all right, Major Bradford.

"So, you know him," Hans concluded.

Paul shook his head, "Nah, only that he stayed there. I might recognize the bloke, but I never met him, have I."

Sir Harold leaned forward and held onto the back of the seat. "Why are you inquiring about this Bradford fellow?"

"We have him," Hans replied. "He arrived at the farm looking for you. His papers say he is American, but make no mistake, he comes after you. He claims to work for the Allied command."

"Of course," Phil spoke up. "He wants Paul here and me. They mean to stop us. Wasn't that your mission, Sir Harold?"

"No names," Hans reminded him.

"My only mission was to keep you out of the way for a time," Sir Harold told him. "That's all. I never counted on any of this, you see."

"Now, I have a question," said Paul. "If this bloke only aims to keep us from the Jerries, and here we are doing a job of avoiding them on our own, why is he still after us?"

"That's a good one, my friend," The MI6 man patted his knee. "Unless, he was really up to something more."

Phil looked back at them and suggested, "Like keeping us quiet, permanently."

"Exactly!" Sir Harold slapped the back of the seat. "By George, there's no reason we should want to meet up with him. None whatsoever."

Gestapo Field Office, Venlo

Schellenberg sat at the head of a table, a cup of coffee at hand, and a multi-paged report titled "*Landelijke Organisatie, 1 Juni 1944*" before him. Across from him sat the new Chief Inspector, Werner Ullrich. To his left was the deposed Georg Weber, and on his right, agent Peter Maas, who specialized in monitoring the Dutch resistance.

"*Please, Maas,*" the general said as he picked up the report, "*Spare me this, and tell me directly the results of your inquiry last night.*"

The agent nodded. "*Herr Oberführer, I went to the latest suspected L.O. location and they were gone. It seems they have moved somewhere they've never used before. However, I made observations and inquiries, and the Augustinian convent yielded some useful information.*"

Schellenberg was becoming impatient. "*And that was …*" he prompted.

"*One of the nuns there told me that last night, a woman was brought in near death. And as it turns out, she is the wife of the farmer who helped the fugitives.*"

"*Did she live? Did you speak with her?*" blurted Ullrich and quickly he eyed the general.

Schellenberg said coldly, "*It's okay, Herr Inspekteur. Two good questions. Well, Maas?*"

"The farmer's wife had already been moved by the L.O.," the agent continued. "However, the nun had heard that, when she recovered, the woman said something about an American pilot coming to the farm. Apparently he was injured and the farmer returned there to help him."

"Did the American ever appear at the convent?"

"I asked, and the nun didn't think so. The farmer returned at about midnight and she went to bed after that. When she awoke, the room where they had the woman was empty. I tried to discover where she was taken, but it was fruitless. It was dawn when I returned to make my report."

"A good effort, Agent Maas," the general said, "but it is not enough. We need to locate the resistance and determine where my prizes have gone. How do you propose we do this, gentlemen?"

Weber spoke first, "We must interrogate the nun further. She may be hiding something."

The general pursed his lips. "Shall we beat her within an inch of her life until we find out what that might be? Would this work, Maas?"

"No, sir, I believe she offered all she knew." He avoided Weber's stare. "I say we need to find out what happened to the American."

"Yes," Ullrich agreed. "If he was sent to save the Englanders, he may lead us to them."

"But sir," Weber insisted. "I believe the nuns know something more. We should interrogate them."

"Are you suggesting we torture the entire convent, Weber?" the general sneered, deliberately turning his back on the former chief inspector. "Now, Ullrich. Go and trace the farmer's path. Determine where he took the American."

The Belgian Border near Maastricht, the Netherlands

The German soldiers at the crossing south of Maastricht were indeed more intense in their inspection than the guards at Venlo. They ordered the four men out of the Citroen and expertly patted them down. After meticulously checking their papers, they questioned each of them. Hans, Sir Harold, and Phil all passed their test. Hans correctly claimed that he was merely a driver who planned to return to Venlo immediately after dropping off his passengers. Harold and Phil used their assumed names and gave their occupations as valet and maître d'hôtel, respectively, Phil's French being good enough to satisfy the German guard who was accustomed to the multilingual character of the area.

When it was Paul's turn, the guard asked his name and why he was entering Belgium. In perfect if somewhat stilted German, the postman answered that he was Gunter Hamm, on his way to Brussels to cook at a large restaurant there. He was glad the German common phrase book had included references to eateries, kitchens, and meals.

When the soldier returned their papers and the improbable team was free to carry on, Phil got back in the car and checked for the weapon he had stashed under the seat earlier.

The Border at Leuth, Germany

Ullrich and a team of agents from the Venlo *Gestapo* went to the Dekker farmhouse to verify that the wife was no longer there. Finding nothing else of importance, they worked their way back toward the Dutch border. Tracks in the plowed soil, matted grass, and broken twigs marked the path of Jan's trips back and forth. The inspector was looking through his field glasses, surveying the nearby forest when one of the agents shouted, *"Here, over here! I found a body!"*

He and two of his men rushed to discover a dead man who appeared to be an enemy pilot. The uniform was right, but Ullrich, wondering how he ended up there and what or who had killed him, leaned over the body and carefully checked the clothing. The flight coveralls were no doubt RAF, but the uniform underneath was clearly United States army issue. Puzzled, he ordered two men to carry the corpse to the vehicle. Ullrich returned to his car and radioed the good news to his office as the team headed back to Venlo.

At the same time, a search party from the German border patrol unit was working its way along the frontier between the two countries trying to locate Will Koenig, a private who had not returned from his rounds that morning.

When the inspector arrived back at the field office, he found General Schellenberg in an ebullient mood. *"So, Ullrich, that was short work. Let me see this American trophy you bagged."*

"Yes, Herr Oberführer, the men have brought the body to the interrogation room."

The pair walked down the hall to the dreary room where an agent was adjusting the arms and legs of the dead flier lying on the table.

The general regarded the corpse. *"Ah! So this is your American. Do we know what killed him?"*

"Sir, we do not know that, but we do know why he died." The agent pulled the head up by the hair and released it, letting it flop back down to one side.

"It seems only the man's ligaments and skin are keeping the head attached to the torso."

"I see. Were there any papers on him?"

"Unfortunately not," Ullrich told him. "However, we believe he arrived here in a British aircraft, as evidenced by his outer garment."

The general stepped closer and felt the cloth of the flight coveralls. "Yes." He pulled the material aside. "And underneath, the uniform of an American army major." He looked directly at Ullrich. "Herr Inspekteur, does this man look old enough to be a major? He appears to be no more than twenty."

Ullrich shrugged nervously. "I do not know, Herr Oberführer. It is possible with the Americans. They are crazy."

Schellenberg used both his hands to open and inspect inside the corpse's mouth. "Come. Look here both of you. You see this silvery tooth? Is this not the work of our own dental corps?" Loosening the tie and opening the man's collar, the general reached inside the shirt and pulled out a chain with two dog tags stamped with the name "Edward D. Bradford," along with his serial number, shot record, blood type, and next of kin. In the lower right corner, a "C" indicated he was Catholic. The general let the dog tags drop and turned his attention to the dead man's feet. "Schnürschuhe!" He exclaimed as he raised the corpse's left boot, displaying an array of hobnails in its sole. "Do these look American? Of course not. They are Wehrmacht issue. Yes?"

The inspector looked as though he had just been sentenced to go before a firing squad. "I am so sorry Herr Oberführer. It was my entire fault. I should never have rushed to judgment."

"Find out who this man is and return him," Schellenberg said, going to the door. "A border guard would be my guess. We have wasted enough time here. I am going to the convent. Ullrich, you drive."

Brussels, Belgium

The Citroen entered the city from the northwest and drove along the *Chaussée de Louvain*. Hans eventually turned the vehicle south onto the *Rue Royale* and navigated a maze of streets to the famous *Grand Place*, the great marketplace square enclosed by the town hall, guild halls, and the King's house. Their front elevations, festooned with Nazi flags, gave mute evidence the city was under German occupation.

"Not many signs of the war here," observed Paul as they passed buildings, churches, and other facades that looked relatively untouched by bombs and battle scars.

"I believe Jerry may not want to render his usual havoc here as he aims to annex the Low Countries to Germany," Sir Harold explained.

"That, and it isn't much of a strategic target for the Allies," Phil remarked as the driver negotiated several more turns and they found themselves on a narrow street lined with brick buildings.

"At last, the bakery," Hans announced, pulling up in front of a shop with the sign *Boulangerie - Bäckerei*. "You stay and I shall go prepare the way."

The trio did as they were told, but it took some willpower because the aroma of baking bread reminded them it had been many hours since breakfast in Venlo.

Hans returned to the car and looked up and down the street. There were a few bicyclers and a woman carrying bundles, but no sign of Germans. He opened the car door. "Come, casually so as not to arouse suspicion."

The group entered the bakery and was escorted to a back room where they met Jacques Du Bois, a medium-height, wiry Belgian with stringy black hair, and a moustache. He wore a faded blue apron over baggy tweed pants and a frayed but clean white undershirt.

"Years we have waited, and now here you are," he said with a heavy French accent, holding out his hand. "Welcome. I do not know why you are here, and I do not want to know. That you are running from the German pigs is all I need."

"Right-o," Sir Harold replied. "We would appreciate anything you can do that would help us to return to England by the fastest and safest route possible."

Jacques smiled. "Of course, what is fast, is not always safe, you see."

Hans interrupted. *"Jacques, I need to radio back to Venlo."*

"Oui, oui." He called into the hallway, *"Louis, venez ici s'il vous plait."*

The sound of footsteps and grumbling preceded the appearance of a lanky, brown-haired young man with blue eyes and sallow skin. *"Ah, mon ami!"* he exclaimed, embracing Hans who, after introducing him to the others, asked to use his radio.

"So, we must make a plan," Jacques said as the two disappeared into another room. "But first we eat and drink. You must be strong, my friends, very strong because who knows what lies before you."

The Convent at Venlo

A group of twenty-three nuns, seated around a large table, had just finished their insubstantial lunch of thin soup, bread, and cheese when their superior, Mother Elisabeth, pushed her chair back and stood up at the head of the table. The others all rose and, as the head nun led them in blessing themselves with the sign of the cross, the door swung open and there stood General Walter Schellenberg.

Behind him, a young, novice nun signaled an anxious apology for the interruption before scurrying off as another *Gestapo* officer, Ullrich, brushed past her.

The general approached the table. *"Good afternoon, ladies. I apologize for interrupting your meal, but I have come for information I believe you can provide."*

Mother Elisabeth forced a smile. *"I would be happy to talk to you, Herr General. Please, sisters. Clear the table and leave us."*

"I am afraid I would like to speak to all of you," the general told them. *"I understand you had a certain visitor last evening. A woman who was injured in a fire, is this correct?"*

"General, with the war, we have many such people," the mother superior responded. *"They come to us for help, we minister to them, and they leave when they are well enough."*

"Was there one such woman last night?" asked Ullrich, only to shrink back against the wall when the general turned and glared at him.

In an awkward moment of silence, Sister Marie offered, *"Yes, we had a woman last night. She came to us with injuries, but not from a fire. We treated her and she went away after she was much improved."*

"Were there others with her?" Schellenberg persisted.

"Her husband who brought her here."

"Was he alone? Or maybe there was a German soldier with him."

Maria looked down at her empty bowl. *"I am not sure, but they all left. They are not here any longer."*

"How did they leave? Did someone else come for them? Did they leave on their own? Did the soldier accompany them?"

Sister Maria began to cry. *"I don't know. They left, that is all."*

Mother Elisabeth demanded. *"Please, General, you are upsetting all of us. Haven't we said enough?*

"One more question, if I may," he replied. *"Was the Landelijke Organisatie involved in any of this?"*

The mother superior touched the cross that hung from her neck, *"General, we know nothing more. We are religious sisters dedicated to the greater glory of Jesus Christ. Now, please, if you are finished."*

Outside the convent, Ullrich asked, *"Herr Oberführer, you were masterful, but what was gained by this visit? We know little more than when we came."*

"It is quite simple Herr Inspector. We confirmed that the nuns were involved, we can deduce the American came here disguised as a German soldier, and despite the mother's protestations, I suspect they are working with the L.O."

Brussels, Belgium

In the bakery cellar, Jacques Du Bois stood in front of a wall map marked with pencil lines and annotated in French. The three Britons sat around a long table, each with a glass of wine in front of him. Two men with rifles slung over their shoulders leaned casually against the wall, eyeing the visitors. The group shared the room with stacks of flour bags, sacks of sugar, tins of baking soda and yeast. A sleek, black cat resting atop one of the sacks opened his eyes periodically, waiting to discover a furry intruder.

"So, we agree." Jacques moved his index finger along the coastline from Oostende, Belgium to Brest, France. "It would be foolish to try to cross such a well-fortified and well-patrolled area. The entire Atlantic coast here is a forbidden area. I suggest you go to Paris and contact *La Résistance Française* where you can arrange transport to a safer coast such as Brittany. They will know best I am sure." He paused for a sign of feedback and when the threesome nodded, he went on. "*Bon.* Next, we must choose transportation. There is car or train."

"What? No boats?" Paul quipped.

The Belgian took the question seriously. "There are rivers and canals, but they are a poor consideration. Slow and you cannot trust that the way will be open."

Sir Harold eyed the map closely. "It seems to me, motoring there is preferable. More autonomy, you know."

"Right-o," Phil agreed, "we can choose the route and not get stuck on some railway in the middle of God knows where."

"All true," Jacques folded his arms before him and moved away from the map. "However, there are other considerations. By car, there are more checkpoints along the roadways, and you each will be one of four being inspected. You see, much of the area south of us is also forbidden. We believe the chance for discovery is reduced on the train where the examination of you and your papers will be one of many and it is much more routine. There are also fewer checkpoints along the railway." Leaning forward, he put his elbows on the table. "But the choice is up to you. If you choose auto, I will provide a driver and reliable machine. This will take some time, so you will not be able to leave until morning. By rail, you can depart this evening, once we make certain your papers and appearance are in order."

"What about the language?" Paul asked. "I speak English and a bit of German, but I'll need French, won't I?"

"It would help, my friend. But there is little time to teach you. You should ..."

"Jacques, the chap has a striking memory," Sir Harold interrupted. "Recalls anything he reads."

Phil spoke up. "A tourist guide book would do. I can help with pronunciation."

"Of course, we have one." Jacques smiled and clasped his hands together. "Now, what more?"

Sir Harold reached into his trouser pocket. "There is a matter of money. Among us, I dare say, we have plenty, but all British notes."

"We can also see to this," Jacques assured him. "It will be no problem; however, I will be honest, the many difficulties you will face cannot be so easily settled."

☆ ☆ ☆ ☆

The Brussels *Gare du Midi* train station, a walk of less than a kilometer from the bakery, was busy with all types of commerce and travelers, but mostly German troops.

"Not to worry," Jacques assured Paul, who was visibly anxious on seeing the enemy uniforms. "You will be fine. Many are young farm boys, Serbs and Poles who have been sent to prop up their withering army. They are most frightened themselves."

Escorted by the Belgian partisan, they lined up at the ticket booth and individually bought their passage to Paris, each surmounting the language barrier without any difficulty. According to the tickets, they were due to leave in less than an hour and would arrive in the City of Light by ten-thirty that night. After Jacques had each of them commit to memory the address of the French underground, in case they got separated, he left them with a *"Bon voyage et bonne chance, mes amis."* The fugitives took over a bench that became available when a train departed and waited their turn.

"Oy, it's been a smooth run so far, I'd say," Paul observed. "What about you blokes?"

Sir Harold scanned the crowd carefully. "Too smooth, if you ask me. First of all, we were more or less talked into taking the train. Moreover, I don't like the way we were dropped off. We're sitting ducks, as it were.

"What exactly does that mean?" Paul asked him.

"It means we might not want to be lingering here," Phil told him, frowning.

"Well, we got to wait for the train, ain't we?"

"Look!" Sir Harold pointed with his chin at the two German soldiers headed directly for them. They appeared to be more mature and battle worn than many of the youthful recruits around them."

A shiver shot up Paul's back. "Blimey!" he exclaimed. "Not again."

"Lieutenant, do you still have that Jerry weapon?" Sir Harold asked.

Phil patted his lower left chest. "I also picked up some ammo at the bakery."

"Good, we may need it." The MI6 agent had barely gotten the words out when one of the soldiers approached them, a cigarette hanging from the side of his mouth."

"Excuse me," he asked in German, *"would anyone have a light."*

"Aber, ja," Sir Harold responded, and proceeded to commit an inexcusable error. He dipped into his jacket pocket and pulled out a lighter with two British half pennies embedded in it. There was a sailing ship on one side and the likeness of King George VI on the other. Catching his blunder, he cupped his hand hoping the enemy soldier would not notice the emblems.

The soldier caught the flame on the end of his cigarette and inhaled. *"Danke,"* he said as he blew out smoke and glanced at the two others sitting there before turning and walking away.

When the pair got out of earshot, Harold grabbed the jacket sleeves of his compatriots. "Come on boys, it's time we disappeared." He pulled them into the passing crowd just as the two Germans stopped and looked back for them. Before Phil and Paul could make sense of it, Harold had hustled them out of the terminal. The agent used his evasion skills to lead them away before the soldiers were able to spot where they had gone. They hustled down a side street and paused at a flight of stone steps in front of a large, red door.

Paul sat catching his breath. "What in hell is going on, mate? There we were, all set."

Harold admitted, "I rather think there'll be no train ride for us tonight, and it's all on me. I buggered it up."

Phil sat. "Sir, what happened?"

Harold wiped his forehead with his sleeve, pulled the lighter from his pocket, and showed it to them. "This!"

Paul examined it. "Here, that's a dead give away now, ain't it."

"When I awoke yesterday morning, I didn't expect to end up on this side of the channel." Harold dropped the lighter down a grate in the sidewalk. "Damned poor excuse, what!"

Phil looked down the street and saw four German soldiers heading their way. "Looks like they're still after us."

Harold pointed to the door. "Inside, at once."

The Englishmen scurried up the stairs and entered another world. They found themselves in an elaborate foyer, but before they could fully appreciate their new surroundings, they were greeted by a mature woman with black hair piled atop her head, blue eyes, and full lips accented by bright red lipstick.

"*Good evening, Gentlemen. I am Monique,*" she said. "*Please, come right this way.*"

The vision of this other world continued when they entered a large room with marble columns, damask rose wall covering, and baroque white and gold decorations. The trio instantly focused on the most interesting adornments in the place—the scantily clad women standing about and sitting on sofas. Some smoked, while others sipped wine, and all gazed seductively at the new arrivals.

"Good God," Harold said out of the side of his mouth. "A bordello."

"*Now, gentlemen,*" Monique announced, "*you may select your pleasure.*"

"*Non, non, Madame.*" Phil began to explain that they were not there for pleasure, but he stopped short when he saw the German soldiers enter the foyer, laughing and frolicking.

As the madam glided back down the hall to welcome her new guests," Sir Harold issued a directive. "Step lively," he said, "and just pick one. No time to be choosy." He took the hand of a freckled redhead who looked half his age and headed for the steps. Phil, who was considering a couple of well-endowed blondes, chose the more buxom of the two and followed Sir Harold. As he did so, he saw Paul stalled among the bevy and called back, "*Emmenez-le et je vais payer un supplément,*" whereupon a perky brunette with big, dark eyes set down her glass and took Paul's arm. The escapees and their companions disappeared behind the safety of separate boudoir doors.

Venlo, the Netherlands

Ed Bradford, still wearing monk's robes, paced back and forth from one end to the other of a small room furnished only with a cot and a stand holding a water pitcher and bowl. Outside the open door stood a resistance fighter with a rifle.

Frustrated, the major strode over to the guard. "Look, I don't know what's going on here. I'm an American officer on a very special mission for a general, and I'm treated like dirt?"

"Please, major," said the guard as he wielded the weapon, "I follow orders. You stay here and Hans returns. It is better."

Ed looked at his watch and saw that it was already after four. "It's late and the men I need to catch up with are getting farther away by the minute." The remark elicited no response. "Shit, I may as well be talking to the wall." He sat on the cot, pulled out his pack of Luckies and Zippo, and lit up.

He was taking a last puff when Hans entered the room. "Finally!"

"My friend, how are you?"

Bradford shot up. "Friend my ass! I'm fed up, that's how I am. I need to get out of here. The whole friggin' war may depend on it."

Hans put a hand on his shoulder. "We detain you no longer than necessary," he assured him. "However, you do understand I cannot allow you to follow the others without knowing who you are and your motives."

"But I gave you my papers," Ed said impatiently.

"Papers are proof of nothing. We know this well. Remember, when we met, you wore a German uniform."

"I don't get it. I'm on a priority mission, and I'm stuck here going nowhere fast."

"We are attempting to contact your headquarters," Hans told him. "Is there someone other than this General Terry to speak to?"

"I don't know. He gave me verbal orders. I doubt anyone else knows where the hell I am."

"Do you have any other identification?"

"No! I left my dog tags on that Kraut whose neck I wrung."

"Ah, yes, so you said."

SHAEF Headquarters
Office of the Supreme Commander

"Butch, we appear to be getting better and better at softening rail and roadway targets," General Eisenhower told Lieutenant Commander Harry Butcher as he pored over the day's reports. "I'm damn glad I insisted on a transportation plan as part of Overlord. Now, here's something ..." He was interrupted by the buzzing of his intercom and the news that he had a call from Admiral Ramsey.

"Ike, it's the PM," the admiral told him. "Ever since the St. Paul's briefing, he's been insisting on going along to observe the invasion."

"Well, he has every right to ask," Ike replied wearily, having tried many times over the past few weeks to deal with this problem. "After all, he is Prime Minister and the Minister of Defense, to boot."

"I thought we could handle it," Ramsey went on, "but the more I consider his request, the less sense it makes. He damn well may be putting Neptune and the whole of Overlord at risk. If his ship is hit, several others will have to abandon the fight to rescue him. It could spell disaster."

"I don't disagree," Ike assured him, "but the fact is, I don't have the horsepower to dictate what he does. If it helps, please tell him the supreme commander says 'no' and explain that his presence would require extra resources we just cannot afford. I'll have a face-to-face meeting with him to smooth any ruffled feathers."

"Thanks Ike, will do. Oh, and be aware that he's gotten wind of this Whitehall incident involving BIGOT papers. He's hopping mad over it and wants to know what's being done about controlling the breach. I explained about MI6 being in direct contact, but I don't think it soothed him at all."

"Butch, what is the status of the lost BIGOT papers at the War Office?" Ike asked after he hung up. "I know they were all accounted for, but was it ever determined if this postman was involved in a security problem?"

Butcher folded his arms. "Well, sir, the latest I heard from General Smith is that the two suspects and the MI6 man were taken back to Germany."

"What?" Ike frowned. "Dammit, Butch, why am I hearing this now? Do we know if it's true?" He picked up his phone. "Please get me General Smith on scrambler. I believe he's at the War Office." He lit another cigarette from the butt he was smoking and let some steam subside. "Sorry, Butch, I know you're only the messenger."

When, a minute later, the phone rang, Eisenhower grinned at hearing the voice of a man he trusted deeply. "Listen, I have a few things to go over with you, Beetle," he said. "First of all, Churchill is still pushing to go."

"I know, that's the word floating around Whitehall."

"Speaking of floating around Whitehall, what's the latest with those BIGOT papers?"

"Ike, we got a report from the G2 man who was following the three Brits. Terry's Major Bradford was flown to Germany in pursuit. The Mosquito chase plane actually shot down the German cargo plane taking Eisenhower, this Brit Lieutenant Davis, and the MI6 guy."

"So, that's that."

"Not quite. It turns out the three of them had already gotten free and parachuted before the Mosquito caught up with the plane they were in."

Ike took a deep breath. "Was there a kill order?"

"No, sir, not at the time. The Mosquito was attacked and the pilot had no choice but to return fire. He took out the enemy in one pass, knowing the Brits weren't aboard."

"So where do we stand?

"According to Bradford, the three of them were taken in by a farmer. The Mosquito pilot has returned with a full report and I've seen reconnaissance photos of the area around the jump site. We have nothing further, but we assume they are in friendly hands in either Germany, where they dropped, or close by in Venlo, Holland, just over the border."

"Is there any way we can pick them out of there?"

"Venlo has a large military compliment. The German airbase there is one of their biggest. So, I'd say it would be risky. The MI6 agent is probably the saving grace in all this, as far as avoiding the Nazis goes."

Eisenhower shifted in his chair. "Do we know for certain that no one has spilled the beans?"

"Terry's boys have been monitoring it and the Brits have a close eye on Enigma message traffic. So far, there is no indication of a leak."

"Correct me if I'm wrong, Beetle," Ike replied, "but we aren't even sure Eisenhower or Lieutenant Davis has any knowledge of the plan."

"That's a fact. We only know the postman had access to it, not that he ever read it, and we're not at all sure where Davis fits in."

"So, let's see to it they're kept out of circulation."

"Except that Terry gave his man authority, based on dire need, to take out the two of them, but not the MI6 agent. As far as we know, the spy doesn't know anything, and if he does, the Krauts will have one hell of a time getting it out of him."

Ike ground out his smoke. "Try to contact the underground and ask them to put these guys on ice for a week or so. Meanwhile, I'd like to keep them all alive. This Eisenhower fella, any word on him?"

"G2, in their spare time, mind you, was able to trace his family back to Pennsylvania and confirm they came from the Saar region of Germany in the eighteenth century."

"It all sounds very familiar." Ike picked up a document from the PM's office and shifted gears. "Oh, and I have a letter here from Churchill bellyaching about the travel restrictions. We can go over that tomorrow. I think you'll get a chuckle out of it."

It was, he thought as he hung up the phone, one of the few things anyone was likely to get a chuckle out of until this operation was safely over.

The Brussels Bordello

The Englishmen each had a very different experience at the establishment of *Madame Monique*. Harold, being some twenty-five years older than the prostitute he had chosen, opted to ignore her charms and since she happened to be German, simply chat with her. He was careful to tender nothing factual about himself, while offering her a chance to give a full accounting of her life, during which she managed to manipulate the situation in such a way that, ultimately, their talk turned to matters of sexual preference. As a result, the famous Jackdaw rediscovered a level of arousal he had not experienced for more years than he cared to remember.

Phil's adventure took an entirely different route, albeit to the same destination as Harold's. He approached it with bravado after feeling cheated when the "sure thing" date he was on a few nights ago had ended so abruptly. Besides, being somewhat fatalistic about his chances of surviving the invasion, which he still fully expected to participate in, he felt justified in making the best of the moment at hand. What the girl accomplished with her mouth and other warm orifices brought him to such a height of pleasure, he imagined the experience could never be duplicated. The young man swore that if he did survive this ordeal, he would spend the rest of his days trying to do just that.

In the third room, Paul sat on a small bench next to the bed explaining, in his recently acquired tourist-book French, that he did not wish to participate. His thoughts kept going to Emily and the realization he was falling in love with her, and that his only desire was to be back home with his congenial neighbor. The charming, deer-like damsel writhing sexily before him did her best to entice and arouse him, but his lack of interest finally convinced her he was having none of it. She adjusted the few items of lingerie she was wearing and sat on Paul's lap, cuddling him as a child would a father.

Concluding, on the basis of the banging and moaning coming from the nearby rooms that the Germans were still going at it, Sir Harold gathered up the team and prepared to abandon this other world and reenter a far less pleasant reality.

The Brussels Bakery

Jacques was kneading a large blob of sticky dough when he heard a whoop from the back room and ran to join Louis just in time to hear the BBC announcer on *Radio Londre* saying, "*... longs des violons de l'automne.*"

"*That's it, Louis!*" Jacques cried. "*They will come soon!*"

The men grabbed each other's arms and danced around the room like two fools, until on their third circuit, they saw Paul, Phil, and Harold in the doorway. For a long moment, no one spoke.

Finally, Jacques said, "You must pardon us and not get the wrong idea. We celebrate good news. But wait. You should be gone, no?""

Paul took off his cap. "We would have been, but for some Jerries."

The baker's face paled. "*Mon Dieu*, what happened?"

"Jacques, *mon ami*, I must confess I bungled it in two ways," Sir Harold said sheepishly. First of all, I used a cigarette lighter that may have tipped them off to us." He held up his hand to ward off the baker's response. "Worse yet, I had my doubts about you and your motives for shuffling us off on the train as it were."

Jacques slapped a hand to his chest. "My motives? I want to help you escape, nothing more."

"I know that now, and I apologize."

Louis went to the rack and selected a bottle. "Now, we celebrate, so long as we are all okay." He held up the bottle in tribute.

Jacques put his hands together as if in prayer. "No one followed you here, did they?"

Harold assured him, "We doubled back twice. You are quite safe."

Phil added, "So are we, for the moment. But we don't want to go back to the same railway station on the chance they'll be waiting for us."

"No, of course not," Jacques agreed. "We can drive you to Mons. The trains will stop running for tonight, but we go in the morning. Now, tell me, how did you avoid the Germans?"

It's a very long story," Sir Harold told them, "altogether too long to bore you with."

Phil and Paul heartily agreed.

Venlo, the Netherlands

With his boots up on the chief inspector's desk and a glass of mineral water close by, General Schellenberg was going over the report from agent Maas about the convent when Inspector Weber appeared at the office door.

"*Herr Oberführer, there is news,*" he announced excitedly. "*OKW reports Radio Londres has announced the message alerting the resistance to the invasion.*"

"*The French poem?*" Schellenberg pushed back and let his feet drop off the desk.

"*Yes, sir. The first part.*"

The *oberführer* stood and looked down at the report. "*Maybe interrogating the nun is not such a bad idea after all,*" he said reflectively. "*Desperate times call for desperate measures. Get Ullrich and Maas in here.*"

Moments later, the chief inspector returned with Weber. *"Yes, Herr Oberführer, what is it you need?"*

"Where is agent Maas?"

"I believe he returned to the convent," Ullrich replied.

"Very good! It is precisely where he needed to go. I want you to go there too and make sure you both return with the nun who first told him about the farmer's wife."

The general stepped close to the inspector. *"And Ullrich, if you manage to fuck this up, I will replace you with Maas. Understand? He seems to be the only one who is accomplishing anything around here."*

Once Ullrich left the room, Schellenberg turned to Weber and demanded to know if he had any suggestions as to how to proceed.

"Sir, I believe there are other ways to discover where the L.O. is hiding. Informers—street urchins—who see many things and will tell them for a price."

"Can you locate these people?"

"I have my contacts, and this is the active time of night for them. There is money in the top left drawer."

Schellenberg pulled out a stack of *reichsmarks.* "Ah, *lucre. Oil for the gears of intelligence gathering."* He handed it to Weber.

"Thank you Herr Oberführer, I shall use it wisely."

"Being wise is far less important than being effective, Herr Inspekteur."

Perhaps the Oberführer would care to accompany me."

"I think not, Weber." Schellenberg lowered himself into the desk chair and laced his fingers. *"Look upon this as an opportunity to redeem yourself. It will be a much greater accomplishment on your own. You may go. And remember, I want results, and I want them now."*

As he approached the convent, Ullrich eased his car no closer than fifty meters of the gate so as not to interrupt any surveillance his fellow *Gestapo* agent might be attempting. He crept to within sight of the entrance where Maas, whose handgun was on the ground beside him, was trying to reason with Mother Elisabeth as she expertly wielded a shotgun.

"It would be a mistake to think I do not know how to use this," she warned. *"I was a rider and hunter in my youth."*

"But Mother Elisabeth, I only want to speak with one of your nuns for a moment," Maas said. *"I mean no harm."*

"*The convent is closed for the evening,*" she told him. "*It is after curfew. You may return in the morning, but be assured she will have nothing more to say.*"

Hiding behind a thick holly bush, Ullrich pulled his Lugar pistol from its holster and took aim when there was a flash of gunpowder and a loud blast.

Clutching his upper right arm, Ullrich fell to the ground, writhing and screaming, "*The pain, stop the pain! I am dying!*"

"*Werner, you are not dying,*" Maas, who had rushed to his aid, assured him. "You have been wounded, but you will live."

"*That whore of a nun! I hate her. I hate them all. Burn the convent. Burn it down! I demand ...*"

He broke off as the nun, who had joined Maas, aimed her gun at him.

"*No, no Mother, we would not harm you,*" Maas assured her. "*We would never harm the convent or your nuns. Believe me, I am Catholic. I do not want to burn in hell for eternity.*"

She backed off and Maas helped Ullrich to his feet, supporting him as they made their way to the car. Ullrich wondered fleetingly, through a blur of pain, whether eternal damnation might not be the better alternative.

Weber had been walking the streets and alleys of Venlo trying to make contact with his informers, but so far, he had struck out. When he had finally located a few, they claimed to know nothing of the latest L.O. location. It was after midnight when he decided on a last resort, and made his way to *De Grot*, a local nightspot tucked away in the cellar of a little dry goods store. Entering there was a trip into Dante's inferno, complete with a cloud of cigarette smoke, drunken arguments, brawls, lewd dancing, and a variety of indiscrete sexual encounters, all abetted by jazz music coming from a wind-up record player sitting at the end of the bar.

"*Shultzy around tonight?*" he asked the bartender who indicated that the person in question was somewhere in the mass of humanity crammed into the confines of the damp, candle-lit walls. Sure enough, there he was. The nervous little man with frizzy brown hair, crooked horse teeth, and gray popping eyes was in the process of burying his head between the huge breasts of a woman who was at least twice his size. Weber worked his way to the corner where the improbable pair was going at it, and pulling on Shultzy's hair, brought him up for air.

"*What the hell do you think you're doing?*" was the reprobate's first response, followed by, "*Oh, Inspector! How the shit are you, my friend?*"

Weber towed the little man through the crowd and up to the top of the stairs for some sorely needed fresh air and enlightenment.

"*I need some information, and I'm prepared to pay more than usual,*" he said, propping his source on the railing by the steps. "*You will be able to buy any woman you want. Come on. Snap out of it. See these bills? Do you want them or not?*"

The sot grabbed for the money, but Weber pulled it away.

"*The L.O. Where are they hiding these days? Come on. Sober up. Do you know or not? If you don't, I'll stop wasting my time. Their last know location was the basement of the monastery chapel, but now they've moved, so don't give me that one.*"

"*If you're talking about the big guy, Hans,*" Shultzy replied, swaying uncertainly, "*I saw him early this morning. I was going home, and he was getting in his car. You know, the black one.*"

"*Idiot, they are all black!*" Weber said impatiently. "*What else? Anything?*"

"*He was getting into his car with these three men. Looked like workers. I don't know where they were going.*"

"*Where were you when you saw them?*"

"*Let's see. I was going down Hoogstraat. That's it. I went to turn onto Gildenstraat and I saw them. I think they came from the shop right on the corner.*"

"*Gildenstraat and Hoogstraat,*" Weber repeated. "*Anything else?*"

"*Nichts,*" he burped. "*They drove away and I kept walking. But it was him all right.*"

Weber pealed four bills off the stack, stuck them in Shultzy's jacket pocket. "*You may return to your sweetheart.*"

The weasel took out the money, looked at it, hesitated, then staggered down the street.

Chapter Six
Friday, 2 June 1944

Gestapo Field Office, Venlo

"*Stop it, you weakling!*" Schellenberg shouted as Ullrich let out a groan from the office couch. "*It is only a flesh wound and from a nun of all people. I suppose you expect a medal for your injury.*" Putting his face close to the whiner, he promised, "*You will get nothing for this but a reputation as a failure. Maas here is now the new chief inspector for this office.*"

"*Yes, Herr Oberführer. It is an honor,*" the promoted agent said.

"*Honor my ass. You are no better than the wretch on the couch. You merely have not blundered as badly as he has. Here it is almost one in the morning, and we have made no progress.*" Schellenberg stomped his foot. "*Believe me when I tell you, I will not allow myself to be brought down by your incompetence. You …*"

He broke off as the door opened and Weber appeared, wearing a big grin which faded when he saw Ullrich.

"*Never mind him,*" Schellenberg roared. "*What have you got for me?*"

"*Sir, I learned the latest location of the L.O.*"

"*So!*" The general's mood lightened. "*Tell us.*"

"*An informant told me where they are,*" Weber said proudly. "*He saw the L.O. leader, possibly with your three Englanders, this very morning. Or rather, yesterday morning.*"

"*Is this source of yours reliable?*" asked the general.

Weber nodded and continued with growing confidence. "*I had my doubts, sir, so I went there, and it definitely looks promising. There was no activity, but it appears correct and I believe we should set up surveillance immediately.*"

Schellenberg inhaled deeply. "*Aahh. This is a breath of fresh air, Weber. If it works out, I will see that you are restored to your previous position. Oh hell, if this works out, I will have you promoted!*"

L.O. Location, Venlo

Ed Bradford was sleeping soundly on the cot when Hans entered with good news. "Time to wake up," he said, shaking the major's shoulder. "We have made contact. Yes, that's right. We finally got through to SHAEF by wire. They verified your mission and General Terry wants you to contact him. I have arranged for it."

Bradford was suddenly wide awake. "Well, now you're talking," he said, bounding to his feet.

"Come this way." The L.O. leader showed the major to a radio room where the man at the set was listening intently. He looked up at Hans and shook his head. "*Niets. We have lost it. The wire is no more and radio signals across the Channel are jammed.*"

The major sized up the situation. "Look, Terry can wait. I have no time. I need to get to these Brits before one of them blabs. Right now, I need to know everything you can tell me about the three of them."

"I drove them to the underground in Brussels," Hans explained. "Maybe they go from there into France, then back to England. I avoided learning the details."

"But I have to know where they went," the major pressed him. "Tell your radio guy to try to contact the Belgian underground. Next, since they have such a big head start on me, I need a fast vehicle. I absolutely must catch them."

"The most rapid is motorcycle. You can ride one?"

"Why not?" Bradford said with a shrug. "I mean it's no more than a bike with a motor, right?"

Hans was perplexed. "One might say this." He regarded the American. "But you must not go as you are."

Ed looked down at the brown monk's robes. "Yeah, I see what you mean. Can you help?"

"We can, and with money and papers also."

"Will it take long?"

"An hour, maybe two, no more. Meanwhile, we will attempt to contact Brussels."

Ed smiled and decided maybe things had finally begun going his way.

Maas and Weber arrived at the Hoogstraat stake-out location riding a BMW-built motorcycle with sidecar. Maas drove, since he was the one who suggested using the vehicle in case there was need for a speedy pursuit. Accompanying them was a Horch military truck with six armed soldiers. Parking the vehicles out of sight, they set up covert surveillance of the shop and apartment on the corner of Hoogstraat and Gildenstraat. The two inspectors, neither of whom had been to bed for more than a day, alternated their watch; whereas the troopers with them were fresh and alert, waiting only for a signal to move in on the location.

Brussels, Belgium

Outside the   bakery, the three English fugitives were about to be chauffeured to the Mons railway station in a ten-year-old Renault Monaquatre. Paul got to ride up front since he had the fewest language skills and Jacques was next to him if he needed cover. Sir Harold and Phil occupied the comfortable back seat where they both immediately settled in for the journey.

"We are off, my friends," Jacques announced as the engine sputtered awake. "Mons is one and one half hours away. We cross no border so there are few checkpoints. We will arrive in time for the early train. Your greatest danger will come after you board and must be cleared to go through the forbidden zone."

During most of the trip, all was silent. Sir Harold and Phil slept in the back seat, while Paul, riding shotgun, alternated between dozing, thinking of Emily, and trying to make sense of it all.

As they approached Mons, the three passengers became animated and Jacques reported, "Something I have neglected to tell you. We learn from Hans at the L.O. that a General Schellenberg is among those pursuing you."

"I say, I do know the name," said Sir Harold. "He's a favorite of Hitler's."

"I believe I've heard of him as well," Phil said, yawning. "Something about an abduction."

"Well, I wouldn't give a fig if Adolf himself was after us," Paul declared. "One more bleedin' country, and then home. Can't come too soon for me."

"Do you not love my homeland?" Jacques chided.

The postman realized his *faux pas*. "Ah, … yes, a lovely place it is. Alls I'm saying is I'll be happy to get away from the Jerries, won't I."

"As will we all," Jacques agreed. "As will we all."

L.O. Location, Venlo

It was twenty-five minutes to five in the morning as Hans continued to prepare Major Bradford for his trip. After briefing him and providing deftly forged papers designed to get past any guard, he drilled Ed on his language skills. The major thought of his high school German class and wished he had paid more attention instead of always thinking about football. His questionable skill with the language prompted the Dutchman to recommend he say as little as possible at the checkpoints. On a more positive note, he added, "My friend, we believe we can raise Brussels. The conditions have improved."

Having double checked the appearance of the Yank officer who was now dressed as a common laborer in dark trousers, a gray jacket, and a flat hat with a black leather peak, Hans suggested a change of shoes, but once again Ed chose to keep his GI-issue boots.

"Those will never do," said Hans. "Too military. Please, remove them so we may correct their appearance." He had one of his operatives scuff the boots with a heavy wire brush to the point they resembled suede. Then the man smeared a dull, black substance on the once shiny brown leather.

Bradford's heart ached when the refurbished boots were returned to him. The many hours of spit polishing he had done when there was little else to occupy his time, all gone for naught. As he laced them up, the radioman announced, "I have Brussels."

"Jacques, my friend," Hans said, after donning the headset. *"Oh, Louis, it's you. Listen, can you tell me of the three travelers? I have someone here who must contact them immediately. Do you know the route they took?"*

Faint sounds followed, after which Hans signaled the radio operator to cut it off. He turned to the major and shrugged. "Like us, they are cautious. He wanted to ring us back to know he speaks to friends."

Ed nodded. "I understand."

A short time later, Louis made contact, and satisfied he was speaking with the Dutch L.O., revealed where Jacques had taken the English trio and what their destination was in Paris.

Hans unfolded a map and recommended that Bradford sneak back into Germany and ride south to *Saarbrücken*, thus avoiding the forbidden zone and leaving him with only one major border crossing.

Calculating that the suggested route would add three or four hours and most likely require him to refuel, Ed opted for a more direct approach despite the greater number of checkpoints and zone restrictions.

As part of his preparation, Hans had him memorize the directions to the French resistance unit in Paris and reminded him to make very certain he was not being followed before going there. "It is the best kept secret in all of Paris," he explained, "and many lives depend on it remaining so."

After rechecking the American major's papers and his appearance, Hans led him out to the street and disappeared into an alley. Ed casually lit up a final smoke before the long trip while Hans wheeled a well-used motorcycle to the curb.

As Ed sat astride the machine and started it up, Hans gave him some final reminders and wished him luck. "Thanks, my friend, for everything," Ed said, shaking hands sincerely with the partisan before adding with some gusto, "Victory is coming!"

With Ed's words of hope ringing in his ears, and the stammering sound of the motorcycle echoing down the street, Hans headed back inside just as his radio operator came racing out to get him.

"We have finally re-contacted General Terry."

"He's a bit late," Hans said with a shrug.

"Only a single message made it through, sir," the operator explained. *"It was most urgent. I've jotted it down here. It says, 'Kill authority withdrawn.'"*

After trading rest periods several times, it was Weber's turn to watch. A moment after he took over, the door next to the shop opened and the tall, blonde man he knew to be Hans Rijkers emerged followed by a slightly shorter figure who appeared to be a common laborer. The worker waited, smoking, while the first man disappeared into an alley then emerged wheeling a motorcycle.

Seeing this, Weber crept back to the truck and alerted his fellow agent. *"Peter,"* he jostled him. *"Wake up, they are there."*

Maas responded immediately and the pair of them watched as the big man appeared to be giving information and instructions to the worker who was now straddling the machine. *"They are speaking English,"* Maas observed, *"but the accent of the man on the motorcycle is not British."*

Weber listened for a moment. *"No doubt, he is the American—the man Oberführer Schellenberg wants followed."*

The cyclist removed his cap, donned goggles, and drove off haltingly, before getting the machine up to speed. The other man watched for a few moments then went back inside.

"*I will go after the rider,*" Weber said, as he went to the motorcycle, "*and you go inform the oberführer, and find out his wishes. Help me detach the sidecar.*"

"*Dammit, Georg! What do you mean you will follow him? This was my idea, and I am still the chief inspector. Did not Schellenberg appoint me such after Ullrich got shot?*"

"*But it was I who saved the day with this information about the resistance location,*" Weber retorted.

"*May I remind you that you will be the hero only if we find the three Englanders. As of now, I am in charge.*"

"*I soon will be.*"

As the stalemate continued, they both realized, the man they needed to pursue was slipping out of their reach.

"*It is settled, then.*" Weber climbed into the sidecar. "*We both go.*" He waved over the soldier in charge. "*Corporal! Inform Oberführer Schellenberg that agent Maas and I are following the American, and leave the other men here to observe and report on any activity.*"

Hans watched out the first floor window as two men on a motorcycle rode off after the major. At the same time, German soldiers took up watch from nearby doorways as a military truck appeared from a side street and drove off.

"*It looks like our American has attracted unwanted company,*" he told the radioman, shrugging. "*Once again, we must move.*"

"*An escape to the rear?*" offered the operator.

Hans shrugged. "*What else? Alert the others.*"

Railway Station
Mons, Belgium

Watching the Britons purchase tickets to Paris, Jacques recalled how he had made similar arrangements over the past few years, most often for Jewish exiles seeking to go north to Sweden or Denmark to escape the Nazi concentration camps. Suddenly, an alarming thought struck him. What if these men, who looked much like those he usually helped, were taken for Jews trying to enter the forbidden zone? As they walked to the waiting area of the terminal, he asked casually, "My friends are any of you *circoncis,* ... ah, circumcised?"

Paul stopped short. "Blimey," he exclaimed, "What sort of bloke are you, asking such a question?"

"A simple yes or no, it is important," prompted Jacques, and when, to a man, they answered in the negative, he simply said, "*Très bon.*"

The hour was early, and the station was far less active than the one in Brussels. It seemed that much of the commerce in Mons had to do with food and flowers. Again, there were other travelers, including a few civilians who might have come from the countryside, but only a sprinkling of soldiers dressed in the gray of the *Reich.* The train was due to depart at 0645, affording them about a half hour to visit the café at the far end of the station and get coffee to complement the fresh rolls Louis had packed for them.

The coffee, actually a chicory and barley concoction, was strong and bitter, and there was no sugar to be found. Sir Harold and Jacques went for the straight brew, but Paul and Phil got theirs *au lait,* made with hot, skimmed milk.

As the hour for their departure approached, Jacques told them, "Now, you must be ready immediately as you board. The French border is near and you will be checked here before you depart. Stay calm. Speak only if spoken to. The papers will pass, but the guards will look for other clues. Do not give them any. And if you need help along the way, try contacting partisans through small shops, bakeries, and such."

Their train arrived about five minutes late, and amid an air of excitement, they boarded. Sir Harold felt a sense of *déjà vu* since, until a few years ago, he had used such railways to crisscross Europe in service to the Crown.

They had barely settled in when the compartment door opened and an SS lieutenant demanded their proof of identification. "*Sind sie Juden?*" he asked scornfully as he flipped through their papers.

"*How dare you say this?*" Sir Harold demanded in German, grabbing his crotch. "*We will all submit to an examination in front of your supervisor. When we are shown to pass, I will recommend you be sent to the Russian front.*"

The officer held up his hand, and moved on just as the conductor came by collecting tickets. With two major hurdles behind them, it all seemed to be going very well until suddenly the door opened again and the German lieutenant popped his head in and asked, "*Excuse me, does anyone have a cigarette?*"

"*Nein,*" Sir Harold answered, looking at the others and shaking his head until they picked up the movement, making it unanimous. The officer grumbled something and closed the door.

"Sly bastards," the MI6 man observed. "If any of us had produced a pack of the wrong brand, it would have cooked our goose."

Phil and Paul nodded, but didn't say a word.

"Oh, come, come, gents speak up, the threat is over for now. We shouldn't be bothered again for a time."

Paul exhaled the breath he was unconsciously holding in. "Here, that was close enough, wasn't it."

"I'll say," Phil agreed. "Give me combat, any day. This covert business just isn't for me." He leaned back and tried to get comfortable.

Sir Harold eyed Paul. "Say, old man, I'd like you to tell me about yourself."

"Me, Guv? I'm a simple postman."

"Tell me where you live, your work and home life, about how it was growing up, your family, that sort of thing."

And with what seemed to be an idle query, the MI6 agent began laying the groundwork for his backup plan.

The Road to Paris

Ed Bradford had had no trouble getting past the Venlo guards, and as the kilometers mounted up, he gained confidence in his ability to operate the infernal machine. The cool, moist air pressing against his face and the lack of traffic along the route brought with it the hope that his mission would soon end in success.

The *Gestapo* agents following him less than a kilometer back were careful not to be spotted and yet painfully aware that tracking the American to the British fugitives was vital to them, their futures, and, according to Schellenberg, the fate of the *Reich*. To this end, earlier, when they had reached the Venlo checkpoint, Weber ordered the officer in charge there to send word to all crossing posts along the various routes south through the Netherlands, Belgium, and into France, to allow the cyclist to pass. He gave a complete description of the man and machine, assuring the guard the *Gestapo* would be following the motorcycle.

When Ed arrived at the border crossing near Maastricht, the ease with which he was allowed to enter Belgium came as a surprise, but he wrote it off to continuing good fortune, even though, until now, he had concluded there was no such thing.

RAF Molesworth Airfield
Cambridgeshire, England

The flight crews of the 303rd Bomb Group, known as Hells Angels, filed out of the mission briefing room. They were the men of the 358th, 359th, and 360th Bombardment Squadrons, and included Lieutenant John Wilson and his crew from the 360th. As they chatted casually about the assignment for the day, men from a few of the crews could be heard singing with bravado to the tune of Lili Marlene, "We're goin' on a mission, we know we'll all be back. We don't mind the fighters and we don't mind the flak. For we're the Hells' Angels tried and true, we're going up in to the blue. We're goin' on a mission—we know we'll all be back."

"Hey, Johnny," said Lieutenant Neil Costa, the co-pilot, "they said this is our first tactical mission. We're actually going after weapons for a change."

"Yeah, Noball means we'll be hitting Kraut rocket sites," the pilot replied. "Anyhow, that's the plan. How's it look, Rolly?"

"Not a problem," assured bombardier Lieutenant Roland Green, who was bringing up the rear carrying a satchel with charts and mission maps. "So long as the weather holds, it should be a cinch."

The crew piled onto a jeep and were taken out to their aircraft. She was called "Miss Liberty," a B-17G identifiable by her tail number, 42-31340, and the nose-art painting of a curvaceous female bather captured in a swan dive. When they arrived at the plane, Wilson, Costa, and Technical Sergeant Dominick Carbillano, the flight engineer, performed a walk-around and preflight visual check with the plane's crew chief. Meanwhile, other ground crew members worked with the flight crew to ensure the bomb load was correct and the ammunition and machine guns were in order. Once the other men climbed aboard, Carbillano checked the top turret gun for which he was responsible, and then watched over the pilot's shoulder as Wilson and Costa went over their preflight checklists. The co-pilot called out each item and one or both of them confirmed it with the word "check" as they made certain the batteries were functioning properly, all switches and levers were in the correct positions, and the myriad gauges worked and were displaying acceptable readings.

When the rest of the crew reported in, the pilot verified that the ground crew fire guard was posted behind the correct engine. The co-pilot called out, "Clear left," and Wilson held down a starter switch that brought the first of the plane's four engines gasping to life. As it achieved a rhythmic idle, he and Costa repeated the process three more times, in strict accordance with engine run-up procedures. Meanwhile, as other B-17s moved out in a procession, the crew chief signaled Miss Liberty's turn to taxi. He saluted the plane and its crew as they passed to join the parade of aircraft to the end of the runway. The 167th mission of the 303rd Bomb Group was underway.

It was an uneventful flight over the Channel, as the British and American fighters providing cover were doing a good job of keeping them out of danger. The gunners on Miss Liberty were ever vigilant just the same because German aircraft were known to appear instantly out of the glare of the morning sun.

Below them, more and more heavy clouds gathered, blocking the view as they approached the shores of France until finally Don Stollinger, flying the unnamed lead ship, radioed all crews that the primary target of a V-1 launch site was socked in solid. "Undercast is ten-ten, proceeding to alternate," said the voice on the crew's headsets, sending the bombers to their secondary target—the railroad tracks and marshaling yards at Laon, France.

The Train to Paris

The border from Belgium into France passed virtually unnoticed while Sir Harold drew from Paul a detailed biography. During the postman's narrative, the agent took particular note of his gestures and speech patterns.

As for Phil, he alternated between sleep and watching the countryside slide by outside the coach window, thinking that becoming familiar with the lay of the land might be useful when it came to future missions. Oddly, the phrase brought him back to the bordello and the blonde. He chuckled to himself. "Now, there was the lay of the land."

More than an hour later, all three Englishmen were napping to the rhythmic clackity-clack of the wheels and the sway of the coach when, suddenly, the brakes screeched and Phil and Paul were thrown onto Sir Harold. The jolt woke the MI6 man with a start and a series of loud rumbles, cracks, and thumps echoed down the length of the train as it screeched to a stop.

Once things settled down, they traded questioning looks, unaware that several kilometers ahead, the tracks and yards at Laon had been heavily damaged, compliments of the Hells Angels. The repairs needed to set the rail line right meant the train would not be going to Paris anytime soon.

"Please, stay in your seats until we determine the cause of the delay," announced the conductor as he walked by their compartment.

Paul nudged Sir Harold's knee. "Let's go," he said. "We're in France, aren't we? I say we bolt now and head for the coast. Once there, it's Bob's your uncle and we're home."

"And, no more frappin' checkpoints," Phil added.

"Sounds like a smashing idea," Sir Harold agreed, "but we should never do it without help. Otherwise, the way to the coast is quite impassable. I say we go on to Paris and find the resistance, as planned. With their support, we can make a good run at it."

"Here!" Paul insisted. "Either way, we get off this bloody train."

After checking the corridor, Sir Harold waved them on, and doing their best to go unnoticed by the other passengers, the team headed for the exit. Climbing down the steps, they found themselves among the tall bushes that ran along either side of the track. More importantly, they were on French soil. Once the Englishmen pushed through the lush foliage, they spotted a village a few hundred meters away.

Phil drew a long breath. *"Ah, la belle France."*

Paul looked around. "I'd say this is Picardy, mate. We sang about roses bloomin' here in the first war. One more border and we're home."

Sir Harold brought the pair back to reality. "That border just happens to be the English Channel," he said. "We have miles to go before there's any hope of seeing it."

"There's always some bloke waiting to rain on the fete," Paul observed as they trudged across a field to a roadway. Appearing as farm laborers, they made their way past a sign for the village of Chambry.

"I doubt there'd be any support for us here," Sir Harold observed. "I'd say we need something larger."

"Oy! There's something grand on that hill," Paul called out. "See. Over there."

"Right-oh! I think I know it," Phil said, grinning, "It's the *Notre Dame* cathedral of Laon."

Paul nodded and added, "If I recall the map correctly, it means we're only about 150 kilometers from Paree."

SHAEF Advance
Near Portsmouth, England

With H-hour of the invasion creeping closer, General Eisenhower was spending less time in his formal office at Bushy Park, and more at the location known as "SHAEF Advance" set in a forest near Portsmouth. This forward command post fell well short of the opulence of Southwick House, the nearby mansion used by Admiral Ramsay for Operation Neptune; however, Ike preferred this less assuming, more remote location. He had been given the choice of using rail cars, but wanting to avoid the likely logistical chaos, chose trailers and tents instead to house communications and weather forecast gear, staff quarters, and mess and latrine facilities. Because of the almost constant dampness, there was a smell of musty canvas that penetrated the sinuses and stayed with anyone who spent more than a few hours there. Ike's trailer, or caravan as the Brits referred to it, included a study, living room, and small kitchen. There was an adjacent command tent and one for meetings, but when the need arose for larger accommodations, such as confabs with the Allied brass, he used Ramsay's headquarters.

It seemed no matter where he chose to be, the prime minister was close by. Churchill had gone so far as to have rail cars pulled into the area from which he could operate, and to some degree, participate. He had taken to dropping in on Ike almost daily and often at the most inconvenient times. This day was no exception.

The general had just sent Butcher to arrange an informal visit with departing troops when the sometimes cherubic, often cantankerous, master of the English language showed up with Field Marshal Smuts in tow.

As the visitors entered, Ike put down the daily activity reports he was reading and greeted them warmly.

"You know, Ike, I cannot justify, but I can abide, not sailing with the invasion force," Churchill announced, sinking heavily onto a chair and relighting a half-smoked cigar. "I must say, His Majesty was surprisingly adept in his argument that, if I went, he too would have to go along. An utter impossibility."

"The King was unexpectedly sly, what?" Smuts agreed. "More of a force than one might have guessed."

"I feel I must say you yourself should abandon any thought of attending, my dear general," the PM said from amid a cloud of smoke. "While there are no pertinent decisions I might be required to make regarding Overlord, it is likely you will be called upon for that very thing. I am sure you should not leave your command post during any of this. I say this with your best interests in mind."

The field marshal punctuated his friend's words with, "Best interests, yours and those of the war effort, don't you know."

Eisenhower smiled. "Gentlemen, rest assured, I have no intention of going anywhere on D-Day. I'll be right here until we have a clearer picture of the outcome. I believe with all my heart it will be positive. However, I am ready to accept failure and any blame that goes with it, although I certainly do not want to in any way contribute to it."

"Well put, Ike. Very well put," Churchill commended him.

"As you know," the general continued, "I believe in eliminating or at least mitigating all the negatives. None of us can control the weather, and it seems to be working against us."

His statement drew two knowing nods.

"Perhaps you would like to attend the meeting I have scheduled for later today with the SHAEF staff and the meteorology folks."

"A distinct possibility," Churchill replied grimly. "I have been watching the skies and none of it looks good. I must say, the weather concerns me, as well." The PM leaned forward and tapped his cigar on the lip of Ike's ashtray, "Now, tell me. Is there news on the affair involving this other Eisenhower?"

"Sir, as far as we can determine, there has been no breach of security," Ike replied, momentarily caught off guard. "As I'm sure you have been informed, an MI6 man is with the two suspects and controlling the situation. One of our G2 men is also on the case. They are not in German hands, and in days, the whole episode will be moot."

"Moot indeed. I should wish the same for my terrible fears in this regard. Please keep me informed." He turned to Smuts. "Well, Field Marshal, I don't know about you but I'm a bit peckish." Then to Eisenhower, "Ike, care to join us at the mess?" He hoisted himself up out of the chair. "Too busy I expect. Then you won't be upset if I ask the delightful Lieutenant Summersby to accompany us."

The general shook his head. "Not at all, but promise you won't tell her anymore of your bawdy jokes."

Churchill winked, "I shall leave her undoing to you, my friend."

Smuts chortled, and the pair left without further comment.

They found Kay in her office tent close by Eisenhower's. She stood when they entered and ever the gentleman with her, Churchill asked, "Mrs. Summersby, we should be honored to have you join us at the mess?" He winked. "I have cleared it with your boss."

"I would love to." She left what she was working on and picked up her hat, brightening the moods of both men.

However, the glow of Kay's personality could not overcome the PM's worry over the weather when, as they crunched along the cinder pathway, he looked up at the darkening skies. "Tell me there is a silver lining somewhere."

They enjoyed coffee and pastries at the mess, and the conversation was light enough, but the overriding concern with the climate could not be conquered. After the snack, Kay continued her small talk with Smuts, but Churchill became downright gloomy. Calling the weather, "the hidden enemy," he withdrew from the group. His mood improved for a time when one of the cats that had adopted the camp appeared. The prime minister attracted the orange and white feline to the table with a saucer of milk and stroked its fur as it lapped up the treat. He played with the docile creature and became quite jolly, until anxiety over his hidden enemy once again hijacked his mood.

Laon, France

The three Englishmen roughly followed the railroad line as they made their way toward the hill with its great cathedral. On the way they saw the extensive damage Allied bombs had inflicted earlier.

"We can forget about using any more trains, gentlemen," Sir Harold observed. "We must surely endeavor to find some local help."

Phil indicated a sign labeled, "Ville Haute" and concluded, "We can either try down here, or …" he pointed to the cathedral, "… up there."

Paul urged, "I say we try the kinds of shops the Belgian bloke recommended down here before climbing that bloody mountain."

He'd made his point, and off they went on to the lower section of town. They walked less than a kilometer before spotting a *Boulangerie–Patisserie*.

"Good show!" Phil exclaimed. "A bakery—and, with tables." He was referring to the two wooden stands out front with stools around them. "It's a good bet they have other food as well."

As they walked up to the bakery, they saw a gaunt man in a wrinkled blue shirt and dark trousers leaning back on a stool against the wall of the building. A cap similar to the ones they wore shaded his eyes. He appeared to be sleeping.

"Okay," suggested Phil, "I go in and buy some bread or rolls, and meat, if they have it. Then, I hint at my discontent with the occupation and see what response I get."

"Oy," said Paul, "if it ain't a good one, we move on. Who knows how long we have till they catch up with us."

"All good advice," Sir Harold commended. "If this fails, there is a row of likely spots down the road just there. But first, Lieutenant, give this a go, and we'll see where it takes us."

And take them it did, but not as they had planned. Phil had not been in the shop for more than a few minutes when one of those strange coincidences that punctuated the terrible war occurred.

Augustine Campana & Marco Di Tillo

Major Ed Bradford, feeling a huge emptiness in his stomach after riding the beastly machine for more than six hours, decided to stop for food at the next opportunity. Seeing the cathedral on a hill, he realized with relief that he must be nearing a town of some substantial size. Although he approached from a more easterly direction, Ed ended up on the same street the Britons had taken, and like them, discovered the bakery. He pulled his weary body off the bike and entered the shop, paying little attention to the man sleeping against the wall and barely glancing at either of the two workers at a table out front or the one exiting as he entered.

"Bonjour!" said the chubby baker, and asked how he could serve him. Ed pointed to a baguette. Figuring the locals were used to the language of the occupiers, he tried out his rusty German. When the man held up the long, crusty bread, he nodded and asked, *"Sie haben fleisch?"*

The man behind the counter looked puzzled for a moment. *"Ah, oui, viande. Jambon, ist gut?"*

"Ja," said Ed, and a woman appeared and began slicing pink meat off a ham bone. While he waited, Bradford looked idly out the window and saw that the worker he had passed on the way in had joined the two other men, one of whom looked strangely familiar.

Outside, the lieutenant reported that the baker was not part of the movement and had little knowledge of it.

The stool leaning against the wall flopped forward and the man got up and walked by their table. As he passed, he said something in French, indicating the direction with his eyes.

Phil translated for the others. "It seems we might find what we are looking for at a café called *Le Chat Bleu* down the street."

"After lunch I hope," Paul said as he dug into the fixings and put together a sandwich. "Anything to drink?"

"Vin ordinaire," Phil answered. "A plain table wine."

"That might be a fitting touch," said Sir Harold, prompting Phil to return to the bakery.

Shortly, he came out with a wine bottle in one hand, three glasses in the other, and Ed Bradford's .45-caliber handgun stuck in his back.

The major ushered the lieutenant to the table, and keeping his weapon pointed at him as they sat, got a closer look at Paul and recognized the older version of the face in the post office photo. "Look," he said. "I don't know how the hand of God put us all here in the same place at the same time, but I accept it. Now, I need some answers. Let's introduce ourselves. I'm Major Ed Bradford, U.S. Army, SHAEF G2. I know these two, and I'm guessing you're the MI6 guy."

"At your service," Sir Harold said, extending his hand to the major. When Ed ignored it, he continued, undismayed, ""Look, old man, we're on the same team here. We need to work together if we are to have any hope of protecting what Eisenhower here knows of the Overlord plan."

"Eisenhower? I thought you all knew. Well, at least this postman and the lieutenant."

"I don't know a bloody thing and I shouldn't even be here," Phil told him. "All I did was run into this bloke's bicycle."

"And the poor bastard riding same!" added Paul.

The major put away his gun.

From up the street, the *Gestapo* agents observed from an alley where they had secreted their motorcycle. *"He talks to these three other men,"* Weber said, lowering his binoculars. *"Are they the oberführer's fugitives? Could it possibly be this simple?"*

Maas looked at him and shrugged. *"Or, maybe they just met and he is passing the time of day with them. They do appear to be nothing more than laborers."*

"Fool, do you expect them to be wearing signs, 'We are the enemy'?"

"Okay genius, what should we do?" Maas looked again.

"Continue observing. If he goes on, we follow him. If he does not, we capture them all and report to Schellenberg." Weber's face screwed up into a warped smile. *"You see, it isn't very difficult when one has a logical approach."*

"You are a dangerous piece of property my friend," Ed told Paul once he had heard the explanation. "Expendable, if you know what I mean."

"Here, what about yourself?" Paul replied. "I would guess you have something they might want as well, don't you."

Sir Harold agreed, "He does have a point, Major. You are at least as valuable. BIGOT cleared, I should assume. It's one of the reasons I passed up the clearance."

"So, we all need to stay out of their hands," Ed concluded. "Look, I never wanted to kill any of you. I say we work together."

"Most definitely!" Phil agreed, slapping the tabletop.

"Oy, we're like the three musketeers, and D'Artagnan," observed Paul. "All for one and one for all."

Sir Harold cautioned, "Before joining us, Major, you first need to give the slip to the pair following you. Don't look, but they are up the road watching from an alleyway. I spotted them when you arrived. My guess is they reckoned you would lead them to us, and so you have. Our advantage is they may not know it for certain."

"So, they let me go after you. And here, I thought the border guards just liked my face and sunny disposition," Bradford wisecracked. "What do you suggest I do?"

"We must convince them this was an innocent gathering, no more," Sir Harold replied. "We'll leave before you finish eating. Then, continue on down the road for at least twenty miles—thirty-five or forty kilometers— so as to draw them well off, and then make your move, say at a crossroads or around a curve. Double back and we'll join up."

"Where do we meet?"

Phil chimed in, "There's a café called *'Le Chat Bleu'* just down from here. We believe there may be a resistance contact there."

Weber and Maas watched the three workers get up from the table, shake hands with the American, and walk off in the opposite direction.

"*So,*" Maas taunted his companion, "*your logic says we both follow the major. But what if the three are the ones we are seeking?*"

"*What do you suggest,*" Weber frowned, "*that we split up?*"

"*Of course. You follow the three and I will continue after Bradford on the cycle.*"

"*Oh no!*" Weber protested. "*Following him was our mission and I will do it. The three may be nothing. I say we do as I proposed.*"

As their bickering continued, from down the street, there came the unmistakable rumble of a motorcycle starting up.

"*Shit, he is leaving!*" Weber exclaimed and both agents went for the bike. Maas again took the controls and Weber climbed into the sidecar as they resumed their assignment—tailing Major Bradford.

The three Englishmen arrived at *Le Chat Bleu* where they found coffee and pastries for sale. After trading *"Bonjours"* with the man behind the counter, the others found a table while Phil ordered coffees and éclairs then went to join his companions. On the way to the table, he considered ways he might communicate their real purpose for being there. When the man arrived with the desserts and coffee—real coffee since German's patronized the place—Phil told him they had been sent there from the bakery up the street.

The server grinned. *"Ah, oui. Camille makes our fine pastries."*

"Actually, a patron at the bakery told us about you," Phil said as he pulled a pound note out and tendered it.

"I am sorry, I cannot accept this."

The lieutenant continued to hold the money out. *"Maybe, you can direct me to someone who looks to the day when he is able to accept it."*

This gambit drew a cynical stare. *"Who are you, and why did you come here?"* the man demanded.

Throwing all their cards on the table, Phil answered in English. "We are harbingers of the invasion," and then, after repeating his words in French, added, "Paul, the first part of the poem, if you please."

The postman thought for a second then, like a school boy, recited, *"Les sanglots longs des violons de l'automne."*

The man's eyes widened, but before he could respond, two German officers entered. *"Enjoy your treats, my friends, while I serve these,"* he scowled, *"gentlemen."*

The Road to Paris

Keeping an eye on the bike's noisy odometer and verifying its reading with the kilometer markers along the road, Bradford, began looking for a chance to lose his pursuers when he was forty-five kilometers from the bakery. Since the route was tree-lined, it was difficult to spot side roads; however, a long curve ahead gave Ed the chance he needed. Speeding up in order to give himself a greater margin of error, at the midpoint of the curve he rode into the trees and brush alongside the road. Ducking down, he waited until the pursuers' motorcycle chugged past. When they were out of sight, he turned back for Laon.

The maneuver worked, but not as well as Bradford had hoped. Shortly after the *Gestapo* agents negotiated the curve, they realized they had lost contact with the major's motorcycle. They sped up for a time, believing he had outrun them, but after three kilometers, when the road ahead went straight as far as they could see, they knew they had been duped.

By then, Ed had opened the machine up as fast as it would go and was well ahead of the two *Gestapo* men. Once he was back in Laon, he quickly located *Le Chat Bleu,* and after stashing his bike behind two trash barrels, went inside. There were a few customers but no sign of Paul, Phil, or Sir Harold. He went up to the counter and, greeting the fair, blue eyed woman behind it, asked, in stilted German, if three workers had come in together earlier.

She eyed him carefully. "Bradford?"

Shocked at hearing her say his name, he nodded.

She indicated a curtained doorway and said, "Your friends await you through there."

"*Well, Georg, what now?*" Maas demanded as they crept along the main street of the lower section of Laon.

"*We report to the oberführer,*" Weber told him. "*The three at the bakery must have been the ones. We know they are all here, so we have done our job. Come, the city hall may have a local office, as in Venlo. I saw a sign indicating it is up above. We go there and contact Schellenberg.*"

Maas bristled. "*So, my genius, what do we tell him when he orders us to capture them?*"

"*No need to say we do not have their exact location. This is not Berlin, or even Venlo,*" he said, adding as they passed *Le Chat Bleu* cafe, "*Where can they hide that we cannot find them?*"

Regent's Park Road, London

Standing in the garden she shared with Paul, Emily looked up at dark clouds and decided there was no need to water today. She ran over to Paul's door and let herself in just as a heavy downpour began. "Bikits, bikits," Old Frank squawked as she let him out of his cage.

"Miss your master, do you?" She asked the bird, adding as he flew to his perch, "I know. So do I. He's a good man." Hearing herself say the words, her thoughts lingered on his knack for interesting conversation, his gentle and unassuming manner, and his almost comical uneasiness with her femininity. Her eyes widened, "My God," she said, "I really do miss him."

By the time she finished feeding Odette, the rain had let up, making it possible for her to take the basset for a stroll in the backyard.

From a window two floors up, came the scratchy voice of Gladys Grimes, the resident busybody. "Hello, Miss Crowley. How you be?"

"Oh, hello, Miss Grimes. Just fine."

"Haven't seen you in a few days, I had to go to my sister's in Watford. She's been ailing, but well enough now."

"I'm happy to hear it," Emily replied as she walked the stubby legged hound to her preferred spot in the yard.

The old woman continued nattering about her sister before adding, "I'm not the only one who has been away, I see. Isn't your Mister Eisenhower off on holiday? Blackpool was it?"

"Oh, now, he's not my 'Mister Eisenhower'. He's just a friend whose pets and plants I'm tending for the few days until his return."

The old lady stuck her head out further. "What do you think of all the interest his trip has gotten? First the woman and then a Yank soldier coming around asking about him."

"Oh, I'm sure it's nothing. You know how they often check on workers for the Crown." She opened Paul's door. "Nice talking to you."

"Just thought you'd want to know."

Emily went inside and curled up in Paul's easy chair. Odette sat nearby, while Frank was occupied with his seeds. The old biddy's words bothered her and she found herself hoping Paul hadn't gotten into a twist over the travel authorization. Then an odd feeling of contentment overtook her. It was, she decided, rather a luxury to worry about the man she was beginning to think of as, "My Mister Eisenhower."

Laon, France

Maas and Weber followed the road up the mesa to a maze of streets that eventually brought them to an open plaza. There, they were heartened to see two large flags with swastikas hanging on the façade of the imposing town hall building. As they had hoped, there was a *Gestapo* office within, and since his credentials still showed him as Chief Inspector, Weber was given access to the radiophone.

The operator reported, *"Herr Inspekteur, we have your general in Venlo."*

He picked up the receiver and announced himself twice, but heard only silence in return. He waited and groaned before a voice on the other end of the line responded, *"Schellenberg here."*

"Herr Oberführer, this is Weber. Maas and I are in Laon, France. I am happy to report the American led us here to the fugitives you seek."

"So, you have them in your custody, Weber?"

"Not yet, Herr Oberführer, but it is only a matter of time."

The line exploded, *"TIME! We do not have any more time. The invasion is at hand and we still do not know where or exactly when it will come. It is not a matter of time. You are out of time, Weber! Where is Maas? Why is he not handling this?"*

"We are working as one, very closely," Weber assured him.

"But not very effectively!" Schellenberg paused to bark orders at someone who was apparently in the room with him before returning to the telephone. *"Weber, I am coming there. I will arrive at the airfield at ..."* again, his voice faded out and in *"... where exactly? Ah, the base at Laon-Athies. I shall be there in no more than three hours. In the meantime, arrange for my transportation and spend every minute you have finding and arresting the three Englanders. I want them in custody when I arrive, and do not even ask what the consequences will be if you fail!"*

Despite his wish to avoid ascending the 120-meter hill to the top of the Laon mesa, Paul found himself, along with Phil, Sir Harold, and Ed, climbing a steep, bush-lined, gravel path, interrupted occasionally by steps. The group was led by Corinne Bouchet, a partisan Frenchwoman in her twenties. She had introduced herself as "Cori," and was carrying a rucksack and wearing a sweater and skirt. A dark blue kerchief covered enough wavy, brown hair for two women. Her lips were full, her brown eyes bright, and she had the nose of a Grecian goddess. Obviously, the lovely guide was also very fit as she paused every so often for the others to catch up. Phil was the only one who was keeping pace, staying directly behind her, and clearly enjoying the view of her swaying backside.

More concerned with the business at hand, Ed caught up with her to ask if she was sure his cycle had been safely hidden. "I wouldn't want the Krauts finding it and tracing us here," he said anxiously.

After reassuring him, to the major's surprise, she waxed philosophical. "We would be wise to look to the future. What is past is past. We have only what is here today and what will come tomorrow."

Ed recalled the famous Santayana aphorism about those who did not remember the past being condemned to repeat it, but he let the subject drop as she continued urging them on to the top.

When they reached the next set of stairs, Paul sat, declaring he needed a rest.

Cori shook her head and pointed up to the street just meters above them. "We need go only there."

Paul's groans told her he wasn't going to move until he was good and ready. The prospect of spending a bit more time with the Frenchwoman led Phil to join Paul, and Sir Harold had to admit that he too needed the break. Ed had a different reaction to the climb after spending so long on the two-wheeled beast. He was ready to forge ahead, but when Cori retrieved a bottle of wine from her sack and pulled a cork which appeared to have been reused dozens of times, he found a seat on the steps. They all shared the warm, ruby-colored libation until the green glass container was drained.

The respite helped, and when they cleared the final steps, Paul looked around and exclaimed, "Crikey! It's a whole other town up here."

"But of course," said Cori, "It is the center of the ancient city. Not only the great church, but the shops, homes, and the place of government is here."

"Including the city hall, I suppose," Sir Harold noted, adding with disgust in his voice, "The place no doubt is infested with our Jerry friends."

Phil asked, "But why have you taken us straight into their midst?"

"Oy, right to the bloody enemy," agreed Paul.

"I take you to the safety of the resistance. You all must have trust, please."

"A matter of keeping your friends close and the enemy closer, I imagine," said Sir Harold, as he recalled what a great Chinese general had said centuries earlier.

"True," said Cori, "and as you will find, it is the *géologie*, also." She looked at the face of her loose-fitting men's watch. "*Alors,* we must move on quickly now."

"Indeed!" agreed Harold.

"Cori," Phil asked, "will we go by the church? It's a lovely example of Gothic architecture. It was part of my studies."

"Of course," the young woman pointed. "This way." The street went past a wall to an alley that led to the cathedral.

Phil was delighted when he saw the beautifully buttressed nave with its windowed clerestory. "There it is, four tier construction. Smashing!" He paused, savoring a moment he had hoped for since Paris.

Cori pointed to the right. "The Romans originally fortified Laon. The area was a, how do you say, *champ de bataille.*"

Phil translated, "A battlefield."

"*Oui.*" She regarded the lieutenant with a glint of admiration in her eyes. "A battlefield of Caesar is nearby, and many from other wars, including the last one with these German bastards." Standing so close to a house of God, she quickly covered her mouth then blessed herself.

The visitors could not help but pause as they entered the forecourt of the cathedral, with its 800-year-old stone façade, remarkable rose window, and majestic towers rising into a gray, cloudy sky.

Cori urged the group on and led them to a nearby street called, *"Rue du Cloître."*

"A cloister!" Phil said. "You're taking us to a convent?"

"Ah no, *mon ami, we* go just there." She pointed to an indentation in the wall between two facades. It was not much more than a meter high and half as wide, and sealed with a rusty metal door. "For this we must thank the ancient conquerors and the *vignerons*—the winemakers. They left us many caves and passages. The occupiers know little of them."

After looking up and down the street to ensure they were not being watched, she kicked the heavy metal panel twice, waited about three seconds, kicked again, and repeated the entire signal one more time. The door creaked open on rusty hinges and the four guests were admitted into a lair of the aptly named French underground.

Once they were safely inside, there were introductions all around. The unit leader, Gaston Seurat, was elated to meet and help these forerunners of the long-awaited Allied invasion. He took them deeper into caverns that were surprisingly dry but had a musty odor which might have lingered since the time of the Romans. The walls, carved from the limestone that comprised most of the mesa, were cool to the touch, and the curved ceiling they supported arced to some three meters at the center. Electrical wiring strung from glass insulators spaced every few meters led to hanging, bare light bulbs which cast a yellow-orange glow on the passageways, chambers, and cubbyholes of the hideaway.

They were hustled along the main corridor of the complex, passing rooms filled with ordinance that included large and small weapons, ammunition, and explosive components, the sight of which caused Paul to avert his eyes. There were also storage places for general supplies, food, and the ubiquitous green bottles of wine stored on racks which appeared to be remnants from a distant past.

Cori and Gaston led them to one of the larger chambers, furnished with three tables, a desk, and radio equipment, and invited them to sit on chairs apparently once part of some 19th century drawing room. From a side cabinet that might have once belonged to Louis XIV, Cori brought two bottles of wine and glasses.

"First, we drink, and then you tell your story," Gaston announced. "After, I shall see how we can help you, yes?"

The Laon Bakery

Inspector Weber held a knife to the throat of the baker's wife while, from behind, agent Maas bent back her husband's arms, pressing them into his chubby body. The bakery door was closed and its shade drawn to discourage customers during the interrogation which was being conducted in German.

"What do you know of the men who came here earlier?" Maas yanked the baker's arms causing him to scream.

"Nothing," he cried in the language of his torturers. *"I know them not at all. They buy food here. It is all I know."*

Weber pressed the blade of his knife against the wife's marshmallow skin. *"Maybe now,"* he suggested, *"you will talk."*

The baker screamed louder. *"Please, please do not harm her. I and she have nothing to tell."*

Maas pulled again on his arms. *"What did they say when they bought the food?"*

"Please, the man he did not like the occupation."

Weber kept pressure on the knife. *"There, see? You do have something to offer. Now, what did you tell this man about the resistance?"*

"Nothing. I know nothing of it. Only a baker am I."

Weber drew the knife and caused a small stream of blood to trickle down the woman's neck.

"Aaaay," she shrieked and spit out the word, *"Cochon!"* before fainting in the agent's arms.

"Jacqueline! My Jacqueline!" the baker cried as Weber let her slip to the floor. *"You kill her, and for no reason. Nothing more do I know."*

At a signal from his companion, Maas released him, and as he collapsed in grief, kicked him.

"She is not dead," he snarled. *"You will both be allowed to live, so long as you help only us and never the enemies of the Reich. Do I make myself clear?"*

Laon-Athies German Air Base

The *Messerschmitt* Me 410 carrying *Oberführer* Schellenberg landed at 1746 hours and taxied to a camouflaged hangar where a man in a dark suit and fedora stood beside a Citroen sedan. The canopy of the deadly fighter-bomber swung upward, and once the twin engines of the aircraft spun to a stop, Schellenberg emerged from the rear of the cockpit, climbed down, and was greeted with a Nazi salute.

"Sir, I am Chief Inspector Gerhard Lehrer, welcome." He tended the rear car door for the general, then climbed into the front seat next to the military driver.

"To the headquarters—hurry!" he said before looking back over his shoulder. *"We are honored by you presence, Herr Oberführer. All our resources are at your disposal."*

"Thank you, Herr Lehrer, but what of the two Venlo agents?"

"They continue searching Laon for the three Englanders. As of minutes ago, they had not found them. Herr Weber would have accompanied me, but he did not want to take time from the pursuit."

The general sneered, *"Huh! Maybe he is learning."*

As they passed the base gate, the guards stood at stiff attention and issued precise military salutes. Schellenberg returned their gesture and the vehicle sped on to Laon.

"It does not surprise me the fugitives remain on the loose, Herr Lehrer. They have avoided capture for days."

"Weber reports an American is suspected to have joined them."

The general frowned. *"Damned Allies! They are formidable dogs when they work together."*

When they arrived at the *Gestapo* post, the general was shown to a room where Weber and Maas saluted him, only to receive a withering stare in return. No one sat.

"So, my two fools, how could you both be so inept?" the general demanded. *"All you needed to do was follow the American!"*

Weber bowed his head. *"Herr Oberführer, if I might, we did exactly that. Just as you predicted, he did lead us directly to your fugitives; however, before we could correctly identify them, he continued his journey and drew us away from them."*

"What?" the general spat out the word.

"Herr Oberführer, we returned to Laon because we now know for certain the Englanders are here, and so, we suspect, is the American."

"We have searched the entire lower district with no results," Maas added. *"And here?*

"We are now on our way to investigate this upper area," Maas replied. *"We have been assured there has never been any activity in this section, but we will go just the same."*

Schellenberg opened the door and stepped back. *"Don't let me detain you a moment longer,"* he said as the two men rushed past him, nearly running into an entering Inspector Lehrer in their haste.

"Can I offer you something, Herr Oberführer?" Lehrer asked.

"A mineral water will do, and any files you have on resistance activity in the past six months. Immediately!"

French Resistance Headquarters, Laon

The table held one empty wine bottle and another that was less than half full. Gaston raised his glass and the others at the table did the same. *"Santé. I now understand your situation, my friends,"* he said. *"We must devise a way of delivering you back to England. So here is what I propose. First, your idea to go to Paris is sound. However, attempting a direct route to the seacoast would be foolish, and I do not recommend it. In Paris, it can be arranged to transport you by a merchant boat. In this way, you can follow the Seine to Le Havre and then out into the channel."*

"I knew we'd get to boats eventually," quipped Paul.

"Is it the surest method?" asked Sir Harold.

"Nothing is certain," Gaston shrugged and added, "but we have used it before with success. There are tunnels to the river in Paris, and the German patrols are accustomed to seeing such boats. They carry supplies, produce, and seafood into the city." Gaston awaited more questions, and receiving none, continued. "You will go as seamen, probably using your current papers. Such will be decided there."

Ed Bradford spoke up. "How about getting to Paris? What's the plan? Can we go by bus, car, what? We know the train is out. The rail yards have been bombed to hell."

Gaston smiled. "It was an attack we called for."

As the three Britons looked knowingly at each other, Cori added, "I believe fate has brought you here. There are forces larger than we can imagine on our side." She looked directly at Phil, *"Il est vrai, oui?"*

The lieutenant agreed, "*Oui*, it is true!"

Gaston continued. "So, you will go by delivery lorry carrying produce, cheeses, and meat. It is typical for one to go in the evening for a delivery to Paris. You will be among the parcels. Corinne will drive and one of you will ride beside her. The other two will hide in the rear."

"Hey, what about me?" Ed asked.

"There is room to conceal no more than two in the lorry," Gaston said. "We will prepare your motorcycle."

The major rolled his eyes at the prospect of more hours on the mechanical creature.

Sir Harold nudged him. "You and Eisenhower are the ones among us who know the plan. Separating you makes sense. Eggs in one basket, what?"

"Precisely," Gaston agreed.

"When do we leave?" Phil asked.

Cori had a ready answer. "The dark comes in several hours. We must leave well before in order to avoid violating curfew." She said to Ed, "You will precede the truck, and we watch for anyone who might follow."

"I feel like a piece of bait," observed the Yank.

"Not at all," Gaston assured. "It is only a precaution."

"Oh, well." Ed came up with one of the few French phrases he knew and it was apt. "*C'est la guerre.*" He picked up his glass of wine and drained it.

SHAEF Advance

Ike sat at his desk ruminating over the fact the seventy-two hour clock for the invasion had started that morning, and there were still huge doubts about the weather. Pressure was on him from all sides. He was, after all, the focus of responsibility for the success or failure of Overlord—the one who would decide to send hundreds, maybe thousands, of men to their deaths. More than this, the recent meetings with the exiled governments of the Netherlands and Belgium underscored how the invasion might determine the fate of the European countries and the history and traditions of their people.

Ike picked up a cowboy novel by Zane Grey, considered it, and set it back down, opting instead for a cigarette. He leaned back, ran his hand over his thinning hair, and blew smoke at the ceiling.

Harry Butcher knocked and entered. "General, the staff meeting is set for 2100 hours at Southwick. The meteorology briefing will be at 2130."

"I hope to hell we have some good news for a change," Ike observed. "Have you sniffed out anything from the weather folks?"

"Group Captain Stagg has polled all his people and no one is certain of anything. Our weather guys paint a rosier picture, but nothing we can count on."

"If it stays this way, we may have to postpone," Ike ground out his cigarette. "Nothing's as powerful as the hand of God in these matters. I invited Churchill and Smuts to sit in, but I doubt they will. The PM has been edgy about the same thing for days, and I expect he doesn't want to hear any more bad news."

"Yes, sir."

"Get Kay, and let's go over there now. I'm damn sick of sitting here thinking about things I can't have an impact on."

Gestapo Field Office, Laon

Schellenberg sat across from Weber and Maas with Inspector Lehrer at the short end of the table to his right.

"*The mystery goes unsolved as the clock continues to run,*" he growled, glaring at the two agents.

"*Herr Oberführer,*" said Weber, desperately trying to save his career and, according to certain reports about the general, possibly his life, "*we have investigated every potential hiding place. We have interviewed anyone who might remotely know of the resistance.*"

"*And you have found nothing!*" Schellenberg reminded him. "*Absolutely nothing!*" He addressed Lehrer. "*Herr Inspekteur, what is your force size here?*"

"*Sir, working out of this office for the Aisne region, we have six inspectors, thirty-six agents, eight SS officers, and fifty-two enlisted.*"

The general slapped the top of the desk. "*With the local police, you must have a fifty-to-one advantage. I would like every one of them who is available to be part of this hunt, now. Understand?*"

"*Perfectly, sir.*"

"*For a town of this size, we should be able to station men at close intervals to watch every move made, upper and lower. I want the Englanders found! Now!*"

Schellenberg stood and the agents came to attention. "*When I say 'available', I mean nothing less than death or dying as an excuse. If they are at home, no matter what they are doing—reading, on the toilet, in bed with their wives—tear them away. If they are drinking, sober them up and get them here. If they are with a whore, pull them off and bring them. This has gone on long enough!*"

His left eye began to twitch as he shot a wilting stare in the direction of Weber and Maas. *"If you have any chance of ever redeeming yourselves, you will work with Lehrer's men and achieve success. Brief them on what you have done thus far, and tell them anything and everything you have learned, good or bad. But keep one thing and one thing only in mind. I want results. They are all that matter!"*

Southwick House
Portsmouth, England

Eisenhower, Beetle Smith, and the British flag officers who comprised the leadership of SHAEF occupied settees and easy chairs in a library which had been converted to a briefing room. They had just concluded going over the status of the naval, ground, and air forces scheduled to be deployed before, on, and just following H-hour.

Ike sat hunched over with his elbows resting on his knees and hands clasped, like a quarterback setting a play. Respecting the wishes of Montgomery, he was not smoking. "Gentlemen, I believe we have it well in hand. The clock has started and the gears have been set in motion for the fifth. If the weather holds, we are go."

As if on cue, Group Captain Stagg entered carrying a case crammed with weather communiqués and charts. After explaining the various sources on which his information was based, he proceeded to describe the meteorological events expected to be moving over England and the French coast in the ensuing hours and days. In the end, he could offer no assurance of anything, other than the unpredictability of current and future conditions. A reliable forecast never passed his lips, and when Eisenhower asked his opinion on the matter, the weatherman replied that offering such would make him a "guesser, not a meteorologist."

Ike rubbed his chin and ended the meeting early, requesting Stagg to provide weather briefings twice daily until further notice. If conditions did not improve or at least become more predictable, the 5 June date for D-Day would have to be changed.

French Resistance Headquarters, Laon

At the same moment the SHAEF meeting convened in England, the four fugitives were enjoying some much needed sleep in the unit's oversized chairs when Phil, trained to remain vigilant, awoke at the sound of Cori's voice. She was telling Gaston they were ready to leave; however, there were troubling reports about heightened *Gestapo* activity all around them.

"*It seems the entire force has been posted here,*" she concluded.

"*This cannot be good,*" Gaston replied. "*It is unusual for Lehrer to take such action without orders from above.*"

"*Such may be the case. We are told there's a German general in town who may be directing this.*"

Her words fully roused Phil, who asked in French, "*This general, would his name be Schellenberg?*"

"*Why yes, exactly!*"

"*He's the bastard who's been after us.*"

Paul awoke and grumbled, "Oy, what's all the yammering about?"

"Wake the others," Phil told him. "They need to hear this."

As Sir Harold and Ed shook off their grogginess, Phil reported that the *oberführer* was hot on their trail and most likely controlling the local *Gestapo*.

"Security is such we should not chance departure tonight," Gaston told them.

"Oy, we can't wait another day now, can we," Paul demanded.

"It will be a difference of hours," the resistance leader assured him. "You shall leave early tomorrow."

"The lorry sounds quite risky," Sir Harold observed. "Is there a way we can measure the opposition before we attempt an escape? You know, discover what they might throw at us."

"Right," Ed agreed. "Test them and see what they've got."

Gaston looked at his watch. "We have forty-three minutes before curfew. After, we can attempt nothing until morning."

"I can take the lorry," offered Cori. "It is stocked and ready, so we have a convincing story."

Gaston stood. "I don't want you going alone. Besides, there are usually two—the driver and a delivery man."

"I'll go!" Phil volunteered as he flashed Cori a furtive wink. "I would likely have been the one to ride up front had we left tonight. It will be a good test."

"Here," Paul jumped in, "you're one of us, ain't you."

"I don't know a thing, remember?" Phil reminded him.

"Ah, let him go," Ed said.

Gaston gave a nod and it was settled. Before the pair left, the resistance leader held the young woman close to him and cautioned not to be caught out past curfew.

The Streets of Laon

The open staff car carrying *Oberführer* Schellenberg and Inspector Lehrer was chauffeured by a young corporal.

"There," said the general, pointing to the towers rising above the rooftops. *"Go there. I want to see the cathedral."*

As they drove the narrow streets from the town hall plaza to the great church, Schellenberg was pleased to see troops and police posted at intervals all along the route.

Lehrer smiled proudly. *"As you can see, Herr Oberführer, we have the area well covered."*

"What matters are results, Herr Lehrer. We must learn the details of the invasion for the Führer. If we fail here, I fear all might be lost."

When the car arrived at the forecourt of *Notre Dame*, the general had the driver stop so he could get out and look at the wonderful façade in the waning daylight. He had no idea he was standing only meters above the resistance caverns and the Englishmen whom he had so doggedly pursued.

A portion of the passageways of the hideout ran under the cathedral square and one led directly to the church. It was the same corridor the four allies would have taken had they left that evening. Rarely used as an entrance because such activity could attract unwanted attention, it was a perfect exit point since the occupiers did not account for people entering and leaving the cathedral during the course of a day.

Inspector Lehrer was surprised to see Schellenberg walk up to and enter the magnificent house of worship through its center door. The general did so not only out of curiosity about the interior architecture, but also to feed the faint flame of spirituality remaining in him after years of service to the Nazi cause.

Taking off his hat, he ambled down the aisle for a closer look at the rose window above the altar in the apse, its colors muted by the dwindling sunlight. As he stood admiring the work of hands and minds that had been still for hundreds of years, a woman and man appeared from the right transept area, genuflected when they reached the center aisle, and passed directly by him on their way to the exit. The man carried a cap in his hands and the woman wore a blue kerchief on her head. They were both young and appeared to be of the French working class. Seeing them brought the general a fleeting moment of envy for the simple life of a peasant and the satisfaction of having something greater than himself—greater even than the *Reich*—to believe in.

The delivery van rumbled noisily away from the cathedral, but the driver and her passenger were silent, each lost in personal thoughts about what had just happened. Cori was careful not to rush or show any sign of nerves as she guided the van past the observers posted along the same streets the German staff car had traveled minutes earlier.

Phil was the first to speak. "*That was likely him—Schellenberg.*"

"*My God, what was he doing in Notre Dame?*" she asked, negotiating a corner.

"*Maybe he fancies churches. I don't know.*"

"Speak English," she urged. "I need the practice."

"At least he didn't discover us. Our mission might have been over before it started."

"If he had come a moment sooner, he might have seen us come from the tunnel. *Mon dieu!* What could we do then?"

"Cori," he touched her hand, "Rest easy. It didn't happen." Phil caught sight of the city hall. "Why are you driving here? Isn't it the *Gestapo* headquarters?"

"It's part of the plan," she told him. "Wait and see what happens." As she drove past, at least two agents noticed the truck. They were Weber and Maas, who had just returned from a second, more detailed, albeit fruitless, patrol along the street where the bakery was located. They had even stopped at *Le Chat Bleu* and came away with little more than the bittersweet taste of pastry and *café au lait* in their mouths.

"*Where is a delivery van going at this hour?*" asked Weber. Maas shrugged as he sucked his teeth.

The inspector insisted, "*I say we follow it and see what it is up to.*"

"*It's dusk. I don't want to drive the motorcycle in the dark.*"

"*Come, Peter, there is plenty of daylight left. We must leave no possibility unexplored. God help us if we do.*"

With that, the Venlo agents returned to their motorcycle and followed the van.

Cori checked her rear-view mirror. "*Alors*, our bait has worked."

Phil looked back. "A motorcycle and side car at our six o'clock."

"Why do you speak of time? It is much later."

He smiled and touched her hand again. "It means they are directly to our rear."

Cori shrugged and drove carefully down the hill, eyeing the police and SS troops along the side of the road as she went. They reached lower Laon without incident; however, the *Gestapo* agents stayed with them as they turned onto the road to Soissons and Paris.

Less than five minutes later, Maas overtook them and waved for the van to stop. She pulled over and set the brake. "Here is our test."

Phil checked his jacket for the German weapon he still carried.

When Weber approached the truck and, in passable French, asked for their papers and what they were doing out at this hour, Cori explained they were making an early delivery in Paris. The inspector signaled for Maas to check the contents of the truck. His partner did so and, in short order, waved an okay.

Seeing nothing irregular about their documents, Weber told them they could go, but as Phil observed when they were on their way again, "We're not out of the woods yet. They are still following us."

"What can we do?" Cori asked, as she checked the mirror and accelerated.

"Stay the course, I reckon they must go back at some point."

Another ten minutes passed before Weber and Maas turned their motorcycle around.

"Ah, finally," Cori said. "But it's too late for us to return to Laon without risking a curfew violation. We will wait until the light returns." She steered onto a dirt road and into a grove of poplars.

Phil looked to the rear of the van. "You stay here, and I'll make do back there. I see some canvas bags."

She reached over and pulled him to her. "We shall make do together, *oui?*" And turning her face up to his, their lips met in a tender kiss.

"Wait," Phil stammered, backing off. "Look, you don't want to get involved with the likes of me. We hardly know each other."

"You do not like me?" she pouted.

"I don't even know you and you don't know me."

She looked directly into his eyes. "I know you are a brave soldier who is fighting for the same things I fight for. I know you are artistic with your love for architecture. I also know you will not take advantage of me, otherwise, we would not be speaking as we are." She touched his face, "Above all, I understand it was fate that brought you here. There is a magic I cannot explain. Have you not felt it?"

Phil nodded. "Of course I have. I first thought of you as a conquest, but the magic you spoke of showed me this was different. It's precisely why I don't want to ruin it by moving too fast. Besides, what will Gaston say? I saw how he looks at you."

"Gaston?" She smirked. "He is my half-brother, and he worries about me."

The lieutenant looked into her eyes. "See. I really don't know anything about you."

"Some things you need to know can come later," she said, pulling him to her.

This time he did not resist.

Chapter Seven
Saturday, 3 June 1944

The Countryside near Laon

Dawn was gray and dull, but bright enough to awaken the lovers. Cori opened the rear doors of the van and looked out, oblivious to her own nakedness. Phil simply enjoyed watching her. She was a true beauty, inside and out, and she had stolen his heart.

When she looked beyond the trees to misty fields, recognition glowed in her eyes. "Philippe, we are by the *Chemin des Dames,* a very famous battle area of the great war. Someday, when this is over, we shall have a tour. The *Cavern du Dragon* is where underground battles were ..."

He ended her commentary by pulling her back down to their makeshift bed where they again made love. Later, wearing each other's musky scent, they returned to Laon. When they entered the lower village, they saw neither *Gestapo* nor SS troops posted. There was activity at the city hall headquarters, but they drove by without incident. Maas, who had given up trying to sleep and was reporting in early, recognized the van and assumed it was returning from its run to Paris. If he had taken a notion to stop them, he would have discovered the same articles on board as those he had checked the night before. It might have spelled disaster, but good fortune rode with Cori and Phil and they successfully returned to the hilltop lair of the resistance.

"Ah," Gaston said when he found them having coffee and rolls in the small dining area. "*You have finally returned. We assumed you had been picked up.*"

Cori greeted him with a kiss on each cheek and explained what had happened with the *Gestapo.* "*By the time we could turn around, it was past curfew.*"

"*I see,*" he said with a raised eyebrow. "*So, is there anything else to report?*"

"*The ploy worked. Had we known, we could have all made it to Paris last night.*"

Gaston pressed, "*I trust you slept well, because we leave within the hour. Oui? I have already sent the major down to the café to pick up his motorcycle. He will depart at seven hundred hours. And now, we must prepare for whatever lies ahead, n'est-ce pas?*"

Gestapo Field Office, Laon

"*Is it conceivable that our vigil yielded nothing?*" the *oberführer* grumbled, pacing back and forth before Maas and Lehrer who were standing at attention.

Weber rushed into the office, out of breath and looking disheveled.

"*Ah, Herr Weber, so good of you to join us,*" he said his words dripping with sarcasm. "*I was just recounting the utter failure of last night. I will not waste one more hour here. I suspect they are attempting to get to Paris or may already be there. So, that is where I will go, where I am confident the agents will be more effective locating the fugitives.* He pointed at the two Venlo men. "*And no, you will not accompany me. You two are finished. Do not even bother to return to your office. There is nothing left for you there.*"

Weber's face turned pale, frozen with shock at the prospect of execution. "*But sir, we can help you. We have seen them. We know their ways.*"

Trying to soften the impact of the general's words, Maas added, "*Herr Oberführer, Weber and I are dedicated to finding these spies. Please, give us another chance.*"

Schellenberg put his hand on his pistol holster. "*Go!*" he shouted.

Once the pair left, his tone mellowed. "*Now! As for you, Herr Lehrer, I need help, and you are the one to provide it. I want a plane to take me to Paris as quickly as you can arrange one. Inform the office there of my plans and tell them I want to know everything they have on the local resistance operations. Alert them that I am pursuing three Englanders and an American, and explain this has the highest priority. The Führer himself has a personal interest in their capture.*"

Lehrer had taken out a small notepad and pencil and was recording the general's every word. "*Sir,*" he said, "*the other agents mentioned the appearance of the escapees. Do you have photographs of them?*"

"*At the moment, we do not; however, one of them, an MI6 agent, is known to me personally. The records of the British and American soldiers have not been readily available, but the Gestapo office there may be able to help with that. Finally, we have a description of the postman Eisenhower supplied by our agent in London.*" He thought for a moment. "*Alert Army Group B of my presence. Generalfeldmarschall Rommel may be able to help. His headquarters is outside of Paris.*"

The inspector made a few more notes and looked up. "*I will tell them everything and request full support in your name, Herr Oberführer. And if I may say so, sir, it was right to get rid of Weber and Maas. They were weak and unassertive.*"

"*So, what would you have done differently, Lehrer?*" Schellenberg said, squinting.

"*I would not only have followed the American, I would have captured him and forced him to tell what he knew about the destination of the three Englanders.*"

"*You may yet have the opportunity. I want you to accompany me. Consider yourself my aide.*"

"*Sir, you honor me,*" Lehrer replied. "*I will be proud to serve you, and I promise, we shall succeed.*"

Outside, Weber and Maas were also strategizing. Realizing Schellenberg had not given them any direct orders, other than to get out of his sight and not return to their office, they concluded they had leeway to decide what to do next. After all, they were still fully documented members of the *Gestapo*, and their mission was of the highest priority.

"*So, my dear Peter,*" concluded Weber, "*we have the chance to redeem ourselves. Instead of working at odds to please the oberführer, I say we work together and save both our skins.*"

Maas got on the motorcycle. "*We are off to Paris.*"

And Weber, climbing into the sidecar, declared. "*To Paris it is.*"

When his watch showed a few minutes before 0700 local time, Ed Bradford wheeled his motorcycle out of the alley next to *Le Chat Bleu* where it had been stored in a small lean-to. As he passed by the front of the café, he waved to the people inside who'd helped him. They had given him advice about checkpoints at Soissons and the other towns along the route, put some bread and cheese in the pouches which passed for saddlebags, and wished him *"bonne chance et bon voyage."* As the engine of the balky machine labored at evening out, something it never fully did, he stuck his hat in his pocket, put on the goggles, and rode off.

French Resistance Headquarters, Laon

After saying goodbye to Gaston, Cori, Phil, Harold, and Paul made their way through the tunnel to the cathedral and climbed a flight of worn steps to a wooden panel. Cori undid two latches and opened the panel, revealing the inside of a closet where liturgical vestments hung. Carefully pushing the holy articles aside, she cracked open the closet door and, finding the room empty, slipped out and signaled the others to follow. As they left the vestry and made their way to the transept, they saw that mass was being celebrated.

"It is okay," Cori whispered, putting a finger to her lips. "It will end shortly. Remain in the shadows, then we shall leave with the others. We go one at a time, as if we attended mass. Space yourselves and respect the sanctity of the cathedral. Outside, the lorry is in the alley on the left. Go directly, do not wait for anyone."

When the mass ended, she walked into the main area of the nave, genuflected, and made her way along a side aisle to the cathedral entrance. She left and was followed by the three Englishmen, all of whom made it to the van unnoticed.

Phil took the front passenger seat and Cori helped Harold and Paul into their hiding places in the back. She piled groceries against the panels then took the driver's seat. Within minutes, they were on their way to Paris.

Château de La Roche-Guyon, France

Erwin Rommel sipped his tea as he gazed out a *château* window onto a view of the Seine valley bathed in patches of sunlight.

"The conditions appear to be improving, Lang," he observed. *"Do the forecasters continue to report bad weather on the way?"*

"They say it will not be long before things get increasingly worse, sir," his aide replied. *"In fact, a major storm is predicted."*

"That damned French poem tells us the Allied assault is at hand," Rommel groused. *"Can it be the invasion and the foul weather will come at the same time?"*

"Perhaps Oberführer Schellenberg will shed some light on this when he arrives."

The field marshal set the cup on a nearby table. *"Apparently, he is on some mission to discover the details of the invasion for the Fuhrer."*

"Yes, Generalfeldmarschall, and those details may make clear what the next step should be."

Rommel patted his aide's arm, *"We can only hope such is the case. Come with me to the tower. I want to enjoy the view while the weather is good."* Adding under his breath, *"And before the enemy destroys it."*

The Road to Paris

Ed Bradford's American impatience and the fact that his motorcycle was not burdened with a side car and passenger brought about the inevitable. Just south of the town of Soissons, when coming out of a long curve, the road straightened and he saw the two Venlo agents barely more than one hundred meters ahead.

By chance, Maas glanced in his rear view mirror and spotted him. *"Georg! We may be redeemed. I believe our American major is directly behind us."* He went for his pistol. *"Pull off now!"*

As soon as he saw them, Ed opened the throttle as far as it would go and sped by, but he couldn't outrun the bullets blazing at him from Weber's *Luger*. The first slug hit his watch, bruising his wrist, and when the second tore into his left shoulder, he was forced to brake, fighting for control of his machine as it came to an abrupt stop.

"Well, Major Bradford I presume," Weber said as he climbed out of the sidecar, his gun trained on Ed who did not respond. "Come, come. You are merely wounded. Do you play the possum?"

Taking the *Gestapo* man's cue, he let himself tumble off the bike, allowing it to fall one way and he the other onto the gravel along the side of the road. Other cars passed them from both directions, but the drivers knew better than to interfere with Germans in dark suits.

Ed was playing for time. The van was minutes behind him, and he knew he needed to stay visible from the road if he had any hope of being rescued. With his watch destroyed, he began counting—one Mississippi, two Mississippi—to estimate how long he had been there and how much longer it might be before help would come.

"Georg, we should take him somewhere to be interrogated," Maas announced. *"You ride his motorcycle, and I will put him in the sidecar."*

"Peter, I don't think this will work," his companion replied. *"First of all, where would we go? Back to Laon? It is almost an hour away, and Paris is farther in the other direction. We know nothing of the towns in between. Do you know where*

an office might be in Soissons? No, of course you don't. Nor do I. He may die before we can deliver him anywhere."

Maas folded his arms. *"Okay, Herr Genius Inspector, what do you suggest?"*

Weber pointed to a tree just off the side of the road. *"Help me move him over there and then we conduct our interview."*

Ed continued counting as he feigned unconsciousness, hoping he could delay long enough, and praying neither one of them would take the time to move the cycles from the road's shoulder. Someone lifted his feet, and when a pair of hands went under his arms, the shooting pain in his left arm brought him very close to actually passing out. He forced himself to think of his life back home—his wife and two kids in South Carolina, the job he left as a real estate agent, playing golf, enjoying friends and family—it all helped him to stay conscious. When they propped him against a tree, the pain subsided to a tolerable level.

Ed's count was at three hundred and forty-seven when, suddenly, smelling salts were passed under his nose causing his eyes to pop open and fill with tears. He coughed from the acrid odor and the pain in his shoulder worsened.

"So," Maas observed, "You are fine then, Major?"

"How the hell do you bastards define 'fine'?" he gasped, wishing he could get up and rip the heads off these two idiots.

"Now," Weber bent over him. "If you will tell us what you know of the location of the three Englanders."

"My name is Edward Bradford, Major, United States Army. Serial number O-6833568. That's all you get."

"In civilian clothes, you could be shot as a spy, but first I think you know something." He grabbed Ed's wounded arm and raised it, causing him to scream. "Now, you will tell us where are the fugitives. Say it and you may go free." He raised the arm higher, eliciting another shriek.

"What are you, a fucking madman?" Ed groaned. "I don't know where they are. I've been looking for them myself. It was my job to silence them. I came across them back in Laon at the bakery, but I didn't know it was them. They looked like laborers having lunch."

By his count, he estimated almost six minutes had passed since he had been attacked. Where the hell was the van?

"They had me fooled," he continued, "but later I realized where I had seen one of them before. I recognized him from an old picture. That's when I turned my cycle around and returned to Laon. I searched, but never found them."

Ed was pleased with his facility for mingling truths and lies despite the pain, but he sensed Maas wasn't buying it.

"Do you mean to say you go to Paris on a whim?" the agent demanded.

"I figured it was their original destination. Until I remembered this guy's face, I was hightailing it for Paris myself."

The doubt on Maas's face grew. "So, Major, where did you rest last night?"

"In an alley next to this café. The chat something."

"*Le Chat Bleu*? You lie. We searched there thoroughly."

"There's a little storage shed. I jimmied the lock and spent the night in there with my cycle."

The two agents conferred in German. What Ed got out of it was they were buying his story. The bad news was, if they believed it completely, he would no longer be of any value to them, and they might kill him. He decided to pull the old switcheroo and lead them down another path. Before he could do so, Maas grabbed his lapels and opening his jacket, searched the inner and outer pockets, then went through his pants, coming up with nothing more than the .45 caliber pistol and forged identification. Throwing the gun aside, he waved the papers in the major's face.

"What are these?" he demanded. "Who gave them to you?"

Without skipping a beat, Ed responded, "Allied G2. They knew I'd need some sort of cover." In response to which Weber accused Bradford of telling more lies, pointing out that when they found the German soldier, he was dressed in Ed's uniform.

The Yank major took a chance and told them a small Allied air drop near Leuth had supplied him with papers and the clothes he was now wearing.

Weber fingered the material of Ed's jacket collar and checked for a label. "Most authentic," he declared.

By now Ed was beginning to panic. Ten or more minutes had passed and still no van.

"Were you not at the convent as a German soldier? Explain this!" Weber sneered, inches from his face.

Between spasms of pain, Ed managed to spin out story after story, including an explanation of why he had been at the convent in the first place until Weber pulled out his gun again. He told Maas he was tired of the major's lies, and the time had come to finish *dieser kerl* off. But before the *Gestapo* agent could turn the weapon on Bradford, the van pulled up and Cori leapt out carrying a machine pistol.

"*Arrêt!* Stop!" she shouted, "*or you are dead. Both of you.*"

"*Well, well, another delivery to Paris?*" Weber punched the gun into the side of his captive. "*I will shoot him.*"

"*And I will kill you. I don't know who he is, but I am certain you will die. Are you ready to do so for your crumbling Reich?*"

When Phil showed up brandishing his gun, Weber relented and let his *Luger* drop to the ground.

At the same time, Maas made a foolish move. He got off one round at Cori but she dodged it in time and the bullet whizzed by her head. She turned the pistol on him and three plumes of red splashed across his chest. As Maas went to the ground, Weber edged toward his own gun but froze when he heard Phil cock his weapon.

"Would you like to try also?" asked the lieutenant.

Weber shook his head. "Please, I have wife and family. I beg your mercy."

Cori aimed her weapon at the inspector. *"Phillipe, please see to the major."*

The other Britons came out of hiding as Phil went to help Ed. The howl of pain when the lieutenant pulled off the major's jacket prompted Cori to change roles.

"Wait, I have a kit in the van," she said, handing Paul the gun. "If he moves, shoot him."

The postman nervously accepted the weapon. The last time he had held any gun was for qualification to serve in WWI. Fighting off nerves and a sudden queasiness in the pit of his stomach, he knew he must control the *Gestapo* agent.

Cori returned with the medical kit and while she and Phil worked on Ed, Sir Harold asked Paul, "Would you like me to take over, old man?"

"Oy, would I ever," he said, gladly ridding himself of the weapon.

The MI6 man instructed. "See if you can find some twine in the lorry to truss him up."

With Ed patched up, and his gun and papers back in his pockets, they began clearing the scene. After taking all identification off of agent Maas, Harold pulled his body into the bushes and Phil followed with the *Gestapo* motorcycle. Next, there was the question of what to do with the remaining agent. They agreed he should be taken to Paris, and this raised the dilemma of who would sit where in the van. Phil resolved it by volunteering to drive Ed's motorcycle the rest of the way. It was decided the wounded major would ride up front with Cori even though Harold's command of German made him a more likely choice to ride shotgun. A couple of hours rolling about in the rear or crammed into a small compartment might have killed Ed.

Paul and Sir Harold finished tying up Weber and stuffed him into one of the hiding places while the postman took the other compartment and the MI6 agent sat on the floor, ready to play the role of delivery man if called upon.

As Phil readied the cycle, Cori asked, *"Do you know where you are going?"*

"They gave us an address to memorize in Brussels."

She looked at him expectantly. *"Say it."*

"Fifteen Rue du Parc Royal."

She was satisfied. *"Ça va. I wanted to be sure in case we get separated."*

They kissed and the lieutenant waited for the truck to leave before falling in behind. The trip to Paris resumed.

They had travelled for more than an hour, when the beast Phil was riding began to cut out, causing him to slow to a crawl. He watched the truck growing smaller in the distance as he nursed the motorcycle along for several more kilometers, searching for nearby towns where there might be help. There were none. When the machine finally stalled for good, Phil found himself quite literally in the middle of nowhere. Estimating his speed and the time since he began his ride, he figured Paris was about thirty miles ahead. He stashed the motorcycle and set out walking along the desolate, rural road with little chance of getting a ride any time soon. As he trudged along, he comforted himself with the thought that Cori would surely come back for him.

It was an empty hope. As the drive progressed, Cori had become more and more fascinated with Ed. Of course, he did not have the romantic appeal of Philippe, but here he was, right next to her, a major in the American army. Having never met a Yank before, she asked him every question she could think of about his personal life, the United States in general, the Grand Canyon, the Wild West, and the cities she had heard so much about: New York, Chicago, Dallas, San Francisco, and of course, Hollywood. She wanted to know about American food and baseball. Did he like hot dogs? Had he ever met Clark Gable or Joe DiMaggio? She was hungry for information about a land her own countrymen had helped make an independent nation. Almost 20 minutes had passed since the last time she'd checked the mirror for Phil. When she finally did so, he was nowhere in sight. *"Mon Dieu, I have lost Phillipe."*

"Naw," Ed looked back, "he's probably just lollygagging along. Slow down and let him catch up."

Cori eased off the gas pedal, but after running at half speed for more than 15 kilometers, Phil never appeared, while ahead, the skyline of Paris grew in the misty distance.

After hiking about three kilometers, Phil spotted a farmhouse just off the roadway. He found it deserted and began searching the grounds, locating a bicycle behind the combination barn and house. It looked to be in good working order, and feeling justified by the circumstance, he wheeled it into the yard. Taking a wad of *reichsmarks* from his pocket, he peeled off what he guessed were more than enough to cover the cost of a new bike. Setting the bills under a stone on the steps leading up to the living quarters, Phil looked around one last time, and pedaled off.

As he made it to the road and started away from the farm, Phil saw a tractor heading his way pulling a wide cart with hay on it. The man driving and the woman riding atop the hay both gave him long looks as he rode past. The irony of it all struck him. This whole mess had begun with an incident involving a bicycle and now here he was riding a similar one, trying to get back to where it all started. "How long ago was that?" He calculated and was shocked to find that only five days had passed. He began recounting the events of the recent days to himself, but his reverie was rudely interrupted when the tractor he had seen earlier, now without the cart, caught up to him, and the irate man driving waved for him to stop.

"*You stole my bicycle!*" he shouted as he got down from the seat and pulled out a rifle. The gaunt, typically Gallic man with a faded blue shirt and baggy trousers pointed the weapon at Phil and growled, "*You are a thief, and we shoot thieves here.*"

"Wait," Phil jumped off the bike. "*I did not steal it. I paid for it.*"

The farmer pulled the *reichsmarks* out and waved them. "*What, with this shit! This is payment for nothing.*" He threw the money to the ground.

"*It was all I had. It is good money here, isn't it?*"

"*Never! I shall never call the notes of the German pigs good for anything.*" He motioned with the rifle for Phil to step away from the bike. "*Walk on ahead. Back to my home, where we will await the police.*"

Gestapo Headquarters
Paris, France

Mid-morning saw the arrival of *Oberführer* Schellenberg and Chief Inspector Lehrer. As this was one of the larger and more efficient field offices of the *Gestapo*, the general and his aide received every courtesy and accommodation. When they arrived, the office head, Wilhelm Jung, a paradigm of a *Gestapo* chief inspector, showed the visitors to a spacious conference room with a large table surrounded by comfortable chairs. A stack of folders sat at one end, and in the middle of the table there were carafes of water, coffee, and tea, along with all the necessary utensils and linens. A bowl of fruit and a basket of rolls and pastries finished off the lavish assortment.

"*Herr Inspekteur,*" Schellenberg said to the office chief as he regarded the pile of folders. "*Tell me what you know about the French resistance. I have no time to sort through these documents.*"

As he listened closely to the crisp report which followed, the general zeroed in on the fact that there were more than thirty suspected resistance sites in and near the city. "*Jung,*" he asked, "*if I wanted to escape to England, how would I go about it?*"

"*But you would never want to do this, sir.*"

"*Of course not, but what if I did? Say I am an Englander trying to return home.*"

Jung peered up at the ceiling. "*Sir,*" he said finally, "*I would go to the coast—Normandy, possibly Brittany. The Mediterranean route is complicated. Cherbourg and Calais are too well-fortified. As there are, of course, no English aircraft available here, I would have to get there by motor vehicle or boat out the Seine to the coast, then across the Channel.*"

The general smiled. "*Very good. Wouldn't you agree, Herr Lehrer?*"

"*Quite so, Herr Oberführer,*" the Laon agent replied. "*And I would then have to ask, where are the resistance units most likely to support such an escape? The ones close to the Seine, for example.*"

Like a spectator at a tennis match, Schellenberg nodded and looked to Jung for his volley.

Again the Paris inspector consulted the ceiling. "*Let's see. There are three that fit this scenario. I think if I were trying to prevent someone from executing such an escape, I would post guards in the three areas where we know such activity might occur.*"

"*It will take caution,*" Lehrer warned. "*If we are at all obvious, the attempt may never occur. We must allow them to reveal themselves.*"

The *oberführer* sat back. "*Good, then we have a plan of action. Jung, make the necessary arrangements, but first, I would like to see where these suspected resistance sites are.*"

Jung opened a wall panel revealing a detailed map of Paris. He first pointed to the *Île de la Cité,* famous for the Cathedral of *Notre Dame de Paris,* then to the *Île Saint-Louis* nearby, and finally to the *Île Saint-Germain* located just outside the city at *Issy-les-Moulineaux.* "*Sir, these* present the most likely areas from which the resistance might attempt an escape by boat."

"Of course, each is in the Seine," Schellenberg observed. "It makes sense. But we must move with haste. There is some chance the fugitives have already arrived here and they may make their attempt very soon. We will need at least a dozen of your agents and police at each location immediately. I trust we can rely on the local law enforcement."

"Absolutely, Herr Oberführer," Jung replied. "They do as we direct."

Jung's positive responses were precisely what the general wanted to hear. He could only hope this time they would lead to success.

Paris, France

The remainder of the trip had gone well for the group in the van. Their papers and assumed identities were never questioned, and Ed, denying his pain, successfully presented the appearance of a hardy delivery worker at each of the four checkpoints they had encountered. Fortunately, he never had to use German or fabricate a reason for his presence in the delivery truck.

Cori turned a corner onto Rue du Parc Royal, a quiet, cobblestoned street, and pulled up before a large, stylish residence a few blocks from the Seine. A guard at the entrance opened the wrought iron gate and they were allowed to drive into the courtyard. As they stopped at the front door, a footman directed them to a side entrance where they could not be seen from the street. Once she parked the van, Cori orchestrated the delivery of breads, cheeses, produce, and the three allies.

When Jean-Paul, a butler with a distinctive British accent, asked if there was anything else, Sir Harold handed him the papers they had taken off Maas and said, "Oh yes, old man. Behind the right panel you'll find a *Gestapo* agent your master might wish to speak with."

"Very good, sir. I shall see to him immediately."

The butler's words made Sir Harold realize how much he missed the air of civility and confidence only a good man servant could provide.

They were led through a large kitchen, busy with preparations for lunch, and into an anteroom with paintings, statuary, and rococo decoration to rival sections of Versailles.

Sir Harold took it all in stride, but Paul gawked at every detail and risked neck cramps looking at the ceiling frescoes. Ed was equally impressed with the fine piece of real estate, but more than this, he was happy to be alive and, for the moment, out of danger.

After a few minutes, a door disguised as a wall panel opened and a stunning woman appeared. She was in her late thirties with short, black hair that shined like patent leather, pale skin, and twinkling blue-gray eyes. The draped blue chiffon dress she wore was right out of an Erte painting.

"*Ah, mes amis,* it is so good to have you here," she greeted them. I am Genevieve du Lac, and I will do everything I can to see you succeed in returning to England. Gaston has informed us of your plight, and we have developed a plan. With fortune on your side, you will be home in no more than a day or two."

Cori recognized their hostess immediately and was thrilled to be in the company of one of her country's most famous and successful actresses. While the two Brits and the American were all smiles, she guessed they had no idea who she really was. Genevieve du Lac, as every Frenchman knew, had begun her career as a teenager during the latter part of the silent film era. Unlike others who failed to make the transition to "talkies," her voice was soft and sexy and her success blossomed throughout the 1930s. She had become an international star, but quit acting when the Germans arrived; although, it was said, she was a favorite of the *Führer* himself. As the wife of the automobile magnate, Charles Velon, she shared her husband's hatred of the Nazis and worked secretly with him to privately subvert them at every turn. Since the occupation, they publically supported various *Reich's* causes with relatively small contributions of their wealth, throwing lavish parties for them, and going so far as offering to host *Herr* Hitler during his 1940 visit to her city. All the while, the couple provided major monetary support and the use of their home to the French underground.

The sad end of their loving partnership had come a year ago when her husband succumbed to the effects of a stroke. Although devastated, she continued to work with the resistance and had become more directly involved with the operations in her home. Despite the efforts of the local *Gestapo*, the location had never been discovered or even suspected.

"Come, we have a small luncheon," she told them with a graceful wave of her hand, "and then we shall discuss your future."

The locations suggested earlier by Jung were being watched by teams of *Gestapo* agents, and the *oberführer* toured each site, demanding that any activity even remotely related to the men he sought be reported immediately. As the afternoon wore on into evening, the surveillance results were disappointing, almost nonexistent, but the general refused to let another day pass without finding his prey. He ordered Jung to have patrols set up all along the shores of the Seine and told him to assign every available police boat to interdict any and all river traffic.

The stone and concrete basement of the Velon-du Lac mansion was neat and as clean as a hospital, with passages lined with rows of wine racks holding hundreds of bottles of various vintages. The corridors led to chambers full of arms, radio gear, uniforms, and one, marked by a red door, where ammunition and explosives were stored.

In one of the larger rooms, Madame du Lac sat in a wing chair, her usual place for such meetings, while the others arrayed themselves on benches around an old oak table large and wide enough to accommodate at least twenty people.

"The plan is simple," the partisan leader who had been introduced simply as "Achille" was saying. "This evening, Madame du Lac will host a cruise on the Seine, a *soirée* for German officers and *dignitaires*. You will go too, except you will be below the deck."

While the others were visibly uneasy with the idea of escaping on a boat carrying the enemy, Sir Harold smiled confidently at the dark, powerfully built man describing their escape.

"Of course," Achille continued, "madame's boat cannot take you the entire way to *Le Havre*. We will anchor for a time at *Île Saint-Martin* before turning back. There, you will slip away and board a fishing craft. By tomorrow morning, before you will lie *La Manche*, the English Channel."

Sir Harold slapped one hand into the other, and Paul exclaimed, "Right-o." Ed was less demonstrative, since the throbbing pain in his left shoulder had returned.

"You must understand," Achille went on, "it will not be easy. There will be many hurdles, so you must never let your guard down. I trust you will see to them, Corinne?"

"*Certainement,*" she replied. "I know the meeting point well and will accompany them to ensure there is not a problem. Continue to await Philippe, will you? I know he will come."

Deep down, Cori and the others had to face the fact they might never see the lieutenant again.

A Farmhouse Northeast of Paris

The farmer sat at a table drinking milk and eating an omelet, not bothering to offer any to Phil who was tied to a kitchen chair. The man's wife had pity in her brown cow eyes for the poor prisoner who had tried to purchase their bicycle in such an odd manner, but she knew better than to try to sway her stubborn husband in the matter.

"How long before they arrive?" asked Phil in French.

The farmer grimaced. *"They are busy men. Who knows?"*

"Oh, isn't this simply smashing," the lieutenant mumbled to himself.

"It will do you no good to complain, thief! They come when they come."

It was hours before a member of local law enforcement arrived. Phil was still tied up, his stomach growling, and feeling a bit lightheaded. He found comfort in the thought that if he did go to jail, they might at least feed him.

The officer listened to both sides of the story—how Phil had been in desperate need of transportation, and how the farmer had found his bike missing and discovered this young man riding it along the road. Phil concluded with, *"I wished to buy the bicycle and I left ample payment for it."*

"Dirty reichsmarks!" shouted the farmer.

The police officer moved closer to the distraught man. *"Now, you know by law we must use the currency of the Reich."*

"Not on my farm. This is my land and on this land we do not use such shit, not even to fertilize!"

"Enough!" the policeman exclaimed. *"Suppose we can make a compromise. I will convert the money to francs for you and that will be that."*

"What about my bicycle. I need it. I do not want to sell it."

"You can have the motorcycle," Phil offered. *"It's just down the road from here. It will be easy to repair, I am sure."*

The farmer leered and slowly nodded, signaling an accord. The transaction was completed under the watchful eye of the police officer, after which Phil resumed his bike ride to Paris and continued uncertainty.

Paris, France

Schellenberg and Lehrer stood in the wheelhouse of a patrol launch making regular passes up and down the Seine, having already stopped several other craft on the river with no positive results. When the increasingly frustrated general ordered the boat farther east, they passed *Île de la Cité* and were heading for *Île Saint-Louis* just as Schellenberg saw a large motor yacht about to cast off from a dock on the far shore.

"*Lehrer,*" he asked, "*what do you make of it?*"

The inspector pulled his field glasses up from around his neck, and examining the sleek, wooden craft, could see a number of well-dressed people aboard, all celebrating.

"*A party, Herr Oberführer,*" he said, and to the driver. "*Move in for a closer look.*"

When they drew nearer, Schellenberg was astonished to see a number of German officers among the revelers.

"*My God!*" he exclaimed. "*We are at war. What is this?*"

"*It is Paris, sir; it is Saturday evening,*" Lehrer looked up at the sky, "*and the weather seems to be …*"

The general cut him off. "*I want to board. I must find out precisely what is going on.*"

From the hold where he and the others were confined, Sir Harold Kane watched through a porthole as a patrol launch eased up to the side of Madame du Lac's yacht, and an SS officer boarded. "My friends," he said in a low voice. "Prepare yourselves. The notorious *Oberführer Schellenberg* has just come aboard."

Above them, Genevieve du Lac also recognized the man she had met at various functions early in the occupation, and greeted him accordingly.

"Ah, General Schellenberg," she said warmly, as he bowed over her extended hand, "What an unexpected surprise. As you see, many of your compatriots are here. We will be so pleased if you can join us."

The *oberführer* regarded the crowd on deck with an expressionless gaze. "I am afraid, Madame, I am here for other purposes. There are fugitives from the *Reich* who must be apprehended immediately. We suspect they are attempting an escape by boat. Therefore, we are checking every craft on the water this evening."

Without missing a beat, she made room for him to pass, saying, "Please, feel free to inspect mine. Perhaps you would care to have some of the other generals of the *Wehrmacht* help you."

"No, no," he told her, "that will not be necessary. I only wished to inform you of the possible danger."

For the next forty-five minutes, the former actress charmed Schellenberg with all the skill at her command. She also led him to mingle with other German officers, some of higher rank than himself, French dignitaries, such as a former minister and a leading *notaire*, and members of the Vichy government.

By the time they reached *Île Saint-Martin, Oberführer* Schellenberg had been seduced by the gaiety of the evening, the camaraderie of the guests, and the awesome magnetism of Madame du Lac. The movie star with a taste for champagne and a bubbly personality to match seemed to hang on his every word, making him feel like the most interesting person aboard. Of course, he would never allow himself to be taken in by her flattery, but this was a most delightful respite from the days of concern over the invasion. Her attention and the sparkling wine she plied him with, despite his usual aversion to alcohol, lowered the general's guard and dulled his senses. He was unaware the men he wanted so urgently were escaping from the very vessel he was on.

As the yacht dropped anchor and its prow turned east into the flow of the river, a dinghy carrying the two Britons, the American, and the French partisan appeared off the stern and made its way along the shore of the island.

Paul and Sir Harold paddled the little boat for several minutes before Cori pointed to a wharf where a fishing vessel was moored. In the same instant, a voice amplified by a megaphone warned, *"Stop! You are all under arrest. You must not make another move. If you do, you will be shot."*

Sir Harold translated with, "Bugger, they've got us."

This was it, Ed Bradford thought to himself, the "ah shit!" moment they had been avoiding. No one moved as the launch pulled next to them.

The activity downstream attracted the attention of the ubiquitous butler, Jean-Paul, who worked his way around the edges of the crowd on deck and calmly approached Madame du Lac. He eased closer to her as she held forth, bemoaning the frivolities of the United States with Schellenberg and a group of other SS officers. "If I may, Madame, there seems to be a problem in the galley."

The actress excused herself and, when they moved out of earshot of the guests, Jean-Paul revealed what he had seen. She immediately sent him to get on the radio and notify Achille.

Southwick House, Portsmouth

It was just after 2100 hours, British Double Summer Time, and once again, the Overlord chiefs were gathered in the library. As before, when Group Captain Stagg described the anticipated weather conditions, the faces around the room turned grim. His report, integrating the disparate forecasts from his various sources, was not encouraging. He had, he explained, hoped to predict conditions for the following several days, but the conflicting data made it impossible to forecast even one twenty-four hour period. His sole conclusion was that the storms brewing out to sea could bring some of the worst circumstances imaginable for the planned invasion date of 5 June. The only glimmer of hope was a high pressure system caught between two lows over Iceland. Unfortunately it was not expected to arrive in time.

When Ike asked Stagg if things might improve by tomorrow, and the group captain assured him they would not, the consensus was to delay D-Day one day until 6 June. Wanting to be absolutely certain, the supreme commander decided to let the ships embark as planned and added, "We'll take one more look at it at the zero four thirty meeting."

During the small talk after the meeting broke up, Ike learned that the Associated Press had mistakenly announced that the Allies had landed in France. "It seems," said General Smith, "a tape typist sent the message as a test and it got wide play before the AP could cancel it."

"Sometimes," Ike confided, "I feel like I'm trying to organize chaos. We have to get this thing moving forward before there are any more loose ends."

"I agree," Smith replied, "but I do have some positive news. From the French underground, we learned the postman and the others went to Paris and are working an escape via the Channel."

Ike ran his hand over the top of his head. "Why in hell can't they just lay low for a few days? What they may or may not know becomes meaningless after that."

"The *Gestapo* is hot on their trail, and a General Schellenberg, the head of Hitler's foreign intelligence, is directly involved. They're turning over all the stones."

"Schellenberg? Isn't he the one who abducted some Brit agents?"

"Right! By all accounts, he's a real smart cookie."

Ike crushed his cigarette in an ash tray and headed for the door with Beetle by his side. "Look, is there anything we can do to help our guys?"

They both paused as Smith answered, "According to the resistance, they've done just about all they can for the moment."

"If the information leaks at this point, we're in big trouble," Ike said, reaching for his pack of cigarettes. "Damn it! I hate feeling so helpless, but it seems our fate is in the hands of the weather, a Brit lieutenant, and a postman. Lord help us."

German Patrol Boat on the Seine

"You were fools to believe you could escape in such a tiny boat," Inspector Lehrer sneered, clearly unaware they had come from the du Lac yacht. This was only a glimmer of sunshine indeed, but it was something to be thankful for. It would have done great damage to have the beloved French actress directly linked to the resistance.

"We didn't think the patrols would spot our small boat," Sir Harold said quickly. "We expected to simply slip past them."

"Obviously, you had not counted on my powers of observation," Lehrer replied, preening himself as he called to the captain and ordered him to overtake the yacht so he could display his catch for Schellenberg. A few minutes later when they pulled alongside, he was greeted from the rail by the general himself with Madame du Lac at his side, holding a bottle of champagne in one hand and a half-full glass in the other.

"Sir, I am happy to inform you we have them," he reported. *"The lieutenant is not among them yet, but it is only a matter of time."*

Schellenberg smiled crookedly when he saw the bound-up prisoners, and raised his glass in a toast. *"Congratulations, Herr Inspekteur!"* he said, *"Please continue on to Generalfeldmarschall Rommel's and await my arrival. He has a special facility for such prisoners."*

As the patrol boat pulled away and headed down the Seine, Lehrer radioed in to the Paris *Gestapo* office and informed Inspector Jung that all but one of the fugitives had been apprehended. He recommended they continue to patrol the river areas for the British lieutenant, and informed him he would be taking the captives to Rommel's headquarters at La Roche-Guyon. For his part, Jung was relieved, as he did not appreciate having SS generals come into Paris and upset the efficiency of his operation.

The four unfortunates were taken below and laid in a row on the gray wooden slats of the deck between which sloshed water that stunk of beer, urine, and vomit. Ed was on the left, then came Sir Harold, Paul, and Cori.

"Blast!" Sir Harold erupted. "We are in for the worst of it, and we need to plan now, while we still can." He turned to Paul, "Do you know the distance from the island where we were to land to this La Roche-Guyon?"

The postman thought for a few seconds. "Not a very detailed map now, was it. But I reckon we have eighty or so kilometers—say fifty miles."

"Then, we have time. At least one of us needs to get away." The MI6 man looked to Cori. "Do you have any concealed weapons on you?"

"They took everything," she answered, coyly adding, "Everything except my crucifix with a small blade inside."

"Good-oh," said Sir Harold, as he listened for sounds coming from above. "There's too much activity on deck at the moment. Let's wait and see if we can't lure lady luck to our side in a bit."

The Velon-du Lac Mansion, Paris

Phil was happy to have arrived at the gate while it was still light out. It had been years since he had pedaled about the grand city, and finding an unfamiliar address would have been doubly difficult in the dark.

"*I am Lieutenant Davis,*" he said, wheeling his bicycle up to the guards who eyed him suspiciously.

"*We were told you would be arriving by motorcycle,*" one of them said. Phil patiently explained what he'd been through and was allowed to pass. He rode to the rear door where a footman led him into the residence. The grandeur of the place appealed to his eye as an architect, but he had little time to fully enjoy it before he found himself being hustled down a long hallway. He entered a door behind a large breakfront, and went down two flights of marble steps to the basement surging with activity. Men and women were moving weapons and ammunition, consulting and marking maps, working the radio, and parceling out supplies.

There, he was introduced to Achille, who greeted him with sadness in his voice. "I am sorry to say, my friend, the others have been captured."

"Oh, bollocks! When? How?"

"A short time ago. They were escaping on the river when the *Gestapo* caught them. It was a nearly foolproof plan, but the police activity on the river was much greater than ever. A General Schellenberg has come and shaken things up."

"Bloody hell! We can't seem to break free of the bastard."

Without asking, Achille poured two glasses of wine and slid one in front of Phil.

"What of the Laon woman?" asked the lieutenant.

"She was with them to make a contact down the river. It was there they were taken."

"And Schellenberg has them," he concluded and slapped the table.

"No, at least, not yet. They go to *Château de La Roche-Guyon.* It is Rommel's headquarters. This is all we know, except our benefactor has assured us Schellenberg is being handled."

"Goddamn Jerry," Phil muttered. "What can I do? What are *you* doing about it? The Nazis cannot be allowed to interrogate this postman Eisenhower. The whole bloody invasion might be compromised."

"Easy, my friend," Achille assured. "We have not been idle, and I am well aware of the consequences. We shall depart for *La Roche* very shortly. You are welcome to come. However, you must abide by our rules. You cannot go off on your own to display the heroics. Do you agree to this?"

Phil nodded glumly.

"*Bon.* There is an excellent unit there. Only you, I, and maybe one or two others go from here. The rest have their own missions. As you must know, the message alerting us of the invasion has set off many operations. This is our main concern right now. But I assure you, we will do everything possible to rescue the hostages before they are interrogated."

German Patrol Boat on the Seine

When Lehrer's prisoners were reasonably certain they would not be interrupted, the wheels of an escape from the patrol boat were set in motion. After due consideration, it was decided. Ed and Cori would make the attempt, for it was clear they were perceived by the Germans as having the lowest intelligence value, and, therefore, were least likely to be hotly pursued. Of course, Ed's BIGOT information was a primary factor in wanting to get him away before he was found out.

The first task was to open Cori's cross and get to the blade. This fell to Paul, who was the only one next to her. The Frenchwoman rolled in Paul's direction and it became the postman's assignment to use his teeth to undo her blouse. He leaned close to her and the Frenchwoman's warm muskiness filled his senses as he worked from one button to the next. By the light of dusk coming through the portholes, the soft, white tops of Cori's breasts resembled those of an alabaster Venus. Determined not to be distracted, Paul stayed focused by keeping an image of "his Emily" in his thoughts.

"The cross. We must get it off me. Be certain you grasp the top," Cori instructed.

Paul clenched down on the crucifix as she jerked away, breaking the chain.

The others raised a small cheer when they saw the postman come up with the cross still in his teeth.

"The bottom slides off," Cori told him. "I will bite down on it and you will pull." She moved closer to his face, and with her breath warm and moist on his lips, clamped her teeth on the base. "Ready?" she mumbled. He nodded and pulled, and there it was—a small, sharp cutting edge.

As the twilight continued to fade, and footsteps sounded on the stairs, Cori spit out the bottom of the cross and Paul quickly pulled the blade into his mouth. When he pushed it to the side with his tongue, it stabbed his inner cheek, releasing a taste of blood, but that was the least of it.

Lehrer had come down carrying a lantern and was standing over them. He held the light by Sir Harold and checked his ropes. Moving on to Paul, the inspector saw Cori's half-bare bosom and went to her instead. He leaned over and deliberately let his hand wander across her chest as he slowly examined the Frenchwoman's bonds. When he was done, he buttoned her blouse and went back up the steps, never uttering a word.

Once he felt it was safe again, Harold nudged the postman. "Pass me the blade and I'll cut the major loose. He can then free Cori."

"Here, not by mouth, I won't," Paul objected through clenched teeth as he tried to avoid being poked again.

"Let it drop to your belly, as far down as possible," instructed the MI6 man. "Take care it doesn't fall into the muck."

Paul did what he was told and the blade ended up just above his crotch. Harold boosted himself up onto the postman, and after some groping, which failed to please either of them, grasped the top of the cross and climbed off.

"Major, turn the other way like a good chap," he said and proceeded to cut away at the Yank's ropes.

"That had better be the rope and not my wrist," Ed wisecracked, despite the screaming pain in his shoulder.

The rest was easy. By the time daylight had completely disappeared, Cori and Ed were free and ready to make their getaway. Agreeing with Sir Harold's wise suggestion to split up and take separate routes back to Madame du Lac's, they crept toward the hatch and felt their way along the bulkhead until they reached the stairs where they slowly eased up the steps. Ed, who was in the lead, expected to see the night sky, but instead found the silhouette of Inspector Lehrer looming above him. There was just enough light to catch the blue steel finish of the gun he held.

"My, my, you Americans and French are so very resourceful," the inspector snarled. "Did you suppose it would be easy to escape the *Gestapo*? I would shoot you both, but I shall leave this decision to the *oberführer*. Now, get back down there."

Paul muttered, "Bloody Jerries," and Sir Harold let the cross top with its blade drop into the muck.

SHAEF Advance

General Eisenhower, who was in the habit of writing memos for the record, was reviewing some recent ones to ensure they expressed exactly what he had in mind. One referred to the terrible weather and the impossible circumstances it was causing. Ike wasn't one to assign blame, but he certainly didn't want the impact of climate on Overlord to go undocumented. Another discussed the difficulties he had encountered in trying to deal with General Charles De Gaulle. Ike was well-aware of President Roosevelt's caution not to present the general as the leader of post-liberation France, preferring to leave that decision to the French people.

He set the memos aside and looked at pictures on his desk—his wife Mamie, his parents, and his family. Pulling out a pack of cigarettes, his thoughts shifted to Kay, who had been diplomatically rationing his supply of smokes. What a blessing she had been for him.

Reaching into his desk drawer, he retrieved a typed message he'd drafted to be broadcast and sent to all Allied troops just prior to the invasion. To the last sentence, "beseeching the blessing of Almighty God," he added, "upon this great and noble undertaking." And then, marking it for final typing, put it in his out-basket.

Regent's Park Road, London

Emily Crowley turned first on one side, and then the other, beat her pillow, and laid her head down for the umpteenth time trying to get some sleep. The redhead had been restless all night and she really couldn't pinpoint why. It had been an ordinary day of piano lessons, shopping, taking care of Old Frank and Odette, and checking Paul's garden. Wait a minute. Paul! That was it! He should have been home from Blackpool today. Slipping into her dressing gown, she walked to the window facing the garden and her neighbor's flat, moved the blackout curtain aside, and listened to the distant drone of bombers—a sound she was hearing more and more frequently. "Oh Lord," she prayed, "I hope nothing has happened to that sweet man."

Chapter Eight

Sunday, 4 June 1944

Château de La Roche-Guyon

Although the castle was close to the river, Inspector Lehrer had radioed ahead for transportation and a contingent of guards. He was riding with a civilian doctor named Maximilian Folkstein, a short, balding man in a tweed suit, wearing wire-rimmed glasses, and holding a black medical bag in his lap. The captives, who were now in shackles, rode in the rear of a utility vehicle being closely followed by a personnel carrier with four armed soldiers. The inspector had requested a medical person to administer what he referred to as, "interrogation aids," and the *Gestapo* chief had delivered the perfect man for the job, calling him, *"an expert in such matters."*

It was after midnight when the entourage rolled onto the castle grounds and pulled up at the entrance off to the right side of the facade. While the agent stayed with the car and two of the soldiers took positions on either side of the entryway doors, the prisoners were ushered up the steps and into an anteroom. True to his strict regimen, Rommel had gone to bed hours earlier, so they were met by Captain Lang.

Lehrer introduced the doctor to Lang, gave a brief, purposely unspecific, overview of what had taken place, and repeated *Oberführer* Schellenberg's order to bring the hostages to this headquarters. *"He said the generalfeldmarschall would have a special place here for them."*

"Ah, yes. So we do," Lang said. *"We call it the dungeon although it is in the tower. But I am certain the generalfeldmarschall will want to speak to them first. There are other rooms for tonight. Come, right this way."*

"Wait! There is no time for rest!" Lehrer exclaimed. *"We must begin the interrogation now!"*

"*As you wish, Herr Inspekteur,*" the captain said, picking up a phone and contacting the sergeant of the guard.

"*Yes, Eks, this is Captain Lang. We need immediate access to the bunker. There are nine of us, including four prisoners, a Gestapo inspector, a doctor, and myself. We are accompanied by two armed guards. Please alert the clinic. We need it for… interviews. Oh, and one of the prisoners is wounded. Have someone ready to see to him.*"

Captain Lang led the group to the back of the castle and out across a dark expanse whose aroma hinted it was a garden. They next entered the bunker area consisting of caverns which housed all the facilities necessary for Rommel's command center and the support of his personal troops. Posted guards stood in silence, and the area was eerily quiet except for the hum of generators and the faint sounds of sleeping personnel. "*This way.*" Lang pointed to one of the few caverns with a wooden partition and a doorway over which hung a sign with the word, "*Klinik.*"

"*And the dungeon?*" asked Lehrer.

The captain looked up, "*It is many steps above us. Quite a good climb.*"

The clean, efficiently-staffed treatment facility, which was nothing less than a ten bed hospital, was more than Lehrer had expected. Indicating a side cubicle, he told the guard to take the prisoners there. "*Herr Professor,*" he said, turning to the doctor, "*Ready the serum.*"

"*There is enough here for one application,*" Folkstein said, taking a vial of clear liquid and a hypodermic needle out of his bag. "*I will need more for all four of them. You have a supply here, of course.*"

"*I do not believe so,*" the captain replied. "*We have no need for it, and the generalfeldmarschall is not in favor of mind altering drugs.*"

"*Folkstein!*" Lehrer fumed. "*Why have you brought so little?*"

"*It was last minute, and I assumed you would provide it. I never have more than the amount made for each use. It needs to be fresh as it may weaken when stored. Never mind. This will do for now. I can have more made in the morning, when the chemist is available.*"

"*Shit!*" Lehrer seethed. "*You will go at daybreak and obtain what you need. Understand?*"

"It seems there may be some sort of reprieve, at least until morning," Sir Harold whispered as Lehrer approached.

"Which of you is Eisenhower?" the *Gestapo* inspector demanded, staring down at them.

Before Paul could respond, the MI6 man jumped up, "Oy, Paul Eisenhower here. A simple postman is all."

Cori didn't budge, but Sir Harold's charade stiffened Paul and he banged his head against the wall.

Lehrer ordered the guards to take the man who claimed to be Paul Eisenhower, and they led him away, laid him on a surgical table, and strapped him down. Folkstein administered the so called "truth serum," and when it had taken effect, the inspector began his interrogation. Of course, he had no idea he was grilling a man who had built up a resistance to amobarbital and was trained to withhold information, regardless of consequence or form of persuasion.

After a series of fundamental questions—name, residence, job—Lehrer asked, "Now, what do you know about the planned invasion of France?"

The answer was relatively easy for Paul's pretender because it was true. "Only what I read in the papers or hear on the wireless."

The inspector frowned. "Explain."

"There will be one. We see bloody equipment and Yanks all over England, don't we."

"Did you ever come to find a document containing invasion information?"

"I did."

Lehrer stepped back and paced. "So, did you determine what the document contained?

"Never. I never read it."

The inquisitor became agitated. "You claim you know nothing more of the specific plans for the invasion?"

"Nothing."

Lehrer looked to the doctor. *"More, give him more. It is not working!"*

"Herr Inspekteur, I have administered a full dose. There is no more."

"We cannot allow failure!" Lehrer shouted, backing the doctor into the corner and threatening him with his fists. So absorbed were they both in the drama of the moment, neither noticed the satisfied smile on Sir Harold's face.

The Velon-du Lac Mansion, Paris

Achille entered from the corridor and tapped the sleeping lieutenant on his shoulder. Phil had learned to rest sitting up as part of his glider crew training, but he was not happy about being taken away from the dream he and Cori were starring in.

"Here, what's that for?" he demanded.

"We must go now."

When Phil asked if they had gotten any information from the Venlo *Gestapo* agent, the resistance leader shook his head. *"Only that he asks for asylum. All along, he claimed to have a wife and family. Suddenly, he is a bachelor and he wants to be taken to England."*

Phil stood up. *"Certainly not with us."*

"We shall hold him until the Allies arrive. They can decide." Achille waved Phil on, *"Now, we go to La Roche-Guyon."*

As they walked down the hall, the Parisian added, *"We have just received word of a Doctor Folkstein, a specialist in interrogation, being summoned to the château. If your friends are already being examined, it may be too late. We had counted on them waiting for Schellenberg. His distraction by Madame du Lac should have afforded us more time."*

When they climbed the steps and reached the main floor of the mansion, they were greeted by the actress herself, wearing a white dressing gown with a fluffy collar and silver and diamond ornamentation. Despite the busy day she'd put in, she looked fresh and radiant. There was no need for an introduction. Phil instantly recognized her from his days attending the cinema in Paris.

"Oh my!" he exclaimed, bending to kiss her outstretched hand. *"Miss du Lac, this is a great honor."*

"The honor is mine, Lieutenant," she told him. *"Soon, thousands like you will win us our country back. I am humbled by your presence. Bonne chance."*

As they walked out, the Frenchwoman put her hand on Achille's shoulder, *"Our guest is resting comfortably. Although I was prepared to make a great sacrifice, he passed out and I was spared. I will keep him here as long as I can, but I fear he will bolt once the champagne wears off."*

Southwick House, Portsmouth

At 0430 on 4 June, General Eisenhower and his staff received a briefing from the meteorologist in order to determine whether or not to delay the initiation of Overlord.

No one was in the mood to wait another day, least of all Montgomery. As a result, when Stagg confirmed his prediction that the weather would, in fact, worsen starting sometime later that morning, Monty pushed hard to go anyway. Leigh-Mallory objected, firmly stating he would not be able to provide proper air support considering the expected amount of cloud cover. Ramsay also worried over the weather and finally, the entire group voted for the delay, even though Eisenhower was painfully aware this decision would also add one day to the time Paul and the others were in jeopardy and the security of Overlord at risk.

Resistance Location
La Roche-Guyon, France

As in Venlo, the locations of the La-Roche-Guyon underground were fluid, but the operation was well-organized and comprised of dedicated fighters, both French and foreign, who were committed to the cause of overthrowing the Germans.

Before sunrise, the local partisans were already mapping out a rescue strategy. While they truly wanted to save the unfortunate captives, uppermost in their minds was stopping an interrogation which could spoil the invasion that was years in coming.

"We may be too late already," announced Chev La Mer, the tall, broad-shouldered local leader dressed all in black. *"The doctor has been there for hours. We never saw him leave. Of course, it could mean his work is not done."*

"Wait!" the radioman in the corner exclaimed. *"Here is a report from Sacha. The doctor has left the château and a car is taking him into the village."*

Chev picked up the microphone and pressed an earpiece to his head.

"Sacha, follow him," he said. *"If he goes home, his work is probably done. If not, do not intercept him, but do your best to foil the interrogation, no matter what."*

Château de La Roche-Guyon

Field Marshal Rommel looked out his window at a dawn sky filled with churning clouds. *"Any minute, we will have rain,"* he observed, turning to Captain Lang. *"This makes the invasion impossible for the Allies. Our trip to Germany is most likely. Let von Templehof know."*

"Yes, Herr Generalfeldmarschall, I alerted him when I saw the morning forecast. It said there will be several days of continuous storms."

"Any other developments overnight?"

"Sir, four prisoners have been brought here at the request of Oberführer Schellenberg."

"Has he arrived?"

"Not yet. He is expected. His representative, a Gestapo Inspekteur Lehrer, accompanied them."

"What are we to do with these prisoners?"

"Oberführer Schellenberg wants them interrogated. They have engaged the services of Professor Folkstein for this purpose."

"Folkstein!" Rommel fumed. "I do not like that man! To my mind, he practices the dark arts with those terrible drugs of his. What is so important as to require his services?"

"They believe one or more of them has vital information about the invasion, sir."

"Do they indeed?" the field marshal questioned, his eyes narrowing. "Come with me, Lang. We shall see about this."

The Village of La Roche-Guyon

It was raining steadily when Sacha, a brute of a man with a scraggly black beard, saw Doctor Folkstein get out of a *Gestapo* car, deploy an umbrella, and bang on the door of the apothecary shop of Andre La Grange. Sacha motioned to his armed compatriots to go around to the back of the building. He also instructed his radioman to notify Chev what was happening as he watched the activity at the shop's entrance.

After a long delay, La Grange answered the door and let Folkstein in. "You call too early, Doctor. What can be so important?"

"I need my serum once again, my friend. Only this time, I require a quantity of six for a very special purpose." He pushed past the chemist and closed his bumbershoot.

"An order so large will take some time. Please, have a seat."

Folkstein sat primly on the edge of a chair, knees together, humming an odd little tune.

Sacha crossed the street and tried the pharmacy door. Finding the chemist had failed to relock it, he entered. "Good morning."

The strange little man returned his greeting.

"The chemist, is he here?" Sacha asked.

"In the back, preparing an order," offered the professor.

There were no further exchanges between them and Sacha passed the time casually looking about the shop and examining little packets of cold, headache, and stomach remedies.

When La Grange returned, he had a small package in one hand and a decidedly frightened look on his face. He eyed Sacha. "Sir, I regret, I am not yet open for business."

The partisan opened his jacket just enough to reveal to him the holstered gun. The chemist forced a smile and raised the package. "Here you are, Doctor. A special order of six."

Folkstein thanked him, told him to add it to his account, grabbed the umbrella, and left. The chemist exhaled as Sacha approached him.

"You were smart to have cooperated, La Grange. Soon, they will all be gone."

Sacha's henchmen emerged from the back of the shop. One left with their leader while the other stayed behind to ensure the chemist made no contacts.

Château de La Roche-Guyon

Field Marshal Erwin Rommel and his aide Lang arrived at the clinic as Lehrer was preparing for a second round of interrogation. He immediately recognized the famous military man and saluted. *"Heil Hitler! Sir, it is a great honor to meet you. I am Inspector Lehrer."*

"Ah, yes. Please, I want to know about these captives of yours—or rather of Schellenberg's. Do you know for certain whether any of them may be able to tell us the invasion plans?"

"Herr Generalfeldmarschall, I personally have no knowledge of it, but the oberführer has learned of an Allied security breach and one or more of them was involved."

His words still lingered in the air when the door opened and General Schellenberg entered. The usually fastidious SS officer looked rumpled and his eyes and face showed the effects of a lingering hangover; however he quickly assumed a more military manner when he saw the legendary Desert Fox and went out of his way to defer to him. They stepped off to one side and the *oberführer* related the entire story, explaining why Rommel's headquarters had become the escapade's current venue. His words were most persuasive, and the chance to learn any details of the invasion prompted the field marshal to agree to the plan.

At the same time, Professor Folkstein returned and guards brought Sir Harold, Paul, and Cori down from the dungeon. The doctor announced he had acquired enough serum for the current prisoners, and one or two more, if needed. As a sign the professor was now back in his good graces, Lehrer introduced him to Rommel and Schellenberg. The *oberführer* gave an off-handed nod while the *generalfeldmarschall* offered an icy glare.

Looking over at the captives, Schellenberg demanded, "Lehrer, where are the others?"

"Sir, the wounded American is being cared for in one of the clinic's rooms," explained the inspector.

"I see," said the general, *"and what of the other Englander—the lieutenant? Has he not yet been apprehended?"*

Lehrer grunted uncomfortably. *"No, sir. It appears he has vanished in the wind."* He forced a smile. *"However, we still have the postman. We began interrogation last night, but with few results. More of the chemical was required."* He turned to Folkstein. *"Doctor, prepare Eisenhower."*

When Schellenberg saw Folkstein direct the guards to bring Sir Harold to the gurney, he shouted, *"What are you doing? He is not the postman! He is Jackdaw, an MI6 agent. You would get nothing out of him. Idiots! I continue to be plagued by idiots!"*

Walking over to Cori, he took her by the arm. *"This one is most definitely not a postman, is she, you fool?"* Lehrer shook his head awkwardly and the general continued. *"The American is not a postman."* Again, Lehrer agreed. *"Then, as their famous detective, Sherlock Holmes would say, when you eliminate all other possibilities, you are left with the truth."* He grabbed Paul by the back of his collar. *"This is the postman!"*

As the guards brought a terrified Paul to the table, Schellenberg made an aside to Sir Harold, *"You must have known it would never work. Why did you even try?"*

"Time, General," the MI6 man replied. *"Playing for time."*

Meanwhile, the doctor strapped Paul to the table and injected him with the contents of a vial he had obtained that morning.

When, after minutes passed and he felt no effects, Paul feigned a trance just like the one he'd seen a hypnotist cause at a revue in London. Apparently the ploy worked because he heard the doctor asking his name, where he lived, and where he was employed, all questions which he could answer truthfully. When the subject arose, he even admitted discovering and reading the classified invasion plans. And then Lehrer asked the jackpot question, "Where will the invasion of the Allied forces take place?"

Paul answered in a clear voice, "The Pas de Calais. It will happen at the Pas de Calais."

"So, the mines and obstacles at Normandy will go for naught," Rommel commented to Lang. *"It was a gamble. It is always a gamble."*

The inspector followed up with, "And when will the invasion by the Allied forces take place?"

Paul's answer, pulled from thin air, was, "The thirteenth of June."

"The tide will be high, as I also suspected," Rommel said, nudging his aide.

"Wait!" The crafty Schellenberg cautioned, *"We must have verification."* He looked at Cori, who remained impassive and un-intimidated even when Schellenberg came so close to her she could smell the stale champagne on his breath. "We know the resistance is not privy to the details of Allied

planning. They are puppets who respond to the messages from *Radio Londres*. Only recently, it broadcast a poem telling them an invasion was coming. But nothing so definite. For them, it could be days or weeks off." He took Cori's chin in his hand and she defiantly pulled away. Pointing at Lehrer, he ordered, *"The American! Get him!"*

Ed Bradford was wheeled in from a nearby room and, as they waited for the shot to work, he made the same discovery as Paul—the drug had no effect. When Lehrer questioned him, he too answered the initial questions honestly, giving his name and rank, and adding to his credibility, admitted working for G2 intelligence. But that was it! Everything he said next was a copy of the fabrication he had overheard from Paul.

Schellenberg exclaimed. *"There it is! This is most heartening news."* He walked over to Captain Lang. *"I'd like to inform higher command immediately. Then, please arrange a car for me back to Paris. I have ..."* he searched for a delicate phrase, *"... shall I say, unfinished business there."*

"Lang is leaving with me shortly for Germany, Herr Oberführer," the field marshal said. *"My chief of staff, General Speidel, will see to your needs."*

The one remaining question was what to do with the prisoners now that they had served their purpose. *"If they are no longer of any use,"* the doctor said, *"I have some strychnine with me. It would be a simple matter."*

The saner, authoritative, voice of Erwin Rommel cut him off. *"Finish treating the American and send him to an oflag. As for the woman, let her be sent there, too, but keep the other two here as they may be bargaining tokens for the return of some of our people."*

Of course, the inspector agreed with Rommel's decision, while Schellenberg frankly didn't care what happened to them. He had gotten what he wanted, and was satisfied that he would be a hero in the eyes of the *Führer*. The Jackdaw would have been a grand prize, but since it was not to be, he consoled himself with the undeniable fact that he was the victorious gladiator who had achieved such a great success.

Église Saint-Samson
La Roche-Guyon, France

From the bell tower of the stone church, Chev la Mer watched through his binoculars as Doctor Folkstein walked out of the *château*, waved off a driver, and continued to the gate. *"Shit,"* he said to Sacha, who was observing out the other side of the tower, *"The doctor is leaving on foot. It is all over."*

His burly companion shook his head. *"We can only hope he used the vials from the chemist."*

"This would be good news, my friend, but we cannot be sure of it."

The sound of footsteps on the rough, wooden stairs sent Sacha to the handrail. *"Who is there?"* he called down into the dark abyss.

"Achille," said a familiar voice. *"We are here."*

"Ah, good!" Chev joined Sacha and the two greeted their friend from Paris as he completed the climb. Behind him came Phil Davis, whom the two locals eyed cautiously until Achille made appropriate introductions.

Chev shook Phil's hand and greeted him in accented but clear English, "You are most welcome, Lieutenant."

Sacha also offered a warm, if a bit hesitant, "Hello, we be happy to have you here," and Phil had to grab the banister and steady himself from the big man's friendly slap on his back.

Achille advised the two La Roche men, *"The lieutenant speaks our language, my friends,"* before turning serious and asking, *"So, Chev, where do we stand?"*

"It is not good; the doctor who did the interrogation has just left."

Sacha, who had returned to observing, pulled his field glasses from his face and called excitedly, *"More activity. It may be Rommel. There is a group by his staff car."*

Lang and the others who would make the trip to Germany waited by the field marshal's Horch 901, while Rommel took time to bid goodbye to his personal staff and discuss some last minute matters with Major General Speidel.

"Hans, see that our hosts are not disturbed," the field marshal said, referring to the *La Rochefoucauld* family whom he had allowed to remain living in the upper floors of the *château* when he took it for his headquarters. *"Remember, we are their guests. And make sure Schellenberg's prisoners are not mistreated. I have learned the Englanders were kidnapped from their country and brought here. They are not to be considered spies. The American and the woman were apparently involved in facilitating their escape, no more. I have directed them to an oflag. The others are your responsibility. Keep them away from that bastard Folkstein. I don't want to see him here again."*

"But sir, did he not help obtain information about the invasion landings?" Speidel asked in a low voice.

"He did, however, I detest his methods. He is a madman, and we already have more than enough of those."

Chev watched as the Horch followed by another car and a *Kübelwagen* made their way out of the *château* grounds. When his view of the motorcade became obscured by a building, he tracked back to the entrance just as two other *Wehrmacht* vehicles pulled up. The first was a Horch similar to Rommel's, while the other was a troop carrier.

Achille and Phil also observed through field glasses as soldiers brought two bound figures from the castle.

"Cori!" Phil shouted. *"That's Cori!"*

"And the wounded one must be the American," Achille added.

The two captives were ushered into the back seat of the lead vehicle and Chev asked, *"Where do they take them?"*

"Who knows?" Achille shrugged, *"But at least they are alive."*

Chev called to his comrade, *"Sacha, get the others and follow them."*

"I want to go with you," Phil told them.

The big, bearded man nodded. *"We can always use help."*

As the men headed for the stairway, Chev reminded them, *"Do no more than follow them at a distance. A rescue attempt could put the postman and the agent in danger. Our one concern now is to get them out alive."*

Château de La Roche-Guyon

When Speidel arrived at his office door, he found the *oberführer* on the phone at his desk. *"Schellenberg, what the ..."* he was about to dress down the junior general for his impudence when he caught the gist of the conversation and realized he was speaking with Hitler.

"Yes, my Führer, we are elated at this breakthrough as well." He stood. *"Yes, Excellency, it has been an honor."* He hung up the phone and moved to the front of the desk, where he apologized. *"Forgive me Herr General, I needed to contact Berchtesgaden."*

"So, what did Berchtesgaden have to say?" Speidel asked.

"It was most happy to get the information; however, there was some doubt as to why the poem would be broadcast so many days in advance," Then, dropping the pretense, he added with a smirk, *"It seems our Führer*

second-guesses everyone, and everything, including the facts. In the face of my assurances that we have obtained irrefutable information, he clings to the idea of an invasion at Normandy.*

Schellenberg gathered up his things and offered the more senior general a jubilant, *"Auf Wiedersehen."* Once he'd gone, Speidel called in his aide, Lieutenant Colonel Franz Euler, and asked him to bring the two English prisoners.

The Bell Tower of Église Saint-Samson

"Maybe this is a waste of time, my friend," Achille suggested as he and Chev continued to observe the activities at the *château.*

"I think not," his companion said, keeping his field glasses trained on the side entrance. *"Schellenberg is leaving with another man who appears to be Gestapo."*

Achille used his own binoculars as the pair entered a staff car and drove away. *"That may be Lehrer, the bastard who captured them."*

"It appears to be over," Chev speculated, *"but there is no sign of urgency. They are proceeding as though an invasion is not coming at all. Rommel leaves, Schellenberg leaves. One must wonder why."*

"I don't know about Rommel," Achille replied, *"but I assume the general is returning to Paris. Madame du Lac made quite an impression on him. She has a way with German generals, even though she despises the lot of them. If she continues to see Schellenberg, it will be to keep him out of circulation and I suspect she will also try to find out what he has learned about the landings."*

"From the head of intelligence? Impossible!"

"She may have to invite him to her boudoir, but if anyone can seduce it out of him, she can. It would be a great help. As of now, we know too little, and I am not prepared to guess."

"My God, she is a real patriot," Chev exclaimed. *"Also, I must assume an accomplished lover."*

"That I would not know," Achille declared, avoiding his companion's gaze. As they went to the stairs, he suggested, *"Let us talk instead about your sabotage plans. I suppose, like us, you have been working day and night since the message came through. I need not remind you the outcome of the war may depend on everything we are doing now."*

Euston Station, London

Emily Crowley was at a window pleading with the ticket master. "But sir, please understand. He is a day overdue and the last I knew, he was going to Blackpool. That was almost a week ago. He was due back yesterday. I've gone to other stations and they sent me here."

"Sorry, Miss, this isn't Scotland Yard, is it."

"Can you please see if he bought a ticket? He said he was going on business for the Royal Mail."

"Ah, an official courier. Why didn't you say so? What was the name again?" The agent pulled out his logs.

"Eisenhower, Paul Eisenhower. It would have been on Tuesday. Last Tuesday, May 30th."

"No, Miss," the man said, after running a finger down a list. "No courier named Eisenhower went north from this station, not on that day." He smirked. "Would you like to try for Churchill?"

"Oooh." The frustrated music teacher grabbed her handbag and strode away from the window in a huff. When she got outside the station, her exasperation turned once again into concern for Paul. Pulling a handkerchief from her bag, she dabbed the tears that had suddenly filled her eyes and found a seat on a bench.

A gray haired lady at the other end edged closer to her. "There, there, deary. It can't be all that bad, can it?"

"I may have lost someone special," Emily sobbed.

"There's a lot of that these days. Consider yourself lucky to ever have someone who means so much." The woman patted her hand. "Ain't many can say that now, can they."

"I suppose not. He's such a kind, innocent man."

"There now, the Good Lord watches over the innocents. Always has."

Emily smiled and hugged the woman.

Château de La Roche-Guyon

General Speidel was going over the latest intelligence report on Allied deployments which seemed to confirm the recent revelation that the landings would come at the Pas de Calais. He opened two large panels and consulted a detailed map of German army deployments, *Luftwaffe* bases, specialized bunkers, mine and hazard placements, and hardened sites along the Atlantic Wall. Concluding they were ready for any eventuality, he was content knowing the final deployment decisions for Army Group B would be up to the field marshal himself.

As he examined planned and existing locations of V-1 and V-2 rocket emplacements, there was a knock on the door and Lieutenant Colonel Euler announced, *"Sir, here are the two Englanders you wanted to see."*

The general scribbled something on the report, turned it over, and closed the panels, covering the maps and deployment information; however, the few seconds of exposure was all Paul needed. Much of the information that was now behind the panels had already been imprinted on his memory.

"Gentlemen," Speidel addressed them in fluent English, "I want you to know the field marshal and I consider you our guests. There is no danger, and we want your stay here to be most acceptable. Regrettably, the so-called "dungeon" is all we can offer, but I will see to it that your time there is tolerable."

Once again, Paul unwittingly verbalized his inner thoughts. "Well, Guv, it's better than some places we've had, isn't it. We was like moles underground."

"We do greatly appreciate your hospitality, General," Sir Harold said immediately attempting to dilute the awkwardness of Paul's remark.

Taking a seat behind the desk, Speidel folded his hands before him.

"You know," he said, "this war will end someday, and then we shall be friends. Maybe we can begin a little of this here."

The cordial meeting continued for some minutes before a signal from the general told Euler it was time for his guests to return to their accommodations in the tower.

When they arrived, they saw the cots now had mattresses and linens. There was a supply of water for washing and drinking, along with an assortment of sausages and cheeses, as well as packs of cigarettes and a box of matches. Even the wall sconces about the room had new candles in them. As Euler and the two guards left, the metallic click of a key turning in the lock reminded the Englishmen they were still prisoners.

Sir Harold put his ear to the door and signaling that a guard remained outside, moved close to Paul and whispered, "I say, you did get it, didn't you?"

"Well, didn't I just." He pointed to his head, "It's all up here. No more complicated than some postal routes."

"We must see to it the Allies are informed. The fact that Jerry got the landing information from you may be offset by what you learned."

Paul threw up his hands. "But I didn't."

"You just told me you got a good look at the maps, did you not?"

"Right-o, but I never gave them the landing plans. Not the proper ones, now did I."

"What?"

"I don't know why but the serum never worked on me, and I'm guessing on the major either. It was all an act."

"So, it isn't Calais?"

"And not the thirteenth. It's sooner by quite a bit, so we need to get out of here before they find out."

Sir Harold considered this revelation for a moment and concluded it would be too late for the Germans to do much once they did learn the truth, but Paul disagreed.

"Remember what Schellenberg said to Cori about the poem." Harold nodded and he went on, "If the Jerries knew what the first line meant, they'll know when the second part comes, the invasion is on. And trust me, Guv, we need to get out of here because that second half can come anytime. When it does, they'll suss out that I lied and we'll be deader than doornails."

Sir Harold scowled as he looked out an arched window that offered a view of the forest behind the *château*. The opening showed the wall to be at least three feet thick and it was filled with a sturdy casement. "The resistance is our one hope," he concluded.

Paul went to the other window and looked down at the courtyard, the gardens in front of the castle, and the Seine just beyond.

"That bloody river can take us home, if we can only break out of this ogre's den." He went for the cigarettes, opened a pack, and took one. "Me mum always said to make the best of it." He struck a match and lit up, but the smoke caused him to cough and gasp. "Blimey! These are terrible!"

Paul was about to throw the ghastly smoke on the floor when his cellmate held up his hand. "Wait! They're strong, but you can get used to them."

"Like hell I will." Paul let the cigarette drop and crushed it under his foot. "All the more reason for keeping those bloody sons of bitches out of England."

Sir Harold went to the table and picked up the box of matches. "Just as well not to waste any of these, they may come in handy."

The postman was grim. "If it all doesn't come a cropper before dark."

The Velon-du Lac Mansion, Paris

The doorbell rang and Jean-Paul found General Schellenberg standing there. He appeared rested, wore a neatly pressed uniform, and was holding a large bouquet of mixed flowers.

"Good afternoon, sir."

The general grinned like a teenager picking up his date for the prom. "Is Madame du Lac at home?"

"She is, but I'm afraid she is not seeing anyone at the moment." Schellenberg's look of disappointment prompted the butler to continue, although he would have enjoyed toying with the German officer for a bit longer. "She did say you might drop by and she asked me to see that you were entertained until she became available."

"So, I was expected?"

"Quite so, sir, but last evening wore her out considerably and she needs her rest. Please come through."

Schellenberg handed Jean-Paul the flowers and removed his hat as he entered. "Where would you like me to wait?"

"The library is one of the most entertaining rooms in the house. If for nothing else, I can project Madame's motion pictures there."

"Well, that sounds wonderful. Lead the way, Jean-Paul, isn't it. I remember from the cruise last night."

"Yes, sir." He opened the door to the spacious room filled with shelves of books and movie memorabilia. On the fireplace mantle were several cast models of cars once manufactured by *Velon Moteurs*.

"Would you care for something to drink, sir?"

"Champ ..." the general caught himself. He wasn't going down that road again. "Mineral water will do nicely, thank you."

The butler left and Schellenberg took the opportunity to look around the room. When he came to a shelf full of mementos and photos of the actress in all her glory he could feel a warm glow in his loins. *"God, what will it be like? I can hardly wait."*

The Road to Strasbourg, France

The 1935 Peugeot 601 the partisan rescuers were traveling in was large and powerful, but so heavy it was slow to respond to the accelerator. In many respects, it matched the physique of its driver, Sacha, but certainly not his ability to react. Phil rode in the front and the two resistance fighters from the chemist shop sat in the back quietly observing the passing landscape. The lieutenant leaned over for a look at the odometer. *"How far have we come? Are we close to the German border?"*

The big man kept his eyes on the two vehicles about 200 meters ahead. *"There are another 150 kilometers,"* he said, tapping the gas gauge, *"However, we are low on fuel. If we wait much longer, we will have to stop and may lose them."* Looking to the back seat, he said acerbically, *"Someone neglected to bring the gasoline container."* The two henchmen in the rear seat both gave dismissive hand gestures. One added, *"Why must we think of everything? We brought what is most important."* He patted a packed rucksack.

"Bêtes," Sacha grumbled as he pressed on the accelerator and the lumbering automobile began gaining on the small convoy. *"Now, everyone, get down. We will go five or more kilometers ahead of them and set up an ambush. Be ready."*

They were nearing the Peugeot's top speed when they passed the two German vehicles and, in less than twenty minutes, had opened a gap of several kilometers. Sacha slowed the big car and pulled across a spot in the roadway by a narrow bridge, blocking the way. The men in back jumped out carrying their sacks bulging with explosives and arms, and Sacha gave Phil a choice of weapons. The lieutenant selected a well-used double-barreled shotgun while the burly Frenchman grabbed two machine pistols for himself, one for each of his large paws, and they joined the others in the bushes.

When the two enemy vehicles arrived, the element of surprise gave Sacha and company a tactical advantage. The lead Horch stopped and the officer in charge stood up and ordered the men in the second vehicle to clear the car off the road. But before any of the soldiers could climb down, Sacha's men hit the truck with grenades from both sides, killing them all. The driver of the lead car leapt to the machine gun mounted on the back, just above where Ed and Cori were hunkered down in their seats. He sprayed the bushes with bullets until Sacha caught him straight on with both pistols and sent him to his maker.

"*Wait,*" the officer shouted in French as he aimed his *Luger* at Cori and Ed. *"I will kill them if you make another move."*

Recalling a movie he had seen about the exploits of Sergeant Alvin York in World War I, Phil began gobbling like a wild turkey. When the German officer turned toward him for a split second, he pulled both triggers and, as he recovered from the jolt of the recoil, watched the bloody enemy soldier collapse into the well of the front seat.

Having neutralized the threat, the lieutenant and the resistance fighters rushed to the staff car.

"The cavalry has arrived," Ed quipped as Phil grabbed Cori and held her close for a moment before removing her shackles. Sacha freed the major, and they all did what they could to move and cover the remains of the destroyed vehicles and their occupants. After herding everyone into the Peugeot, Sacha got back behind the wheel and they sped away.

When Phil embraced Cori again, she clung to him. *"We must cherish what we have today for who can say what tomorrow may bring,"* she told him, *"especially now when the enemy has the invasion information."*

Phil frowned and held her away from him. "So, they broke the postman. We were afraid of that."

She gripped his hand tightly, "My love, they used a drug on Paul and the major and forced them to reveal the secrets of the liberation."

Ed shook his head. "Wait a minute. They didn't succeed."

"What! What do you mean?" Cori asked.

"I can't say much more, but the Krauts don't have crap," Ed said. "Look, I don't know what happened, but the crazy doctor's injection didn't work, on Paul or on me. He gave the wrong date and place and I confirmed it."

"You must thank the three of us for that!" exclaimed Sacha. His two compatriots let out a whoop and his face broke into a self-satisfied grin.

"So, you knew it was wrong, Major," Phil asked Ed.

"Of course," he replied, "and, I can tell you, it may come sooner. Much sooner."

"Bloody hell!" Phil said. "Paul did let it slip a bit. He was about to warn me I would never make it back in time for my mission. Which means …"

"Mon dieu!" Cori grabbed Phil's arm as she came to a realization. "The poem. We await the second verse every day, but the Germans wait for it also. Remember, Schellenberg talked about it, so they must know. If it comes very soon …"

Ed finished the gloomy thought, "They'll know Paul and I lied and all hell will break loose. He and Sir Harold could die."

"And so we must rescue them immediately, *n'est-ce pas*?" Sacha concluded as, with grim determination, he floored the gas pedal.

The Velon-du Lac Mansion, Paris

Schellenberg was mid-way through a second Genevieve du Lac film, when the lovely actress made an appearance in person. She opened the library door and the light behind her outlined her seductive body beneath the layers of the diaphanous material she wore. Jean-Paul turned up the lights, and the *oberführer* stood to greet the vision in dusty rose.

"Ah, General, I am so sorry to have kept you waiting. One must get her beauty rest you know and yesterday was long and trying for me." She walked to him and presented her hand, which he kissed. "My parties are most amusing, but the preparation does take much out of me." She winked at him. "I hope you enjoyed your evening."

"Dear Genevieve, it was wonderful, and I must say, your respite has rejuvenated you."

She smiled and eyed the projector. "I see you have been watching me in my absence."

"Your films are most entertaining."

"Well, since you now have the real person, what would you like to do with her?"

He cleared his throat, certain he was blushing. "I really couldn't say." Schellenberg thought for a moment. "I have been to Paris before, but I have never really seen it. Perhaps …"

"It is a bit early." She put her finger to her chin. "Of course, we could visit the usual places—the *Arc*, the *Torre Eiffel*, the *Champs-Élysées*, but it is so much more exciting after dark. *Wouldn't you agree, Jean-Paul?*" she called to the butler who was busy arranging film reels and preparing to stow the camera. She often tried to catch him off guard, but rarely succeeded.

"As you say, Madame, much grander at night," Jean-Paul answered without looking up.

"So," she stroked Schellenberg's face, "I propose this. We stay here until dark and enjoy each other's company. I have asked the chef to prepare a light meal for the garden. Then, I can take you on a tour of my home. We have many works of art, as well as fine architectural features."

His smile concealed the vision of exploring her fine architectural features in the bedroom. "It sounds delightful."

"Good, I suppose you need a break from your duties, and I will do what I can to provide a fitting respite." She looked about. "By the way, what did you do with your heroic inspector? He appeared to need some diversion also."

"I left him at the local office. His idea of a good time is doing the work of the *Gestapo*. Some people never understand how to enjoy the finer things of life."

She slid her arm under his, and led him to the door. Her touch and alluring scent completely disarmed the smitten *oberführer*. Someone might have warned Schellenberg that, while her feminine appeal in a movie was enchanting, off the screen, it could be devastating.

SHAEF Advance

Kay Summersby and Harry Butcher sat at a table in the mess tent. She was drinking tea, while he had coffee in front of him and was puffing on a cigar. "So, how do you think he's getting on?" she asked.

He played nervously with his spoon. "I don't know, Ike's a strong guy, but I can see the pressure taking its toll lately. Today has been the worst of it. On top of all the worries about the invasion, he had to host De Gaulle."

"I understand the scene was glum, with the Frenchman refusing to do the broadcast."

"The Frog even had the nerve to criticize the general's planned address to the troops," Butcher told her. "I was with them when it all happened. Then, when we went to the War Room, Ike showed him the maps and talked about invading Calais."

"So, De Gaulle is still in the dark."

"Even so, he questioned the boss about tactics and pushed for more involvement of the Free French. That's when I politely left."

"I also heard Churchill had lunch with De Gaulle earlier, and got nowhere," Kay said. "I would love to have seen their little *tête-à-tête*. The clash of two giant egos."

"Yeah, but although the PM is tough, you can reason with him," Butcher said, rising. "In the meantime, I'd better get back into the fray. How about a little bridge later?"

She put on her military cap. "Maybe we can get the boss to relax."

"I doubt it. His schedule is maddening. He wanted to go to the embarkation points this morning. I had all the passes arranged, but something came up, and it never worked out."

Kay looked up wistfully and sighed. "He hasn't got time for anything, anymore."

As they agreed to catch up later, rain began pounding the tent canvas. The hidden enemy seemed relentless.

Resistance Location, La Roche-Guyon

Chev and Achille sat at a table with the ritual bottle of wine and two partially filled glasses, examining an old map of the village. Tracing a path from the church next to the *château* up the mountain to the tower holding Paul and Sir Harold, Chev suggested an ancient tunnel as their best hope. *"Of course,"* he added, *"it may be a problem if the Germans found it when they built the bunker; otherwise, it provides good access."*

Achille was about to ask if they would exit the same way when a radio operator interrupted and told them Sacha was calling from the unit in Nancy.

They raced to the radio room, and Chev grabbed the microphone. *"Sacha, give me good news."*

"We could not wait." The big man's voice crackled in the speaker. *"We had to move quickly and have rescued the woman and the American. But there is something you should know. The American major has told us the Germans were fed the wrong information and the true invasion date could come very soon."*

"But the second line of the poem has not been heard yet," Achille reminded him.

"That's just it!" Sacha shouted. *"The Germans know the signal. As soon as it is broadcast, they will realize they were lied to."*

Achille drew a finger across his neck, *"It will be over for our friends."*

Chev asked excitedly, *"When will you arrive? I need you here."*

There was a pause before Sacha responded. *"From here, it is usually over five hours. We will do better and fly like the wind."*

"Can you make it before tonight's Radio Londres broadcast?"

"It will be close."

"Good luck, my friend."

As the call ended, Achille asked to contact the Velon-du Lac mansion.

The Velon-du Lac Mansion, Paris

The lothario general had a superb afternoon getting to know the French actress and her domain. They first toured the garden, with its diminutive version of the famous statuary of Versailles. However, as they walked a stone path, rain began to fall and the tour was moved indoors where they explored the mansion's halls, chambers, and artwork. With feigned interest, Schellenberg examined works of Dutch and Flemish painters, the early impressionists, and pieces of Renaissance art, all the while aching with a need to enjoy the finer points of the classic beauty at his side. Motivated by lust, he convinced her to extend the tour into her living quarters.

As they strolled a baroque hallway, they passed a sitting room and a study with shelves of books and a great wooden desk. The corridor ended at an anteroom off which there were four large bedrooms. Schellenberg looked around. "Let me guess which one is yours."

"Dear, Walter, this is far too easy. If you peer inside, you will see the guest rooms are full of covered furniture. As for this one ..." Her voice caught as she pointed to a closed door. "... this room belonged to Charles. It has not been used since his death." She bowed her head and sniffled. Schellenberg held her close and was stunned and delighted when she melted in his arms.

They kissed and she quickly backed away. "I am so sorry. Please forgive me. It was a weak moment."

The kiss had put Schellenberg well past the point of no return. He took her in his arms again and kissed her harder and deeper than the first time. She started to resist but let her defenses fall away as he scooped her up and carried the actress into the bedroom he knew had to be hers.

"Oh, please," she purred. "Please be gentle with me." It was a scene from one of her early films titled, *"La Victoire du Cœur,"* about a World War I heroine who allowed herself to be seduced for the sake of liberty.

She swooned on the soft, feather bed, one hand dramatically resting on her forehead as he pulled off his tunic and shirt. Not wanting the moment to pass, he left his trousers and boots on and lay down next her. He stroked the soft airy material of her dress and eased the top of it down to her waist. She let him lift her camisole over her head and smiled at his reaction to her perfect breasts. He became a child anticipating a favorite dessert.

The amorous general pulled her to him and entered nirvana when her hard nipples rubbed on his chest. She moaned as he rolled her on top of him and worked her dress down below her knees. Holding her above him, he hungrily tasted her nakedness. As he moved down to the silky softness of her abdomen, there came a tapping at the door.

"Madame, excuse me," Like a storm cloud, the butler's words drifted in and doused the moment with cold water. "I have a most urgent message."

Genevieve moved off of the general, slipped into the camisole, pulled up her dress and went to the door.

Jean-Paul whispered, *"Madame, according to Achille, they know what the Germans learned and there is no longer a need for you to pry it out of the general."*

With barely a pause, she gasped and exclaimed in English, "Oh, no! Not my sister. Oh, this is terrible." She closed the door and looked at the general. "Walter, I am so sorry, but I must leave immediately. My dear Antoinette has had a serious accident." He nodded, unable to speak or move thanks to the exquisite pain growing in his scrotum.

Jean-Paul was waiting for her as she went to the stairs. *"Madame, there is more to the message. He also said they want you to keep Herr Schellenberg here. They are concerned what could happen if the second line of 'Chanson d'automne' is broadcast tonight."*

"I must get away from him, at least for a little while. He fancies himself a great lover, when, in fact, he tests my acting skills."

Jean-Paul smiled. *"So, I am happy to have interrupted when I did. It was indeed urgent."*

"I know I could have gotten the German degenerate to talk, but you say my sacrifice would have been for naught." She stroked her hair and adjusted her dress. *"Now, I only want to go to the cellar and hide like a rat."*

"Perhaps you can allow him time to cool off before returning."

"Yes, and make it plausible to explain my sister's difficulty."

"May I remind you, Madame does not have a sister."

"What does it matter? He does not know it. I will go back and say the emergency is over."

Genevieve waited almost ten minutes before returning to her bedroom. When she got there, she found General Schellenberg hugging a pillow and snoring loudly. His pants and boots were off and there was a sticky, wet mess next to him.

"Well, that takes care of that. He didn't wait for me." She shivered at the sight of the stain and curled up in a boudoir chair.

Regent's Park Road, London

When the doorbell rang, Emily was at her piano crying as she played a piece called "Melancholy" by Edvard Grieg. At first she thought it might be Paul, but her momentary joy vanished when she opened the door to find Jimmy. The lad said his mother had sent him over with the two shillings for his last lesson which, captivated by the treat Emily had prepared, he had forgotten to give her.

"Have you been crying, Miss Crowley?" he asked.

"It's just the piece I've been playing," she told him. "It's called 'Melancholy.' Someday you may wish to play it."

"What's a melancholy?" he wanted to know.

"It's a feeling of loneliness—of emptiness, like when you miss someone or something."

"Like when I miss my dad. Is that the way you feel, Miss Crowley?"

His innocence made her want to cry again. "Yes, Jimmy, I suppose I do, and I'm glad you're here to help me chase it away. Come over to the piano and let's play a happy song. How about 'Chopsticks?'"

"That's a happy song, for sure," he said as he slid onto the piano bench beside her.

And sure enough, the melancholy did go away, at least for a time.

Château de La Roche-Guyon

Paul and Sir Harold passed the time playing a game of pick-up with the wooden matches. One of them would dump the fire sticks into a small pile and the other had to remove them, one at a time, without disturbing any of the others. Sir Harold decided it was an opportune time to bring up something that had been on his mind since visiting Speidel.

"I say, old man," he asked, "are you ever going to tell what you saw down in the general's office?"

"Oh, that." Paul worked at removing one of the top match sticks. "Not saying a bleedin' word about it is me motto."

The MI6 man pressed the issue. "Look, shouldn't it be better to have two of us with it? Greater odds we'd get it back to where it will do some good."

"Here, I wouldn't know what to tell you if I wanted to. I have a picture in me head, is all. I don't know what any of it means now, do I. It ain't like a book or news article. There was some Jerry words, but mostly symbols."

"If you had a map, maybe you could …"

The door lock clicked and two guards they had not seen before entered carrying wooden trays of food. One of them pushed the matches aside to make room and set down plates of potatoes, slices of some kind of roasted meat, a green vegetable resembling spinach, chunks of bread, and a glass of white wine for each of them. There was even decent flatware.

"*Guten Appetit!*" said one of the soldiers as they left and locked the door after them.

"The condemned eat a hardy meal," quipped Sir Harold. "This tells us they can't be on to us yet."

"Or they might be doing us like Hansel and Gretel, tryin' to fatten us up," Paul suggested. "If they'd brought us a flipping steak knife now, maybe we could get the bloody hell out of here."

"Eat up, man," Sir Harold told him. "It'll be dark in a few hours. Then we'll have our chance." He didn't bother to add how slim he believed that chance might be.

Resistance Location, La Roche-Guyon

Chev sat at the console next to the radio to which the operator was listening intently, having tuned the set as he had done on so many previous nights. Achille stopped pacing when the announcer began, "*Ici Londres. Before we begin, kindly listen first to a few personal messages. The dog has caught the cat. The voices of the night make my heart sing. Jean-Luc is no longer in love with Marie. It is hot in the Suez. We say twice. It is hot in the Suez.*" And so it went. There were dozens of seemingly mundane, sometimes poetic, often nonsensical phrases. Most of them were insignificant, but some held special meanings for resistance fighters within range of the broadcast signal. An important few prescribed specific acts of sabotage.

As the announcer droned on, a familiar voice sounded in the hallway, and Sacha could be heard proclaiming, "*Chev, we are here!*"

As tales were told and bottles uncorked, Achille came with the news that the poem had not been announced.

Chev raised his glass. "I now celebrate the heroes and the ones they rescued," he said in English, mindful that Ed did not speak French.

"I must add my gratitude because now we have time to save the others," Achille added.

Sacha took a swallow and asked, "The operation is ready, yes?"

"It is, my friend," Chev replied, positioning himself next to a hand-drawn map of the *château*, the tower, the nearby church, and a roadway behind the tower leading to the river.

"The bell tower of the church is our best vantage point," he told them. "From there, we observe the enemy, as we did earlier. We can also see the *château* tower and, with luck, we are able to signal the prisoners from there. It will be a great help if they can know the plan as well. Even if we cannot contact them, we will proceed. Darkness is our friend, and we must succeed tonight or risk having the message come tomorrow."

Phil, Cori, and Ed had been quietly getting over the chaos of the past six hours and preparing for the challenge ahead, when Ed spoke up. "Speaking of messages, I need to contact my general and fill him in."

"Sadly," Chev responded, "as of now, nothing gets through to England. But we can try, just the same. Come with me."

Gestapo Headquarters, Paris

"So, Gerhard, you think the oberführer has a certain interest in our famous movie star?" Jung asked Lehrer as they both sat on fine leather enjoying Napoleon brandy in the chief inspector's lair.

"Interest! The man is absolutely besotted. As we have seen, he spends all his free time with her. He is likely there now." Lehrer took a swallow and cradled the snifter in his hands. *"I must admit, she is charming. I, myself, have watched many of her films."* He took another sip. *"You know, for a time we suspected her of being a Jewess."*

"Really," Lehrer responded with raised brows.

Jung continued, *"She was cleared, but I would have enjoyed interrogating such a fine piece of ass."*

Lehrer chortled, *"I suspect the supply of Jew women for such purposes has dwindled quite ..."*

The thought went unfinished when an agent appeared at the door holding a paper in his hand.

"Come, come." Jung waved him in and reached for the paper. *"What is this?"*

"It is for Herr Lehrer." He handed it to the other man. *"The information you have been awaiting, sir."* The agent did a casual about-face and left.

As Lehrer read the copy, Jung asked, *"What is so important?"*

"I requested some additional background information on the postman," Lehrer told him. *"Our agent Thor, who knows him very well, has finally responded. As always, the Enigma process takes time."*

"So, why did you ask for this? Is the episode not finished?"

"After the interrogation, I considered whether this Eisenhower was himself an operative. It was too convenient to me the way we suddenly were provided the invasion information. Now it seems Thor has sent an extensive commentary on him, and there is no indication he is other than what he claims to be. The only detail of any note is his ability for total recall."

"Such an ability would be a problem only if he had access to any of our classified documents," Jung observed.

Lehrer put down the paper. *"And then only if he got the information back to England. As of now, he and the MI6 agent languish in the château dungeon. Besides, he never saw anything more important than the interiors of the clinic, the hallways, and the tower."*

"In that case, Prost!" his companion said, raising his glass.

SHAEF Headquarters

General Bill Terry had just returned from SHAEF Advance aiming to clear up some routine paperwork when Sergeant Dave Goodson, one of the men Terry referred to as a "ball-bearing secretary," caught up with him in the break room to tell him of an urgent call on the scrambler.

"This is Captain Phelps, Enigma liaison," he was told when he answered the phone. "We just got word from Bletchley Park. They intercepted a strange signal going to the *Gestapo* in Paris. It gives background on Eisenhower and says he's a postman who apparently has a photographic memory. Are they talking about Ike?"

"No, Phelps, but it is interesting news. Send me a typed copy, pronto."

Hanging up, Terry rubbed his chin speculatively. So the postman had jumped into the mix again. Now the only question was, did the Nazis have him or are they still looking. The answer to that one was important and he wished to hell Bradford would check in.

Southwick House, Portsmouth

General Eisenhower and his team assembled for yet another weather briefing, at which Group Captain Stagg was finally able to present a promising forecast. Based on a consensus, he reported that a high-pressure system and an atypical June cold front would bring a period of reasonable weather for air and sea operations. British air marshals Leigh-Mallory and Tedder debated whether they could go forward, whereas Admiral Ramsay was in favor of pressing on with naval operations since not doing so would cause a two-week delay and myriad unforeseeable problems. Montgomery also supported proceeding, as did Beetle Smith, who rated their chances as better than average. Weighing all of it, Ike concluded the order should be given for the invasion to begin on 6 June. Still leery of the hidden enemy, he scheduled a final decision meeting for early the next morning.

Église Saint-Samson, La Roche-Guyon

It was nearing dusk when Chev and Phil returned to the bell tower carrying a battery operated signal lantern and binoculars. Once they reached the top, they pulled field glasses from their cases and scanned the looming dungeon section by section. Chev concluded, *"No activity. In a while, we shall attempt contact."*

"Are we even certain they're up there?" asked the lieutenant.

The Frenchman looked up at the heavy clouds overhead. *"The dark approaches. We will soon know."*

Their watch continued for another forty minutes and then they saw it. A faint glow moved past a window, spawned a second glow, and faded out, leaving only the one.

"Someone lit a candle," said Phil. *"It must be them."*

"Now, they need to see us." Chev handed the lantern to Phil. *"Something simple in your language."*

Having learned Morse code as part of his Army training, the lieutenant flashed two long, two short, a long, and four short, the code for MI6, and he did it over and over.

He nudged Chev, who was looking through his glasses. *"Anything?"*

"Nothing yet. Keep going and pray they see it."

"And this battery holds up."

"Do not worry," Chev told him. *"It is new and good for many ... Wait! The candle moved. It is at the window! Contact made! Now this is the message I want you to send."*

Sir Harold held the candle in the cell window and passed his hand before it, responding to the code coming from the church tower.

When he paused, Paul asked, "What are they saying, Guv?"

"It seems they are coming for us later tonight. We are to be ready to move out sometime after midnight." He replaced the candle in a sconce and joined Paul at the table.

The postman still had doubts. "The Jerries will have a thing or two to say about it, won't they."

Sir Harold banged his fist on the table. "Jerry be damned! This has to work or I'm afraid this may be our final resting place."

Sacha and his men, along with Cori, Achille, and Ed were gathered in the church vestibule when Chev and Phil returned to announce they had contacted Harold and Paul. Amid the ensuing moment of celebration, Father Flambeau, an intense man with white hair, mournful eyes, and blotchy skin, approached from a side aisle. Greeting Chev by name, he beckoned to the group, *"Follow me."*

"Wait," insisted Sacha, *"We have other business."* He and his men picked up their rucksacks. *"We must go now."*

"Not yet." Chev stopped him and turned to the others, "Everyone, give them your guns. We have no need for them and shooting will bring the Germans. Besides, for the climb, they will only get in our way. Knives, if we must. We will not be returning this way, it is too dangerous. You will get your weapons back later, up on top."

Phil eyed the bulky sack Achille was carrying. The Parisian held it up and explained, *"Implements for the escape, oui?"*

The lieutenant nodded and added his German handgun to the weapons collection being bagged by Sacha and company. With a wish of good luck, the three men and their sacks left the church.

Father Flambeau led the others to the sacristy off the main altar. He pulled a thick candle from its brass and gold holder, lit it, and produced a key from his cassock. Opening an oak cabinet door, he quickly removed two shelves and a dark back panel. Behind it was a meter-square hole which, when he poked his candle inside, revealed a dusty, spider-webbed crawl space.

"It leads up to the tower," the priest explained. *"It was once used for escape from the dungeon. Fortunate for you, it works in this direction, also."* His unexpected witticism eased the tension of the moment.

"Come, I will show you." He held the candle before him and entered the hole.

The group crept almost twenty meters before the tunnel grew into a space large enough for them to stand. The open area could not have come soon enough for Ed Bradford, who felt his world closing in on him during the initial crawl. They then proceeded up a long, winding ramp with ruts that sufficed for steps until finally they reached a chimney like shaft with a weatherworn wooden ladder that rose into darkness. Water dripped from the opening, forming a small stalagmite on the cavern floor.

Father Flambeau caught his breath and pointed up the shaft. *"One final climb and you will be there."*

Chev checked his watch. "We must wait for a time. The guards patrol the base of the dungeon until midnight. After, they do not return until four in the morning. Please, rest now. Our friends know when to expect us."

"I must go now," said the priest, *"but you are very close, and I am certain you will succeed."* He blessed them with the sign of the cross, *"May God be with you."*

As Father Flambeau went back down the rutted tunnel, the light from his candle grew faint and finally disappeared.

The Dungeon
Château de La Roche-Guyon

Sir Harold was lying on his cot, awake with his eyes closed, as his cellmate paced nervously. "Damn it. Sit down old boy! You'll wear yourself out."

Paul stopped and put his hands on his hips. "Here, it ain't every day this happens to a bloke like me, is it. I'm bloody sick of being captured and rescued, and running, and hiding, and being stuck with needles. Who knows, maybe even poisoned." He burped. "I feel I need to …"

"Now that'll be quite enough!" The MI6 man warned as he sat up. "The food was perfectly fine."

The postman wasn't done. "I didn't ask for a bit of it."

"You did the minute you read the plan." Sir Harold reminded him.

"Hah! It wasn't that, at all. It was when the lieutenant knocked me off me bike and on me arse. That's how I came upon the bloody thing in the first place."

"Paul," Harold said in a calm, low voice, "that isn't exactly what happened. The Yank major doesn't say much, but he knows the whole story. He was there when it took place and told me how it all began when a breeze sent the plans flying from a War Office window. Apparently one got mixed in with your post."

"Not me post, some Home Guard papers I was doing a favor picking up. Hah! A good turn, like hell." He paused to consider his cellmate's words. "So, in truth, Phil had nothing to do with it at all, did he."

"Correct. If anyone shouldn't be caught up in this mess, he's the one."

The Home of Professor Folkstein
La Roche-Guyon, France

The doctor's day had begun with a successful interrogation using one of his favorite drugs, but it rapidly deteriorated afterward. He had established his practice as an expatriate in the 1930s and, although he preferred working in the lab with animals, the clinic was his main source of income. Most days were humdrum, but this one had become especially annoying. There were the doting mothers with their runny nosed kids contaminating his sanitary facility with their snot and screams. As annoying were the whining hypochondriacs who demanded his attention. The few truly sick patients who came were readily diagnosed and sent off with appropriate drugs or prescriptions, but the others were bothersome for a multitude of reasons. Worst of the bunch was the obese woman who insisted she had a goiter when it was nothing more than her own ugly fat. When his nurse went home ill just after noon, the ensuing mayhem caused him to abandon his public persona as a calm, medical professional. He abruptly performed a version of triage and sent those with unthreatening and imagined illnesses home.

Visions of the previous sixteen hours swam in his brain when he laid his head on the pillow, as he did every night at precisely 10:00 p.m., only to enter a terrible cycle of tossing about, fluffing his pillow, and changing positions dozens of times over. Sleep never happened, and when the wall clock told him it was 11:45, he knew the night would get no better unless he did something to help himself. He went for his black bag and injected himself with the same barbiturate he had used on the prisoners earlier in the day.

Seconds passed, then minutes, but nothing happened. Absolutely nothing! More agitated than ever, he picked up the hypodermic needle, squeezed a drop of the remaining liquid onto his finger, and tasted it.

"Water! This is what I gave them? Plain water?"

Red faced and trembling, the doctor went to make the call he knew he must make.

Gestapo Headquarters, Paris

Having finally given up on seeing the *oberführer* any time soon, Inspector Lehrer was asleep on Jung's leather sofa when one of the night shift agents shook him awake. Professor Folkstein from LaRoche-Guyon was calling.

"He said it is most important that he speak with you or the oberführer." He continued, *"And Oberführer Schellenberg has not yet returned."* The agent pointed to a phone. *"You may take the call there."*

Lehrer picked up the receiver and got an earful from the doctor. The inspector reeled as the ramifications of Folkstein's words sunk in. By now, the entire *Reich*, including the *Führer* himself, had been told the invasion would come on 13 June at the Pas de Calais. *"So, the information may have had no validity at all, as it originated with two Allied swine, neither of whom had been under the effects of the drug,"* he said, grim faced. *"Speak to no one about this. Obtain a supply of the proper serum and wait at home to be picked up. Mein Gott! I must find Schellenberg!"*

Paris by Night

Genevieve du Lac had used her celebrity status to arrange a gay evening in the City of Lights. Her plan was to detain the amorous German general as long as she could while keeping the oversexed bastard out of her boudoir.

Earlier, they had visited the usual tourist attractions, including the Eiffel Tower, where they enjoyed cocktails and the view, and later motored around the *Arc de Triomphe*. Jean-Paul had taken over as chauffer of her 1937 Velon 900 limousine in order to watch over the actress and help her fend off the general's advances. He next drove them to *Le Moulin Rouge* in the Montmartre district. The Germans had taken ownership of the famous nightspot just after they occupied Paris, and Schellenberg was treated most deferentially when he and the actress arrived. From a table close to the stage, Schellenberg ogled the girls as they did their risqué dances.

Madame du Lac was relieved that, for the moment, his lust was not directed at her. She sipped her drink one last time and suggested they leave. From the look on Schellenberg's face, she was certain he was imagining a return to her bedroom. He made a show of ushering her out then led her to the limousine where Jean-Paul hovered. The butler held the door for them, but before they could enter, a car pulled alongside.

Lehrer stuck his head out the driver's side window. *"Herr Oberführer, at last. Please, I must speak with you."*

The general stepped close to the *Gestapo* vehicle and the inspector gave an intense and not-so-private recital of the events of the past two hours. *"Herr Oberführer, I believe we must return to Rommel's château immediately."*

Schellenberg, torn between duty and sexual conquest, reluctantly agreed and offered Madame du Lac unctuous apologies before driving off with the inspector.

As the *Gestapo* car raced along the streets of Paris on the way to La Roche-Guyon, the *oberführer* told Lehrer, *"I believe we can rectify the mistake before morning and undo the damage by obtaining the correct information from the postman."*

"Thank God he is still in custody," the inspector said. *"We might have had him killed, thinking he would be of no further use to us."*

"The professor, we shall pick him up and ensure he has the correct drug."

"Yes, sir. There will be no further mistakes."

Recalling the fate of Admiral Canaris when he gave the *Führer* bad intelligence, Schellenberg nodded as he sat forward, elbows on knees. *"So, possibly, the postman was actually an agent working with the Jackdaw. How could we have missed it?"*

"Herr Oberführer, I had similar doubts so I contacted Thor in an effort to discover the truth. Having known Eisenhower for years, he assured me he is truly a postman who lives the life of a dormouse. The man's only attribute of any note is his memory. He apparently can recall anything he reads."

"So," Schellenberg concluded. *"He deliberately lied to us but the true facts are in his head, and we will make certain that this time he shares them with us."*

Chapter Nine
Monday, 5 June 1944

Château de La Roche-Guyon

Just after midnight, the rescuers went over the next phase of their plan. Chev, Phil and Cori would free Harold and Paul from the cell, Ed was to be responsible for watching for any signs of enemy activity, and Achille would deploy the rope ladder over the back wall of the tower down to the bushes below.

Chev climbed up the shaft first, pushing open the grate at the top, and crawling into a dark niche next to the stairway that led to the tower door. He confirmed the absence of guards before signaling the rest of the team.

They gathered in a terrace at the base of the tower where Ed found a vantage point from which he could observe both the steps and the yard below. At the same time, Achille went to the rear wall and searched for anchor points for the ladder.

Meanwhile, Cori slowly opened the tower door and moved like a cat up the steps to the cell door. She emerged a short time later and informed Phil and Chev of a single guard who appeared to be dozing.

When Chev instructed her to stay behind and relay any alerts from Ed, while he and Phil took out the guard, she protested. *"Why? Is it because I am a female, you do not believe I can handle that pig?"*

Phil tried to reason with her, *"Not at all, my love. Three of us are too many for the task, and we need someone here if Jerry shows up. Chev and I will use our knives."*

Cori pulled a long blade from its sheath. *"I have one as well. You stay and I shall go."*

Chev sighed and directed Phil, *"You stand watch, and she can come with me. It seems this is a matter of honor."*

Cori led as they crept up to the landing where the guard was seated, his feet up on a second chair and his chin on his chest. Flattening herself against the wall, she eased closer to the German, only to misstep, sending loose shards rattling down the stairs.

Waking with a start, the guard leaped to his feet and raised his rifle, but before he could pull the trigger, the handle of Chev's dagger popped out of his chest. Gasping, the German fell to the floor, spitting blood as he went down.

Going to her knees, Cori dug through the dead man's uniform and came up with an iron key with which Chev opened the door to find Paul and Sir Harold waiting.

When the foursome got to the terrace, there was a moment of silent celebration before they descended the ladder and joined Sacha. Once the group assembled, they walked in the semi darkness through trees and bushes to a dirt path and ultimately to a larger *route des crètes*, or ridge road, where Sacha's men were waiting beside two vehicles—the big Peugeot from the earlier rescue, and a smaller Citroen. One car would return to Paris and the other would head for *Le Havre* where a trawler would take the four allies back to England.

Phil had different plans. Certain it was too late for him to arrive in time for his mission, and wanting to spend more time with Cori, he volunteered to stay in France. Chev agreed and Sir Harold said he would so notify the lieutenant's commander.

When Sacha's men redistributed the sack of weapons, Paul accepted a small handgun, frowned, and quickly jammed it into his inside jacket pocket. After a sad but hope-filled parting, Sir Harold, Major Bradford, and Paul accompanied Chev and Sacha to the Peugeot while Phil and Cori joined Achille at the Citroen. Sacha's compatriots watched in silence as, with their lights off, the cars drove away in opposite directions.

The Courtyard of Château de La Roche-Guyon

Inspector Lehrer drove the staff car carrying General Schellenberg and Professor Folkstein into the courtyard. The doctor sat next to the inspector, bag in lap, doing his best to avoid any contact with the *oberführer* he had so deeply disappointed. When they pulled up at the side entrance, the general bolted from the sedan, rushed up the steps past the guard, and into the foyer. The place was eerily quiet, and by the time Lehrer and Folkstein

234   Augustine Campana & Marco Di Tillo

got there, Schellenberg was demanding that the prisoner Eisenhower be brought to him immediately.

"*But sir,*" the young duty officer paled, "*we have strict orders not to disturb him or the other man. General Speidel made it clear we are to treat them as guests.*"

"*Guests! They are enemies of the Reich! Get him at once.*"

"*But Herr Oberführer, General Speidel said …*"

Schellenberg picked up the phone. "*Shall we awaken him and see what he has to say?*"

"*Sir, the general just turned in for the night. There was a late dinner party.*"

Schellenberg waved the phone at him. "*Your choice. Either get the prisoner and take him to the clinic or I wake Speidel.*"

The officer rushed off and Schellenberg chortled, "*Hah! He finally recognized the urgency of the matter!*" His face hardened. "*And this time, Herr Professor, there is no room for failure.*"

Sacha had driven no more than four kilometers when the *château's* klaxons sounded in the distance behind them, and looking back, they saw the tower bathed in light.

"A bloody air raid is it?" asked Paul.

"Damn it all!" Sir Harold groused. "I believe they are onto us."

Chev shook his head in disgust. "I had hoped your disappearance would not be detected until the guard changed at four. Now, the river is our best bet."

"A boat waits ten kilometers away," Sacha said, urging the car up to speed. "We must get there before they block the way."

The bunker was a scene of turmoil, with armed soldiers rushing from their quarters and pouring out into the courtyard where trucks and *Kübelwagens* were assembling. The open vehicles had their canvas tops deployed against the rain that had begun falling.

Inside the *château*, Schellenberg ordered Lehrer to pull the car around then addressed the doctor. "*Folkstein, stay available. I want to grill that British son-of-a-bitch, Eisenhower, as soon as we catch him.*"

"What the hell is happening, Schellenberg?" Major General Speidel demanded when he arrived.

"Sir, the prisoners have escaped. It appears they had help, and went out behind the tower."

"So, why all this urgency? Why order a full alert, when they are of little value to us any more? You got the information you wanted, did you not?"

"I regret to say, it was probably incorrect, sir," the oberführer replied. "The serum the doctor used was ineffective. We must assume the postman and the American major lied about the invasion coming at Calais on the thirteenth."

Speidel went to his office and Schellenberg followed. "You are causing all this for an assumption? I had the postman here for a conversation after you left. He seemed harmless. Also, wasn't the information verified by the American major?"

"It is quite possible Eisenhower was sly enough to distort his answer. The major could simply have followed his lead."

"I see." Finally satisfied there was some cause for alarm, Speidel opened his wall map panel and ran his finger from Paris to Le Havre. "The logical escape route would be to the port."

The level of Schellenberg's alarm doubled. "Herr General, Eisenhower did not have a chance to see this, did he?" he asked.

"I closed it as he and the MI6 man entered. Maybe for the slightest instant. Why do you ask?"

"Oh, no reason. I was simply curious."

Speidel fumed uncharacteristically, "Schellenberg! Is there something you are not telling me? Perhaps I should alert Rommel."

"We can avoid disturbing him if we capture the postman quickly."

The major general waved him away. "Then go! You may use whatever Army B resources necessary."

The oberführer immediately commandeered two of Rommel's Horch vehicles, one similar to the generalfeldmarschall's staff car for himself and the doctor, and the other a troop transport, complete with six armed soldiers.

"I want you to make certain they have not taken the route to Paris," he told Lehrer. "Do it yourself. Take a detail if you must! But hurry!"

He ordered the entourage on and turned to Folkstein. "Well, Herr Professor, do you see what you and your incompetence have caused?"

"It was the chemist, sir," Folkstein said, cowering in the seat beside him. "He made the mistake. This time, I mixed the formula myself."

"You had better pray we have the opportunity to use it, or your future is very uncertain, indeed," the general warned. He called to the driver, "Follow *the Seine along the route to Le Havre. My instincts tell me they will attempt an escape by boat. And sergeant, get me the local Gestapo on the radio at once!"*

Near Vernon, France

Sacha navigated the big car past the towers of the *Château des Tourelles,* a ruined castle from the era of Richard the Lionheart, and up to a wharf where a dozen sail and motor boats bobbed and sloshed. Chev leapt out and spoke with a short, fat man wearing a dark outfit and a red fisherman's cap. After a moment, he waved the others on to a small cabin cruiser and introduced them to the chubby man, Poupin, the captain of the vessel they would take to Le Havre and one step closer to home.

"Welcome aboard *Le Pégase.* Please, make yourself at ease, yes?" said the captain.

As they boarded, Chev said his goodbyes, promising to inform the contact in *Le Havre* of the change of plans. As he left, Sacha arrived from the Peugeot carrying two large rucksacks.

They found the boat surprisingly comfortable, with plenty of seats, a small galley, a toilet, and, of course, a table where they could play cards, smoke, and drink wine.

"The engine is more than *deux cent chevaux*—two hundred horsepower," announced Poupin proudly. "It will get us there with great swiftness."

"Can't be fast enough for me," cracked Paul.

The engine roared to life and the craft eased out of its slip as Poupin called down from the wheelhouse, "With the current, we make forty-five or fifty knots."

"Easy," Sacha cautioned, *"we do not want to attract attention. Go slow and stay safe. An hour more will not matter. Our only goal now is to get them there safely."*

"Oui, mon commandant! It is a large goal indeed."

The Road to Paris

Meanwhile, the trio in the Citroen driven by Achille was well on its way to its destination when they detected faint lights behind them. Phil, easing himself out of Cori's embrace, recognized the German vehicles. *"Something must have gone wrong!"* he shouted.

Achille purposely slowed and let the *Gestapo* staff car and the *Kübelwagen* behind it pass. The pressure seemed to be off until, excitedly, Cori told them she had recognized the inspector from Laon.

"If they had stopped us, he would surely have known me," she said.

"We have no choice but to go on," observed Achille. "For the moment, we are safe."

Ten minutes later, everything changed when lights ahead signaled trouble. They stopped well back from the vehicles blocking the road and could see the Laon inspector standing by his car. One of the four soldiers lined up in front of the *Kübelwagen* came forward and beckoned the Citroen closer, but Achille held it at the edge of the light from lanterns aimed at them. Cori quietly distributed weapons from the rucksack.

"I have him," whispered Achille, indicating the closest soldier. "*Corinne, the inspector is yours. Lieutenant, you take out the others by the truck. On my signal.*" Once they were out of the car, he shouted, "*Ça va!*"

The German corporal was no closer than ten meters away when Achille riddled him with bullets. Phil and Cori dove away from the Citroen as return fire tore into its windows and open doors. Phil's machine gun quickly cut down the three other soldiers, and Achille moved from his original target to the inspector whom he brought down with a single round. Because all but one of the lanterns had been shot out, it was too dark to tell for sure, but a deathly silence said the job was done. Achille and Phil returned to the car, but where was Cori?

Anxiously, Phil ran for the last functioning lantern and cast its light along the pavement where he discovered his beloved lying in a pool of blood. She was still alive but her body had been ravaged by bullets.

"Oh, my Cori, please. Oh, God!"

He lifted her into the car and Achille produced a kit containing medical supplies. As the bullet-ridden Citroen sped away, Phil tried to stem Cori's bleeding and he kept reassuring her that she was going to be okay. Yet, doubting his own words, he prayed for divine intervention.

The Road to Le Havre

The rain had stopped and Schellenberg ordered the Horch's canvas top rolled back. Imitating a famous photo of Rommel, he stood, raised the field glasses that hung around his neck, and swept the Seine for boat traffic as the car rolled parallel with the river at a moderate pace. With two hours to go before daylight, all he could make out were occasional red and green lights, dim interior glows, and the indistinct outlines of vessels moving on the river. Deciding the surveillance was fruitless, he ordered the driver to go directly to Le Havre.

Southwick House, Portsmouth

It was 0400 on 5 June when the SHAEF staff reassembled in the library meeting room. The weather conditions had been terrible when General Eisenhower awoke to prepare for what could be his most important decision related to Operation Overlord. Thanks to the driving rain, he and the others had arrived in wet overcoats and windbreakers that matched their dampened spirits. Montgomery was the exception. His signature sweater and beret were soaked, but his determination was far from wilted and he was fully in favor of charging ahead.

Stagg's latest information also supported the earlier "go" decision. In his final pronouncement, he declared conditions would improve and hold sufficiently well for the invasion.

After his staff gave their blessings to one degree or another, the room turned silent and all eyes fell on the supreme commander. At 0415, Eisenhower said simply, "Okay, we'll go," and D-Day was on. From that point forward, Ike became a very interested observer of the operation which had dominated his life for months. The excruciating detailed planning, and bulk of the calculated decision-making were over. As Churchill had correctly predicted, although Ike would be called upon for top-down guidance, implementation was in the hands of his chiefs and the thousands of subordinates down the chain of command to the ships complements, air crews, and the privates, corporals, sergeants, and officers who comprised the first line of battle—those who would go toe to toe with the enemy. Most of what remained for General Eisenhower to deal with was the worry.

The Velon-du Lac Mansion, Paris

The Citroen pulled into the courtyard where Madame du Lac and a trusted doctor awaited its arrival. Cori was carried to the living quarters and made comfortable in the hospital bed once used by Charles Velon.

At her bedside, Phil took her hand and felt a weak grip as she murmured, *"Philippe, my darling, I will always love you."*

"And I you, forever," he replied, kissing her cheek softly. *"Now, rest and the doctor will make you well."*

"Stay with me." She tried to reach up to touch his face, but her arm went limp and dropped to her chest as the morphine the nurse had administered took effect.

As Phil watched, the doctor saw to Cori's lower wound which appeared to be the most serious. He made a small incision and observed that a bullet had gone completely through her. Although his probing revealed no major organ damage, a further examination exposed an oozing gash in her abdominal aorta. The nurse carefully applied pressure to curtail the bleeding, but the vital artery was too far gone, and when the doctor tried to suture the damage, the aorta ruptured in a fountain of blood, splashing the doctor, the nurse, and Phil. Despite the medic's heroic attempts to staunch the flow, in seconds, life drained from the brave Frenchwoman.

When Phil felt Cori's hand go limp and saw the doctor shake his head, he covered his blood-smeared face with his hands and sobbed. Barely able to give her one last kiss, he slumped to the floor and stopped trying to hold back the torrent of tears.

"It is a terrible loss," Madame du Lac said, stroking his hair. *"You must love her always."*

"I'll get the bastards who did this," Phil said, his eyes fixed on Cori's lifeless body. *"I'll get them or die trying."*

Le Pégase

As dawn broke, Sacha and Poupin manned the wheelhouse, while Ed and Sir Harold watched as Paul transferred images from his memory to one of the captain's charts of the coastline of France, Belgium, the Netherlands and the waters of the English Channel. The postman put the finishing touches on a row of rectangles east of Calais, then drew a box and inked in the characters, "V-1."

Ed ignored his aching shoulder and peered at the map. "Holy crap, Paul, this is amazing G2. It's the kind of stuff men die to get their hands on."

Seeing the hundreds of boxes marked with Vs, Sir Harold exclaimed, "I say! Those all appear to be missile launch facilities! We know Hitler was preparing what he called his *'Vergeltungswaffen,'* his weapons of retaliation, but we had no idea there were this many sites."

"Here, alls I'm doing is me best to draw what I saw," Paul countered. "Besides, I thought you steered clear of such things."

"That's true regarding the invasion," the MI6 man replied. "But this is different. It has to do with defense." He looked closer. "See how many sites are annotated with the word *'gefälscht.'* It means those are dummies put in place to confuse our bombers. We must get this to the top brass immediately, before the invasion, if at all possible."

"Oy," Paul responded, "I'd say it all depends on the enemy out there, now doesn't it."

Sir Harold peered through his binoculars at the shoreline emerging in the growing light. "Blast it, nothing at all," he exclaimed. "It's all too bloody simple. This is Jerry we're up against. He should never have given up this readily. They are either pursuing us or preparing some sort of trap."

Ed chimed in, "According to the captain, at the speed we're going, they'd have plenty of time to set one."

"That's it, then!" Sir Harold said as he climbed up to the wheelhouse.

Interrupting a chat between Sacha and Poupin, he tugged the big partisan's sleeve. "Look, old man, I believe our pace will put us in grave danger when we reach Le Havre. If they're on to us, they'll have time to plan for our arrival."

"Then we must go fast," Sacha said matter-of-factly. *"Poupin, how long if we go at her top velocity?"*

The captain's response was immediate. *"Half the time. Maybe less."*

"Okay, do it," Sacha ordered as he raised his thick eyebrows at Harold. *"Et voila!"* he said as the engine pitch got louder and higher, the prow of the vessel rose, and the scenery began to move by in double time.

The question still gnawing at Sir Harold was, what were they rushing toward?

SHAEF Advance

After a few hours rest, General Eisenhower was ready to attack the day. He had already eaten breakfast and was in his command tent when Lieutenant Commander Butcher arrived carrying a satchel.

"All set, General. You're cleared to visit the South Parade Pier at Portsmouth. Brits are boarding LCIs there."

"Good going, Butch. How about our boys? I want to see as many of them off as I can."

"Yes, sir. We had talked about the hundred and first down at Newbury. I know the press is chomping at the bit to go along."

"It's to be expected." Eisenhower walked out of the tent and Butcher followed. "Is Kay ready with the car?"

His vivacious driver appeared from the other direction. She stopped and saluted. "All set, General."

Ike returned the salute and nudged Butcher. "Well, there's a ray of sunshine." He looked up at the gray clouds. "Now, if we can only get some of that up there."

The general's spirits were up considerably after having made the decision to proceed with Operation Overlord. It still deeply concerned him, but effectively, it was too late to turn back, and he knew the responsibility for the mission rested squarely with him. Ready to accept the full blame if it failed, he was prepared to accommodate the many who would step forward to claim victory when it succeeded.

As they climbed into the staff car, he stopped and reminded Kay, "I want to go by Ramsey's later to see how things are going there." Regarding the two of them, he added, "You know, I have to thank all of you—T.J., Tex, Mickey, and the fellas who keep me fed and clothed, and of course, you two for getting me through this. I know it wasn't easy for any of you, but it's done, at least for the time being. Now we'll just have to wait to see if this is another damn beginning to the war, or the beginning of the end for the enemy, but whatever happens, we've all done our best."

Regent's Park Road, London

Emily threw on her dressing gown and slippers, and hurried across the courtyard, her heart full of hope that "her Eisenhower" had somehow returned during the night. She let herself into the postman's flat and was greeted only by a sloppy nuzzle from Odette and the penetrating squawks of Old Frank.

"I'm off to the post office then," she told the animals. "They simply have to know something."

As she set about taking care of Paul's pets, she tried not to show them her tears.

The Seine at Le Havre

It was after eight in the morning when Poupin pulled back on the throttle, muting the engine roar and slowing his boat. He watched warily, knowing that, in less than ten minutes, they would move beyond the confines of the river and into the broad expanse of the Seine estuary. *"If there is a trap, it must close very soon,"* he told Sacha who had been concentrating on the river traffic which had increased since daybreak.

The chart with Paul's markings had been stowed and the table now held an assortment of weapons, including handguns, rifles, automatic weapons, and two bazooka rocket launchers. On the benches, canvas bags contained hand grenades and ammunition.

After checking the opposite shore of the river approximately one kilometer away, General Schellenberg barked into a walkie-talkie, *"The troops have not yet arrived. What is keeping them?"*

A gruff voice came back, *"The other unit is on its way, Herr Oberführer, but the boats should already be there, sir."*

As the general located the patrol boats with his field glasses, a sergeant called out, *"A suspicious craft approaches, sir!"*

Schellenberg looked up the river and observed a small cruiser with several men on deck, all watching the shoreline. Despite the distance, he thought he recognized one of them. "Jackdaw," he murmured.

"Signal the men, sergeant!" he shouted. *"I believe our quarry has arrived."* As the soldier got on the radio, the general added, *"They are not to harm the passengers. Shoot for the driver of the boat. The others are to be spared until we can sort them out."*

Bursts of machine gun fire tore a line of holes in the prow of *Le Pégase*, smashed the windshield, and struck Poupin's head, killing him instantly. Sacha ran to the cockpit and slammed the throttle as far forward as it would go, throwing the others aft in disarray. Crouching down, he held the wheel straight, knowing there was open water ahead.

Sir Harold recovered first and grabbed one of the bazookas. He loaded it, connected the ignition wiring, and aimed at the source of the gunfire on the left bank. The rocket hit low, but it rendered sufficient damage to gain them time to get past the point of greatest jeopardy. As the four patrol boats came after them, firing their weapons, he reloaded and put the lead boat in his sights. This time he was on target and the enemy craft was blown out of the water.

A driving rain and a constant hail of bullets splattered the deck as Ed joined Sir Harold and returned fire. Paul, repulsed at the thought of handling a weapon, scampered up to the wheelhouse where Sacha was steering with one hand and firing an automatic pistol with the other.

"Here, I'll take that!" Paul shouted, grabbing for the wheel and trying not to look at the bloody mess that had once been Poupin.

"Do you have it?" asked Sacha. Paul nodded and got a grip on the helm and his runaway terror.

As the three remaining patrol boats bore down on them they entered the estuary. Ed prepared the second bazooka and managed to aim it despite his shoulder. The blast hit the closest patrol boat low on the prow and set it afire. There followed a series of bright flashes amid black smoke before a huge explosion tore it to pieces. Some of its seamen could be seen escaping an instant before the craft blew and scattered debris and less fortunate crewmen high into the air. Sacha continued to fire automatic weapons at the remaining two pursuers, but the metal cladding of the enemy boats could not be penetrated and the bullets simply ricocheted off. It was Ed who fired another bazooka round and hit the cockpit of the third boat, causing it to spin crazily out of control before going dead in the water.

✯ ✯ ✯ ✯

"*Order the last boat back!*" Schellenberg barked to the sergeant. "*And have them pick me up there,*" he added, pointing to a dock about 200 meters away. "*The Englanders must not leave the harbor.*"

Jumping into his Horch, he found Folkstein cowering behind the front seat, gripping his medical bag.

"*I am protecting the serum, Herr General,*" he explained in a quavering voice.

Schellenberg shot him a contemptuous look and ordered the driver to head to the landing where he boarded the remaining patrol boat.

"*Tell the captain to go after them, but take measures to avoid their goddamned missiles,*" he commanded, steadying himself on the rain-slick deck. "*And remind him, I want the fugitives spared.*"

✯ ✯ ✯ ✯

"It appears we have escaped!" Sacha shouted as he surveyed the wreckage behind them.

"We aren't rid of them yet, lads," Sir Harold replied, pointing to the patrol boat leaving the pier. "Look there."

Ed asked, "Can this thing outrun those bastards?"

"She's all the way," Paul responded, jiggling the throttle, his face drenched with stinging rain. "Are they gaining on us?"

"I think not," Sir Harold shouted, "Just keep it steady as she goes, and you'll be fine."

"As she goes? I don't know where in bloody hell I'm going now, do I." "

Before long, we must head to starboard," Sacha told him. "To the right and into the harbor where a fishing trawler waits to take you across."

Suddenly, a stream of slugs tore a line of nasty holes in the port side of *Le Pégase* aft of amidships. The boat's powerful engine sputtered, whined, and died.

"Blast! I knew it was too good to be true," moaned Paul.

"Yet another 'ah shit' moment," observed Ed. "Give me those grenades, Sacha. They should do the trick. They're GI issue MK-2s."

He grabbed one of the bomblets. "When the Krauts get within forty or fifty yards, I'll lob a few of these babies. Just like my good old days on the gridiron. Follow my lead boys and aim for the windows, away from the armor."

Meanwhile, Paul kept trying to start the engine, but it was for naught.

The German boat was less than 100 meters out when Sacha and the MI6 man began firing. Ed remained out of sight until Sir Harold shouted, "Tally-ho!"

Ignoring the return fire, the major stood, pulled the pin, and sent the first grenade in a wobbly spiral toward its target. Before it landed, he quickly picked up another and threw it in the same direction. Both grenades found their mark and two glorious blasts tore into the German boat's cabin and wheelhouse. The gunfire ceased as the crew scattered and Ed sent two more perfect passes on their way for good measure. "That should take care of them."

"Good work, everyone," Sir Harold shouted.

Paul leaned on the wheel. "Oy, good work, but what in bloody hell do we do now?"

"The current will take us close to where we need to be," Sacha told them. "We can attempt to repair the engine while we drift. If we can make it work even a little bit, we should be fine. Search for a tool kit."

Meanwhile, Paul held the wheel cut hard to the right to keep the boat from drifting out into the channel as the smoldering wreck of the German patrol boat was doing. Neither he nor anyone else aboard *Le Pégase* noticed the lone swimmer moving steadily toward the left bank of the Seine's estuary.

SHAEF Advance

It was mid-morning in England, and, having made the most important decision of his career, Ike was sloughing off pressure by having a game of Foxes and Hounds with his aide. Between them were a checkers game board, cups of coffee, and an ashtray with several dead cigarette butts and a smoldering cigar.

The general placed four red checkers on the four black squares directly in front of him, while Butcher put a single black checker on a black square in his first row. As with everything he ever tried, Eisenhower enjoyed mastering the game and winning, which he did quite regularly.

"I really felt good about our outing this morning," he said pushing one of his "hounds" to an adjoining black square. "The Brits showed a lot of warmth and heart."

"With all that cheering and calling for 'Ike,' you'd think you were running for PM, sir. Your move."

"It takes a special type to be a Churchill," Ike told him. "I don't know if I'm cut out for it. Too much politics and being beholden to people. Speaking of politics, De Gaulle is reneging on doing the radio broadcast again. By the time it was all over yesterday, he had agreed to it, but now, he is apparently backing down. Sometimes I think it's a good thing he's over here so his resistance people can do their jobs, but don't tell anyone I said so. We have enough on our hands as it is."

Le Pégase

They had been drifting for almost an hour with Paul keeping the boat tracking toward the harbor. The weather was moderating, the wind had died, and a soft rain was falling when the banging and clanking noises from below ceased.

Sacha called, "Okay, *mon Capitaine*, try it!"

The other men, with greasy hands and faces, watched anxiously as Paul pressed the button. The starter motor whined and the engine sputtered, but nothing more.

"Give it another go," Sir Harold shouted. "Blast, it has to work."

The second try yielded the same response as the first, but just as the whine of the starter motor began to die, the engine chugged, kicked over, and gained revolutions. As it crescendoed to a most welcome roar, the erstwhile mechanics cheered and congratulated each other.

Sacha wiped his hands on a rag and joined Paul. "*Succès!, mon ami*," he said as he took over the helm. "Now I deliver you to the boat to take you home." He navigated *le Pégase* past rows of anchored war ships and approached a dock lined with trawlers. Eyeing each as he passed them, he pointed, "See, there it is, the one called *'La Mouette'*."

With Paul's help, Sacha secured *Le Pégase* to the dock and he and the three allies began the transfer to *La Mouette*. Suddenly, bullets splattered around them. Three slugs caught Sacha and he went down. As the others dove for cover, Ed landed back on *Le Pégase* which, being smaller than the two trawlers on either side, was relatively sheltered from the gunfire coming from the head of the dock. He grabbed a machine gun and returned enough fire for the others to join him just as the *Kübelwagen* rolled up. It was followed by Schellenberg's Horch staff car carrying two soldiers, the doctor, and a soaked but undaunted *oberführer*, gesturing and shouting commands.

Once aboard, Ed and Sir Harold went for weapons. "Time to face the music, old man," the MI6 man told Paul, pushing a machine pistol into his chest. "Click that safety down and you only need to aim and squeeze the blasted trigger."

"Here," Paul replied, "I don't like guns, but I never said I wasn't able with them."

The men in *La Mouette* were also returning fire and two of the soldiers from the *Kübelwagen* vanished, seemingly out of the fight. However, they reappeared moments later and rained grenades onto the deck of *La Mouette*, tearing open the trawler and engulfing it in flames.

Ed grabbed the bag of grenades and attempted an encore of his earlier performance by pitching them over the trawler at the *Kübelwagen*. Two missed their target, but a third effectively neutralized the threat. The only remaining gunfire was coming from the staff car.

"Cover me," Sir Harold told Paul. When the postman hesitated, the MI6 man shouted, "Blast! Do as I say if you ever want to see England again."

Screwing up his courage, Paul aimed in the direction of the Horch and sent bursts of bullets at it before drawing return fire and giving Sir Harold a clear shot at one of the remaining gunners in the Horch. The soldier went down and in the brief lull that followed, Ed jumped onto the shattered dock and hauled Sacha back to the boat. Paul pulled the Frenchman into the cabin, where he saw he'd been shot once in the upper thigh and twice in the gut, but he was alive. Ed joined Sir Harold on the dock and continued firing until the last of the soldiers in the Horch was downed.

Looking around, Sir Harold wondered aloud, "What in blazes became of the general?"

"He's right behind you." They turned and saw Schellenberg brandishing a machine pistol.

"Back to the boat," the general ordered. "We have some business to complete, yes?" As he ushered them onto *Le Pégase*, he shouted, *"Professor! Come! It is safe."*

Folkstein arrived in short order, carrying his black case, and wearing an evil smirk. *"So, I see the American and the spy, but where is the postman?"*

"Eisenhower!" the general shouted. "Get out here! This time you are going to tell the truth!"

There was no response.

Schellenberg backed up to the cabin and leaned into the open hatch while keeping his gun trained on Sir Harold and Ed. "Eisenhower, it is over. Come out or I will kill these …"

Suddenly, the cold steel muzzle of a pistol pressed against the general's temple.

"Let it drop, you bastard!" Paul shouted, adding when Schellenberg complied, "I'm done with this bloody injection business!"

Sir Harold picked up the general's weapon and pointed it at him, allowing Paul to come on deck. As he did so, Folkstein bolted for the dock. With the skill of a seasoned marksman, the postman nonchalantly sent a round into the doctor's leg.

Amid Folkstein's shrieks of pain, Schellenberg pleaded, "I would not have harmed you. It was never my goal. I only wanted the information."

Ed stepped up, putting his nose an inch from the general's. "And once you got it, you would have killed us all, you Kraut bastard!"

"No, please. I was doing my job, but for many of us there is a sense of futility. Himmler himself has plans to sue for peace. The *Führer* has become ineffective. There have been plots to remove him."

Sir Harold asked, "Do you know these things for fact?"

"Yes, of course I do. We who serve do so because we love our country. For the Fatherland. But the *Reich* is falling and many of us realize it is only a matter of time."

"I say," Sir Harold eyed the general up and down. "He's a grand catch, indeed."

"I'm for taking him along," Paul chimed in. "Speakin' of which, we needs be getting out of here."

"What about the doctor?" Ed asked seeing that the little man had passed out.

"Set him on the pier, but we'll hold onto this." Sir Harold picked up the black bag. "I should think it contains some rather interesting items."

After they had bound Schellenberg's hands and tied a rope around his bootless legs, Paul helped Sir Harold lift Folkstein onto the dock like a sack of potatoes. He then returned to the helm and piloted *Le Pégase* out of the harbor.

While Harold and Ed treated Sacha's wounds, Schellenberg worked the ropes on his legs loose and, choosing a moment when his captors were most distracted by their task, dashed to the stern and dove off. With his hands still bound, he porpoised his way toward the line of moored ships.

Ed looked up from bandaging Sacha's leg, grabbed a machine gun, and aimed at the man wriggling away.

Sir Harold grabbed his arm. "You fire now and it might well bring the German Navy down on us. In case you haven't noticed, those were Jerry ships back there."

"Then let's turn around and go after him," Ed insisted.

"Oy," Paul called from above, "hard enough keeping this thing going straight ahead. Now you want a bloody loop de loop, do ya? I say we go on."

"Crap!" the major exclaimed. "My boss would have shit a brick if we walked in with that Kraut." He went up to the wheelhouse. "Look, you do know where we're going, don't you?"

"Not to worry." Paul pointed to his head. "I have it right up here."

Sir Harold joined them. "I'm sure you do, old man, but you may need help just the same. Can you read a compass?"

"Guv, I just keep it running west. Can't miss England. It's just there." He pointed straight ahead.

"We want to get to Neptune H.Q. at Portsmouth and deliver your map," Sir Harold said as he moved Paul's arm to a more northerly direction. "I'd say there."

"Ike's forward command post is near there too," Ed added.

Sir Harold slapped his hands together. "All the better. Let's see the chart so we can set a proper course."

Within minutes it was done and, with the route firmly implanted in his memory, Paul shouted, "England, here we come."

But alas, England was still a long way off, and Churchill's hidden enemy wasn't cooperating in their direction either. By the time they reached the open waters of the English Channel, the weather had again turned blustery. *Le Pégase* was tossed about violently, and her passengers, soaked from the driving rain and the cold waters of the channel, fought off the effects of *mal de mer*. Hours passed before the churning swells calmed enough for Harold to get a fix on their location. As he did so, the weather calmed and soon billowy white clouds rose above a distant mist along the horizon.

Ed had done all he could for Sacha. Now, the rest was up to God. He blessed himself and said a prayer over the fallen Frenchman, then went out on deck and enjoyed the warmth of the sun.

Sir Harold watched the distant mist thicken and looked through his field glasses at what appeared to be great cliffs. "Impossible. We shouldn't be there yet. Eisenhower, do you see what's directly ahead?"

Paul steadied the wheel with one hand and used the binoculars. No doubt, there was something huge out there that had captured the horizon. "Is it land?" he asked.

Ed got wind of their conversation and rejoined them in the wheelhouse. Using Paul's binoculars to look for himself, he shouted, "Yahoo!" and beamed. "That, gentlemen, is part of the Allied armada, coming right for us. D-Day is on!"

SHAEF Advance

General Eisenhower sat behind his desk handling one final detail. While failure was not an option, the fact was, Operation Overlord might not succeed. Ike hated to think negatively about it, but he knew he had to be prepared. He had just finished scrawling a brief message saying the landings, initiated based on the most complete information available, had failed despite the best efforts of the troops, and that he alone accepted all responsibility. As he folded it and put it in his pocket, the phone rang. General Smith was calling with the amazing news that the postman and the others were safe.

"They were picked up by a Brit ship out of Portsmouth and are being brought to Ramsey's HQ now."

Eisenhower's brow furrowed. "That's great, Beetle, but do we know if Overlord was compromised?"

"According to the report, they gave the Krauts the wrong information. Told them it was on for Calais next week."

Ike grinned broadly. "My God! Are we certain of it?"

"Wait, there's more. They got out with a map of all the latest German emplacements and troop positions, including the V-1 and V-2 stuff."

"Beetle, this sounds too good to be true. Can these guys be double agents? Were they turned?"

"That's why they're being taken to Southwick for the intel boys to question. But I have to say, it sounds like the real deal. The MI6 man backs it up. They should be out of the debrief in a couple of hours."

Ike called in his aide. "Butch, it looks like things are starting to go our way."

Southwick House, Portsmouth

The supreme commander and a small group which included Butcher and Kay were greeted by General Smith who explained that Ike's namesake and the two other men would be meeting them outside Ramsay's operations room. As they walked, he added, "Right now, each of them is in a separate room being debriefed. They should be done shortly. I've listened in, and their reports are consistent in terms of fact. The postman is the main focus since the other two were sent to pursue him. Kane, the MI6 guy, is a stalwart whom the Germans could never turn, and the American is an Army major out of our own G2 shop."

"What about the Brit lieutenant?" Ike asked as they arrived at the operations room door.

"He stayed behind, working with the resistance. According to what Eisenhower said, the Davis fella never knew anything right from the start. Kane verified this."

"So, it all came down to the postman."

General Smith nodded. "It did, and he skunked the Germans."

"Damn! It sounds like an awful lot of good came from a potentially disastrous situation." Ike pursed his lips. "Maybe it's an omen."

A moment later, Paul appeared and Beetle ushered him to Ike. "General Dwight Eisenhower, may I present Mister Paul Eisenhower."

Paul took Ike's outstretched hand and shook it vigorously. "Sir, I am very pleased to meet you."

"I'm the pleased one. I understand you became quite a hero over these past several days."

The postman blushed a bit. "Weren't nothin', sir. For the good of the country was all."

The general put him at ease with small talk, and as they discussed their ancestry, Ed and Sir Harold showed up. Once again, Beetle handled the introductions.

Ike pointed to the operations room door. "Are we okay to go in? I'd like to show these fellas what they were protecting."

They entered the large, smoky room bustling with personnel and bursting with telephone gear, wires, desks, and tables. A full-wall map used for tracking deployments and ship positions was being monitored and updated by plotters of the Women's Royal Naval Service. As staff officers looked on, a team used the chart from *Le Pégase* to add Paul's details to their map.

Ike raised his brows to Beetle, who explained, "This new intel is being sent to all the war rooms. It's less than thirty-six hours old, right from Army Group B. Oh, and we also learned Rommel is away in Germany."

Ike chuckled. "Good news, but Monty isn't going to like it. He's been crowing about meeting him again on the battlefield."

From a few paces away, Kay nudged Ike's aide. "Butch, I haven't seen him this content in a very long time. It's like Christmas morning."

"Exactly," the lieutenant commander agreed, "and on the eve of D-Day. It couldn't have come at a better time, and we have another Eisenhower to thank for it."

The Velon-du Lac Mansion, Paris

The radio announcer gave the usual "*Ici Londres*" greeting, and Achille, Phil, Jean-Paul, and Madame du Lac listened to the litany of notices, anxiously awaiting the one message that could spell the beginning of the end for the German occupation. Then it came. "*Blessent mon coeur d'une langueur monotone.*"

The radio operator let out a yelp and the others embraced one another before all of them, Phil included, sang *La Marseillaise*.

"If only Cori could be with us," he said sadly when it was over.

"She is, *mon ami*, she is," Madame du Lac told him. "She will always be with you, and like all who give their lives for France, with all of us, as well."

Regent's Park Road, London

When an army staff car dropped Paul Eisenhower off, he discovered the door to his flat unlocked. The experiences of recent days had taught him to be cautious, so he tiptoed in and discovered his lovely neighbor, her back to him, feeding Odette while Old Frank watched from her shoulder.

"Emily!" he said softly. "I'm back."

"Oh, my Lord!" She whirled around, eyes wide with disbelief. "Paul! Are you all right?"

"Alright," Old Frank repeated and flew to his perch while Odette woofed twice and rubbed her master's legs.

"We're all so happy to see you!" she cried. "When you failed to return Saturday … were you detained? Was it that authorization? Did you get to Blackpool? Just look at your clothes! And where is your luggage?"

"Oh, Emily, you're all I thought of the whole time," he said, opening his arms wide. They stood holding each other, not saying a word for long moments, and then they kissed. It wasn't the polite peck of days ago, but a sincere expression of love.

"You're a changed man," Emily whispered breathlessly.

"Maybe so, but I say, it's for the better."

She stepped back. "Lord, what happened to you up there?"

He took her hand in his. "It wasn't 'up there,'" he told her with a grin. "It was over there. A long way over there. And it's a long story, too, but let's save it for later. Right now, the only thing you should know is that I'm one happy bloke."

RAF Greenham Common
West Berkshire, England

It had been an impatient two-hour trip for Ike. Kay was driving lead for a three-car entourage carrying staff officers and members of the press corps.

"Butch," Ike asked from the rear seat, "Did you pass the word—no ceremony? I just want to say hello to these fellas."

When they arrived at the airfield, the supreme commander didn't wait for Kay to open the car door for him as he usually did. Instead, he leapt out and, dispensing with military formality, stepped over gear and weapons as he waded into a sea of blackened faces belonging to the men of the 101st Airborne who would be among the first to jump and ride gliders behind enemy lines. The general was caught off guard when the soldiers recognized him and began cheering and shouting his nickname. Kay later recorded that the reception was spine tingling for her, and she could only wonder how it made General Ike feel.

Hands crammed into his pants pockets and a reassuring smile on his face, Ike spoke with as many of the men as he could get to. At one point, a photographer captured the moment in what was to become one of the most famous snapshots of the war.

Later, after visiting other airfields, Eisenhower returned and he and his retinue stood on the roof of the headquarters building. They watched proudly and anxiously as more than 80 C-47 Skytrain transports carried the men of the 101st and their commander, Major General Maxwell Taylor, off to Normandy and their appointment with destiny.

On the way back to the car, Ike looked up with teary eyes as the last of the planes closed into a V formation. "Well," he murmured to himself, "no one can stop it now."

Chapter Ten
Tuesday, 6 June 1944

Regent's Park Road, London

The weather outside was gloomy, but there was sunshine in Paul's flat. The wireless was playing a happy tune about life returning to normal after the war as the peripatetic postman gazed across the kitchen table at the beauty wearing his dressing gown. It was like living a dream. He could scarcely believe any of it and was absolutely certain he'd gladly repeat the past nine days if he knew he would come home to Emily.

The two lovers had talked well into the night, with Paul revealing all the pertinent aspects of his adventure and sparing her the more gruesome circumstances. He skipped the bordello escapade entirely. Content but exhausted, he had fallen asleep in her arms to be awakened hours later by the warmth of her touch as she made sweet love to the man who had come to mean so much to her.

Emily was carrying a double portion of egg in the basket to the table when the music on the radio was interrupted by an announcer saying there would be an important message in three minutes.

Paul grinned. "I guess we know what that might be, don't we."

"You helped it happen," she said, bending down to kiss him. "Oh my, I'm so awfully proud of you."

A short time later, they heard BBC Home Service read SHAEF communiqué number one: "Under the command of General Eisenhower, Allied naval forces, supported by strong air forces, began landing Allied armies this morning on the northern coast of France."

Paul smiled broadly. "He would be me cousin, Eisenhower."

She held his face in her hands. "And you would be me lover, Eisenhower."

Hitler's Berghof, Obersalzberg

The *Führer's* piercing gaze fell upon the two senior officers he had ordered to his retreat after learning of the possible Allied landings taking place in Normandy. Hitler pointed to a map which had been hastily prepared by his naval aide, Admiral Karl von Puttkamer, and demanded, *"Well, can you tell me? Is it or is it not the invasion?"* Field Marshal Wilhelm Keitel, head of the OKW, the German high command, and Colonel General Alfred Jodl, Chief of Operations, tried to tell him they lacked sufficient reliable information to answer his question, but he was having none of it. Fuming, he stomped out of the room and slammed the door.

Hitler called for Blondi on his way out to the terrace—a place he knew he could find relief from a war no longer in his favor. He sat on a cushioned white lounge and patted the faithful dog next to him as he took in the alpine panorama which never failed to bring him peace.

"Crack!" A sound flew up from the forest below. Then another. The dog emitted a low growl as the noises continued. A final crack was followed by an almost birdlike screech, then a mournful moan. Dog and master rushed to the wall.

In the clearing at the forest's edge, Hitler saw a buck, its antlers stained with blood, standing over the wounded stag—the one he and Blondi had watched and enjoyed so often. Looking up at the leader of the "Master Race," the victor defiantly pawed the earth and snorted before trotting into the underbrush. Meanwhile, the fallen stag made several attempts to stand. Each time, blood from its wounds dripped to the ground until finally, with all strength drained, it tried no more. The great animal expelled a last breath and was still.

The *Führer* beat the invisible podium before him and ranted, *"I want the attacker killed immediately!"* And then, burying his face in his hands, *"It cannot end this way."*

Inside the Berghof, Field Marshal Keitel received word that the Allied invasion of Normandy had been confirmed.

Epilogue

Operation Overlord succeeded in giving the Allies a foothold in Europe from which they would establish a western front and execute a sweep into the heartland. Sadly, this success came at a terrible cost. While soldiers such as Jimmy's father eventually made it back to England and their families, far too many like Tony, Ray and myriad others, would never return home. The price of victory over tyranny was dear, and many paid for it with their lives, while for others, the quality of the rest of their lives suffered immeasurably. The men and women so affected by World War II could never be honored highly enough for their sacrifices.

The D-Day parachute and glider operations succeeded with a far lower loss rate than the seventy percent Air Chief Marshal Leigh-Mallory had feared. While some jumps and glider landings were off the mark, and too many troops were killed as they landed, their brothers pressed on and accomplished their missions.

One airborne assault that was right on target involved members of Lieutenant Philip Davis's unit, D Company, 2nd Battalion, Oxfordshire and Buckinghamshire Light Infantry Regiment. Shortly after midnight on 6 June, they landed in Horsa gliders and captured vital bridges over the Caen Canal and the Orne River. Two days later, with the help of the French underground, Phil joined his unit at Ranville, France. He went on to distinguish himself in combat throughout their remaining missions. As the Ox and Bucks moved toward Belgium, he received permission to visit a very special gravesite along the way. Months later, after peace was declared, Phil surrendered his commission and returned to Laon to study the architecture of the cathedral and live near his beloved Corinne.

Despite their extensive intelligence gathering, the invasion came as a near total surprise to the Germans. Even after D-Day, some of their generals considered the Normandy landings a feint and continued to believe the major offensive would occur at the Pas de Calais. By the time *Generalfeldmarschall* Erwin Rommel arrived back from Germany to resume command of Army Group B, the Atlantic Wall had been breached. The Allies had established beachheads along the Normandy coast and were installing Mulberry port facilities in preparation for the massive influx of troops, supplies, and weaponry that would follow.

Rommel would only command the army group for slightly more than another month. On 17 July, his car was strafed by an Allied plane. Seriously injured, the Desert Fox returned to Germany and never again held a field command. Days later, a failed assassination attempt on Hitler erupted in a manhunt for anyone even remotely involved. Although Rommel was convalescing and could not have taken part, he was linked to the group of conspirators and forced to commit suicide later that year.

The crew of Miss Liberty completed their full assignment of bombing missions and returned to the United States in July 1944. Their counterparts in the U.S. and British air forces continued to merit great praise for their pursuit and conquest of enemy positions and strongholds, as well as the destruction of strategic and tactical targets. As in the Battle of Britain, the air arm was credited with having helped turn the tide of the war.

Despite constant Allied efforts to destroy enemy launch sites, a week after D-Day, the first V-1 flying bombs, which came to be called, "Doodlebugs," began falling on England. Hitler's ultimate secret weapon brought devastation to both structures and population; however, the hope and promise of the Allied successes helped keep the spirit and will of the British people strong and positive. They were truly indomitable.

The V-1s also brought irony with them. One evening, when the Home Guard unit led by Sergeant Thomas Doyle was on patrol, the distinctive grating sound of one of these precursors of the cruise missile came overhead and went silent. The soldiers scattered knowing that, at any moment, the winged bomb would fall to earth. Tommy ran for the shelter of a brick building, then spotted his mates heading for a tube station entrance and changed direction. Before he got there, the Doodlebug exploded nearby and ended the life of the Nazi spy the Germans knew as Thor.

In late June 1944, *SS-Oberführer* Walter Schellenberg was promoted to the rank of *SS-Brigadeführer*. It seemed his report that the invasion would occur at Calais on 13 June had become diluted in the overwhelming assortment of erroneous information at the time, and he suffered no personal consequence. As the war wound down, he was sent by *Reichsführer* Himmler to seek peace with the Allies. In April 1945, he went to Stockholm to ask Count Folke Bernadotte, an influential Swedish diplomat, to intercede on behalf of Germany. Unbeknownst to the *Fuhrer*, Himmler proposed surrendering to the Allies, provided Germany would be allowed to continue fighting the Soviets. When the offer failed, Schellenberg tried to personally surrender and was arrested in Denmark.

The resistance movements in France and the Low Countries had done their pre-invasion jobs of sabotage well. After the success of Operation Overlord, they helped Allied troops liberate many cities, towns, and villages in their respective countries. Likewise, the Velon-du Lac mansion was a focus of much partisan activity during the days leading up to the liberation of Paris, which culminated in late August 1944. The Germans never learned there was a vital center of the French underground in their midst. Madame Genevieve du Lac continued to use her beauty and acting acumen to charm and misdirect the occupiers right up until their final days.

After the war, at last free of the pretense they had carried on for over two years, the actress and Achille revealed their enduring love for each other. In June 1945, they married in a private ceremony at a chapel in the *Cathédrale Notre-Dame de Paris*. The small wedding party included Jean-Paul and his sweetheart, Maria, a former resistance fighter whom he had met and fallen for during the last days of the German occupation.

Far more impatient than Genevieve and Achille, Paul and Emily wed on Sunday, 6 August 1944, and honeymooned in Blackpool. There, they walked the beach and enjoyed the amusements, the merry ambience, and each other. On Wednesday of that week, they attended a revue starring the sweetheart of the armed forces, Vera Lynn, whose signature song, "We'll Meet Again," held a special meaning for them both, as did the poignant tune, "You Are Always in My Heart." All in all, their stay had been magical, despite the occasional blustery weather and lingering difficulties with rail travel in both directions. The pleasure of each other's company was only surpassed by the passion in each other's arms. Slightly more than nine months after their wedding, Emily presented Paul with a baby boy whom they christened Paul Dwight.

Sir Harold Kane spent the week in Paris he had promised himself following the August liberation. Among a host of other enjoyments, he called at the Velon-du Lac mansion and was warmly welcomed by Madame du Lac, Achille, Jean-Paul, and Maria. He also drove to La Roche-Guyon where he and Sacha drank wine and talked about the Frenchman's plans to restart his life as a gardener.

After returning home, Sir Harold resumed his agent activity. As he could no longer work undercover as Jackdaw, he became an advisor to novices such as Paul Eisenhower, whom he had earlier recommended for a position as an analyst with MI6. The agency was quite happy to acquire the man with such a facility for recall.

Major Ed Bradford returned to his G2 duties wearing the Bronze Star for valor and the Purple Heart medal for the wound he had received during the escape. He also sported the silver oak leaves of a lieutenant colonel. As the war front moved eastward, he went with it ultimately to SHAEF Forward in Reims, France, Eisenhower's subsequent advanced command post. There, the instruments of surrender were signed by Germany on 7 May 1945.

On 12 June, Supreme Allied Commander Dwight Eisenhower was asked to speak at the venerable Guildhall. The Lord Mayor of London, in the full regalia of his office, met Ike's carriage and later presented the general with the sword carried by Wellington at Waterloo. Eisenhower's emotional speech, one of the first he had given in public, was a product of his own hand, flawlessly delivered, and very well received. At a luncheon that followed, Churchill paid tribute to Ike's ability to bring nations together, "in the grim and awful cataclysm of war." The warm responses and cheering crowds hinted at the adulation Ike would receive upon his return to the United States.

Later that same day, General Eisenhower went to Buckingham Palace for tea with King George VI and Queen Elizabeth. He arrived to the traditional pomp and circumstance and was immediately put at ease by the monarchs, just as he had been when he visited during the trying times prior to D-Day. The King appointed the general to the British Order of Merit, a rare honor, especially for an American soldier. After the ceremony, two tall doors opened and there stood Paul and Emily. His Majesty smiled at Ike. "Now, I have something for the other Eisenhower."

The couple entered with all the grace and propriety of persons who had done it many times. They stood side by side as a citation was read and the King presented Paul with the George Cross, an honor he himself had originated. A counterpart to the Victoria Cross, it was the highest civilian award for valor in the entire kingdom.

The tea and conversation which followed was easy and delightful, and, at one point, Ike talked about the Eisenhower lineage he and Paul shared. The general offered an open invitation to visit his farm in Gettysburg, Pennsylvania. Coincidentally, the area was the very same one from which Paul's ancestors had migrated to England.

During another exchange, Queen Elizabeth confided that she had learned of Emily's prowess at the piano. With a coy smile, she said, "We would not want to impose, Mrs. Eisenhower, but perhaps you might favor us."

Paul was bursting with pride as he watched his dear Emily, who had never realized her dream of playing with the philharmonic, give a flawless recital of Handel's *Fantasia* sonata in C major for the King and Queen of England.

Select Bibliography

Butcher, Captain Harry C., USNR, *My Three Years with Eisenhower*. New York: Simon and Schuster, 1946.

Crosswell, D.K.R., *Beetle: The Life of General Walter Bedell Smith*. The University Press of Kentucky, 2010.

Doerries, Reinhard R., *Hitler's Intelligence Chief, Walter Schellenberg*. New York: Enigma Books, 2009.

Eisenhower, David, *Eisenhower: at War 1943–1945*. New York: Random House, 1986.

Eisenhower, Dwight D., *Crusade in Europe*. Garden City, New York: Doubleday & Company, 1946.

Gilbert, Martin, *Winston S. Churchill, Road to Victory 1941–1945*. Boston: Houghton Mifflin Company, 1986.

Green, Brigadier General A.F.U., *The British Home Guard Pocket-Book, 1942*. London: Conway, 2009.

Howarth, David, *The Dawn of D-Day, These Men Were There, June 6, 1944*. New York: Skyhorse Publishing, 2008.

Ryan, Cornelius, *The Longest Day, June 6, 1944*. New York: Simon and Schuster, 1959.

Schellenberg, Walter, *Walter Schellenberg, The Memoirs of Hitler's Spymaster*. London: André Deutsch, 2006.

Shirer, William L., *The Rise and Fall of the Third Reich*. New York: Simon and Schuster, 1959.

Summersby, Kay, *Eisenhower Was my Boss*. New York: Prentice-Hall, Inc., 1948.

303rd Bomb Group (Hells Angels), *Combat Mission Reports*. 1943–1944

Authors' Note

The Other Eisenhower is based on an actual lapse in Operation Overlord security that occurred on a warm morning in May 1944, just days before the start of the unprecedented invasion of France—D-Day. In the story, we have combined documented events and real people with interesting fictional characters and compelling circumstances. We hope you enjoyed this product of history and our imaginations.

For more information about the authors, and photos and discussions related to *The Other Eisenhower,* please visit *campana-ditillo.com.*

Made in the USA
Columbia, SC
08 September 2023

22601465R00148